PAINTING BEYOND WALLS

PAINTING BEYOND WALLS

a novel

DAVID RHODES

MILKWEED

ALSO BY DAVID RHODES

Jewelweed (2013)

Driftless (2008)

Rock Island Line (1975)

The Easter House (1974)

The Last Fair Deal Going Down (1972)

Published 2022 by Milkweed Editions
Printed in Canada
Cover design by Mary Austin Speaker
Cover art by John Edwards ("Various Tulips," 1791)
and Julie de Graag ("Studies of wasps")
Author photo by Anna Weggel
22 23 24 25 26   5 4 3 2 1
First Edition

978-1-57131-141-2

Library of Congress Cataloging-in-Publication Data

Names: Rhodes, David, 1946- author.
Title: Painting beyond walls : a novel / David Rhodes.
Description: First paperback edition. | Minneapolis, Minnesota : Milkweed
    Editions, [2022] | Summary: "As approachable as it is profound in
    exploring the human condition and our shared need for community, this
    is a story for our times"-- Provided by publisher.
Identifiers: LCCN 2022017325 (print) | LCCN 2022017326 (ebook) | ISBN
    9781571311412 (hardcover) | ISBN 9781639550579 (epub)
Classification: LCC PS3568.H55 P35 2022 (print) | LCC PS3568.H55
    (ebook) | DDC 813/.54--dc23
LC record available at https://lccn.loc.gov/2022017325
LC ebook record available at https://lccn.loc.gov/2022017326

Milkweed Editions is committed to ecological stewardship. We strive to align our book production practices with this principle, and to reduce the impact of our operations in the environment. We are a member of the Green Press Initiative, a nonprofit coalition of publishers, manufacturers, and authors working to protect the world's endangered forests and conserve natural resources. *Painting Beyond Walls* was printed on acid-free 100% postconsumer-waste paper by Friesens Corporation.

To Edna,

my wife
companion
friend
critic
lover
muse
advocate
helpmeet
financier
caregiver
manager
guide
coconspirator
enemy
bodyguard
advisor
nurse
counselor
strategist
secretary
priest
chef
scrubwoman
confessor
chauffeur
alter ego
ambassador
scheduler
paramour
architect
litigator
hero
therapist
consultant
banker
competition
druggist
gamekeeper
jailer
liberator
and the *other*

CONTENTS

Without familiar patterns, how will we ever know we're lost? Seek beauty, but no—not over there. Evolution depends on the misfit who fits.

—JAMES NOLAND

PAINTING BEYOND WALLS

A MINIATURE CAGE
SEPTEMBER 2027, CHICAGO

EARLY FOR AUTUMN, yet a few trees had already turned color, surprising the old brick-and-mortar neighborhood with splendid, if unwelcome, harbingers of winter. It seemed too soon for summer to be over, too warm for daylight hours to shorten. But there could be no mistake about the signs. One especially extravagant hard maple paraded in front of August Helm's apartment on Fifty-Eighth Street, its red-orange flora shamelessly monopolizing the window view from his second-floor kitchen. On sunlit mornings, broad avenues of light slanted in from the horizon, and the glowing leaves resembled the innermost chamber in desire's furnace.

Five blocks away, August Helm worked in a biochemical laboratory at the University of Chicago, the same facility he'd been in for four years—almost as long as he'd lived in the Hyde Park apartment. Along with the fifteen other members of the research team, he experimented with adaptive immunization engineering—studies primarily designed by Dr. Peter Grafton and funded through grants from privately owned pharm-conglomerates and the National Institute of Health.

It was a relatively unremarkable time in August's life. He was thirty years old, an inch shy of six feet, and he weighed roughly 150 pounds; his daily routine had a nearly predictable rhythm, and his health remained excellent. He enjoyed cycling whenever he could carve out the time, and on one day rode his Swedish-made bicycle eighty-six miles—a personal record; yet the high odometer reading had less to do with his own ambitions, and more to do with the man and woman he was riding with. Both were older than August, well respected within the scientific community for their grant writing, and wore their fitness like merit badges. Though August generally went out of his way to avoid overt physical competition of all kinds, on that day it seemed important to keep up with them. Two weeks later, when he was asked to ride with them again, he begged off.

Most of the stumbling blocks along August's career path had been overcome, and he anticipated a decade of working in temporarily funded labs before seeking salaried employment with an established pharmacological or biomedical company. Currently, his monthly student loan payments were being waived, yet his income never quite stretched far enough to cover all his expenses—like a twin sheet fitted over a full-size bed. And he accepted this as normal. Nearly everyone he knew under the age of forty lived beyond paychecks, settling old obligations by incurring new ones. Due to a steady trickle of people and businesses from the East Coast, where retreating shorelines seemed increasingly inhospitable, and an even steadier stream of immigration from the drought-plagued Southwest, the costs of living in Chicago had risen.

August's parents had been calling and texting a lot lately, urging him to come home for a visit. His mother had become unusually strident, and recently threatened to take a bus to Chicago by herself if August's father continued to refuse to drive into the city because of the traffic. She complained that if August stayed away from home much longer, they might become strangers to each other.

But August kept putting them off. The tiny village of Words, Wisconsin, where his parents continued to live in the same house August had grown up in, had come to seem to him like a foreign land, nearly irrelevant to the life he'd become accustomed to. Whenever he considered returning home, other activities and schedules always seemed more pressing. He could never find the time.

This dismissive attitude toward the place of his childhood would have seemed quite unfathomable to August seven or eight years earlier, when the urge to flee back to the benign familiarity of home had tormented him unmercifully. For months after leaving Wisconsin, his heart had nearly broken from dislocation. And he'd often dreamt—even during daylight hours—of returning home, coming upon his mother pulling weeds in her garden or reading in her favorite chair, and his father working on gasoline and diesel engines until after dark, smelling of perspiration and oil. Any remembered scenes from home, it seemed, could be effectively mythologized by his loneliness into visions of domestic rapture.

But since then, the unfamiliar had become familiar, and like many other young people who are selected by test scores, sorted by application forms, separated by scholarships, and relocated out of voiceless rural backwaters into urban centers of higher education and technical training, new activities and thoughts gradually consumed him, and for several years now, he seldom thought about his origins.

First, there had been the dormitories, cafeterias, offices, and classrooms to contend with, and many of those mammoth buildings had exuded a grand respectability of age and old-world craftsmanship, with polished granite floors, thick, beveled glass, and hand-carved woodwork. All of them seemed formidable, bursting with people from every corner of the world—many of whom looked and sounded very important. Growing up in a lower working-class family in an extended rural community of other families of similar circumstances had not prepared him for the diversity he discovered at the university. On that first day, in front of the dorms, arriving students had pulled suitcases and boxes out of vehicles that August had never seen before excepting in magazines and movies; but he also saw people who looked like they hadn't changed clothes, slept, eaten, showered or entertained a benign thought in many days. Everywhere he looked, something challenging looked back.

August's assigned roommate—an ultrapolite young black man from Puducherry—spoke in a distinct British accent. He called himself Ishmael, though the name listed on the student registration form clearly read Eugene, and he wore a bright white turban carefully wrapped around his head. His baritone voice conveyed infinite self-confidence, and even his normal mode of speaking gave the impression of making announcements. His smile seemed friendly and upbeat, and at first reminded August of blinking his headlights at the driver of an oncoming car, only to learn his low beams had already been engaged.

When they met, Ishmael assumed the responsibility of explaining to August that Puducherry lay along the southeastern coast of India; and until 1954, Puducherry had been a province of France, previously founded as a trading colony by the French East India Company as early as 1674. Ishmael's family had at one time been spice merchants, or, as Ishmael explained with a short, friendly laugh followed by a blinding smile, "One of Europe's many flavor vendors."

Before August could say where he was from, Ishmael explained that during the previous week he had made inquiries with the registration office and had already learned that his new roommate was a native of Words, a small, unincorporated town in the heart of Wisconsin's renowned yet sparsely populated Driftless Area. Ishmael went on to summarize how the unusually hilly topography of the region around August's home had many briskly flowing streams, and because the rocky geography prohibited most large-scale tilling, planting, and harvesting techniques, dairy farming grew to prominence during the twentieth century, and the Driftless Area became known for cheese. The industry flourished, with local creameries around every hillock.

August interrupted to point out that due to several decades of ruinous government agricultural policies, the number of dairy farms had decreased, and the number of independent cheese makers in the Driftless hills had dwindled.

"Not all of them," announced Ishmael, handing August a Ziploc bag containing eight ounces of cheese curds made in a small cheese factory a short distance from August's home. "I spoke with the head dairyman," said Ishmael. "He seemed like a good chap—well acquainted with your parents. And he assured me the curds would still squeak when you bite into them. I thought you might fancy a familiar taste as we adjust to our new surroundings."

"That was extremely thoughtful of you," said August.

He accepted the plastic bag and offered a curd to Ishmael.

"Sorry, mate, I'm afraid I'm blinkered—lactose intolerant."

"That's too bad," said August. "Here, I have something for you."

He handed Ishmael a small, carefully wrapped box.

Inside was a tiny wire cage, large enough to perhaps enclose a single marble, with a little door that opened and shut.

Ishmael stared at August.

"My mother borrowed a neighbor's jewelry-making kit," August explained, somewhat sheepishly. "She wanted you to have it. I told her it was a remarkably eccentric gift, but, well, she wanted you to have it."

"A miniature cage?"

"Like I said, there was no talking her out of it. When she learned you were from Puducherry, she got excited because a long time ago a yogi named Aurobindo Ghose founded an ashram there, and, well, he was apparently quite prolific during a certain period of his life, and Mom had read a raft of his books."

"The ashram is still there," said Ishmael. "It's a major tourist attraction."

"My mother says," August continued, "that while jailed as a political prisoner, Aurobindo heard a voice in the night saying that India would gain her independence without him, freeing him to devote the rest of his life to spiritual pursuits. My mother wanted to show—"

"I get it, mate. Your mum made me a freedom charm."

"Then you're not offended?"

"To the contrary, it's a grand gift and I will treasure this jeweled cage, though it should probably be noted that Sri Aurobindo attributed the divine voice he heard in the underground prison to a visitation from Swami Vivekananda, and his interest in yoga began at that time. And if you don't mind me asking, what are you hoping to major in, August?"

"Cell science, and you?"

"Criminal justice."

Getting along with people, August discovered, required real concentration. He needed to consistently interrogate the first impressions he formed of new people—to banish unwarranted generalizations and associations before he acquired enough experience to make more useful assessments of character—and to do this while learning to navigate the sprawling campus, disengage his rural reflex that assumed every honking horn and loud voice was aimed at him, enroll in the required classes, acquire textbooks without paying extortionate prices, meet with advisors, fill out financial forms, and assume his work-study obligations.

For months and months, he succeeded in resisting the urge to return home. Since about the age of five, he'd nurtured a healthy fear of failure, and he tried to recruit this fear to work on his behalf.

Still, the new acquaintances he formed remained relatively superficial compared to his friends from childhood, partly because of the profound psychological forces released by early social interactions outside the nuclear family, and partly due to the insular nature of the rural community itself. Nevertheless, he met a few students he genuinely liked, and a few with peculiarities that he could sympathize and even identify with, like working to discover errors in a study guide's optional problem sets and reporting them, unsolicited, to the publishers.

He also met someone who—like himself—had memorized the periodic table in the eighth grade. And once, when he was asked to retake an essay section of a structural biochemistry exam because of his illegibly small handwriting, he found himself completing the makeup work beside three other students.

After two years, he moved out of the dormitory and into a rented room in an old house shared with four other undergraduates. And by the time he received his Bachelor of Science he had lived in three different apartment buildings with a variety of other renters, always looking for better, quieter domestic arrangements.

After receiving a Master of Science, August was accepted into a doctorate program in structural biochemistry—the study of chemical processes inside living organisms. The advisory council overseeing his thesis and student teaching also rotated him through several laboratories needing short-term research assistants.

Somewhere in the meanwhile, August lost his connection to his hometown. And though he saw his parents at major holidays and other times, over the years his visits home grew shorter and less frequent; perhaps more importantly, the character of his visits slowly changed from resuscitating to obligatory. Sure, he went home, but he no longer felt he belonged there. Everything rural seemed in slow motion. Weeding in the garden with his mother, searching for a subject they could relax inside; at the shop with his father, passing wrenches, screwdrivers, and needle-nosed pliers back and forth as his they repaired a piece of broken machinery; eating cold sandwiches pulled from a dented lunch box; neighbors dropping in and out, delivering malfunctioning lawnmowers and chain saws, greeting August with brief eye contact, quick smiles, commenting on the weather while buying a soda from the machine, exchanging a few words with his father, returning home . . . all August could do was remember an earlier version of himself, a younger edition that was currently, well, gone. And when he attempted to look up his old friends, he couldn't find them. His visits invariably came at the wrong times—when JW was away at a marketing convention, or with Lester in Vietnam, or wasn't answering her messages. Once, at Christmas, August almost linked up with Ivan, but at the last minute Ivan texted that an ice storm had stranded him and his grandfather at the lake where they'd gone fishing.

August could no longer sync; he'd become unmoored from his childhood and couldn't find the place where he used to drop anchor. And the distress this brought to him added another argument in favor of his dislocation.

He felt more at home in Chicago. This was especially true after completing his doctorate and beginning a long-term commitment to the research lab under Dr. Grafton. Along with predictable working schedules, he could finally afford an apartment of his own, a better bicycle, and to periodically eat in his favorite diners and restaurants. He purchased a couple of dress shirts—not pulled from a bargain bin— and experienced a measure of independence, or at least semi-indepen- dence. And perhaps of greater significance, the wider civilization that he had joined had assigned him a token of its acceptance—someone with whom he imagined eventually making a family.

Amanda Clark and August Helm had known each other for a little over a year. She lived in a spacious, sumptuously appointed condominium downtown and worked for a mid-sized financial firm in the Loop. The demands of her job frequently required late hours, and due to their sep- arate residences and professional schedules they often only saw each other on weekends.

Amanda was a delicate, long-legged blonde with extraordinarily beautiful toes, feet, ankles, calves, knees and thighs, which served to support her even more attention-arresting features. While standing in a checkout line, Amanda often knew—within three or four percentage points—the total cost of her randomly chosen items, and to entertain herself she would compare this amount to her average electric bill or the size of the compound interest on the national debt at the current rate of federal lending. Her dreams, especially after long and difficult days, assumed numerical themes, and she sometimes felt inclined to agree with Kurt Gödel's controversial notion from a hundred years before, that integers and other socially constructed conceptual entities actually existed in an objective domain independent of human thought. Her finely drawn facial features were constantly changing, and in her more pensive moments her expression suggested she had almost remembered an amusing incident from her past and was attempting to recover every detail, her cupid-bow upper lip poised like a diver on the edge of a diving board.

Amanda's everyday physical movements often seemed inspired by a self-contented thoughtlessness, as though primordial dances were somehow being routinely generated through her without any specific awareness on her part, only to abruptly conclude in a full-length presentation of striking profile—a pose in which her classically matched legs pressed firmly together, elevated at the heels, with shoulders, back, neck and head impeccably erect, as if yearning for someone with aesthetic authority to perform a rigorous inspection. And August was especially vulnerable to those nearly theatrical poses—brief rallies of irresistible, languorous allure drawn up at the last moment into taut conclusions, abandoning him inside feelings of wounded, crippling awe.

They met at a winter party along Lake Shore Drive hosted by a couple of economic postdocs from the University of Illinois. Neither Amanda nor August knew many people in the crowded apartment, and those they did know they didn't know very well.

They'd each arrived separately, and in their own respective ways they'd been wondering why they'd come, until the infinite wisdom of random body motion within a contained population eventually positioned them in close proximity, a short distance away from a long, satin-finished walnut table offering elaborately prepared and tastefully presented snacks.

It would have been impossible to not notice her. At least it was for August. She wore one of those stylish, disposable dresses made from recycled paper products, developed in California, designed in France, assembled in Bangladesh, imported by a Filipino shipping company, distributed by a supplier in New York, and sold in a boutique on State Street. The redder-than-red material accentuated her hair in such an appealing way that she seemed like a sculptured candle burning with a blonde flame. The ruffled sash around her waist acted like a tourist guide, directing August's visiting glances along two separate avenues of interest. Her height was a little intimidating, it's true, yet merriment radiated from every inch of her stature—a woman not only willing but able to forgive others for always noticing her attractiveness first. And perhaps as stiff remedy to this unusually generous demeanor, her smile—even when partly ignited—annihilated all prospect of her eventual capture.

After awkward introductions, they tried to find something to talk about and accidently discovered—to August's boundless relief—that they had recently read the same book on popular anthropology. Amanda remembered something interesting about the author's personal life and August told her of a book from a decade earlier that examined much of the same archaeological evidence but reached entirely different conclusions. Amanda made a droll comment and August smiled appreciatively. And using the protection of her humor as a guide for further discussion, they talked and laughed through some of the discoveries and assertions cited in the book: Recent hominid fossils uncovered in Eastern and Northern Europe were believed to predate the earliest estimates for Cro-Magnons by over thirty thousand years. These bipedal ancestors of modern humans ranged over the same territory as the larger Neanderthals, whom the author referred to as N-tals. Due to the discovery (or to be more accurate, maintenance) of fire by N-tals, the smaller, flatter-faced, less hairy Cro-Mags were inexorably drawn to the larger creatures and their domesticated flames. In exchange for the warmth of their company, the newcomers traded grooming services, poppy seeds and other foods, and sexual amenities, the latter of which resulted in the eventual extinction of the genetically less dominant N-tals, whose chromosomal contributions were—over time—rendered silent through a deficit of expressed proteins. Consequently, although N-tal's genes were often passed along to future generations—and remnants can still be found in modern human DNA—they serve no useful function and survive as historical relics housed alongside actual working genes. The book's author further speculated that more isolated N-tal clans possibly began to recognize that the physical features they shared with their relatives were beginning to disappear in those relatives' offspring; but noticing this didn't prevent them from falling victim to a similar fate. They simply didn't care, and willingly, cheerfully, bred themselves out of existence.

After refilling their crystal glasses with fruit punch, Amanda and August became squeezed between a group of self-consciously whispering English poets and a larger collection of heavily drinking sports enthusiasts rapidly speaking Spanish. Forced to stand closer together, Amanda and August cautiously attempted to widen the field of their conversation into, hopefully, more fertile topics. They moved like novice swimmers letting go of an inflated life raft and paddling off into open water. After several deeply uncomfortable, pause-laden, word-frantic minutes, they discovered having both attended, along with thousands of others, the same concert in Grant Park three weeks earlier, and then they began talking about the recently completed super train connecting Chicago with Milwaukee.

Her voice, August noticed, maintained a slender yet clear-throated quality, mostly within the alto range, difficult to hear in a crowded room, with a meadowlark's tendency to bend upward at the end of longer phrases. He discovered his attention following the dulcet sound like a hound after fresh, humid trails of scent, only to realize, with horror, that because of his keen interest in the musicale, he'd lost the thread of her speech. And her eyes, he also noticed, glowed like fiery lights beneath transparent layers of green ice, and he often needed to look away from them for self-preservation.

Amanda experienced similar difficulties and was easily led astray by the corners of August's mouth, the hairline creases at the corners of his eyes, and his pale wrists moving in and out of pressed white cuffs. It occurred to her for no particular reason that these movements—the emergence of limbs through tunnels of cloth—could be represented in differential equations, modeled through algorithms, and programmed into pornographic simulations. Thinking about it made blood rush into her face.

Again and again, they became stranded within themselves, separated from each other by the shrubbery of privately imagined possibilities. And they could find no immediate way to address this problem of living double lives—no opportunity to include the deeper feelings growing in a tangential way to the few mundane subjects they were able to openly discuss. The impressions being formed in their minds promised too much, and the outsize manner of their fantasies put them on guard.

Yet they persisted, blindly groping through the fog of not knowing enough about each other and not trusting anything they learned, toward a blurry vision of mutual comfort.

After sixteen minutes of standing, Amanda gracefully lowered herself down onto the rounded arm of a nearby sofa, and from this somewhat precarious position effortlessly crossed her long legs. For August, this speedily concluded repositioning seared a permanent afterimage in his brain, and he strained to remember if he had ever seen anyone sit on a sofa-arm before. It seemed a daring maneuver strategically designed to arouse every nerve ending in his body, cleverly cloaked within a barely civilized art form. He tried to keep his face from showing the unvarnished interest he discovered in the lithe action, while also remaining on high alert for any future performances that may unexpectedly unfold out of her. Thankfully, she seemed unaware of his unmanageable internalizations, and her euphonious voice and tinkling laughter continued to communicate gaiety as effortlessly as porch chimes played by an intermittent breeze.

An hour later, they left the party in search of bar food, jazz, and micro-beers. Amanda's sports car was parked just behind the building,

To August, the snug interior of the two-seater smelled of new leather and felt luxurious in an unfamiliar way, with tiny red, green, and amber lights winking out of the dashboard's electronic jewelry kit. The engine started with a quick-tempered petroleum snarl and idled with a low, sleepy growl. Watching her as she drove, August noticed that she'd removed her heels. At the first traffic light she pressed the brake pedal with her shoeless left foot, an ambidextrous detail of unusual significance, it seemed, and the more he thought about it, the more important it became, though he could not quite resolve what fueled such impending consequence. The light changed and they surged away from the intersection at rocket-launching speeds. The car's engine, she explained, was located both beneath and behind them, which partly accounted for its robust capacity for rapid propulsion.

They parked in front of what looked like an appropriate establishment, hidden among larger but less attractive shops and offices. The door closed behind them with the sound of a vacuum seal, and they experienced the warm embrace of the room. Carefully threading a narrow aisle between crowded tables, they slid into a burgundy-upholstered booth with a small light burning inside a gold-tinted jar. The cushions squeezed up against their thighs, and from somewhere unseen saxophone notes oozed in and out of roaming piano chords, walking bass tones, and the rhythmic background of brushed drumming. Distant kitchen smells mingled with the up-close fragrance of smoky leather, lingering body odor, grease, and candlewax. A waiter inside a black-and-white uniform took their orders, went away, and later returned with steaming food and tall, sweating glasses of locally brewed beer.

Amanda's green eyes never seemed to retire. As though mirroring a sprite-like essence behind them, they darted from spoon to napkin, sleeve button to table edge, cup to saucer, glass to flame, constantly hunting and gathering new sensations. August looked at her as though into a magic lantern, and a cautious smile with teeth glinting between her lips invited him to keep looking. He needed to know everything about her, as though the accumulation of incidental facts might eventually reach critical mass and explain the vital phenomenon seated across the table from him. His whole soul, it seemed, was being absorbed by her mannerisms, her way of being alive, and he felt perfectly incapable of privately sustaining his own existence.

Amanda explained that she had come to Chicago from Massachusetts, where she belonged to a seemingly well-to-do family in a long line of early-fur-traders-turned-landowners, manufacturers-turned-bootleggers, and bankers-turned-speculators, who could trace their presence in the Boston area back to before the Revolution. Proud of their British heritage as well as the brief appearance in their family tree of several female members from indigenous American tribes, the Clarks embodied a familiar mixture of upper-class predilections: the unshakable conviction of being self-made; friendly indifference to nearly all civic involvement, with the exception of generous support for local symphony orchestra performances; and open contempt for middle-class conformity. Her immediate family lived in a superbly located, ingeniously designed home in Woods Hole, and customarily divided their summers between New Hampshire and Europe. Both her parents, she said, while laughing in a parody of self-consciousness, "encouraged my brother and me to think of our family as exceptionally ordinary. I suppose it was a way of suggesting that we belonged where we were."

"And did you?" he asked.

"Did I what?"

"Did you feel you belonged?"

"Of course. It was expected of us." Her eyes once again dashed around the booth, searching for something fresh to settle on. "On my fifth birthday, I remember my mother gave me a locket that her mother had given to her. It had a long chain—as thin as a hair—and it would collapse into a teeny gold pool in my palm. *This is precious*, Mother explained to me with a long, audible sigh. *Treasure it always, but never wear it.* After I blew out the candles on my cake, my great-aunt put them back in the box for next year and my grandmother gave me an extravagantly embroidered envelope with a note inside, announcing a small trust in my name—to become effective on my twenty-first birthday. At the time, I didn't know what a trust was, and because I didn't want to ask, I simply imagined it might be something like a trunk with a heavy lid, a place to keep my locket and other things for safekeeping. I can still see that old thing—the trunk—sitting in my mind like a great overgrown toad in the corner of some dark, dusty room."

August's mouth grew a smile, and his eyes with delicate creases in the corners continued staring into her.

After graduating from an all-girls prep school Amanda had followed her older brother away from the Ivy League universities to a more modestly furnished yet highly ranked college in the Midwest. Her brother encountered difficulties living away from New England and after several years returned there. Amanda, however, fit right in, attracted friends as effortlessly as breathing, and graduated at the top of her class. She then earned a higher degree from another school, found executive-level employment in a Chicago firm with connections to her maternal uncle, and utterly charmed August Helm, a biochemist from a family of farmers, factory workers, mechanics, and preachers.

He'd never met such an enchanted being, let alone privately talked to one. Her relaxed spontaneity gave the impression of being on short-term loan from a far better world where all creatures were as intelligent as shimmering sunlight, perfectly formed, and drove impossibly expensive automobiles with both feet.

"My whole life has been spent preparing for something," Amanda complained. "The trouble is I've never known what that something is supposed to be, and I'm afraid I might not recognize it when it comes. I'm tired of waiting."

"What do you mean?" he asked.

"I'd like to jump into the deep end of the pool without knowing how to swim."

"One summer I worked as a lifeguard," he said, feeling especially heavy, an old buffalo chasing a gazelle through an open field.

"I don't want to be rescued, August. I want someone to drown with."

"Well … ," he began, and then could think of nothing else to say. His pull-down screen for speaking options went completely blank. She laughed and squeezed her earlobe between the thumb and first finger of her hand, an action that seemed both unplanned yet purposeful, like switching on a light while walking into a dark room.

"So, tell me about what you do," she said.

August panicked, immediately recalling a number of embarrassing events that had stained his memory like used oil spilled on white carpet. Talking about his work had always been a problem. As long as he could remember he'd passionately, and perhaps naively, believed in the promise of science; each new discovery added another lumen to the great beam of light that would eventually bridge the gap between what people thought they knew and how and why they actually knew it. When the great chasm of ignorance had been fully illuminated, the last secret revealed, humanity would finally be liberated out of the bondage of seeming and into the real world. All the pain, suffering, hatred, and cruelty that came from the illusions of ignorance would vanish.

But the overwhelming majority of people had no interest in science. They loved technology, of course—gadgetry—but hated science. Latin names and quantifying datum were a plague to sociability. Most people fled for their very lives when someone began to explain the shared characteristics of self-replicating prokaryotic cells. And like many other micro- and biochemists, August had learned to hide his passion for the tiniest valves in the universal machinery, and only revealed that side of his personality within the narrow and somewhat sequestered community of other scientists.

More than anything, he dreaded watching those magnificent green eyes across the table grow dim. Talking about oneself was risky, especially now, when he and Amanda were still uneasy with each other, unsteady—afraid that what attracted them to each other might turn out to be inauthentic, a facade thrown up by excessive hopefulness.

"It's not that interesting," he said.

"I don't believe you. Really, I'd like to know."

As he wondered about the sincerity of this statement a new cheek-creasing smile opened in her face. Her wandering eyes settled on his, and through these sublime encroachments a priceless invitation was offered into the interior rooms of her palace. Ambushed by this sudden development, he noticed tiny flecks of gold in her irises, scattered haphazardly, like campfires burning in a distant valley.

His work, he said, concerned living cells . . . and a good way to begin thinking about them was to recognize two cellular functions vital to the survival of the organisms they supported: dividing and dying at appropriate times.

"Why dying?" she asked, chewing a sliver of peeled carrot.

"Cell death is a necessary part of an organism's development and maintenance. For instance, inside the womb when a fetus's hands and feet begin to differentiate from the larger mass of embryonic tissue, the toes and fingers are webbed. Later, the amphibian veil disappears through the death of the webbing cells. They die and fall away. Cell death is also critical to the ongoing battle against injury and pathogens, which is primarily fought through programmed cellular death. When diseased, injured, and malfunctioning cells die, the damaged and infectious agents they carry are made safely available for digestion by healthy cells. It's how we get better."

"How does that work?" she asked.

"First, the infected cell shrinks and its mitochondria—the organelles inside the cell that produce energy—begin to break down. Then the cell releases various nucleotides into the environment outside the cell. These nucleotides bind to receptors on neighboring cells and serve as messengers, saying, *Hey, look over here, over here.* When the healthy cells arrive, the dying cell displays a protein normally hidden within its fatty membrane, and the signal is interpreted by the healthy cells as *come on, yum, eat me.* And they do."

Amanda drank the last centimeter of her fruit beer and ordered another. "So the infected cells voluntarily commit suicide," she observed. "They're martyrs to the cause, rah, rah."

"Yes, and the process—known as apoptosis—proceeds so methodically that we call it PCD, or programmed cell death."

"How do cells know it's time to die?"

"Well, the chemistry is fairly complicated and not all PCD is activated in exactly the same way, but in the most elemental sense the cell either receives a signal from other cells in the larger organism, or the cell internally recognizes that it is no longer functioning properly, and self-destructs."

Amanda pushed her plate aside, leaned forward, slid her left arm across the table, and in a gliding movement settled the side of her head against it. The pale hairs sprouting along her forearm seemed translucent in the candlelight. "So your work amounts to a suicide watch," she said, looking up at him out of a blond tangle of hair.

Unseen musicians in the other room began playing a bass-heavy ballad from the previous century and the room filled with soft, lazy nostalgia.

"Not exactly," he explained, swallowing a small ocean of saliva. "Difficulties arise when cells either fail to detect that they are internally compromised or do not recognize they are within an environment where they do not belong. That's why many cancers, for instance, have been so tenacious. Cancerous agents injure the cell's fragile DNA and the damaged cell often does not detect anything wrong; it goes on dividing and replicating more DNA-compromised cells. However, if all infected cells would simply self-destruct the problem could be solved. In the lab, we're experimenting with ways to signal malfunctioning cells through fragmented antibodies—to tell them that they are, in fact, compromised, induce the natural death process and make the cancer-producing agents available for digestion by healthy cells."

Amanda yawned and the slender hand on the end of her arm inched closer to August, an invasion that momentarily erased his memory of how to reason and breathe. When her two fingers lightly touched the side of his hand, the sensation caused such enraptured pleasure that he recoiled from it as from a roaring furnace.

Amanda burst into gaiety.

"Why are you laughing?" he asked, embarrassed by his uncontrolled reaction.

"You're so serious, August Helm. Such solemnity must come from carrying the weight of the world. Oh no, and now you're blushing."

"I'm sorry," he said, trying to look calm and unflustered.

"Don't be. Don't be sorry. Never be sorry. See, that's what I'm talking about. I think you and I are the same. Both of us have been doing the right thing for too long, trying to be responsible and productive. We've put off our own happiness. "

Then she sat up, took a sip of beer, and asked, "What if those cells you were talking about don't want to commit suicide? What if they're like us—like people—and decide to go on living anyway? There's probably no way they can be convinced."

"What are you saying?"

"People want to live—even if our bodies are falling apart, inside prisons, concentration camps, or slums, diving in dumpsters, or trapped in caves. We want to keep living. Why should our cells be any different?"

"Cells have no aptitude for wanting or decision-making. In fact, they have no aptitude at all. Cells are cells. They lack complexity of mind."

"Do they? Long ago, Roman slavers advertised humans-for-sale through a simple demonstration. A recently captured individual would be given a sumptuous meal—because it was an ill omen if someone died hungry—and offered a knife or other lethal instrument to take her own life. If the poor wretch did not commit suicide buyers could be confident they were purchasing a slave who willingly accepted her own enslavement The point is—we choose life with a lack of freedom or agency, even abuse or torture over death. And if someone signals us that it's our time to die, we're more likely than ever to persist just to spite them."

"That's not at all a useful analogy," August said. "Cells don't decide or feel spite; they simply react. It's their sole utility. They have no way of knowing whether the larger organism of which they are a part is good or bad. Their participation is purely perfunctory—chemical."

"Yes, but individuals maintain the species."

"On the contrary, genes continue, not species."

"Don't single cells know they're part of a larger organism?"

"Not in the way you're implying."

August could hear his voice rising and was unable to bring it under control. His former confidence unraveled inside him. "I doubt cells know anything, and whatever it is about them that might superficially resemble sentience is better understood as function, regulation and adaption."

"You just said they commit suicide."

"No, you introduced that term, Amanda. I only went along with it, which I can now see I probably should not have."

"Then it's your fault!" she announced triumphantly, and the gold flecks in her eyes became even more pronounced, as though the villagers had heaped more logs onto their distant campfires. She took a drink from her glass of beer, dismissively set it down, and slid it away from her.

"August, your sincerity is touching. By now, most guys I've met would have lied about how much money they made last year, mentioned a famous acquaintance or a wealthy relative, taken several important calls, told me how far they run every morning and how much they bench-press. I like your hands, we're identical in height, and our first names begin with the same vowel and have the same number of letters. The month and day of our birthdays, when added together, are prime numbers, which is—among other things—statistically significant. Let's go over to my apartment. There's a spectacular view from the balcony and it never seems right to enjoy it alone."

"Where do you live?"

"Downtown, overlooking the lake."

"Are you going to be braking with your left foot again?"

"I intend to. And I'll be briskly accelerating with my right."

"Let's go."

The following day as August worked in his lab synthesizing proteins, the better part of his mind resisted involvement with anything other than the dreamlike contemplation of naked events accomplished during the previous night. The ecstatic rapture experienced during those hours seemed significant even in broad daylight—an experience that, when remembered, continued to excite his pleasure circuits, exuding comfort and assurance for the future. Beginning when they first stepped out of the elevator on the twenty-ninth floor and walked into the spacious privacy of her apartment, each incremental act seemed vital to recall and relive. Making love with her had deposited in him a stash of mind-honey; and its sweetness could be sampled again and again. And because of this reentry into previous joys, August discovered a new satisfaction with his place in the world. He floated above himself from one luminous moment to the next in anticipation of even more happiness. A higher priority had been established, and all the loose ends of his life that had been struggling for purpose and meaning united under its bright, colorful banner.

The day after that, however, he was alarmed to notice that his memories had already aged. The somatic impressions caused by the sights, sounds, sensations, and smells from his night with Amanda were losing their ability to reward him for remembering them. His stash of mind-honey was losing its taste. Yes, he could still recall the spectacular view from the balcony, the cream-colored Argentinian leather sofa in the living room, the florid Spanish and Italian paintings on the walls, deep copper sinks in the kitchen and a silent Moroccan fan with long, wide wicker blades lazily circling over the bed. He could remember many endearing phrases that they'd spoken to each other, but he could no longer recall the exact way they had enunciated them. Nor could he recall how each moment of heightened drama had been pushed by another sensation into an even more intimate drama. Also diminished were the specific memories of when he'd first entered her—when the sentience factor of his mind exploded, and the mysteries of living were revealed. He suddenly knew the hiding places of all the missing links in the human evolutionary chain, the quantum origins of stardust, and the shape of a single graviton.

Then, two days later, those things remained as obscure as they had been before he'd met her.

On the third day, the fond intimacy he'd been so certain of sharing with Amanda was called into question, and he wondered: Did they *really* experience a mutual buoyancy of awareness and bliss? Were their appetites for intensity and completeness *really* sated before they came apart and sprawled out on the bed, moaning like contented drunkards? Did they both feel the same way about each other?

These questions could not be answered during phone conversations, of which there had been more than a few. And while it was mostly true that the sound of her voice conveyed comfort, and even inspiration, the modulated noise coming out of his cell phone seemed unable to assure him of what he most needed to know.

After four days, his desire to see her again mushroomed into unmanageable desperation.

When he suggested they see each other again, Amanda agreed, and over the weeks and months ahead they episodically renewed their affection for each other with many brief, yet wildly satisfying encounters.

When not together, their bodies waited for each other like runners only allowed to run on Saturdays—hungry, impulsive, demanding, and wantonly reckless.

PALE, POLISHED WOOD

AMANDA ONLY SPENT three nights in his apartment during the entire time they knew each other. They usually slept at her place—a condominium purchased by her parents in anticipation of perhaps moving to Chicago themselves. The accommodations at his small flat at Hyde Park Apartments were Spartan in comparison. There was exposed parking, for one thing, and the bathroom was inadequately furnished; and perhaps most importantly, the mattress on his narrow bed was too hard.

When it came to sleeping, she preferred everything to be just right and in handy reach. She had a routine and could not properly fall asleep without first taking several natural supplements for relaxation, swallowed with eight ounces of lactose- and fat-free bovine milk. She then needed to assure herself that the window closest to the bed would allow an ample current of air into the room, and if there were any disagreeable odors present, she lit a candle scented with bay leaf, lavender, or cinnamon. After taking her shower and carefully toweling dry, three different lotions were rubbed into her face, and a fourth applied to the rest of her skin until it resembled pale, polished wood. Staring into the mirror from only inches away, she brushed and flossed her teeth, gargled with mint-flavored mouthwash, and lowered a drop of eyewash into each green eye. After squeezing her eyelids together to wring out the excess moisture and dabbing them with tissue, she put on a loose-fitting cotton top that would not pull at her neck or underarms. She then stepped into a pair of equally loose-fitting cotton shorts, drew them up her long legs and secured them around her waist with a cotton draw-cord tied with a simple knot to avoid the lump of a bow. Then she rubbed a fifth lotion into her hands and wriggled them inside a pair of protective white cotton gloves. After climbing into bed, she unwrapped a sugar-free lemon-flavored cough drop, placed it in her mouth and positioned it for all-night dissolving between her gums and cheek. Finding her sleeping mask, she placed it over her eyes, pulled the covers up to her chin, lay absolutely still and took stock of her extremities. Several minutes later she usually discovered that her feet needed more lotion in order to remedy chafing around her toes. When this dryness had been corrected she returned to bed, put the sleeping mask back on, and attempted to find a comfortable position. After several more minutes, she often found that additional lotion had not been enough to satisfy the demands from her feet, which now complained—even in the middle of summer—of being a little too cold. Sometimes this could be solved by a pair of Norwegian socks that did not cling to her ankles and resisted bunching up, but more often a small heating pad was required between the mattress and bottom sheet. Later, after sufficient warmth had developed below her knees, the pad needed to be turned down to avoid overheating, With her feet no longer pleading for attention, Amanda was able to concentrate on the rhythmic sounds of oceanic waves sloshing against a rocky shore, reproduced through a digital device next to the bed and high fidelity speakers in four corners of the room. And if she still could not sleep, she watched a program about the building of medieval cathedrals, viewed through a fur-lined video-visor. Then just as the sleep-inducing narrative succeeded in coaxing her into drowsiness—yet before falling unconscious—she turned the visor off, exchanged it for the eye mask and turned onto her left side with her hip thrust into the middle of the bed. In the morning, her preparations for meeting the new day were even more elaborate.

Needless to say, August could think of only her. Whenever they were together time unspooled faster than he could experience. Activities like sharing a meal, attending a concert, shopping, walking through a museum, watching a movie, loitering along the lake, and making love in new places and positions seemed to conclude almost as soon as they began, and long before they were appreciated. He wanted more of her and there was never enough time for the acquisition. Consequently, he kept feeling closer and closer to her without actually knowing her any better.

Yet when August was not with Amanda, time was never a problem. Without her, temporality accumulated, compounded and overflowed. Eating meals alone, watching movies alone, and touring museums alone became self-imposed marathons, deserts of annihilating emptiness that could only be slogged through by offsetting the boredom with thoughts of Amanda.

Most of August's conscious life, it seemed, was spent reliving earlier erotic episodes, fretting about ways in which his participation in those amorous events may have fallen short, wondering if introducing other sensual and sensuous activities would enhance or distract from the quality of their orgasms, worrying that she might not feel as committed to commingling as he, and berating himself for the enormous amount of time he was wasting while thinking about these things.

In truth, Amanda and August were not well suited for each other. They'd both spent an unnaturally long time in school, and learning to manage their sexual instincts within the larger context of the rest of their lives had been neglected as they acquired the vocabulary, symbols, rules, and skills needed to participate in the provinces of science and finance. Unfamiliar with and unprepared for the tyrannical joys of unlimited sensual commerce with a willing, sane, and avid partner, they had few practical defenses against its pleasures. And though their frequent activities may have shared some resemblance to addictive behaviors, there were no deleterious side effects that either of them could detect. Digestion and brain function remained normal, and the uptake of serotonin, oxytocin, and other social-regulating hormones remained undiminished by the euphoric mental states induced through the manipulation of erogenous regions and the frenzied, blissful emergency that immediately preceded the release of deeply held psychophysical tensions.

They were having fun—a kind of fun that seemed to have been designed for them by nature herself.

Though they mostly spent every weekend together, they rarely discussed their own specialized professions or the melodramas taking place within their workplaces. And while August occasionally remarked on something surprising or amusing at the lab, or on some anecdote involving the primary investigator, Dr. Peter Grafton, whom he particularly admired, Amanda was more adept at keeping to herself everything that did not immediately involve August, which may have been correlated to her unflagging ability to be impeccably dressed and appropriately made-up at all times. Her upbringing had made it clear: only go out looking, feeling and functioning your best. She avoided August whenever her health or the demands of her work left her unable to be at the very top of her form.

Only once was this not possible, and it happened after one of the rare nights when Amanda stayed over in August's apartment.

They were both up after only sleeping three or four hours. Vibrant red and orange beamed into the kitchen from the maple tree outside, surrounding them with festal colors entirely unsuited to their sleepy selves. Still dressed in the underclothes she'd slept in, Amanda sat slumped over the small table, staring into a steaming cup of coffee as though it were a crystal ball.

"More caffeine?" August asked, standing next to her with the metal pot in his hand.

She waved him away with a severe frown. Refilling his own cup, August sat across from her and tried to figure out what to do.

They'd been out all night, had eaten and drank too much, and had slept poorly. Amanda had apparently contracted a flu virus earlier in the week and was now feverish, sniffling, glass-eyed, and aching. Unaccustomed to enduring such awkward moments with August, Amanda seemed especially distressed. For the first time, their relationship could neither be defined nor explained through the strong physical attraction they felt for each other. Their respective genders had no relevance and there were suddenly no prescribed roles to play.

It seemed he didn't know her at all, and August was reminded of years earlier when he'd worked as an insufficiently trained medical aide inside a rural hospital. Upon entering a new patient's room, he never knew what to expect.

Some people, when ill, remained cordial; they accepted discomfort uncomplainingly, gladly tolerated company, and were thankful for whatever assistance came their way. Others underwent more radical changes, seethed against the injustice of their suffering, and viewed everyone and everything around them as conspiring to worsen their misery. For still others, illness bestowed a moral obligation to suffer thoroughly, without any hope of future release; for these folks, it was important to identify the reasons they'd been singled out for punishment, face their shortcomings, and learn from the experience. August was most familiar with this method because it well served both his mother and himself. Still others experienced a solemn anointing, a chance to claim their rightful place among tormented figures of old;

they were convinced their agony far exceeded the discomfort experienced by others with similar afflictions, and took pride in this distinction. The more introverted individuals did not relate to the public world at all, and retreated into an inner arena where they could silently and solemnly engage the primordial enemy without distraction. And other sufferers threw in the towel at the first twinge of discomfort; their last days, last meals, and last breaths were perpetually at hand. There were also people who saw sickness as corporal misbehavior and felt humiliated by someone finding out about their indiscretion of being ill and attempted to hide their symptoms; when asked how they were doing, they invariably said, "I'm fine."

"Can I get you an aspirin, juice or something?" August whispered.

Staring at him out of watery eyes, Amanda said, "You have no idea how to take care of me, August, do you? None. Look at this horrible place. What am I doing here?" She found her clothes from the night before, hurried down the stairs and toward her car, which was parked along the road with a parking ticket lodged under the wiper blade. Once behind the wheel, she sat for several minutes with the engine running, then drove away.

August remained at the table, bathed in orange and red light. Then somewhere in the higher atmosphere, a thick cumulonimbus moved between the sun and planet Earth and the brilliant colors in the room vanished. The leaves beyond the window turned rusty brown and the dismal sight had so little in common with the same spectacle from minutes earlier that it seemed like a different room, different tree, and different world.

What did she mean, "You have no idea how to take care of me"? The statement seemed unfair because, well, how did she know what ideas he had about taking care of her? It wasn't a topic they'd ever discussed.

As the gloom settled in closer, he dialed her number.

She didn't answer.

Unable to remain in his apartment any longer, August found his coat and walked the five blocks to the laboratory, where he needed to turn in a requisition slip he'd forgotten to fill out on Friday. Monthly requests for new supplies went out on Mondays, and it was embarrassing to be stranded without needed equipment or reagents.

The out-of-doors felt moist and cool, lightly laced with a fragrance of smoldering sweetness, the early smells of autumn. Neighborhood traffic was light and unhurried, and like most other Sundays the campus stood nearly empty. Two security guards in yellow Day-Glo vests walked beside each other without talking, and an older man with an unruly sheaf of papers pressed under his left arm hurried northeast across an expanse of mowed lawn.

The Pemberton Building opened to August's passkey. On the third floor, he walked down the hallway, through a locked corridor and into the lab from the rear. The long, marble-floored room was dark, empty, silent, and immaculately clean, and because he was seldom inside it without other people, it seemed strangely unfamiliar. The station for running DNA gels, water baths, orbital shakers, rockers, incubators, and workstations with computers and clusters of paper seemed perversely empty and silent. The nitrogen and carbon dioxide tanks, safety showers, eyewash stations, and shelves of stored chemicals—they all seemed slightly unreal without people milling around them.

He crossed into the smaller room to the side, where the requisition slips were kept in a file cabinet, and at the adjacent table began filling in the appropriate slots.

There was some noise in the primary investigator's office—one room down the hall. It sounded like pieces of furniture bumping against each other, followed by rapid, muffled conversation. Then a short burst of unsteady laughter and another furniture collision.

Usually, when Dr. Grafton was in, he stayed buried under bound and unbound volumes of correspondence with the grant committee, progress reports, compliance forms, and schedules. The man was a textbook of busy. In addition to designing and supervising research, the slope-shouldered fifty-three-year-old professor lectured in the classroom, coordinated graduate seminars, served as department chairman, maintained a private consulting practice, kept a small garden, and jogged a half hour each morning. He had been August's advisor in graduate school and August had taken (and, in later years, helped teach) his courses. Sometimes, August flattered himself in thinking they were friends, at least as much as their respective ages and academic traditions allowed.

Another laugh—this one less restrained—came from his office. August walked down the hall and stood outside the closed door. More furniture bumping came from inside, then a long, drawn-out utterance he could not at first identify. As soon as he formed an idea about the sound, he retreated back to the room he'd come out of, but not before knocking over a carton of cleaning supplies that had been left in the hallway.

The office behind the closed door immediately fell silent. A very short time later, the door opened and Lindiwe Sisulu, the undergraduate lab manager from Nigeria, stepped quietly into the hallway. She gracefully looked up and down the hallway, tucked the ends of her blouse into her skirt, skillfully worked her left foot into her shoe, flashed two bright brown eyes in August's direction, smiled in a dismissive manner, and hurried down the hall.

August returned to filling out the request form.

A short time later Professor Grafton walked into the room and stood behind him.

"August," he enunciated with uncertainty, as if he were unsure of either the name or how he should pronounce it.

"Hello, Dr. Grafton," August replied, turning around.

Dr. Grafton inspected August. "I wasn't aware you came in on Sundays."

"I forgot to fill out my supply request," said August.

The professor walked to the window and looked into the lab, as though to check for other unannounced intruders in his morning. "Tell me again what you're working on, August."

"I'm sure you remember. We talked Friday about the—"

"Right, right, mutation amplification. What do you need to order?"

"Fab fragments."

"Oh, yes, from that Ohio pharma-lab, right, right."

Dr. Grafton came away from the window and sat opposite August at the small table, summoning an even more awkward silence into the room. Cupping his hands, he closed his eyes briefly beneath his unkempt eyebrows, and said, "Look, August, I feel a little compromised here."

"No need," August replied, and when this wasn't having the desired effect, he added, "I'm sorry about that."

"I wonder what you might be thinking."

"I'm not thinking anything, Dr. Grafton."

Another, deeper silence settled around them, and inside it they searched like trapped miners for a way out.

The older man found something to say before August did. "Lindiwe Sisulu has been accepted into the premed program, you know."

"I heard that."

"And she speaks four languages."

"As I recall, Professor, so do you."

"Are you judging me, August?"

"No, I'm not."

"I suspect you believe it's highly unethical and possibly even immoral for me to take liberties with a student, especially an undergraduate."

"Liberties?"

"That's a euphemism."

"I can only assume she was as eager as you were."

"You're right, she was," he quickly replied, the thought apparently bringing welcome, temporary relief. He shifted in his chair. "It was her idea."

"I see . . . what idea was that?"

"Stop playing with me, August."

Dr. Grafton reached across the table, took the requisition form, read it, and slid it back. "We don't do this very often."

"Look, this is none of my business, Dr. Grafton. I only came in today to fill out my requisition form. You really don't need to say anything."

"No, maybe not, but August . . . perhaps if we could talk openly . . . like two people who meet on the street and will never see each other again?"

"That seems a little unlikely with your name on the bottom of my paycheck, but I understand what you mean. What do you want to talk about?"

"Women and sex."

"I'm not sure two strangers would talk about that, but okay."

"It's sometimes helpful to remember how we got into this erogenous nightmare. People didn't always live like this. Before standardized systems of exchange, do you know how earlier societies managed contractual relationships?"

"Gifts?" suggested August.

"Precisely. People gave presents to secure goodwill, obtain a necessary share of the community's resources, confer honor, maintain tribal alliances, and affirm loyalty. Powerful families received the most gifts, of course, but the gifts they received also obligated them to the gift givers."

"Which is probably why we're still reluctant to accept favors of any kind, even among family members," suggested August.

"And the earliest gift giving," the professor continued, "often involved giving away cattle, beads, food, clothing, young women, and girls. Patriarchs exchanged daughters so they could have more wives, or their sons could have wives. In this way, families became interdependent, increasing the likelihood of survival."

Dr. Grafton stood up from the table, walked to the window, and gazed into the lab again. The brief silence he created seemed to want to be filled.

"Where are you going with this?" August asked.

"Right to the heart of the matter, August. Men increased their social status by possessing young females. And women's status was enhanced by being possessed by high-status males. These are still our primal social instincts, and the rest of our so-called civilization has been hung like cheap costume jewelry around those mutual compulsions."

"We stopped swapping daughters a long time ago," August objected.

"That's completely irrelevant to what I'm saying."

"I thought this was going to be a conversation, like two men meeting for the first time on the street."

"It is. I'm the lecturing stranger."

The professor came away from the window. "The endless entanglements involved with forming new social arrangements, broadening familial influence, preserving customs, establishing orderly relations with in-laws, raising children and such, harnessed the human sexual drive to serve the wider community. Excess sexual energy was spent— and is spent—on erecting things like government bureaucracies, educational systems, religious orders, sports teams, economic hierarchies, gated communities, and other means of determining status—all driven by the lure of better sex: rise to the top, win the prize, and you'll get better sex. And that implicit promise has made an orderly society possible."

"This is very overstated," August said.

"These are broad statements, I admit, but let's be frank, how many waking hours do you devote to either thinking about sex or trying not to think about it?"

"I really don't think about it that much."

"That's the universal lie we allow each other to keep repeating. Just look at the effort some religious ascetics consume in trying to overcome their procreative impulses. And what is there to show for thousands of years of vigorously applied sexual suppression—beyond the bitter fruit of lingering misogyny? When the pious fail to overcome their basic instinct by condemning it, they blame women."

"There's probably some truth in that, but all the examples you give are of arranged marriages, which are almost exclusively among prominent families and are obviously public, while sexual relations themselves take place—almost exclusively—in private. Other people don't typically know about them. Men have sex with other men and women sleep with other women; men and women have sex with themselves. Sex happens all the time, everywhere, officially and unofficially, sanctioned by society, ignored by society, and condemned by it, and that's been going on for an eternity as well. People don't even limit their gender identities to conform to binary roles. So it's very hard to generalize about what people are up to sexually, because sex is mostly a private matter."

"August, I'm trying to explain the dynamics of evolving social power structures and how sexuality contributes to their formation. Because sexuality reaches into every aspect of our identity, every facet of our experience of the world and role within it, it never remains a private matter. Our urges are so demanding they can even overwhelm the will to live. Regrettably, some people commit suicide because they cannot foresee ever meeting the insatiable requests made by their libidos to be fulfilled and loved. I'm trying to tell you about *me*."

"I'm still listening," said August.

"In former times, if a lower-class couple had the good fortune to give birth to an unusually attractive, lively, and clever daughter, the whole family would work toward maximizing that advantage, hoping for greater comfort, better health, higher social status, and improved security."

"Didn't work out too well for the Boleyn sisters."

"That was true for Mary and Anne, but King Henry conferred a number of titles on their brothers; and the father later became the maternal grandfather to the Queen of England."

"Slim compensation for having your daughter beheaded, if you ask me."

"Which proves my point, August. Look how far Henry went to replace the woman in his bed with a younger and more enthusiastic participant. He defied his church and his court to secure a prize he couldn't prevent himself from wanting. The desire for the optimum sexual partner is the mortar of civilization, the primal urge working overtime to maintain the species. We flatter ourselves by thinking that economic systems are the engines of prosperity. Markets only provide a context for the old mating impulse to unfurl inside. Having great wealth has always been of secondary or tertiary importance. Without the promise of better sex in the future, the value of wealth diminishes. Our civilization, religions, and economic systems are built upon postponed erotic energy. And those same Marxists who claim we are consumed by our positions within social hierarchies are like attendees at a masquerade ball who choose to focus on the masks instead of the naked bodies beneath the costumes. *Everyone* simply wants better sex, and they want it now and tomorrow and the day after. Sex is the frosting holding all the other layers together."

"So, the folks at the top—in the biggest houses, with the most servants—should be content."

"It may not work out, but that's the promise, and without it, civilization ends."

"This is just an observation, but from the women I've known," said August, "it's hard to imagine them not having a lot to say about whatever arrangements are made for them, even in the most male-dominated cultures. For instance, women have for a long time been organizing their husbands' farms, businesses, households, and all the other details of life. Try to run an elementary school classroom and you'll find out what I'm talking about."

"That's irrelevant, because desirable women want to be in splendid houses with many servants as much as the owners of splendid houses with many servants desire to have them there. The point I'm trying to make is that—historically—decisions concerning young women's and girls' reproductive habits included a lot of people. They were societal decisions, involving neighborhoods, and in the cases of kings and queens, entire countries. But all those checks and balances are gone now. We're adrift with no way to steer the boat. Only recently do women of childbearing age with big eyes, blooming breasts, perfect teeth, and unforgettable behinds walk around in public fully revealed, conscious, smart, and empowered."

Dr. Grafton paused for several moments and looked at August, seeking some indication of agreement. When he did not find it, he frowned.

"I don't think you appreciate the point I'm making, August. And frankly this surprises me. All I'm saying is those earlier sociosexual practices really existed and we are all heirs to them. But women themselves are doing the negotiating now, and, August, we're not ready for that. Before long, these women will own all the big houses themselves, and we'll be standing outside wondering how the hell we're ever going to get in. This is a new age, August, and we're not prepared for it. The mental equipment we were born with is attuned for surviving, adapting, and reproducing in a bygone era. And until we figure this new one out our society will continue to unravel."

"Everyone has choices," August objected.

"That's what I thought myself, until it happened to me. It began with ordinary kindnesses, a smile that stayed on Lindiwe's face slightly longer and seemed more genuine than other smiles—not a lot, but enough to be noticeable. Before I knew it, there were a few playful exchanges between us. They seemed restrained enough at the time, but later, upon reflection, I felt compromised by them. Hugging each other a little too long; laughing together in a liberated way. And as soon as there was something between us to hide, she knew exactly how to amplify the intimacy of those shared secrets, and we became accomplices in something blissfully forbidden, even though nothing yet had really happened between us. The pleasure of seeing her increased tenfold."

August smiled.

Dr. Grafton stood up again.

One of the heavy doors at the end of the hall closed and they could hear footsteps coming toward them. They both turned as Lindiwe walked into the room carrying a bright red file folder.

"August," she said, aiming her voice and fierce eyes in his direction. "You didn't return your requisition form this month. Is that it?"

She snapped up the sheet of paper from the table and inspected it.

"It's unsigned," she said, handing it back. "They must be signed. It's stipulated in the grant's charter. Right, Professor?"

"That's correct, Lindi."

August scribbled his name and returned the form to her.

"Thank you," she said, and inspected the form again. "We've changed suppliers on fabs. They're not available through the Ohio pharma-lab anymore. And the Minnesota lab has been having trouble lately with quality control, so we now obtain fabricated antibody supplies from California."

She inserted the page neatly into the folder. "What were you two talking about?"

"Nothing in particular," said August, looking at the floor.

"Nothing important," said Dr. Grafton.

"Then perhaps we can all talk about it together."

The two men remained silent.

August stole a quick look at her. The only thing changed from when he'd seen her in the hallway was her hair, which had been carefully put back into place, with perhaps a touch of eye shadow added to her eyes. August pictured her standing before a mirror in one of the large bathrooms at the end of the corridor, patting herself into place while her confidence rose. The rich darkness of her face, neck, and arms made her hard to look away from.

"Some of the maple trees have turned color already," August remarked.

"Yes, I noticed that," she responded. "It seems early. Did you notice the trees changing, Professor?"

"Sorry, I didn't."

"I only recently noticed," August added.

The topic died. Her brown eyes settled first on August, waited, and then moved to Dr. Grafton. Both blanched and looked away.

"Well," she added. "If either of you have anything else to discuss with me, I'm available. Professor, we have some work between us to finish, but I'll leave you two alone for now. You'll find me in your office."

She turned and stepped confidently out of the room. Her footsteps moved down the hall and the door to the office opened and closed.

"See what I mean," said the professor. "Women—all women—instinctually know things about us that we don't know about ourselves."

"Oh no, don't include me in this," August objected. "And it's not because I don't understand what you're saying, it's because I don't agree with it."

"Then perhaps some examples closer to home might help," said Dr. Grafton.

"What are you saying?"

"That woman you introduced me to several months ago—at the party following the seminar's end, what's her name?"

"Amanda Clark."

"You seemed quite attached to her."

"I am."

"And what do you imagine will come of that?"

"It wouldn't surprise me if we spend the rest of our lives together. I mean, it sure looks like it might happen."

"Really? That's nice to hear. Now let me be sure we're talking about the same woman I remember—the tall blonde with the mid-engine, twin-turbo Italian, sports car who works for Collins and McPhee Investment, whose family lives in Woods Hole, summers in New Hampshire, and vacations on those small, exotic islands in the South Pacific—the woman who sometimes, while standing in a check-out line, adds up the grocery items in her cart and estimates what that same amount would yield over the average life expectancy for an upper income nonsmoking Midwestern female with no family history of heart disease invested at the current rate of return on government bonds? Is that the Amanda you're talking about?"

"How do you know all that?"

"You told me."

"Sorry, I forgot. Yes, that's her."

"And you think you have a future with her?"

"I'm sure of it in fact."

"Well, congratulations. What's her family like? What do they think of you?"

"I haven't met them yet."

"Oh, why not?"

"No particular reason. I've asked about going home with her to visit, but when we get around to actual dates, well, they haven't yet materialized. But I'm sure it will happen."

"That's understandable, I guess. Her family lives all the way out on the East Coast. So how many times have the two of you visited your own parents? As I remember, August, they live only three hours away. In that Italian vehicle, you could probably cut that time in half. The two of you could drive over and back in a single day—on less than a half tank of gas—and be home in time to catch a bite at the diner and watch a movie before going to bed."

"Well, I suggested it once or twice but—"

"And?"

"Something came up. We're both very busy."

"I see. Then let me ask you this, and I'll try to be as delicate as possible. When you first met Amanda did you ever wonder if she was, well, a little out of your league?"

"What do you mean?"

"Come on, August, be serious. It's one of the first things you notice about a woman—her social standing. As a species, we're attuned to such things—always have been. And we can be deeply hurt, in a psychological sense, when we don't measure up to someone we feel attracted to—a woman especially. I mean, to avoid being rejected a man will harness himself to years—even decades—of difficult and degrading work to eventually be more socially attractive to a particular woman. Issues of rank and class are built into us, and they run deep. We understand them at a reptilian level: sex and power. If you can afford expensive clothes, a big house, and a huge boat, you get to sleep with costly women. It's the Gatsby Syndrome and we all understand it. Most of us learn it in grade school. When we meet someone—in the first few nanoseconds—we notice prominent physical features, deportment, health, age, alertness, ethnicity, personal grooming, intelligence, hygiene, and social class.

We instinctually sense if a person we've just met is above or beneath us; it's genetic, and we can no more turn off those pre-cognitive apperceptions than will our hearts to stop beating. Women know exactly what they're worth; their price tags are in plain sight, and all men know how to read them."

August couldn't keep from laughing. "Oh, Dr. Grafton, excuse me. Women know they're worth more than what's in plain sight, and those who don't are quickly learning. Perhaps it's a generational difference; younger people don't see the world as you do. The instinctual impressions you speak of—the ones we experience when meeting new people: Amanda and I pay little attention to most of them. We don't react in the way you do. It's like in the early days of cinematography— moving pictures, they called them—when terror-driven audiences would stampede out of theaters, trampling over those who could not move fast enough to avoid the sight of oncoming trains. When modern moviegoers watch those same films today, of course they see the same images, but they don't react to them in the same way. Sorry, I don't mean to criticize you—I really don't—but stranger to stranger, those old social ranking standards make no difference to Amanda or me. They're not relevant anymore."

"You've got to be joking."

"I'm not."

"Then you're living in a fantasy world, August. Why do you think Amanda felt safe with you? She knew she could have you in the way she wanted, and that you wouldn't offer any resistance."

"I'm afraid I don't follow what you're saying."

"You've been overtaken, August. She's put you in her jewelry box and you don't even realize it."

"You're wrong, Dr. Grafton, with all due respect. The way you read your present situation, and mating markets in general, doesn't have anything to do with Amanda and me. I have the utmost admiration for you—you know that—and you're of course perfectly free to interpret conventions in whatever manner you want, but you talk as though people have little control over their lives, as though cultural appetites dictate individual behaviors. I don't believe that. There's a way of loving women and of women loving men and men loving men and women loving women that seeks neither station nor power. And while we're talking about this, I might add that all the examples you gave about former social practices ignored the much, much longer periods when human societies moved from location to location in response to seasonal changes and in search of optimal hunting and foraging opportunities—before agriculture, before private property, before priesthoods, before patriarchy, and before women fell under the rule of priest-kings and were turned into chattel. During those much longer time periods people loved each other without the encumbrances of status seeking, and without the imposition of hierarchies of power. That's how Amanda and I love each other right now, freely and openly, in the old way—the real way."

The professor stood up from the table and shoved his hands into the pockets of his pleated pants.

"I apologize if I offended you, August," he said. "It was never my intention."

The new tone in his voice announced that the conversation was over. He went to the window and said, "By the way, I recently learned that Engineering will be installing a new furnace in this building before winter. It will necessitate shutting down the lab for several weeks to avoid airborne contaminants, perhaps for even as long as a month."

"When?"

"Soon."

A GRIEF UNLIKE ANY OTHER

WHEN A ROMANCE first begins to die the symptoms are nearly imperceptible; they hide inside shared habits and other familiarities and can be readily ignored for a very long time. Occasionally, they even completely disappear for indefinite periods of time, while mutual fondness and comforting pleasures remain on course.

Even under the most optimum circumstances, it's hard to hear the discordance—a tiny, insignificant sigh so fragile it does not even leave a memory trace. If noticed at all, it's immediately forgotten.

As the decay deepens, it's still possible to ignore it, but some effort begins to be required in looking the other way. The symptoms remain in the background, like transient voltage spikes—a blink in the ambient lighting—a sudden premonition, or groundless fear, a lightheadedness that quickly appears and just as quickly goes away. Something is said that might later—when remembered—be considered sarcastic; a reassuring reply is fully anticipated but not forthcoming; a look appears—for a fleeting moment—to conceal another, slightly more malicious expression beneath it.

Yet benign reasons can usually be found to explain these subtle warnings— stress at work, a disagreeable meal, uncomfortable clothes, poor health, alarming reports on the news, and even inclement weather. And as long as there are no open arguments, lovemaking continues more or less without interruption.

Yet throughout all these rationalizations, the nervous system's deeply buried center of autonomic reckoning keeps processing all the available information, comparing cell-level algorithms generated through nutrition uptake against those spawned by hormonal production and incoming stimulus response, sending out encrypted chains of amino acids that read like unconscious tickertape: *There's a fundamental problem down here.*

Most of the time these cell-level warnings aren't decipherable, but sometimes a particularly romantic individual wakes up from a troubled sleep, climbs from bed, walks to a window, stares into a silent, empty street, and wonders about smoking a cigarette or ingesting drugs to correct an unease that isn't quite identifiable, and a message will sometimes work its way out of the many layers of subconscious quicksand and into the gloaming: *There's something wrong in the most important room in your house.*

At first, August's worry about his relationship with Amanda amounted to nothing more than a worry—a needless worry. His personal history was rife with excessive concern for the things closest to him, and nervous vigilance was one of his most pronounced internal characteristics. On some days, a great majority of his neural activity clustered within the anterior cingulate cortex—the brain's strife center—and what other people might call panic attacks were an accepted part of his daily maintenance schedule.

Nevertheless, August eventually reached a psychological plateau whereon his suspicions that something might be wrong between him and Amanda needed to be openly examined. He'd wrestled with them as long as he could on his own. A direct test probe had to be sent out.

"I'm worried," he told Amanda as they drank sparkling water during the intermission to a lavish theater performance—a contemporary comedy so popular it had been extended into a seventh week. Tickets were hard to get, and Amanda had obtained them from someone at her workplace. The theater was packed.

"Worried about what?" she asked.

Her lipstick left smudges on the rim of her transparent plastic cup, and her eyes darted around the richly carpeted room. Dressed in a snug, low-cut black dress, with a double loop of pearls collaring her neck, and standing in black spike heels, she seemed anxious for the next act to begin, hungry for the lights to go down and the entertainment to continue. She frequently shifted her weight, an impatient, leg-scissoring exercise that repositioned her arched posterior in ways that had been attracting the attention of several nattily dressed men in the lobby along with the dedicated hostility of the women standing next to them. And because Amanda had long ago become accustomed to having a strong effect upon people around her, she remained oblivious.

"Sometimes it seems, or at least it appears to me, occasionally, that we don't get on quite as well as maybe we once did," suggested August, his voice, so far, holding steady. "Do you ever worry about that?"

"Worrying isn't something I do nearly as well as you, dear one," she said. "And why would you ask something like that in a place like this? It's not like we can really talk here."

She was right, of course. And August experienced several things at once, including an agreeable surge of vanity because of accompanying someone so immanently noticeable that people stared at her as though she were sending semaphore from a rescue ship; at the same time he wished Amanda would stand still, and wondered if there was some way to publicly announce that her incessant physical movements were not planned to incite attention or develop a new sign language based on derriere placement, but were only a way of releasing excessive energy generated through an overactive adrenal gland—as unintentional as someone drumming fingers on a steering wheel while stuck in traffic. If humans could be imagined as wind-up toys—and August saw no reason they couldn't be—Amanda's main spring had been given extra turns. And in addition to these thoughts, he was openly engaged in ocular swordsmanship—thrusting quick stares at the most aggressive male onlookers in the lobby and forcing them to look away.

"Perhaps later then," he said.

"Yes," she agreed. "We'll talk about it later."

But of course, they didn't.

While brunching the next morning at a place not far from Amanda's condominium, August asked if she'd like to accompany him on a short visit to his parents' home in Wisconsin. "It isn't far. We can drive up and back on the same day."

"That sounds wonderful," she replied. "Let me think about it for awhile." She adjusted her smart watch, lowered a tiny dollop of honey into a cup of mint tea, and stirred. The metal spoon piped against the thin sides of her cup.

Because of the rain, which had been steadily falling all morning, only a few other people were in the diner. Without enough customers to keep them busy, the waiters talked with each other behind the cash register, and a dishwasher periodically wandered out of the kitchen, leaned against the counter, and stared into the wet street.

"I was also wondering if you'd like to spend next weekend at a B&B on the lake. We could get out of the city, sleep late, have a couple home-cooked meals, and—"

"I'd love to, but department heads are flying in from New York. I'm part of the team chosen to show them around."

"All weekend?"

"We'll be at the convention center on Saturday for policy briefs, cheap entertainment, and overpriced food. On Sunday we're taking them on a charter boat to Michigan for catered dinner with an open microphone. One of the vice presidents apparently has a comedy routine she likes to perform."

"Too bad."

"I know. They pay us well, though, and I've never been asked to do this kind of thing before. It could mean they're thinking about promoting me."

The tip of Amanda's index finger adroitly pushed the last bite of brioche into her mouth. "After the New York honchos leave I'll have some time off and we can get together—next week."

"But that's just before we close down the laboratory," August complained. "We're under pressure to compile our data and Dr. Grafton is expecting an outline for a transmembrane signaling monograph that he can putter around with and eventually publish."

"You could write it now."

"I'm already doing that, but he wants to include an experiment he's still working out."

Amanda frowned and cautiously tested the yolk bump rising out of her poached egg with the prong of a fork. When yellow fluid gushed out, she frowned, abandoned her fork beside the eruption and took a sip of tea. "We'll have to wait."

During the next week, waiting became increasingly difficult for August. And midmorning the following Saturday, he packed sandwiches, an apple, and a bottle of water and rode his bicycle downtown.

It seemed a long time since he'd last ridden, and the lack of familiarity in the required muscle movements added to the pleasure. The air seemed crisp, and the hum and crackle of hard pneumatic tires running over pavement and dry leaves added to the general perception of a fine morning. It was one of those autumn days when sunlight sprawled across the streets and lawns like golden blankets. He liked cycling and wondered why he didn't do more of it. The sounds of the neighborhood rang with bell-like clarity.

As vehicle traffic thickened, he chose his paths more judiciously, moving between sidewalks, streets, bus lanes, open lots, and alleyways. He wove in and out of other bikers, pedestrians, sidewalk tables and chairs, kiosks, and hydrants. At the park, he locked the bike into one of the public racks along the sidewalk.

Many people had decided to take advantage of the warm day. All benches with a lake view were occupied. Joggers with strained faces ran around dog walkers, and exercisers shared the grassy spaces with teams of young people in street clothes playing touch football and tossing Frisbees. Couples spread blankets on the ground and pulled lunches out of woven baskets, and wine bottles from narrow paper sacks. Three jugglers entertained onlookers by tossing rubber balls and elongated bowling pins through the air.

August found an empty bench across the street from the entrance to Amanda's condo building. Placing his pack beside him, he took out a cucumber and lettuce sandwich, bit off a corner, and resumed reading an article about charting neuropeptide behavior during protein formation.

It wasn't that he didn't believe Amanda when she said she'd be at the convention center. He did, or at least his mind's majority did; but the minority had become so shrill lately that to appease it he'd decided to spend several hours riding his bike, hanging around the park, doing some reading, and proving his insecurities unfounded.

After sitting for fifteen minutes, he took the last bite of his sandwich, looked up from his reading material, and watched Amanda step through the double doors of the building across the street, accompanied by a tall, athletic-looking man. They were both laughing. His right hand was at her back. Once outside, they turned left and Amanda performed one of her gravity-defying skipping hops as she synchronized strides with her companion's, taking hold of his arm. Setting a leisurely pace, they seemed completely absorbed in their conversation, barely noticing anything else around them.

August's soul collapsed. Watching them move in and out of the flow of other pedestrians—as a single, rehearsed unit—he thought about death. His and theirs. It seemed that any crime, no matter how heinous, could be forgiven if it took away the unbearable torment he experienced. Adrenaline rushed into his veins, evoking in his mind a silent, murderous rage. Every muscle fiber in his body stiffened.

He went after them. At the first intersection, they waited for the light to change, stood close together, and stared into each other's faces. The man beside her took a card-sized object out of his jacket pocket and handed it to her. They both looked at it, smiling. Then Amanda pointed across the street. Her companion's head turned and they both began shouting and waving.

By this time August was less than thirty feet away. "You go," he heard Amanda say. "I forgot my phone. I'll catch up."

Her companion walked briskly across the street and was immediately embraced by an older man and woman standing under a wide yellow awning. All three were tall and dressed in expensive clothes.

Amanda turned back toward her building.

When she saw August, they both stopped.

The expression on August's face accurately conveyed the exaggerated hormonal situation inside him, and in the first moment of recognition Amanda looked frightened. Then she regained her composure and rushed forward.

"August, what are you doing here?" she demanded, her eyes moist, her cheeks glowing with color.

"Who is that guy?"

She seemed perfectly composed, self-contained, and August realized that sometime in the last year she had learned how to swim.

He was drowning.

"What guy?" she asked.

"The one you came out of your building with."

"That's my brother, John. What are you doing here?"

"Your brother? What about those visiting department heads?"

"My plans changed. John drove up from Kansas City to meet our parents. They flew in this morning. That's them across the street."

"Your parents are here?"

"Yes, right over there. Look, I need pictures and forgot my phone. Wait right here. Everything will be fine. Wait right here. I'll be back."

Amanda returned to the building, running in her heels.

August stood in the middle of the sidewalk and attempted to digest what had happened. At first, relief flooded over him and he felt like an extinguished fire. Across the intersection, John talked to his parents. They looked like an advertisement for standing under a yellow awning in coordinated fall colors—relaxed, friendly, intelligent, and fun-to-know.

After thinking several feet deeper into his situation, August became acquainted with a pressing urge to flee. The compulsion grew stronger as he pictured Amanda returning with her camera, joining the advertisement on the other side of the intersection . . . and like a spectator to his own actions, he hurried to the park bench, took up his pack, yanked his bicycle from the rack, and rode away.

Back in his apartment, he spent most of the next two days trying to force unmanageable feelings back into their stalls. Meanwhile, he kept expecting to hear from her, and every hour that she didn't call he promised himself to call her.

But he didn't.

Why and how did his affection for Amanda—the pleasure he took in her company, his appreciation for her quick mind and extraordinary attractiveness—change into an illusion of ownership? By what dark alchemy did his good fortune in knowing her turn into unbearable torment? What insanity had convinced him—without a shred of actual evidence—that he could claim her as a rightful part of his future? And most shameful of all, when he saw her holding the arm of another man with whom he imagined she might be enjoying the same intimacies that had so much enhanced his own life, why was his first thought to kill them all? Out of what black cave crawled these contemptible reactions? And as his fickle heart made and unmade his happiness he could only stand to the side and watch.

He felt out-of-place in his own company, an obstacle to himself.

Unable to sleep, August tried to begin the outline for the monograph Dr. Grafton needed at the end of the week, but there seemed little connection between his thoughts and the sentences appearing on the monitor.

Leafing through the last four days of mail, he found an official-looking envelope from the university. Inside, the letter explained that due to changes in the grant from the National Institute of Health, his lab position would expire at the end of the month. It was on Biochemical Department letterhead, signed by Dr. Peter Grafton, and initialed, in bold, at the bottom, L. S.

Reading the letter again, August put it back in the envelope and the intercom rang. "Buzz me up," said Amanda's voice.

He went down to meet her and encountered a freezing wind. Frost bristled like tiny white horns on the ground outside.

She was alone, wearing one of his favorite outfits—red and orange silk, gathered at the waist in rows of ruffles, ending several inches above her knees. One of her most stylish bags hung from her right shoulder and irregular splotches of cold-color marked her neck, face, and arms. She looked vulnerable, lovely, and he at once felt rage, joy, remorse, fright, repulsion, lust, and astonishment.

"Come on up," he said.

"I was in the neighborhood and saw your light on," she replied, laughing self-consciously and following him up the narrow stairs.

She hung her handbag from a kitchen chair and surveyed the room with a glazed expression.

"I need to use your bathroom," and she disappeared inside it.

August put a kettle of water on the stove, imagining that boiling tea might dampen the sound of his beating heart.

When she came out, she looked fresh, revived. Glancing at the monitor on the corner desk, she asked what he was working on.

"Nothing important."

"Why didn't you call me?"

"I wanted to . . . but I didn't."

"Why did you leave the other day?"

"I couldn't think of anything to say when you came back."

"I brought you a present." She went to her handbag, took out a wrapped package, and handed it to him.

"Go ahead, open it."

"Would you like some tea?"

"Yes, but open it first."

It was a solid-state pocket phone, waterproof, paper-thin, very expensive. He set it down on the table.

"I already put my number in. Don't you like it?"

"Tea?"

"Don't be angry with me, August. I'm sorry I lied to you, but it wasn't altogether my fault. You've become possessive. It's not fair to me."

"I can't help it."

"You'll ruin everything."

"I can't help it."

"You've changed."

"Why can't you feel about me like I feel about you?"

"I do when we're together. Why isn't that enough?"

"It just isn't."

"Okay, I admit it, I've been saving you from my family. You really don't want to have anything to do with them. You really don't."

"It seemed like you and your brother were having a pretty good time together. They look like nice people."

"They're my family, August. Of course I get along with them and of course they look like nice people. But meeting them would be like running a gauntlet naked. Every competitive and protective fiber in them would bristle and gouge. They'd reduce you to wheat chaff within five minutes, and they can't help it. It's just how they are. It's gone on for generations. Why do you think I moved away? They're embarrassing in every way, like a Druid clan. Maybe someday I'll marry someone who understands what belonging to them entails, someone who comes from the same sort of family and is prepared for the constant belittlements and knifings that go along with becoming indentured to them, because that's the way they see it. But August, that isn't you. You have no instinctual defenses other than those primitive reactions you put on display three days ago. You wouldn't last a single afternoon with them before you were reduced to chopped liver. Besides, we already have what we need in each other."

"I want more of you."

"Yes, I know. But we can get through this, I promise." She turned around and backed up against him. "Help me with that zipper back there, dear one. Seeing more of the real me will help you feel better. It always does. Hurry now, I'm wet-tingling inside."

"It's after midnight. Where were you earlier, Amanda?"

"That has nothing to do with us, I promise. Come on; unpeel me. You can arrange me however you want. We can do everything your favorite way."

RED ROOSTER CAFE

August began looking for a new lab position, scanning university postings and science journals, calling acquaintances.

He soon discovered he lacked the will to continue searching.

Then the lease on his apartment ran out.

He wanted some time away, and he realized that he needed to visit his parents. It had been years since he'd been home.

The same lab worker who had just bought his bicycle drove him over to Chicago's northwest side, where a consortium of Planet Three and other NGOs rented out electric and alcohol-powered cars from a parking lot behind a secondhand store. After choosing a model somewhere between the cheapest and almost the cheapest, he merged onto the interstate and toward Wisconsin.

Within ten minutes, the traffic clotted and slowed to a crawl; after a half hour of creep, stop-go-wait-start-stop, he became reacquainted with why he didn't own a car. Unlike other time-consuming activities, the heart of traffic slowness—for August—contained a low-volume death rattle. Consequently, he only drove when absolutely necessary.

Finally, the jam began to loosen, and the yardage gained with each slow lurch forward became longer and longer. In this way, he progressed through the suburbs.

As more traffic drained off down curling exit lanes, longer views began to appear on both sides of the highway. And as the empty spaces in the highway became more frequent, larger and larger tracks of farmland extended toward the horizon. Harvesting machines from the month before had left rows of brown stubble running in dotted lines through the fields, and after several hours of driving August began to notice that the flat, empty spaces and open sky were evoking memories—not specific recollections of past events as much as attitudes that he associated with being younger—like the cohabitation of longing and fear.

The past waited for him just over the curvature of the Earth, and each additional mile brought him further into it. He slowly became steeped in once-familiar landscapes, half-remembered dramas, paths to freedom that had proved too difficult to follow, the haunting of old relationships abandoned An almost pleasant melancholy surrounded him, and he searched for a music station with an appropriate accompaniment, and then resumed driving in silence.

Crossing the Wisconsin River felt like passing through a doorway into a more personally relevant room. The scenery assumed the role of signage—psychic messaging trying to open a candid dialogue between the present and past.

A short while later, entering the Driftless Area, his familiarity with the passing sights seemed to jump a quantum level. He became conscious of an abiding tension between two versions of his life: In Chicago, his oldest personal history—as represented to others as well as to himself—read like a children's book of comforting tales, a thinly bound, carry-anywhere resume of wholesome vignettes, stories of dear friends and family interwoven with easy-to-understand descriptions of amusing episodes, all in perfect narrative form.

In stark contrast, August's past—as experienced and remembered within the actual geographic area in which it had been composed—contained too many pages to number, too much complexity to organize, and weighed too much to carry into a different region—a sacred yet sacrilegious tome so filled with indecipherable details, emotional entanglements, and passionate contradictions that it could only be wondered about, never understood, formless and raw.

The contrast between the two versions was more than a little unsettling. In the shorter, Chicago edition, August was transparently good-natured, intelligent, confident, and competent. In the older edition, he remained a victim of unresolved tensions and ever-haunting dreams.

Turning off the divided highway, the roads began to narrow, darken, and plead for repair. One by one, the local towns of his youth appeared—gatherings of buildings and homes that at one time had seemed like world centers of commerce, entertainment, and culture, and yet could be driven through in less time than it took to finish a cigarette.

Beyond the towns, hills began sprouting forests and standing armies of dark trunks rose out of lumpy leaf carpets, releasing a secondary network of bare, branching limbs. The roads curved in among them, seeking level paths while ascending and descending.

The sun fell lower in the sky, hidden at times behind the quickly rising hills, and he drove in and out of light, meeting another layer of himself with each new resurrected memory.

Set off a ways from the road, many of the houses seemed engaged in a war of attrition against the encroaching forests and fields surrounding them. Some, he noticed, had obviously waged their defense more successfully than others.

Only a few vehicles appeared, a couple of slowly moving pickups and older cars waiting at intersections, inspecting him as he went by.

There were still gravel roads here, and pieces of limestone, dolomite, granite, and sandstone were thrown against the floor of the rented car, making clipped, pinging sounds. Slower speeds were required to avoid the larger ruts and depressions in the uneven surface.

By the time August reached the long drive leading to his parents' home, daylight had completely worn out of the sky. Stopping just off the road, he climbed out of the car, stretched, rubbed his eyes, and took several deep breaths. The air felt cool. The spicy-sweet perfume from nearby pines interrupted his thoughts and he consciously filled his lungs enough times to dull the influential edge of the smell.

I should have called, he thought.

But he hadn't.

August became anxious. His insecurities over losing his job and lover extended into how he pictured meeting his parents, who might be terribly disappointed in him.

Coming here was a mistake, he feared.

Soon, the option of driving back to Chicago seemed more likely than continuing down the drive.

In the last few years, he'd often imagined coming home. In the last five or six months he'd pictured returning with the news that he'd found someone to fill the part of his life that had been empty. His father, he imagined, would ask, "What's she like?" and in the version of the imaginary scene in which he brought her with him, he would say, "Here, see for yourself." Then Amanda would step out from behind him, silencing all further questions. August would stand there, proudly, as his parents exhaled a long sigh of relief: their son had finally found someone. After meeting her his father would smile awkwardly, nod several times as though in silent agreement with a range of unspoken statements, and remember he had some unfinished work at the shop. His mother would put on a pot of tea, open her mind's calendar, and begin counting the days before she could hope to introduce a grandchild to her ever-expanding ideas about divinity, proper nutrition, and how the world would be a better place as soon as everyone refocused on things that truly mattered.

But *now*, of course, he'd need to explain that he'd lost his job and had everything he owned—everything he'd acquired during nine years in Chicago—was in the trunk of a rented car. He felt like he'd washed ashore, dumb with exhaustion, unable to climb out of the water.

He hadn't eaten anything today after three stale powdered donut holes washed down with morning coffee. And there was a restaurant-sized town only about twenty minutes away. He could get a meal and return after his hunger and sense of failure had receded to manageable levels. And his parents weren't expecting him anyway, so it didn't matter when he arrived.

He backed out of the driveway and returned in the direction he'd come from.

While driving through the town of Grange he couldn't help noticing an unsightly number of inadequately lit homes, sagging porches, broken sidewalks, scrap lumber piled in front yards, and automobiles rusting on concrete blocks. For his first eighteen years of existence these untidy sights were the standard scenery, and if not standard, they were certainly not unusual. They were simply part of the neighborhood. Abandoned vehicles and stacks of lumber were just temporarily set-aside projects that might be returned to later. Human lives remained in transition, and it seemed only natural that the materials surrounding them would exist in a similar state of flux.

His own father ran a repair shop in the village of Words, and mounds of broken machinery and discarded equipment always surrounded it. Every so often most of it was hauled away and sold for scrap, only to soon be replenished. He never thought anything about it other than to occasionally look through the ever-changing collection of rubbish for interesting and useful objects.

But after living for almost a decade in high-rent areas among people who didn't work with their hands and obeyed laws prohibiting unsightliness, August watched himself recoil in alarm—like a trained monkey—at the sight of the disorder.

How could he possibly have grown up in such impoverished circumstances and not known it at the time? And what ignoble path had led him so far away from his origins that he would be ashamed of them now? Why hadn't he fought harder against an acculturation that recruited him to prosecute himself?

The Red Rooster Café had the same sign hanging in front that he remembered from years before when he and his friend Ivan Bookchester had adopted the eatery in high school. At that time, they had needed public personas to establish that they were adults with purpose and drivers' licenses, and while creating this vital identity they had probably consumed a thousand cheeseburgers with ketchup, mustard, onions, and deep-fried potatoes. The owners—an older couple who also served as receptionists, waiters, and cooks—mercifully tolerated their presence and he and Ivan became quite comfortable there.

The restaurant's sign provided the only light on the north side of the street, and three old cars were haphazardly parked in front, a pickup further down.

The other businesses on the block—at one time there had been a bakery, yarn shop, hardware store, and cheese outlet—were either closed for the day or boarded over with gray-weathered chipboard.

Inside, the café still had the same tile floor, the same beige walls, the same low countertop, the same swinging service gate separating the dining area from the kitchen. Three wooden tables were occupied: a family of four, two middle-aged women busily eating large salads without taking off their coats, and an older man and woman sipping water from straight-sided glasses. When August came in, they inspected him without interest. Unseen pans banged in the kitchen. A very young waitress distributed steaming plates of food among the family members, and in anticipation of eating, the twelve-or thirteen-year-old boy—only a year or two younger than the waitress—took off his trucker's hat and placed it under his chair. His sister—possibly his twin—unrolled her paper napkin and the utensils inside clattered onto the tabletop. Her mother scowled at her, and her father picked up a pickle on the edge of his plate and bit into it. The room held the aroma of hot, greasy food the way the word "skillet" holds a skillet.

Feeling overdressed in the suit coat that Amanda had bought for him and seeking less exposure in case his earlier thoughts about poverty might be read on his person, August took refuge in one of the two wooden booths next to the window. He pulled the thickly laminated one-page menu from behind the chrome basket of salt, pepper, and sugar packets. Prices were one-third the cost of meals in Chicago with similar caloric content, and this realization, combined with the overwhelming familiarity of the room and a need to escape his dejection over losing Amanda and his job, resulted in nostalgia for the simpler, happier times of his youth. Staring into the dark street, he almost remembered what living had felt like ten years ago and realized with some pleasure that the elimination of a decade of experience—most of it acquired nearly two hundred miles from here—made room for a greater sense of opportunity and freedom, a nimbleness of being. Back then, in 2017, despite most of the adults around him experiencing a national political nosedive that held no particular interest for him, an outpouring of hope-filled expectations had influenced his day-to-day awareness. He wanted things in the future and daydreamed about getting them, though not in any detail. Then later, as actual events had replaced imagined ones, the substitution felt like a bargain made in bad faith. And like most other people who are disappointed in their hope and deceived by their expectations, August found solace in the past, savoring the pleasurable innocence that comes from lacking experience.

"Excuse me, mister, but are you going to order something or just keep staring out the window," said the teenage waitress standing beside the booth, a fat menu pad in the palm of her left hand and the stub of a green pencil grasped in the other. Her stringy hair looked dirty and her tired eyes stared blankly out of an exhausted face.

"May I still order from the breakfast section?"

"Yeah, sure, anything on that menu," she replied with a bone-weary yawn.

"Steak and eggs, please. Medium. Scrambled. Any kind of potatoes except hash browns, whole wheat toast, and white coffee."

"That it?"

"Yes."

Finished with scribbling into the pad, the teenager turned around and headed for the kitchen, stopped, came back and asked, "You need jam with that toast, August?"

The shock of being identified ended his brief infatuation with the past and abandoned him inside the awkward immediacy of not recognizing someone who had just recognized him. He studied her.

She responded to his searching gaze by slightly improving her posture. A feeble synaptic sparkle inside August's cerebellum spilled out a hundred vague and jumbled memories involving a six- or seven-year-old girl with long brown hair and blue eyes who, after school, had often visited her grandparents' restaurant before returning home. Recovering her name involved a different neural circuitry and took a full second longer.

"I remember you, Julie," he said a little too hurriedly, and followed this with an even more regrettable comment that he couldn't prevent coming out of his mouth. "You've grown up."

Her expression pardoned him, and for that he was grateful. But then she risked a little youthful charm and smiled, squared her shoulders, and assumed a stance that bravely accentuated her hips and breasts. As the moment unfolded, August reluctantly acknowledged that his earlier comment about her having grown up was partly responsible for this development and he attempted to assume his share of responsibility for the changes taking place between them. While the back room of his mind still reviewed historical material involving the preadolescent Julie, August noticed, with cold horror, that a quicker-acting part of his brain, without any consent on his part, had already complied with Julie's wishes to be taken seriously and was eagerly imagining handholds at various contours along her anatomy, tinkling the piano keys of his hormone receptors and preparing him for imminent carnal conquest.

Forcing his attention back onto the laminated menu, August both marveled and despaired over the wildly amoral nature of his body chemistry. Its randy cunning simply astonished him. Fresh from a severe psychic beating at the hands of Amanda, the urge toward sexual gratification had not only completely recovered from the psychological blow but was now fully prepared to forget whatever lessons learned from such a thrashing and begin anew with an even more wholly inappropriate sexual partner with warning signs flashing from every childish pore of her. He was further distressed to notice that his cherished scrapbook of private experiences with Amanda were now being raided for possible general use. He shamelessly imagined the young waitress standing before him as a substitute for Amanda, as though two completely different women could be interchanged in some fundamental way. The unique intimacy that he and Amanda had carefully cultivated together did not apparently mean a treasured familiarity with another valued individual, but rather an introductory course in common sexual practices. The primal dance, it seemed, cared nothing for the partners themselves, only that they danced.

"No jam, thank you, Julie," and he smiled in what he hoped was not a hopelessly condescending way.

"No jam it is then," she responded, and her expression retreated behind the weary mask she'd worn earlier. "It's nice to see you again," she added, and then managed a small, merciful smile.

In the privacy of his thoughts August weighed the evidence, and anointed her a girl-saint while he tried not to watch her walk back to the kitchen to deliver his order.

She pushed aside the swinging gate, disappeared inside the kitchen for several long moments, then dashed back into the dining room with a shrieking laugh, chased by a man of about thirty with a short black beard and thick ropy arms, wearing a checked work shirt with torn-off sleeves.

"Julie," the man cried loudly, merrily. "Come on, girl, give us a hug. You're the damned most beautiful thing I've seen all day and if you keep getting better looking, you'll need to carry a club to fight me off."

"Leave me alone," shouted Julie, and a blushing smile lit up her face with such candid joy it seemed an invasion of privacy to notice it, at least for August, who moments earlier hadn't even recognized her. Her neck and hands reddened, the flush so genuine, so transparent, so revealing, that it surpassed every iniquitous thought that might have prompted it.

"Okay, have it your way, Little Darlin'," laughed her pursuer, "but get me a piece of peach pie before I bring in the rest of those chickens."

Julie dashed protectively behind the front counter, and stated, "Karl says put them in the back freezer this time. He don't want no chickens in front no more."

"Sure, but get me a piece of that pie first," the man said, and in an exaggerated manner pointed toward what he wanted at the counter.

Still glowing, she opened the glass tower, transferred a slice of pie from the pan onto a small white plate, and set it on the counter next to a fork and napkin.

"Thanks, Little Darlin'. Did you make this?"

"Naw, I just roll out the crusts."

"Then I'll eat that part first—to hell with the middle part."

He sat on a stool, took a bite of pie, and then noticed the older couple sipping water at the table nearest the kitchen. He walked over.

They seemed glad to see him and all three were soon gabbling together like a rafter of turkeys.

August felt a pronounced flicker of recognition flare up in his mind, but he retreated into his earlier privacy and went back to staring outside.

In the kitchen, the cook slid two plates of food through the narrow window and rang a little bell. Julie carried the meals to the couple talking to the man with cut-off sleeves and the four of them clucked together about something. Then the bearded man lumbered back to his pie and Julie walked back behind the counter, ran out a glass of fizzy water from a black hose, and watched him eat.

"Whose leaf burner is that parked outside?" he asked.

She nodded toward August's booth and Ivan Bookchester swiveled around on his stool.

After a short time of studied eye contact, he and August recognized each other underneath earlier, hastily formed assumptions about local louts and overdressed strangers. The gap between the present moment and the last time they'd seen each other opened between them like a shared wound.

At one time, Ivan and August had been inseparable. And even when they weren't sharing the same spatial area they remained together in their minds. They trusted each other in the way a door is hinged to its frame. They thought . . . or rather didn't think at all and just assumed in the way children neither consider nor revere the passage of time but simply believe the things that make living bearable—the people they love—will always be there. Then August had moved away, and . . .

Ivan began to get up, but stayed seated, stunned by the horror that they had become unknown to each other.

Then, as though recovering from a physical blow, he shook his head, stood, and came forward.

"Gus," he said. "You're here."

Climbing out of the booth, August could find no words to speak with. The sound of his shortened name had numbed his verbal dexterity. Ivan was the only person who could pronounce it in a natural way, and August experienced a return of a part of himself that he'd forgotten.

DETERMINED FIDELITIES

"How long can you stay?" asked Ivan.

"A little while, I guess. I don't know. The lab closed; I mean, the lab where I work in Chicago closed so the engineering department could install a new heating system. They said it was necessary. And it doesn't matter because I lost my job anyway and I should have said that first off. I'm afraid I'm giving you too much information. You grew a beard, Ivan."

"Gus," Ivan shouted, throwing both arms around him and delivering a hug that drove all the air out of August's lungs. When the embrace relaxed, Ivan continued to grip his upper arms.

"Now look. I smudged up your new coat."

He began brushing off August's suit jacket. "I'm sorry."

"Don't be," said August. "Never be sorry."

"Here's your coffee," said Julie, sliding a cup onto the table. "Two creams."

"Thanks."

"Bring a black one for me, Little Darlin'," said Ivan, and they sat in the booth and stared at each other across the tabletop.

"How long have you been here?"

"I just came."

"Been out to your folks' place?"

"Not yet. I mean, I was out there, a little while ago, I was out there, I mean, I drove out there, but I didn't drive all the way up. I thought I would. I intended to, and, well . . ."

"You can stay with me," said Ivan. "I've got a spare room. You can see your parents when you're ready to see them. It's hard to go home after you've been away a while—like squeezing a cork into a bottleneck."

"I can't get used to your beard, Ivan. It certainly disguises you. Are you in the chicken-delivering business now?"

"Not really. My grandfather—you remember Nate—sold his semi. To keep busy he and Beulah raise chickens. I told them I'd bring this batch over here, save them a trip."

"And your parents, how are they?"

"They drive me crazy every time I see them, but they're fine. Mother's making turquoise jewelry now, I mean, along with her cleaning and cooking."

"Does your dad still work at the repair shop?"

"It's his shop now, Gus. Your dad retired a couple months ago, turned the shop over to Pop."

"Okay, now I remember hearing that Dad retired. I didn't know Blake ended up with the shop, though."

"Yup."

"Is Blake running it himself?"

"He's got a couple younger guys working for him, but, yeah, he runs it. Your dad comes in once in a while, but not much anymore—after he found the Model T."

"What Model T?"

"He bought one at an estate sale and is fixing it up. Says he's going to restore it and convert the engine to burn leaves—something like that car of yours out there."

August's breakfast arrived and he offered to share it with Ivan, who declined, remembered his pie, and retrieved it from the counter.

They talked. And ate. And drank coffee.

Time peeled off. As Ivan's expressions and mannerisms became more familiar, August's brain began releasing comfort-inducing memories. At least for the time being, the unknown space between them—the things they'd missed during the last few years—didn't matter; they again began to feel like separate organs in a single organism—different agents to be sure, but in service to the same creature, and it had always been like that between them.

August had always liked the academic part of school and scholastic challenge in general; Ivan hated them both. Unsuccessful in most physical activities, August eschewed sports; Ivan shined through them. August was cautious by nature, conventional, often inclined toward brooding; Ivan was reactionary, hostile to authority, a physical risk taker. August's mother had been a preacher during much of his childhood, and his father ran one of the community's only repair shops; and they nurtured in August a heightened social sensitivity. Ivan's mother raised him by herself until the age of twelve, when his father Blake—whom he'd never met—was released from prison. His parents' relationship was fierce and stormy, but they stayed together, proving day-to-day that each was a match for the other. And as Ivan grew older, he grew less and less tolerant of social tension.

While polishing off a second piece of pie and drinking a third cup of coffee, Ivan explained he'd attended a technical school and had trained as a welder. He'd worked in several local plants and then moved to British Columbia and signed on to a crew building a pipeline along the Pacific shoreline into Seattle. When August asked for details, he shrugged. Being away from home, he said, taught him he didn't like being away from home, and he'd returned.

"Here, everything makes sense," he said. "Up there I felt like a zone five plant trying to grow in zone two."

"What happened to JW?" August asked. "Is she still around?"

"Yes, but you can't call her that anymore. You can't call her Jewelweed or JW. It makes her angry. You have to call her Hanh now."

"Was that her Vietnamese name?"

"Yes. It means apricot tree, and happiness."

"Neither of those seem to suit her."

"I know, but that's the way with names sometimes. You have to call her Hanh now."

"How is she?"

"She's fine. You can see her tomorrow if you want. I promised I'd cut her some firewood. Winter's coming and it's hard to get in and out after it snows. And old Lester don't do much of anything no more. Rheumatism, he says."

"She's still with him?"

"She'll be with him until the old guy dies, which might not be too far away because he's been rather poor lately. Hell, she fusses over him like an old hen."

"She always had determined fidelities."

"Well, she still does."

"Remember when we used to think she was a feral child?"

"Of course. What a stupid question, Gus. If someone forgot, it would be you. You moved away."

This stung, but August ignored it. "I'd like to see her again."

"Come with me tomorrow."

Julie shouted from the other side of the room as she shoved the mop and bucket into the closet. "I've got to close up here, Ivan."

The restaurant had emptied out except for the three of them.

"I'll get those chickens," said Ivan.

August and Ivan carried seventy-six hard-frozen chickens—individually wrapped in plastic wrap and brown paper—from his pickup into the walk-in freezer.

Ivan asked Julie if she needed a ride home, but she said she had her mother's car.

August climbed into his rented car and followed the taillights of Ivan's pickup through the north side of Grange and onto a curving, broken blacktop.

About a mile later, Ivan turned into a dirt driveway and parked beside a caved-in bungalow with a front porch covered in opaque sheets of plastic. In the available light August could make out two ramshackle sheds off to one side and a haphazardly fenced pasture in back. Large trees towered over the house, their overhanging limbs protecting the roof from the night sky.

August climbed out of his car. His earlier apperceptions of poverty rose up again and he fought them down. Three cats—two orange and one tabby—raced ghostlike around the house from the back, leaped up the front steps and stealthily positioned themselves like ornaments, watching Ivan walking through the front yard.

"Come in," Ivan said, holding back the plastic-covered front door to the porch while August carried in his two suitcases. "If I remember right, beers are waiting for us in the refrigerator."

At the first appearance of an open slot between door and frame, the cats disappeared into it.

The interior of the house was warm and shabby yet well-kept. Several filled wooden bookcases rose behind a sofa and two stuffed chairs—leather, with an oval rag rug between them. Hardwood floors of narrow and wide boards led to a kitchen, with a hallway to the left. Ivan snapped on the overhead—an electrical appliance escaped from an earlier era that drooped down from the ceiling like a small octopus with tulip-shaped bulbs on the end of metal tentacles.

Down the hall in one of the small bedrooms, August set his suitcases on top of a bed and returned to the living room to accept a foamy glass of dark beer. He watched the cats devouring food from a bowl in the center of the kitchen floor.

"Make yourself at home," said Ivan, opening the back door and stepping outside. "I'll be right back—got to check on something."

The homemade beer tasted strongly of yeast and hops. For some reason the cats surprised him. Having pets wasn't something he'd imagined for Ivan, but after considering this for several moments, he could discover no reason why Ivan would be any more unlikely than anyone else to have them.

In the living room he glanced through the collection of books and sat down with a handful of mildly interesting volumes. Sipping the beer, he tried to picture living here, breathing the same air that had surrounded him in childhood, with his parents living only minutes away.

Impossible.

This area had rejected him, and it felt foreign now. The things he wanted to do with his life couldn't be done here. Sure, there were good things as well, and—

"I'm sorry," Ivan said, coming inside. "Jet Lag ran away again, and I need to find him."

"Jet Lag?"

"He's my donkey and he's out again."

"I'll come," August said, taking another swallow of beer.

"It's turning cooler," said Ivan, tossing him an old leather coat, heavy with sheepskin lining. August put it on. They went out the front door and down the road. Loops of rope and a halter hung over Ivan's shoulder, and August noticed that he didn't bring a coat for himself.

Their shoes made soft, clopping sounds in the empty silence.

Despite the bulk and assortment of identifiable and unidentifiable smells, August was glad for the coat. Cool air stiffened the muscles in his face. The dark sky and stars looked a lot different in the absence of Chicago's light pollution, and it seemed like an altogether larger universe overhead. Cascades of visible streams, swirls of murky clouds, and a billion points of light exploded inside a dome of thick, reeling brilliance, a map of oblivion.

After a hundred yards, they walked past a driveway and then another. At the end of each lane stood a home with a few yellow-lit windows. Mostly, however, there were only trees, dead weeds, and open spaces along the road. August remembered how hard it had been to adjust to living in an urban area, surrounded on all sides at all times by other people, traffic, concrete, and buildings. For the first years, every noise and every sight, it seemed, was meant for him, and it took a long time for his pre-conscious filters to screen out, or at least minimize, sensations that did not directly concern him.

But out here, every sound, sight, and smell was clearly intended for him. Far in the distance, a dog barked, and because there were apparently no other people outside to hear it, the obligation fell to him and Ivan. And unlike in urban areas where some ongoing awareness, however peripheral, must be maintained with other people not directly encountered yet living beyond the next walls, here August could feel an encroaching need to find a satisfactory relationship with the surrounding trees, plants, wildlife, and open space. At one time he knew how to do this, and it was strange how remote everything seemed.

"Why do you have a donkey?"

"That's an odd question coming for someone who once had a pet bat," laughed Ivan.

"Let me rephrase that. How did you come to have a donkey?"

"About four years ago my parents turned their farmhouse into a bed and breakfast. Mother bought two horses and a donkey so guests could feel like they were in ranch country."

"I didn't know that."

"Of course not. You weren't here."

"I'm surprised no one told me."

"It only lasted a year."

"What happened?"

"Dad didn't want to share Mother with anyone after he came home from the shop."

"I doubt that went over very well."

"You're right. Mother refused to give up her new business. She enjoyed it, she said, and they needed the extra income. But the two of them fighting all the time put an end to it anyway. Word spread and no one came. Afterward, they sold the horses, but couldn't find anyone to take Jet Lag. So, I brought him here. We're buddies. I have a soft spot for animals. Unlike people, when you look into their eyes you know exactly where you stand with them."

"I forget, are donkeys sterile?"

"You're thinking of mules," said Ivan. "A donkey has two less chromosomes than a horse. A mule is the hybrid offspring of a male donkey and a female horse, and a hinny—which is more rare—is the offspring of a female donkey and a male horse. Mules are almost always sterile, but once in a great while a female mule can be successfully mated with either a purebred horse or a purebred donkey. A fertile female mule is a molly. Male mules are always sterile because when the male contributes the larger number of chromosomes it leads to embryonic loss."

"I see you read the donkey owner's manual."

"Every word of it. And the hybrid of a male donkey and a female zebra is called a zonkey."

"How are we going to find Jet Lag?"

"He always goes to the same place. It's just a little further, and it's time to start keeping our voices down."

"Why? Will he hear us?"

"It's the guy who owns the place. I'd like to be able to get Jet Lag without him knowing."

"What's the problem?"

"He doesn't want him here."

"Why?"

"No reason and every reason. About five years ago his wife and I slept with each other once or twice and, anyway, it happened before they got together, but it still makes him angry. He doesn't like Jet Lag coming down here and I'd just as soon he didn't know."

"Why does Jet Lag come here?" I whispered.

"He likes to stand around with the goats."

"Why?"

"I don't know. He just likes to. Maybe it's the way they smell."

Further down the road, windows glowed on both floors of the farmhouse. In preparation for new siding, the old siding had been stripped and the first pieces of insulation board put up. The front and side yards were littered with old siding and scraps of packing wrap spilling out of an overfilled dumpster. Behind the house, a barn and several smaller buildings accompanied two silos and a fenced-off feedlot, lit by an orange yard light.

"There he is," Ivan whispered. In the near distance eight white-and-brown goats stood and lay around a water tank under the pole-shed overhang. A short distance away—directly under the yard light—stood the donkey, his long ears slanting backward out of a shaggy, lowered head. He appeared to be sleeping. A weathered board fence set off the barn from the house and road.

"I see him," August whispered. "What's the plan?"

"You stay on the road and keep walking. I'll take Jet Lag out of the gate at the other end of the shed, then along the fence through the field. If anyone comes out of the house, make some noise and draw their attention."

Ivan walked into the ditch, climbed over the board fence and headed straight across the feedlot, moving fast.

It seemed like a poor plan to cross an open illuminated area only a short distance from the house, and August wondered how committed Ivan was to retrieving his donkey without being seen. Perhaps like other people with plans that somehow involved present, past, or future sex, acting in a rational manner didn't quite cover all the bases. August was reminded of his own disastrous plan to sit in the park and observe Amanda's condo building while she supposedly was not inside it, to be assured she was not there.

From the road, August had a good view of the front and east side of the house. A television's blue flicker could be seen in one of the windows at ground level.

Ivan reached the fugitive donkey, fastened the halter around his head, and led the animal through the milling goats toward the back of the pole shed. Before reaching the gate, however, the burro planted his front feet and refused to move forward. When Ivan pulled on the rope, Jet Lag reared back, and brayed. The brash sound filled the night—a noise designed by evolution for wild female donkeys to hear from up to four miles.

A dark figure appeared in one of the downstairs windows. After several seconds, the front door opened, and a woman stepped into the yard. She had a blanket wrapped around her shoulders—clutched together in front like a medieval cloak. With confidence, she avoided the discarded siding and scrap paper, walked to the corner of the house and stood looking into the feedlot.

August continued coming toward her on the road.

The woman walked out when she saw him and waited.

August stopped beside her.

"Is that Ivan down there?" she asked.

"Yes, it is. He came to take Jet Lag back home."

In the starlight, she looked older than Ivan, trim with sharp features and an award-winning smile. Her shoulder-length hair looked almost white as she pulled the blanket closer. Her feet were bare, and August couldn't keep from wondering what she wore underneath the blanket.

"You a friend of his?" she asked.

The donkey stopped braying and Ivan succeeded in leading it out of the gate and into the adjacent field.

"I'd like to think so."

"Do him a favor—fix his fence so that animal doesn't keep getting out. I'm afraid Walt will shoot it."

"Seems a little extreme."

"He's an extreme guy. He'll regret doing it, but that won't stop him from losing his temper and grabbing his gun. He hates Ivan."

"Why?"

"Walt loves me, and he knows Ivan and I once had a thing."

"He'd shoot a donkey because he loves you?"

"You bet. Like I said, he's got a bad temper. You're wearing Ivan's coat."

"You recognize it?"

"It's too big for you . . . and I can smell it."

"Very observant. Well, it's been nice talking to you. I'm going to walk back with Ivan now."

"Tell him hi for me."

"I will."

Jet Lag and Ivan were climbing out of the ditch onto the road when August reached them. The donkey stood about waist-high, with thick woolly hair and very little mane, and a tail more like a cow than a horse.

"Didn't work out quite like I hoped," Ivan said as he watched the woman walk up to the house.

"Anything that can go wrong will," said August. "Murphy's Law."

"Walt must not be home," Ivan said, and they began walking back. "What did she say to you?"

"She said to keep your donkey at home, and she said hi."

"What did you think of her?"

"I'd stay away from her if I were you."

"Why?"

"People who come outdoors in blankets make me nervous."

Ivan's laughter filled all the space around them, much like the donkey's earlier braying, and seemed to define all three of them from horizon to horizon. "City living's gotten to you, Gus. There's no dress code out here. You can walk out of your house in anything you want."

"I'd still stay away from her. She said Walt has trouble with his temper and he also has a gun."

"Everyone has a gun," said Ivan dismissively. "When she said to say hello to me, how did she say it exactly?"

"I told you—she said hi."

"I know, but how did she say it?"

"By forcing air through her vocal cords."

"Was it more like 'tell him hi so he'll come see me,' or 'tell him hi so he knows there are no hard feelings'?"

"Maybe both of those, I don't know. Go back and ask her."

"Nope."

"I think she enjoys making her husband jealous."

Walking between them, Jet Lag's trim feet seemed almost dainty in a hard, hoof-like way, and the sharp clopping sounds against the surface of the road were much louder than their own footfalls.

"There's something you're not telling me," said Ivan after they'd gone twenty or thirty yards. "About why you came back."

"I needed some time to myself."

"You seem depressed, Gus."

"I'm not," August objected, his voice lacking the confidence needed to convince.

The cool night settled more snuggly around them, and for the next ten or twenty yards August thought about what he might say.

"There was someone in Chicago, and she left me."

"What happened?"

"She was beyond me."

"In what way?"

"In all ways."

"Hell, Gus, you'll find someone better."

"I'm not interested in trying again."

"Say what?"

"It's pointless."

"Explain."

"I met this woman, Ivan. We didn't know anything about each other, but we talked for several hours. Because of the crowded party we were attending, it was hard to hear much of what she said, and I'm sure it was the same for her. But I fell for her. What revealing subjects did we discuss? Ha! We made a couple of overly generalized comments about a popular book we had read along with three million other people, and then talked about a public concert we both attended. Later, we exchanged a few superficial and unverifiable descriptions of our childhoods, told a few jokes we'd heard from other people, and smiled a lot. But the deal was done as far as my genetic code was concerned. Every candle in my brain caught fire. Every ounce of me believed that this woman was the one, the only one who could complete my life. If I could only have her, I would have the good life and experience heaven on earth."

"Was she really that good?"

Above them, the flapping of an unseen flock of birds moved east.

"You're not understanding what I'm saying, Ivan. She wounded me in a way I don't wish to ever recover from, and I have no desire to come within a mile of another sexual relationship. The whole thing is rigged, from beginning to end. The people we're attracted to, as well as the feelings we have for them—our reactions to the way they look, move, sound, and smell—are determined by whatever genetic configuration we inherit. They aren't our own feelings and preferences—not a chance. The genes of our ancestors are planted inside us, and we're programed from cradle to grave to act like they did and to feel like they did, and frankly I'm just not up to it anymore. The mating routine was scripted out years ago, before language, before walking upright on two legs; the codes were transcribed into genetic algorithms by an unbroken line of hundreds of thousands of ceaselessly copulating ancestors who demand to go on having their orgasms and experiencing their brand of emotional insanity through us. Amanda and I were simply gene-expressing the algorithms of our breeding progenitors, and for over an entire year we repeated that series of unending movements, and wrestled with those irrational feelings, never content for long, never knowing each other any better, each satisfaction leading to a more unbearable longing. Every insecurity I was able to overcome was immediately replaced by an even more profoundly miserable one—leaving me dangling at the dead end of an exhausted humility. And every episode of bad sex—of which I experienced an abundance—was soon after followed by a demonic promise, coming from inside me, that the sex in the future would be perfect. I'm through with it, Ivan. I'm through."

"I take it you cared about her."

"Sure, if you want to call it that. I couldn't sleep, couldn't think. Being away from her was tantamount to going mad."

"What happened?"

"I began to feel like she belonged to me or *should* belong to me. Rationally, I didn't actually *think* she did, and in fact I *knew* she didn't, but I couldn't turn off the desire to have her for myself. If she could have printed out my thoughts on a piece of legal stationary any judge in the world would have, or should have, served me with a restraining order."

"Then you wanted the wrong things from her."

Jet Lag planted his feet in the road and refused to move forward, and after pulling on the rope for several seconds, Ivan began talking to the animal and rubbing the areas behind its ears. He put his arm around the donkey's neck and gently turned its head to the side. Humming in a tuneless way, he leaned against the donkey's body and when Jet Lag repositioned his back legs Ivan led him around in a circle and they continued walking down the road. After a short distance their footsteps fell into the earlier-established tempo.

"Donkeys have a reputation for obstinacy," August commented.

"Yes, they have a sturdy instinct for surviving. When they're afraid of something they can't be easily talked out of it. Fortunately, if you distract them from whatever it is they're afraid of, they often forget what it was."

"I didn't want anything different from Amanda than any other man would."

. Wispy clouds appeared in the sky, like migrating ghosts, and the sweet smell of an unseen wood fire found them.

"Yes, you did. You're looking for a soul mate, Gus. You want a woman suitable for concentrated companionship and joint ownership—someone to complete you."

"Everyone wants that."

"No, they don't, and you only do because that's how your parents were, and it mostly worked out for them."

"You don't want that?"

"All I want is sex every now and then."

"Surely not."

"That all-or-nothing kind of involvement doesn't interest me."

"You don't want to love someone?"

"Not mixed up with sex. My parents love each other in that overly ambitious way, jealous of each other's time, suspicious, easily offended, often angry, embarrassingly happy when things work out, fighting most of the time, whispering, and flying into rages. They worry about where the other is—who the other is with, what the other is thinking. They're constantly making up, falling out, entertaining hurt feelings, feeling guilty, going at each other like there's no tomorrow, feeling miserable in the morning, worried and anxious. I want no part of it. I'll tell you what I like though."

"Go ahead."

"Every so often I cut my hair and beard, rent some nice clothes and go somewhere no one knows me—a big party, wedding reception, or an upscale club on a busy night in a city I've never been in. While having a few drinks, I'll look for that one gal who shines the brightest, who everyone else notices, a vain beauty who has come for the same reason I have—to take home a prize. When I succeed in convincing her the person she's hoping to catch is me, and we walk out together, well, it's just a grand feeling."

"I'm skeptical."

"These nights don't always end up the way I want, but the challenge is fun and, hey, I'm a simple guy with simple needs."

"I don't believe you've made peace with this. It's what we pretend, I know, but it isn't true. No matter what methods we employ, the tension never goes away. We're being led on by a poison tree that eternally bears fruit. I don't believe you."

"It's true. I've made peace with myself on this, though I admit to feeling like you do now a number of years ago. See, I had a difficult time after you went away to school. I was lonely. Everyone my age was either leaving, getting married, overdosing, or becoming stranger and stranger. I finally signed on to a two-year commitment to the pipeline. I volunteered for exile, you might say, and lived a primitive existence where there was only a couple dozen other people to get along with— very few of them women—and time to think."

"You never told me that."

"You weren't here to tell."

"I couldn't stay here, Ivan."

"I know that."

"You always knew I intended to move away. You'd known it for years before I left."

"Stop it, Gus. I know you had to leave and I'm okay with that. It's one of the things I figured out while working on the pipeline. Friendships don't continue unless sex, money, or power is somehow involved. Friends are always for the sake of something else. Chess buddies are fine while there's chess. Office mates make great comrades as long as there's an office. It's part of that genetic shove you were talking about. We *are* our ancestors. Doing what they did is more important than figuring out why we do it. Money must be made, power used, and sex gotten. Those forces are bigger than us. We don't understand them; they understand us. We only exist through them. We insist that we're free to do what we want but what we want to do isn't freely chosen. We simply follow orders. The only freedom we have is to paint the walls of our individual cells in our favorite colors, adapt in our own way."

A light came toward them in the distance. Growing larger, it was soon accompanied by the harsh, rushing sound of a moving vehicle. The oncoming headlights slowed as the driver became aware of the shapes of two men and a donkey along the side of the road, then dashed past in a rush of blinding light, raw sound, and mechanically achieved momentum. Even after the vehicle had turned a distant corner, the violent nature of two dissimilar velocities in close proximity seemed to linger, and August and Ivan walked in silence until the sense of violated privacy had run its course.

As they neared Ivan's house Jet Lag walked faster, straining against the rope.

"He's hungry," said Ivan. "I usually give him a scoop of oats in the loafing shed when we get home."

They walked into the driveway and continued to the fenced-in area behind the house. Ivan removed the halter; the donkey trotted ahead of them and disappeared inside one of the smaller buildings. They followed. Inside the shed a carpet of straw covered the floor. Taking a fresh slice from the bale in the corner, Ivan shredded it, adding the layered strands to the bedding. Then he put several cups of feed into the empty wooden trough and Jet Lag chewed with audible gnashing.

Like the arrival of a bus with many passengers, all at once August understood why Ivan had agreed to keep the donkey. The sound of the contented chewing inside the little shed, the smell of straw, animal, wood, manure, leather, and dust created a becalming scene, dredging up collective memories.

Ivan and August walked up to the house. The warmth inside welcomed them and they settled into the leather chairs in the living room.

"Tell me more about your time on the pipeline," August said.

"Not much to say, really. I saved nearly all the money they gave me, and they gave me quite a lot. Well, not a lot, but, you know, a lot. And I'm glad it's over. Can I get you another beer?"

"No, thanks. I'm really tired. If you don't mind, I think I'll turn in."

"Sure. The bathroom's right across the hall from your room, and if you need anything, holler."

"I will," August said, getting up. "And thanks, Ivan. It's really good to see you again."

"Yeah, you too."

The narrow hallway leading to the bedrooms seemed at once confining and quaint, features left over from an earlier and more economizing style of homebuilding. Extending his arms, August could touch both walls and the impression was one of traveling along a channel. The sharp yet not unpleasant smell of dust-mold accompanied him, an odor so closely associated with older houses that it seemed like the smell of the past.

Falling asleep in an unknown place had never been easy for August, but tonight there was some hope for a steep slide into unconsciousness. He couldn't remember ever feeling more exhausted. Breaking up with Amanda had abandoned him inside a crisis management mentality, and he'd temporarily lost the ability to do anything in the privacy of his own thoughts other than try to reframe the agonizing episode in a way that a future path could be imagined leading away from it. And though unsuccessful in this effort so far, he'd at least left Chicago, driven over a hundred miles, and worn himself down to numbness.

Brushing his teeth required more effort than August wanted to invest, and he abandoned the activity at the first upper bicuspid on the left. Just keeping his eyes open required strength, and after undressing, climbing between the cotton sheets, and pulling up the covers, a dark and blissful relief unrolled inside him. His larger muscle groups relaxed, and he experienced layered collapsing, much like lying inside a descending elevator that stops at every floor on the way down. Soon, his beleaguered mind arrived at its lowest plateau of self-awareness, a velvety space of thoughts generated through the habitual firing of well-worn circuits, with little intentionality involved. As the imaginative content grew stronger and stranger, his thoughts moved further out of his control until they founded a country of their own and began a vividly colored staged performance; they and he had little in common now, except for a passing interest in each other. And in this merciful manner, sleep arrived.

JET LAG

FOUR HOURS LATER, August woke with such suddenness that all the sensible features of the house accosted him at the same moment: a distant ticking clock, a pane of glass rattling in a loose frame, groaning wood in the attic, hues and patterns of steadily glowing light around the curtained window, the coarse texture of the blanket, an array of aged smells, and the deep surrounding night. In rapid succession, memories of the previous day informed him of where he was, and he took a moment to close his eyes again to become better reacquainted with his circumstances. About halfway through his orientation, the problem of Amanda—or rather the psychological catastrophe occasioned by the lack of her—resumed its insistent demand for resolution. For the first time, however, the shrill urgency of this problem and the dreadfulness inflicted by her departure seemed a little less insistent than before, and he attributed this minor blessing to the curative nature of dreamless sleep.

Climbing out of bed, he stepped into his pants and went looking for the ticking clock. Feeling his way across the bedroom, the sound led him down the narrow hallway and into the living room. Streaks of skylight soaked through the windows.

The source of the sound stood against the wall inside a grandfather clock with a large, elaborately embossed dial. August hadn't noticed it during the day. Both its size and sound were impressive, and he wondered if Ivan had wound the spring while he was sleeping because he surely would have noticed the loud, regimented ticking earlier if the gears had been turning. Closer inspection revealed the time: a quarter after three.

In the kitchen, he drank from the sink faucet, and most of the iron-tasting water hurried past his mouth and into the drain. Looking out the wavy window, a shadowy movement in the backyard caught his attention. Another movement attracted him to a shifting, blurry form beside the fence and he put on the heavily lined coat that he'd earlier worn and went outdoors. The air felt quite cool, the grass frosty under his bare feet.

Jet Lag stood on the edge of yard, nibbling cold grass. A short distance away, the wooden gate was wide open.

Seeing August, the donkey raised his head and hurried back inside the pen. In the distance, greenish light glowed along the horizon, as though many silent, important events were happening in the adjacent time zone. The sky leaned down closer and August once again felt assaulted by the immensity of rural space.

After closing the gate, he reset the loop of wire that Ivan had fashioned for a lock and noted that no animal except perhaps a monkey would be capable of unclasping it.

Back inside the house, he sat in the kitchen, trying to imagine living there. The ticking clock elbowed its way back into his attention, and he adjusted his breathing to its regularity. For an indefinite time, his thoughts wandered.

Several crunching noises came from the backyard, followed by a loud rattle, then stomping. The back door opened, and Ivan walked into the kitchen from outside, and three or four outdoor smells rushed into the room. His face was red from prolonged exposure to the cool air and he breathed deeply, suggesting recent exercise.

Registering some surprise at finding August in the unlit kitchen, he said, "I thought you were asleep, Gus."

"I woke up. Where have you been?"

"Nowhere really." Ivan snapped on the overhead light. "I just needed some air." He took off his jacket.

Taking two empty jam jars out of the cupboard, he half filled them with orange juice, put one in front of August on the table and sat in the remaining chair. Adding several ounces of vodka to his jar, he slid the bottle across the table.

"Jet Lag was in the yard and I ran him back in the pen," said August, pouring in the vodka. "The gate was open."

"Strange," said Ivan with a curious lack of concern.

They drank.

"What do you do around here for work?" August asked.

"I put in some time at the repair shop when Dad gets far enough behind to have Mother call me, and there are a couple of plants that need welders on a short-term basis. I also have some experience with electrical wiring, and though I don't have a license I can sometimes work off the books. And I have money saved from the pipeline. Mostly, I try to balance steady work with steady leisure. Speaking of work, tell me about yours."

"I lost my job."

"You worked in a lab, right? What were you discovering?"

"In general, we were trying to learn about how cells communicate."

"And why do 'we' want to know that?"

"So we can talk to them."

"What did you find?"

"One thing that initially surprised me is that most conversing between cells—and within cells for that matter—is due to the many different shapes of proteins."

"Shapes?"

"Cells communicate by sending proteins back and forth through receptor sites with highly individualized configurations. They sit around on the outside of cells and act like doorways and doorbells. The only molecules they let in, or bond with, are shaped in exactly the right way, like keys fitting into locks."

"And that surprised you?"

"Years ago, I guess I imagined that cell-signaling might predominately involve electrical exchanges, incremental bursts of released energy, fluctuating quantum levels, something like that. And though there is some electrochemical activity because of calcium, potassium, and sodium gradients, most communication along gated pathways is both initiated and accomplished by three-dimensional shapes fitting into other three-dimensional shapes. At micro levels, shapes and behaviors are pretty much the same thing."

"It's sex all the way down," Ivan laughed.

"And a lot of it," August added. "Picture a billion receptors and ten billion neurotransmitters all copulating in a single nanosecond and within the space of a millionth of a centimeter, in order to transmit a single signal."

"Coed dormitories during a power outage," quipped Ivan, and they both laughed.

"So, in your opinion," asked Ivan, "what are those receptors on the outside of cells doing when they're not, you know, hooking up with the right-shaped proteins?"

"They're open, ready, and thinking about it. That's their sole function. It's why they exist."

"There you have it, the secret life of life—having sex. How did you lose your job?"

"I was in the wrong place at the wrong time. I nearly walked in on the primary investigator—my boss—fitting into the receptor site of his undergraduate lab manager."

"Were they studying cell communication?"

"Apparently."

"What happened?"

"A month later my position terminated."

"I mean what happened when you interrupted them?"

"Nothing really. Their embarrassment only lasted a couple minutes. A half hour later they went right back to it. In the meantime, the professor explained, or rather, rationalized, his behavior by saying that modern nubile women trade access to their bodies for class and status elevation, and as an older member of a rapidly changing society undergoing feminization, he was powerless against them."

"What does that mean?"

"Dr. Grafton thinks sex is about status and he's okay with using whatever status he has to get good sex from younger women. And according to him, if sex is not about prestige, price tags, or expensive houses, then it's an exercise in power."

"I suppose he also talked about how women were once traded like shiny beads among tribal patriarchs," said Ivan.

"How did you know?"

"I read the same book. In my opinion it wasn't ever true except in the herd behavior among rich people in the first economy. Down where the rest of us live, it isn't true at all."

"Now you lost me," August said, and took another drink, noticing that each successive swallow tasted a little better than the last.

"It's one of the things I thought about while working on the pipeline. People talk about the economy as though it's one single thing. But there are at least two systems, maybe more. The first economy is for the rich and those who directly work for them. Investments are a big deal in the first economy—making money from having money—and salaries are high; there's emphasis on merit and everyone has degrees and careers, and if they don't, they're pursuing them. In the first economy it's how you look and whom you know that counts. Maintaining the first economy is the biggest reason for the government, which exists in order to protect the rich and enforce the laws necessary to keep them on top. This is easy to see in less developed countries—and by less developed I mean poor—where whole districts are set aside, reserved for wealthy tourists. Inside those heavily guarded zones are all the good things, white peacocks, four-star restaurants, clean water, old wine, the latest available technologies, sustainably raised organic foods, exotic entertainment, and a highly-trained staff of scrubbed, smiling, deferential folks trying to be helpful."

"Working on that pipeline seems to have been more like an extended populist seminar than a job."

"Isolation is good for thinking," said Ivan, draining his jar. "Anyway, all you have to do is wander a mile or two beyond the tourist areas in those countries and you'll begin to find the second economy, and it includes everyone not directly working for the rich. It's a web of small local economies, and though money is still used, it's basically barter and trade. Open sewers, low wages, and temporary jobs are the rule of the day, and reputations mean more than how you look or whom you know. No one has investments, everyone is in debt, and you'll never read about the second economy in the newspapers."

"Where do those in the middle fit in?"

"The middle is the recruiting ground for more servants to the wealthy. Schools of higher learning do most of the work for them, finding kids with promise, taking them out of their home communities and sending them off where they can be watched, trained, and encouraged to compete against each other. Their old loyalties and habits are drained out of them. They learn how to make new friends quickly, to grovel before authority figures without embarrassing them, and to relocate to different parts of the world at the first chance of a better position with an improved salary package."

"I don't like the direction this is headed."

"Why not?"

"You're getting back at me for leaving, Ivan."

"I'm not. I'm explaining why your boss was wrong about sex and status. Trading sex for social climbing only happens in the upper class. Inheritance, dowries, lineage, prenuptial agreements, trusts, arranged marriages, and the attractive daughter's burden of saving the family estate by finding a wealthy spouse has nothing to do with most of us. And anyone who thinks sex is about power must first imagine they have some. Like I said, the rest of us don't play those games. For us, people are simply people, and sex is either shared fun or it doesn't happen."

"Just a little while ago you were telling me about cutting your hair, dressing up, and convincing someone above your class that you were the best she could do."

"Okay, I see what you mean. It sneaks in anyway, whether we see it or not, doesn't it?"

"And then there's rape, which is clearly about power."

"Rape isn't sex."

"Of course it is. It's forced sex."

"No, it's hate crime. Look, Gus, if an attractive woman came through that door right now and you could tell she did not want to have sex with you, and in order to hook up to her receptor you were going to have to throw her down and force your way in, would that appeal to you?"

"Of course not."

"Does the idea of having that kind of power over someone excite you?"

"No."

"Me neither. That's why I say it's not sex. Something else is at work."

"Maybe, but I don't see how you can deny that power and sex are mixed together. Any sort of authority gets used to make sexual demands. Employers, judges, presidents, jailers, loan agents, immigration officers, teachers, sanitation inspectors, soldiers, priests, border guards, coaches, tax collectors, parole officers, insurance adjustors, landlords, senators, sheriffs, principals, psychiatrists, bankers, doctors, billionaires, and junkyard owners have all been known to use their social leverage to get sex. I don't see how you can possibly deny this. Power is a Pavlovian bell for sex."

"I just don't want it to be true," said Ivan.

"Neither do I, but I recently read about a man who coerced sexual favors from his neighbor by threatening to poison her cat."

"God, I hate stories like that," Ivan said, his face turning a shade of powdered white. "It's hard to imagine what fun there could be if the other person wasn't attracted to you. Isn't that what keeps both people moving?"

"Sure, but when you're attracted to someone and she isn't attracted to you—or she stops being attracted to you—it hurts. Being hurt makes you angry and anger works like a worm in an apple, eating out the system from the inside. And remember, the impulse to have sex doesn't care how it happens, or for what reasons, it just wants the deed done—over and over again. Frankly, natural selection pays no attention at all to the most circumspect and sexually timid among us; it's the rapacious individuals who have had the greatest influence over present and future sexual behavior. Their genes dominate; consequently one in every two hundred males is a descendant of Genghis Khan. Our progenitors never stop prodding us to carry out their ancient agenda. I want nothing to do with them anymore. Once you're involved with sex—in any way—you're part of the problem."

"But we can't help being involved," said Ivan. "Sex, money, and power define us. And as much as we may resent those social pressures, without them, there would be no conscious life at all."

"I'm afraid I can't agree with that," said August, and immediately afterward, the grandfather clock in the adjacent room bonged out four o'clock.

"Where did you get the clock?" asked August.

"Someone gave it to me."

"Why?"

"They owed me money, and at the time it seemed like the right thing to do . . . even though it meant sleeping with earplugs until I got used to it."

"You could just not wind it."

"Sure, but then it would be like I didn't have a grandfather clock. You know, Gus, we've got a lot to do tomorrow. We'd better get some sleep."

SAWS

THE NEXT DAY came as suddenly as a turned page. Waking up, August remembered where he was. The window's thick curtain strained to hold out the morning and pointed strands of light—photonic pry-bars—wedged into the bedroom, opening bright lines of illumination along the top and sides. Noises could be heard from a distant part of the house.

While staring at his soap-lathered face in the mirror, August was reminded of how—after they had become more familiar and unhurried with each other—Amanda would sometimes lie down on the bed after a shower, steam rising from her, water beading in places, and allow him to simply admire her. Sometimes she would stretch out on her cream-colored leather sofa. She always pretended, or appeared to pretend, to have no motivation other than her own comfort, seemingly unaware of his presence. Sometimes she walked around the condominium straightening up, randomly dusting off furniture, naked. She knew she looked good and didn't mind sharing the subject of that assessment.

Finished with shaving, he washed off the soap.

Back in the bedroom he finished dressing and went down the hall.

Morning light flooded through the four windows in the living room—a brilliant wash of yellow-gold. The illumination held his attention nearly all the way into the middle of the carpet before the image of Amanda returned, appearing as the memory of a carpel might reoccur to a stamen, an object whose very existence ordained his participation with it.

Looking into the front yard, August noticed his rented car parked next to Ivan's pickup. It looked strange; it was gleaming modernity contrasting with the dated surroundings. There were several flowerbeds running in both directions away from the dirt path to the front door. The brown, collapsed stalks still clung to withered flower heads, blackened by frost. He could not picture Ivan planting them, yet assumed he had. Or at least he'd maintained gardens already begun by the previous renters. Once again, he pictured Amanda stretched over her bed, open for viewing. He wanted to believe she had cherished those times as much as he—that the same incitement to affection that gave him pleasure in seeing her had been expressed in a complementary manner through a pleasure in being seen.

August stepped away from the window and tried to establish himself in the present moment, to fully and immediately exist. But his mind once again tormented him with the image of Amanda stepping out of the shower. She dropped her towel, lay across the bed, moved her legs, changed position to suggest variations on an ever-narrowing theme.

The kitchen was choking in a blue haze of frying bacon, and after entering and adjusting to the eye-watering smell, August watched Ivan fork out a dozen dripping strips of salt-cured pork, one by one, onto paper towels. His hair and beard were wet from a recent shower, and he wore a heavy gray undershirt and workpants. Cracking open eight eggs, he encouraged their shiny, sticky contents to droop down into the hot fat, provoking a spate of sputtering and spitting from the black-sided iron pan. Then he turned to a second steaming pan, and with a metal spatula rearranged two pounds of sizzling onions and potatoes. At the table, a hot cup of coffee was set in front of August, and Ivan explained they needed to stop by the repair shop on their way to cut firewood for Hanh and Lester. There, they could pick up saws and borrow a wood splitter.

"I mean, if you still want to come."

He slathered six slices of toast with butter.

"Sure," August said, thinking he'd stay in the truck while Ivan borrowed the splitter; his father might be there and he didn't want to run into him, or his mother, before he went over to their house.

"I've got some old clothes you can change into."

The bacon was thick and chewy and August couldn't remember having this much of it since the last time he'd seen Ivan. As he took another bite, an image of Amanda climbed into his mind, and he succeeded in looking away from it.

"Does the bacon come from your grandfather?"

"Yup, Gramps cures his own. The old guy takes eating very seriously and makes sure I have more than I need. It's good you're here. I usually don't bother to make a decent breakfast when I'm alone."

"Glad to be useful. And the coffee, also?"

"You remembered," he said, obviously pleased. "He still roasts his own beans in a frying pan—old thing is about two feet in diameter."

Ivan dumped the fried potatoes and onions onto their plates, nearly covering the eggs.

They ate like young lions.

August changed into Ivan's old clothes.

Ivan piled the dishes in the sink, and they went outside to fill the pickup with tools, beer and sandwich supplies.

The morning air felt cool, bright, and the sky held an expectant blue.

They drove through the rural neighborhood into open country. After twenty minutes they arrived in the village of Words and parked in front of the Words Repair Shop; Ivan climbed out and moved away from the truck. His walk seemed slow and random, as though he were thinking deeply about something while his legs plotted their own course through the parking lot. It was the way August remembered him walking from years before.

The whitewashed concrete building looked much as he'd been picturing it, surrounded with a hedge of discarded lawnmowers, four-wheelers, snowmobiles, broken farm implements, and miscellaneous metal shells waiting to be further rusted and eventually hauled away. There was also the sweet smell of oil and grease—detectable from the road—and after noticing it August wondered whether he'd conjured up the smell from the sight of the building. Thinking about the question for several moments, he decided it didn't matter. Spending so many hours in the shop while growing up, the love he had for his father had simply spilled over into other nearby sensations, and whenever he smelled grease and oil—and sometimes rubber—he felt at home.

In the parking lot, three older men stood next to a flatbed truck with a hobby farm tractor chained to its bed. August recognized two of them—inhabitants of Words, living several houses away from the shop. Both had aged, and the melancholy recognition of time passing through flesh joined the more general conspiracy of nostalgia that had been plotting against August since he entered the familiar little village; a mood gathered around him like a veil of indulgent sadness. If only Amanda and he could have stayed together, coming home would have been completely different. Her presence would have checked the advancement of the past into the present. Once again, he remembered Amanda coming out of the shower, dropping her towel on the floor, walking toward the bed.

Ivan stopped and talked with the three men in the parking lot before continuing into the building. They seemed to know him, and one reached out to grip his upper arm before Ivan went inside.

Minutes later, he emerged from the same door, pulling a wood splitter mounted above a single axle with a rubber-tired wheel on each end, carrying a chain saw with a long bar in his left hand. Once again, he stopped to exchange a few words with the three men standing next to the flatbed.

August climbed out to help attach the splitter to the bumper's towing ball. Ivan set the big saw next to the smaller one in back.

The drive to the woodlot followed a blacktop through a meandering valley of brown, already harvested cropland.

Riding beside Ivan reminded August of high school, when sharing the front seat of a moving vehicle with his friend felt like both liberty and camaraderie.

In the corners of the fields where the land became too steep to cultivate, shrubs and trees took over. On the edges of these areas, wild turkeys searched for the grain missed by the pickers. And crows, less fearful of exposure because of their smaller size and quicker takeoff, scavenged through the center of the fields.

The pickup continued over the ridge and down into a valley with only a few irregularly shaped fields. There were frequent stone outcroppings, boggy sloughs with dead cattail, mint, and skunk cabbage, and thick stands of black oak and clump birch, the latter rising out of the ground in inverted tripods, their crooked, papered trunks wraithlike against a background of larger, straighter hardwoods.

Turning onto a narrow gravel road, the splitter followed them as closely as a shadow, bouncing, banging, and rattling over the weather-worn surface, throwing a plume of dust behind them.

When the ruts in the road grew deeper, Ivan slowed down.

"Do you think JW will be there?" August asked.

"She'll probably show up," said Ivan, "but remember not to call her that. She's Hanh now."

"Right. Apricot Tree."

August placed the new name on a prominent shelf in his memory, in front of the old name.

The road grew narrower and less well maintained until it was nothing more than two dirt tracks leading up a heavily forested hillside—a lumber road. Then it ended at a half-rotten wooden gate with Keep Out painted in red brushstrokes on wide boards. They climbed out. Ivan turned a key inside the padlock, removed the rusty chain from the post, and they pivoted the gate around far enough to let the truck in.

"How much further?" August asked.

"Don't you recognize this place?"

"Should I?"

"This is where the militia used to come into the reserve. They held their meetings and ceremonies just over the hill in the next valley. You and I used to come over here and—"

"I remember," August interrupted, not wanting Ivan to venture any further into those memories. He was anxious about meeting JW and trying to avoid being yanked back into those earlier times without anything to show for his time away.

Nevertheless, August recognized the area, and it was hard to believe how much it had changed just by photosynthesis taking its multifloral, skyward course.

They climbed back in the truck and continued along the uneven path up the hill. Saplings grew in the middle of the trail and rubbed against the undercarriage. Overhead, a swelling of warm air rose through a ragged flock of migrating geese, rippling the formation in a succession of undulating bodies.

August wondered what it would be like to see Hanh again and tried to imagine how she might have changed during the last five or six years. But like a jealous lover, his memory refused to give up its earlier images of her, preferring for her to walk into the future forever young and outdated.

"You're quiet today," said Ivan.

"I'm thinking about Hanh."

"I thought you weren't going to do that anymore—you know, think about sex."

"I said I was thinking about Hanh."

"No one can think about her for long and not think about sex. If you remember, after we found out she wasn't a wild boy—for the first couple years after that—we talked about nothing else. She lit our imaginations up with a blowtorch. You were even more attracted to her than I was."

"That was a long time ago. We were kids and that's what kids think about. We'd never known anyone like her, and she had a scar. But that's all behind us now."

"Fat chance of that. She's still who she is and we're still who we are."

"Do you think she'll come around today?"

"I know she will because last night I went over and told her you were here."

"You've got to be kidding."

"I'm not."

"That's where you went last night?"

"Hanh doesn't like surprises and I thought everything would go a little better if she had time to think about you being back."

"What did she say when you told her?"

"Nothing."

"How did she seem?"

"How do you think she seemed? Excited, worried, happy, upset, and indifferent."

"Did you say she still lives with Lester?"

"No, I said she still looks after Lester, makes sure he eats regularly, takes his medications, and gets to his doctors' appointments. She's got her own place now."

"How did that happen?"

"Lester kept trying to get her an apartment in town where she could make some new friends—real friends, he called them, not the online people she talks to on blogs. Your mother was part of the campaign to move her out. They dragged her into every available place in fifty miles. Didn't work, though. She refused to move into town, so Lester had a house built for her on the corner of their property, a cottage as far away from his place as he could put it."

"Where?"

"Next to the stream north of his place. She moved into it right off and, to tell the truth, it suits her. Every day or two she goes back to check on Lester and a couple times a week they share meals together. He turned his ginseng business over to her, which along with his military pension was how they got along until Hanh branched out. You probably don't know this, but wild ginseng is worth a lot more than it used to be. Now the Middle East has developed a taste for it, as well as Asia. Also, that big melon field in front of his place—the one we used to help plant and harvest—she put filbert trees in there and hires a dozen pickers every fall to harvest them."

"How old is Lester now?"

"Somewhere in his nineties, I think. He won't say. His rheumatism and health in general is getting worse, but he's still Lester. He's got a few buddies from the service and they swap war stories, drink a little beer, and piss on the government. Hanh drives him over to see them. So, he's okay. Mostly, though, he just gardens, gets older, and reads history books."

"History books?"

"Yeah, that's what he calls them, and if he happens to come around today don't ask him anything historical. He can talk all afternoon about the fall of the Roman Empire or why nationalism leads to eating cake for breakfast. You have no idea how much useless stuff that old guy has inside him. And if you try to correct him, look out, Hanh will cut you off at neck level with one of her dagger stares."

"I think I'm getting used to your beard," said August. What a place, he mused, looking out of the truck into a thin blue sky that seemed capable of dissolving anything. He'd been back less than twenty-four hours and had already encountered, directly or indirectly, a minor waiting tables wishing she were older, a woman outdoors at night in only a blanket, a donkey that liked to stand around with goats, a man who wanted to shoot the donkey because he loved the woman in the blanket, an old veteran who had adopted a friend's granddaughter from Vietnam only to find she wouldn't move away from him after she grew up, a bearded guy with a freezer filled with his grandfather's bacon who apparently never slept, and his big city friend who came home to visit his parents and found he wasn't psychologically strong enough see them.

Perhaps the Driftless water had something unusual in it.

Ivan stopped at another gate.

"We're almost there."

The truck muscled over and through several sandy anthills. Following dutifully behind, the splitter banged and rattled.

A shelf of land opened in front of them, reaching toward steep hills on three sides. Ivan followed the lane around to a clearing where a bulldozer had pushed over twenty or more dead trees into a giant brush pile. Thick roots were still attached to trunks, clinging to old clumps of dirt like gnarled fists. Limbs tangled together in arrested violence. Much of the bark was still on them.

Ivan parked. They climbed out and pulled the equipment out of the back.

"Hard to know where to start," commented August, looking into the snarl of dead trees.

"It's like that old game pick-up-sticks," said Ivan, "only now we cut up the sticks and work our way in. Try to always keep one foot on the ground, Gus. If a tree shifts, it's best if you're not standing on it with a running chain saw."

"There's a half hillside here. Who pushed it together?"

"I did." Ivan rolled the splitter away from the truck.

"Whose land is this?"

"A guy named Phillips in Minneapolis. He pulls a motor home out here for a couple months in the summer. Parks it right over there. He rented a Cat last year and paid me to run it. Said it would boost the value of the land because buyers could imagine building a home on the cleared area. He was going to burn it but said I could cut firewood out of it first. Lester and Hanh's property is only half a mile away."

"I remember," August said, "when this valley flooded, maybe fifteen years ago. Five feet of water ran through here."

"Put these on." Ivan tossed a pair of leather gloves. "Don't take them off as long as your saw is running."

"It hasn't been that long," complained August, putting on the gloves and enjoying their wornness. "I remember how to do this."

Holding the heavier saw in his left hand, Ivan's right arm jerked upward several times and the engine barked to life in a belch of smoke.

Leaning the fuel, he throttled up and the saw lurched in his hands with a snarl and high mechanical scream. August put on a pair of earmuffs. Ivan pumped another stream of oil into the bar and guided the shrieking, whirling teeth onto a limb a couple feet off the ground. A spray of blond shavings splashed onto his boots. In rapid succession, cylinders of uniform length fell away from the ever-shortening limb and lay on the ground in a fattening, staggered line.

The smell of oil, gas, and freshly opened wood joined them.

August breathed deeply and took the smaller saw out of the back of the pickup. Its compact weight felt strange in his hands. He hadn't done any physical work for years, and though he frequently exercised, this was different. His body, he hoped, would remember how.

After a dozen pulls the saw still wouldn't start. He tried several more times and stared helplessly into the sky.

Ivan set his saw on the ground without shutting if off, where it jiggled and bucked in restrained frustration. "Give me that," he said. Holding August's saw over his head, he shook it several times, pulled the cord, and it started.

"Fuel filter got caught in the wrong place," he shouted, handing it back to August.

"What?" yelled August, cocking aside one of the earmuffs.

Ivan walked back into the tangle of wood, picked up his saw and went back to lobbing off stove-sized cylinders.

Two bright red male cardinals flew low to the ground across the clearing and landed in a bush, where they sat on the uppermost branch and looked ornamental.

August felt some embarrassment over not being able to start his saw, though there was no way he could have known about the fuel filter or how to deal with it.

He assaulted the nearest limb, trying to keep up, log for log, with Ivan. But the harder he tried the farther behind he fell. Bearing down too hard locked up the chain. Ivan cut one and a half and sometimes two lengths of wood for each of his. He had the bigger engine.

The production imbalance continued after a short water break, when they traded saws.

Ivan had always been more athletic than August, his actions more efficient. He was almost a full year older, for one thing—a huge advantage in grade school. For years, August had waited for this inequity to level off, but it never did. Ivan's hands, arms, legs, and feet enjoyed a more pragmatic affiliation with the environment, while August participated in the natural surroundings through an awkward combination of self-consciousness and second-guessing. It often felt as if he were visiting in Ivan's world, and as another log fell to the ground August wondered what role these feelings of inadequacy had played in spiriting him away to Chicago, where manual skills had less influence over success.

And it never helped that his friend's superior physical abilities didn't seem to matter to him—that Ivan took them for granted. The inequality was somehow magnified by Ivan paying no attention to it. *Homo sapiens* were dimorphic and the size difference between males and females was believed to evince eons of male competition. August could not turn it off—this lonely war of feckless striving against whatever it was that made him less than Ivan. Even though he denounced the war and wanted no part of it, he could not quit. It was part of the way men related to each other. There were over a billion sperm cells in a single ejaculation and only the fastest and most resilient had a chance to fertilize the egg. Males competed even when they did not openly admit it, and any fondness or sympathy or cooperation that emerged between them had to be able to live inside that paradigm.

By the time August's chain saw ran out of gas for the second time, his arms ached and three or four hundred logs eighteen to twenty inches in length lay on the ground.

They took off their gloves and sat for several minutes, looking into their sweating, steaming hands and up to the sky. Wood shavings dusted the ground around the logs like a blond carpet. The air in the valley sparkled with clarity, in contrast to the weary colors that announced a closing to autumn and the inevitability of winter.

"Is this enough?"

"It's a very good beginning," said Ivan.

"If she had a bigger stove there'd be less cutting," August remarked.

"True, but larger stoves are less efficient. And she has a little house."

"What's that noise?"

"Someone's coming," said Ivan, staring into the distance.

A black three-ton SUV with an overhead searchlight bar moved into the clearing, following the same tracks that Ivan and August had made earlier. The driver's door had lettering, but neither of them could read it.

A man and a woman climbed out. Both wore crisp, gray uniforms and buffed shoes. Short brown hair spilled out from beneath the female's hard-billed cap. She looked about thirty-five or forty and walked forward in an almost casual manner. Both her thumbs were hooked behind a wide, black belt, to either side of the buckle, and she seemed to assume authority. The older man smiled in a paternal way, like a teacher greeting a new class. Both made a point of keeping their hands away from their holstered weapons.

The woman nodded.

"Hello," said the man. "Nice day."

August waited for Ivan to say something. When he didn't, August stood up and came forward, "Yes, it's a nice day."

"Bucking a little wood are we," said the woman, looking at August with unusual intensity.

"That's right," said August.

"I hope you're finished cutting for the day," said the male. Still smiling, he took off his cap, rubbed his sandy hair, and put his hat back on again. "Is this your property?"

As though wanting to keep their shoes clean, the guards stopped at the edge of the ragged carpet of wood shavings. The breast patches on their uniforms said Forest Gate.

August turned to Ivan who had his blue stocking cap pulled down tightly over his ears and forehead

"No," said August. "The owner lives in Minnesota and he hired my friend to clean it up."

"We know who it belongs to," snapped the woman. "We just wondered if you knew Jack Phillips."

"Why, are you looking for him?"

"The injunction is still active."

"What injunction?"

"Noise levels. It's against the law to be using those old two-cycle saws. They pollute the air and make too much noise."

"What are you talking about?"

The male guard put his hands into his pockets and looked at the ground. He seemed embarrassed by the abrupt manner of the female.

"We can hear your saws at the Gate," she said. "They've upset several residents."

"What? Who?"

The male guard explained. "Bernice Parker, Stephanie Haworth and her daughter Collette were taking their Sunday morning nature walks. Judge Pennington had his boat out and was trying to catch a bass, perhaps the last of the season. They called in complaints."

"Excuse me, but who are these people?"

"Gate owners," said the woman, and she stepped onto the wood shavings, as though crossing a line of demarcation.

"What's the Gate?"

"Forest Gate—just over the hill."

"Never heard of it," said August.

"They completed it three years ago," said the male guard. "Going on four, actually. You must not be from around here."

"I was born and raised here. You have an injunction?"

"That's right," said the female. "The new ordinance was passed over three years ago, and last summer there were serious problems when Mr. Phillips brought in a class four Caterpillar. Noise levels were off the charts. When security arrived, the operator refused to cooperate, and local police had to be called. As I'm sure you can appreciate, Gate owners have a right to their privacy as well as their peace of mind."

"I thought people could do what they wanted in the middle of nowhere."

"We've put a call in to Mr. Phillips in Minneapolis. If it turns out the two of you are trespassing, he may want to press charges. In that case you'll either pay a large fine or not see the out-of-doors again until sometime next spring."

"Oh, I'm pretty sure it won't come to that," said the male guard.

Above them, a tight skein of geese moved southwest across the pale sky. Three crows flew among them for a short while and then, as though impatient with such orderliness, exited the skyway through a downward spiral.

An engine groaned in the distance, growing louder. August looked over at Ivan, who remained sitting, staring at the ground.

Another SUV with a light bar arrived, spraying dirt as it turned and slid to a stop. With the engine still running, a third guard jumped out. Younger and taller than the other two, he seemed predatory. His aquiline features moved with swift, angular cunning and he looked quickly about the clearing as if he were a hawk searching for prey.

"Any trouble here?" he asked when he reached them.

"Not exactly," said the female guard. They exchanged a private look, suggesting a deeper connection beyond their similar uniforms.

"No trouble," said the older male. "Everything is under control."

"I talked to the owner," the hawk reported, his eyes still scanning for developing events. "Phillips said he doesn't remember giving anyone permission to cut wood on his property, but he's not interested in pressing charges . . . says they're welcome to the wood."

"Good, then we're done here," announced the older guard. "These two gentlemen won't start up their saws again, and they can take away whatever firewood they've already cut. Let's go."

He turned to leave, but the female guard wanted the last word.

"You shouldn't be using two-cycles," she scolded, aiming an arrow-like stare at August. "Besides being loud, those oil-bangers foul the air. Next time you two want to come up here, first get permission and then bring some decent equipment. Obey the law and there won't be any problem."

They turned to leave.

"Just a minute," said August. "You're surely not saying that more stringent noise pollution standards apply exclusively to this immediate area, and that a local court has upheld this narrow ordinance. Such a ruling seems inconceivable to me."

"Get used to it, Einstein," growled the taller, younger guard. As though defending the woman's honor, he leaned in, his sharpened face inches from August's. "You two dirtbags poached some firewood today and it looks like you're going to get away with it. Count yourselves lucky.

But you can't use those piece-of-shit saws around here any longer. What is it about that you don't understand?" And with a quick movement that seemed more reptilian than avian he pushed August backward several steps, where August stumbled but remained standing.

"All I'm saying," complained August, "is that such a ruling seems highly prejudicial, and it seems there would be excellent grounds for a successful appeal."

The hawk came forward again, and again shoved August.

Ivan got off the log he'd been sitting on, tossed his knit hat on the ground, peeled his arms out of the sleeves of his denim jacket, and pulled his undershirt over his head.

The action surprised August, who had temporarily forgotten how hirsute Ivan was. Even his shoulders and stomach sprouted hair, some of it fairly long.

Stepping in front of August, Ivan faced the hawk. "Push me," he said in a level voice. When the hawk hesitated, Ivan stepped forward. "Come on. You like to push people. Push me."

The hawk retreated and the chief officer placed her hand on her holstered pistol. The older guard came quickly forward, repeating what he'd said earlier. "We're done here. We're leaving. We're done here."

"Later," snarled the hawk at Ivan, as he was led away by the other two guards.

Within minutes, the sounds of their trucks were gone.

"I think you startled them," August said.

Ivan picked up his undershirt, shook off the wood shavings and put it back on.

"How did you learn to do that?"

"Once on the pipeline I watched a guy take his shirt off before challenging someone, and it worked. I think my body hair helps too."

"You're probably right about that," said August. "Primates such as chimps and bonobos are far, far stronger than humans—pound for pound. In branching off from the more robust apes we basically traded most our strength for a lot of fine motor neurons—essentially giving away brute power for intricate hand control. So, in a primordial sense, it makes good sense for humans to fear anything with much body hair. Animals are roughly four times as strong, given the same relative weight."

"I'm just glad he didn't push back," said Ivan. "That guy looks pretty tough."

"Why didn't you say something earlier?"

"My time with them last summer didn't turn out too well. Luckily, they didn't remember me. I didn't have a beard back then."

"So, we don't have permission to cut this wood?"

"We do, but Phillips wouldn't admit it when they went after him about the noise. He did the same thing last summer with the Caterpillar. Once they started hollering legalities, he caved."

"What's Forest Gate?"

"It's a very large tract of land just over the hill—most of it originally owned by two men from Illinois who managed it as a hunting preserve. All of it, including the adjacent valley, now belongs to developers from Chicago. They dammed the river, made a lake, and bid out lots. There's a gated community up there. It's big—square mile or two."

"A gated community . . . out here?"

"Yes, and as you've seen, they've got their own police force, and there are plenty more than just those three goons. In addition to the lake, they have an airstrip, nine-hole course, clubhouse, backup solar and wind, everything."

"How many live there?"

"I don't know. They guard it tighter than Fort Knox. No one gets in without permission. I'm told there are seventy or eighty homes, maybe a hundred, which is about what it looks like from satellite images."

"Who owns them?"

"Wealthy people from all over the world."

"Do they live there year-round?"

"Some do; most don't. Forest Gate is like an exclusive resort. They've even got their own food service and medical clinic with med-flight."

"So why didn't we bring newer and quieter saws? I know the repair shop has them."

"Didn't think about it, I guess."

"No, you wanted to rattle their cage, Ivan. You forget that we grew up together. You can't pretend with me."

"Maybe. I hate those people."

"Why?"

Ivan brushed off his denim coat before putting it back on, picked up the knit hat and stuffed it into a jacket pocket. "They're interfering with the revolution."

"I don't suppose this is something else that can be traced back to working on the pipeline."

"It is, in fact. I'll tell you about it while we eat lunch."

"Don't we need to split some of these bigger pieces?"

"I'm hungry."

"Is there going to be a problem with the engine on the wood-splitter?"

"Nope. You can hardly hear her run."

Sitting on the pickup's tailgate, they ate lunchmeat, cheese, and lettuce sandwiches, apples, pears, and oatmeal cookies, washed down with beer. The sun moved through the last of the afternoon sky and as the light lost much of its luminosity, it invited orange and gold into the valley. More Canada geese flew overhead, dropping their wraithlike shadows onto the leaf-strewn ground below.

Ivan explained his theory of silent revolution. Men and women from all walks of life were slowly becoming more consciously aware—waking up—and rejecting the greed-based centers of civilization. These fair-minded stalwarts were turning their backs on consumer-based society, its cynicism and political depravity. They were dismissing a culture that aspired to nothing higher than to be entertained—tired of being lied to and manipulated by wealthy people. Consequently, they were leaving the urban areas, stealing through the suburbs with their families, and fleeing into the hinterlands. Their departures represented the most significant social development on the planet, unnoticed by the ruling classes.

"A revolution to save humanity has begun," Ivan said. "To recognize it you have to be part of it, because it more resembles a biblical exodus than an outright revolt, a receding tide—away from the anthills of humanity and into the woods and valleys of deeply rural areas. There, new ways of living are germinating. New thoughts are being considered. New methods of cooperation are developing. The meaning of family and community are being reexamined. More satisfying relationships with nature and other people are emerging. New schools are being founded with teachers dedicated to new outcomes, using new methods, employing new concepts. New technologies are being discovered and old technologies are being differently applied. Sooner or later a new civilization will begin to take hold, founded along entirely different lines."

"Sounds apocalyptic," commented August. "I mean, an exodus no less." He swallowed another bite of sandwich and a wave of relief yawned inside him. A sizable part of the day had just passed, and he hadn't even thought of Amanda, remembered the swell of her hips, her smell, the unsupportable anguish of her absence. For several blessed hours his despair over remaining wounded for the rest of his life had not broken the surface. He felt an immense gratitude.

"Glad you noticed," said Ivan. He opened another bottle of beer and passed it over. "It's the way mankind renews itself when its major cultures begin to decay. All the sacred literature that persists to this day, the Vedas, Torah, Gita, New Testament, Koran—all of them evolved out of these kinds of movements. They were all—every single one of them— inspired by relatively small groups of people escaping the death rattle of dying civilizations, the greed, the hype, the corruption and immorality in the cities, heading into the hills, looking for better ways to live."

"I still don't understand what this has to do with Forest Gate."

"That's because you've been away too long, Gus. You don't see it because it's right in front of you. It's too obvious. Forest Gate is an abomination, a provocation. Before those people came here this whole area—every person—was involved in the silent revolution against the dominant order. In their own way everyone was working toward something better, refusing to serve corporate rulers, trying to hold on to a little dignity and independence. Then the masters of our universe arrived. After despoiling the rest of the earth, they built their private homes here, in one of the last unspoiled regions. They moved into the center of the very place where hope for the future was being worked out. It's almost like they knew a better world was not only possible, but on its way. They could hear the faint heartbeat of something better and came to stamp it out."

"I still don't understand why they want to be here."

"Because this is one of the last relatively unspoiled places. Widespread environmental degradation has alarmed the ruling class, and they hired agencies to search out the best remaining places to live.

This area ranks very high in clean water securities, low pollution levels, moderate temperatures, fertile land, small human footprint, thriving wildlife, and other natural amenities. It's remote, yet only hours away from Chicago, and has the advantage of being mostly unknown—a good place to hide out while the capitalist civilization collapses."

Ivan drained the last of his beer and continued. "Five years ago, before their new lake had been completed, the Wisconsin governor committed the Department of Natural Resources to assisting the developers. And public resources continue to be spent on maintaining water quality and assuring the best sports fishing in the state. Everyone else around here has property taxes based on assessed values. But before those people would build their mansions—which are worth more than the combined value of all the other homes in a thirty-mile radius—their lawyers made provisions to catastrophically limit their tax burden. Concessions were also demanded from the highway commission, who built miles and miles of roads for them and agreed to maintain and patrol them, at the expense of the other roads in the area. And who do you think they found to guard their exclusive resort—to keep the rest of us out? You guessed it—they hired people from right here. They turned regular citizens—ordinary Joes and Janes—into thugs with weapons, salaries, and benefits. I know, it's hard to believe anyone would take a job like that, but money trumps loyalty every time. It's depressing how quickly—and cheaply—some people sell out. And did you hear the way those guards talked about Judge Pennington? He had his boat out, they said, as though Jesus Christ himself had been sighted walking on the water. They revere those wealthy bastards simply because they're rich. And that grunt who shoved you, do you remember him?"

"No."

"I thought you wouldn't. That's Jeff Dranger from two grades above us. He was always a bully and now he's being paid to be one. The overlords can always count on buying people. It's the way they stay in control."

"Sounds like they're coming back," said August, letting himself off the tailgate and drinking the last of his beer.

"That's not them," remarked Ivan.

WORKING WOOD

A VERY OLD truck turned wide into the clearing and backed a long, flat trailer with short wooden sides toward them. Just before the trailer rolled onto the carpet of shavings, the truck stopped and the engine died. The driver slowly and stiffly eased out of the cab.

"Where'd you get the trailer, Les?" called Ivan to the old man in overalls and tennis shoes.

"Borrowed it from a friend," said Lester Mortal, walking with some difficulty toward them. "I heard your saws and thought I'd come over. Who's the new guy?"

August waved.

Lester's face bristled with a week's worth of white and gray whiskers. Creases invaded his face and neck, partly from weight loss and partly from the degradations of time. He looked ancient, his voice a whispered imitation of his former one, his hands knotted with rheumatism.

"That's Gus."

"I know. I know. Hey, August, you look exactly like you did the last time I saw you. Doesn't seem possible. Good to have you back. You've been missed."

"Hello, Lester. You're looking well," returned August.

"You always were a liar," he snapped, pulling a pair of dirty cotton gloves out of his pocket and shoving his hands into them. From another pocket he took a tattered cap, stretched the faded red yarn over his head, and rolled it down to cover his ears. "Let's get to work."

August and Ivan maneuvered the splitter directly behind the trailer. They filled the tank with gas, checked the crankcase oil, and started the engine. It ran with steady, muffled hammer blows.

Ivan carried the largest logs to August, who positioned them on the base plate. Lester ran the hydraulic, moving the wedge forward and back. As the logs were reduced in diameter, August threw them into the trailer. If a piece of wood refused to cleanly split, August broke the halves apart with an ax or maul. When the pieces waiting for August to bust open began to pile up, Ivan carried smaller ones that did not require splitting, and tossed them directly into the trailer.

They worked steadily, discovering a shared speed and rhythm. The purr of the engine provided a steady backdrop for the sounds of the humming hydraulic, wood breaking open, and the clunk of logs thrown onto the wooden trailer. The load rose higher as the sun fell further into the horizon. August wondered if they would be able to finish before their vision became challenged. And once again he felt grateful for the work and companionship. He inhaled the exhaust from the small engine, and indulged in the sight of the dissolving sky, drawing him into the limitless out-of-doors. Cooler air settled into the valley, pulled in by the vacuum of departing light.

When the woodpile in the trailer threatened to spill over the sides, Ivan and August corded a tight row along the back edge. Lester drove the trailer a short distance away and Ivan backed his pickup next to the splitter.

They resumed breaking apart the larger pieces and throwing the rest into the back of the pickup, hoping it would hold it all.

The evening spread its last sheet of darkness and in response the irises in their eyes, ravenous for more illumination, opened wide. Objects within fifteen or twenty feet could be seen. Those further away remained doubtful.

Stars appeared.

As August worked, he occasionally noticed sounds that couldn't be accounted for. At irregular intervals, logs were being thrown into the pickup when neither he nor Ivan threw them. Old Lester couldn't be throwing them. Someone else was helping to load.

"Give me a minute," August said to Lester, and went around to the other side of the truck. Standing still, he listened.

Lester shut off the splitter and sat on a log, resting.

Twenty yards away, Ivan lit a cigarette and the brief flame from the lighter yellowed his cupped hand.

Crows carried on an unseen argument with the night.

Far away, a chorus of small dogs barked. Several more joined in from a different direction, baritones. Then, as though hearing the same signal, they all fell silent.

A short figure walked out of the dark, carrying an armload of wood. A parka's fur-lined hood framed her head. Heavy leather mittens covered her hands. Her eyes reflected skylight. She moved briskly, the fabric in her loose pant legs brushed together, coming toward him.

The name Hanh stuck in August's throat and he couldn't get it out. She walked past him to the side of the pickup and tossed the logs in, where they clattered against other logs. Returning, she stopped in front of him. Grasping one mitten by the other, she pulled out her hand and stretched it forward, palm open. "Hello, August," she said.

Her face visible now, her eyes glistened like dark jewels and the scar down her left cheek and neck seemed deeper than he remembered—a puckered crease from her left ear to where it disappeared into her parka, a twenty-five-year-old wound from a landmine in Vietnam. The slash drew attention to the trim loveliness of the rest of her other facial features, the intensity of her face and her astoundingly brown eyes.

August removed his glove, and they shook hands. Because of the insulation in her mitten, Hanh's palm and fingers felt moist, warm, and weightless. He placed his second hand over hers, as though to absorb more of her. But as soon as her hand became trapped, she pulled it away, removed her magnificent eyes from his, and returned her hand inside the leather mitten.

"Hello, Hanh," he said. "I hoped you'd come. I really did. I mean, I hoped I'd get a chance to see you. I've been thinking about you, and, well, worrying about meeting you. Not really worrying, no, not really, and Ivan said you'd probably be here, or you might be here, at least he said that. He said he came over last night. He told me this morning. But when Lester came with the trailer and you weren't with him, I wondered if that meant you weren't coming. I mean, you didn't have to come, of course. I was just hoping you would, I mean, after Ivan mentioned you might be here. I just thought..." His voice trailed off as the gathering content of what he wished to say outran the possibility of ever saying it.

She looked at him once again, then returned to searching for more pieces of wood in the darkness.

The dogs in the distance resumed barking.

"Let's finish this," called Lester, rising wearily, unsteadily to his feet.

August went back to breaking open the last half dozen blocks of wood and putting them in the back of the pickup.

He'd forgotten how little she was, and her real size troubled him. It was like seeing a fox, which is hardly larger than a housecat. In his mind she had much, much larger dimensions.

When he'd first seen her at the age of eleven, she was only slightly smaller than him. Soon after that, however, she stopped growing, while he had continued.

"Pay attention here," complained Lester, as August stood holding a block of wood, staring at it as if it were an antique lamp.

"Sorry."

He set the chunk into the splitter. Lester sent the hydraulic wedge humming forward. The inexorable squeeze began, the wood groaned, creaked, hissed and screamed before it opened.

August tossed the pieces into the truck. The old man was tired, but he kept at his task of manning the lever.

August knew that seeing her again would affect him—just as seeing Ivan had. But he hadn't anticipated the profound impression she had just made. The sound of her voice unraveled every fabric inside him. Her handshake brushed aside the last few years like crumbs from a sheet of paper. He was an early adolescent again.

Growing up together, Hanh and August had experienced a mutual attraction. They'd cautiously experimented with each other, though never unclothed. August's body for Hanh and Hanh's for August were like unfamiliar toys, sensual objects that could only be awkwardly played with. Still, they had both found comfort, and even refuge, in each other's arms.

But they had not gone all the way into that refuge, and while breaking open the remaining blocks of wood August noticed that this empty fact, this nonevent, stood out in his mind as particularly significant. Somewhere in his brain, sensation accountants were apparently keeping score, and he and Hanh's decision to not allow their affection to secure a final, consummate pleasure before August went away to school now seemed more like a broken promise than a foregone opportunity.

He blamed her. Hanh experienced social phobia during much of her childhood, which, among other things, prevented her from attending public school and speaking out loud until around the age of twelve, when she first began talking to Lester, her adoptive father, and later to August and Ivan, her friends. For her, intimacy had required extensive homesteading, clearing away psychological brush and carefully building trust. At her insistence, August and she had to go slow, make infinite preparations, dismantle the elaborate alarm system that had been installed to protect her against every conceivable human threat. Inch forward. They had enjoyed many wary explorations into giving and receiving pleasure, but had always stopped before rapid breathing arrived, because when their hearts began to throb in unison, Hanh's smoke detectors detected fire. She couldn't help it. Rightly or wrongly, biology's blood drums warned her of impending danger—a trap designed to hang her wild young soul on a tavern wall.

"I hope that's the last of it," said Lester, shutting off the wood splitter. Like an afterthought, the global stillness hiding behind the engine's noise rushed out and surrounded them.

The horizon faintly glowed.

Ivan and Hanh walked out of the darkness, each throwing a final armload of branches into the back of the truck.

August and Lester turned the splitter around and locked it into the trailer hitch.

It started to snow. Out of a clear sky, flakes fell around them like pieces of shredded sheets, disappearing when they touched something solid.

Lester and Hanh climbed into the truck cab and they pulled the trailer of wood behind them, creaking, groaning, and sagging out of the clearing and along the lane to the road. After a short way they turned down a narrow driveway. Ivan and August followed them through ten acres of filbert trees, past Lester's sod house and into the woods. Every so often logs fell off the trailer and Ivan would stop for August to climb out and throw them in back. After less than a half mile, the trailer settled beside a small, unpainted wooden cottage with a ribbon of white smoke curling from a stovepipe in the metal roof.

"What are the utility sheds behind the house for?" asked August.

"Those are for processing the nuts, honey, and ginseng."

After Ivan decoupled Lester's truck from the trailer, Lester rolled down his window in the cab and said, "I'm going home. When you finish unloading, there'll be stew and cider. All of you come."

"We'll be over," said Ivan.

"Do you want to go with him?" August asked Hanh as she stood beside him, her face completely hidden in shadow. "Ivan and I can unload this," he added.

The parka's hood moved from side to side. "I already made the stew, baked the bread, and set the table. All he has to do is heat it up." She turned away from August and began pulling logs off the trailer, stacking them along the back of her porch, her movements quick and efficient. The old truck moved away from them and disappeared.

August and Ivan worked beside her, building a single row of logs, then a wall, then a second row, until the stacked logs grew into the shape of a giant loaf of bread.

"Did you notice Hanh's hives?" asked Ivan as they finished unloading the trailer and began pulling the wood out of their pickup.

To the side of the cottage a dozen beehives rose out of the ground. As temperatures fell, the snow had begun to stick without melting, and now covered the apiary with a uniform layer of white, softening the points and edges and lending the boxlike shapes a sense of conspicuous grouping, a miniature Stonehenge.

"There sure are a lot of them," commented August.

"Hanh works with apiologists in Madison. They're developing a strain of honeybees that will resist super-mites."

"What are super-mites?"

"Mites that have grown stronger from resisting fungicides. Hanh's bees are outflanking them somehow, and the university periodically sends students out here to check on them. Some think it may have something to do with the filbert flowers they mainly feed on during portions of the year. She can tell you. They're talking about importing super-ladybugs to eat the super-mites."

"Interesting," said August.

"And not only that, did you know almost all bees are female?"

"I did know that, actually."

"The males' only purpose is to hang around and mate with the queen, which happens almost never, because she can store semen for months. The males die as soon as they hook up with her. And did you know that the type of female bee that emerges from the larva depends upon what and how much it is fed?"

"Sounds a little familiar," uttered August, who was nearing his limit for physical exertion. Each log felt heavier than the last, while Ivan, he noticed, seemed to be working (and talking) even more efficiently, as though both talking and working somehow filled him with additional adrenaline.

"It's true. Larvae can develop into worker bees, attendant bees, or potential queens, depending on what and how much they eat. And how they are fed depends on how strong the reigning queen's pheromones are, because her health and vigor are communicated through the smells she gives off, which her attendants ingest and pass on to the other bees. If the queen is healthy and keeps busily laying eggs, the young larvae hatch into more drones and workers. But if the queen is lazy or slow in her reproductive duties, select larvae are fed what is called 'royal jelly,' and then they hatch into young queens who fight each other until only one is left."

August stood up, stretched, and yawned. "Interesting," he said.

Ivan kept stacking while he talked. "And did you know that queen bees often do not want to mate at all? They're forced out of the hive by the workers and attendants. It's the only time a queen actually leaves the hive, and while in flight she might mate with as many as fifty different males, and they all drop dead immediately after. Anyway, Hanh can tell you all about it. The university people are very interested in her bees."

"That's great, Hanh," said August, still resting. "That's really great."

Standing at the tailgate with snow covering the top of her hood and shoulders, Hanh turned toward him. "Don't be condescending," she snapped, and returned to cording the wood.

August shivered from the rebuke and became even more aware of how tired, cold, and hungry he was. Every muscle that he could feel, ached.

Hanh had always been able to wound him. Being a couple years older had probably helped endow her with psychic authority, and as a friend she had both given and demanded a lot. Knowing her had been a real adventure; and beginning a relationship with her had sometimes seemed like entering a dark house and discovering that all the lights inside the closets, basement, and attic were on but not detectable from outside, and then, returning for a second visit, discovering that she'd turned them all off.

August remembered when he first moved away from the area; he'd missed her every day, yet he also felt relief for the absence of her acerbic criticism.

"I wasn't condescending," he complained. "In fact, I couldn't be more interested."

Hanh kept working with her back to him, and then moved away.

"Let it go," whispered Ivan. "She'll come around."

After all the wood had been stacked, Ivan and August drove to Lester's house in Ivan's pickup. Hanh followed them a short time later in her three-wheeled electric Kar.

The inside of Lester's home was cramped, fragrant, and warm; the thick walls hung with faded photographs of small Midwestern towns from earlier centuries that reminded August of displays set up by rural historical societies—scenes with boardwalks, old trains, horses, men in hats and suspenders and women in long dresses and lace-up shoes. The rest of the walls were lined with books, mostly well-worn paperbacks, some on shelves and others rising up from the floor in irregular towers.

Looking around, August became aware of another difference between Chicago and here: property management. In the upscale apartments, condominiums, and townhouses that August had become acquainted with in Chicago, the owners were perennially aware of housing markets and the need to be able to rent, sublease, buy, and sell property at a moment's notice, and the interiors assumed an orderly sameness reminiscent of hotel accommodations. Living places were well maintained and frequently updated—available for inspection and new occupants. Here, however, owners like Lester Mortal took a longer view of their property, and usually assumed they would live in their homes until they died, with no thought for future resale, lost deposits, or inspections. Furniture was not replaced after it became unfashionable or unsightly. Walls and doors were okay as long as they kept out summer bugs and winter wind. Abandoned objects remained for months, even years, and every room harbored indelible traces of earlier events. Accumulated clutter—cast-off shoes, tools on staircases, two-by-fours that were headed for the outdoors but leaned temporarily against the refrigerator, books left next to sofas on lamp tables and along window ledges—remained for indefinite periods of time. Lester had apparently set down a case of glass jars filled with nails of different sizes in the middle of the living room floor. The action no doubt justified itself at the time and went on justifying itself. Order, August reflected, meant different things to different people, and one man's order might seem to another like an attempt to hide personal facts.

The eating area was only large enough to accommodate a small table and four wooden chairs. Lester sat near the cooking stove. Hanh sat across from him, her short black hair growing from her head in the shape of a helmet. Around her neck, a bright red scarf made a single turn before plunging into a beige tunic's hemmed collar. To her right, Ivan sat in his undershirt, his hair and beard as wild as fighting grackles. As though feeling some responsibility for entertaining, he talked loudly, improvising with both hands, relating how security guards from Forest Gate had driven over and objected to the noise of their saws.

August sat across from Ivan in Ivan's clothes, his eyes moving, taking in everything, grateful for the warmth and occasionally rubbing his arms and shoulders.

Much had changed since he'd last been here. The four of them now occupied different slots along the timeline, and their lives now connected through different circumstances; August tried to discover what new role he was expected to play. He also tried to make eye contact with Hanh, without success. She guarded her vision and only occasionally allowed her sight to make quick excursions into other parts of the room, though never in August's direction.

Lester served up the stew in wooden bowls and passed around thick slabs of sourdough bread, mugs of hot spiced cider, and slices of aged cheddar cheese. His movements were deliberate, very slow, and almost ceremonial. Despite the new wrinkles, age spots, balding, and a whispered voice, he still seemed fully at home in his body, even though he was clearly shrinking. He occupied about a half of the space he did six or seven years ago. Still, he seemed completely at ease, like someone who had fought long and difficult battles with himself and exacted an amicable armistice. Hanh watched him protectively, but did not interfere with his serving the meal, which he seemed to take pride in.

After describing the visit from the security guards, Ivan went directly into his ideas about the silent revolution and how people inside Forest Gate were interfering with it. Hanh and Lester picked up their spoons. They seemed familiar with the subject. Both listened dutifully, even fondly while they ate stew, and August couldn't tell if this fondness came in response to the subject matter, which they agreed with, or to Ivan himself, or some combination of both.

August chewed a mouthful of stewed potato and cooked carrot. The flavors acted like balm rubbed into his tired mind. The hot cider bit into the sides of his tongue, drawing his cheeks together. He remembered drinking a similar cider at the same table years before, at about the age of eleven when he had come looking for the wild boy, or for what he thought at the time was a wild boy—a child August only saw glimpses of in the wooded hills in the area. Back then, Lester protected Hanh's identity while she hid in another room, and he allowed August to continue imagining a feral boy roaming through the Driftless Area. Then, several months later, after Hanh agreed she was ready to meet him, Lester introduced them. After that, August and Ivan (who had also entertained the fantasy of a feral child) frequently returned to Lester's house to see her. Their lives were enormously enhanced by a friend who never talked in the beginning, and only rarely talked later, as she led them into the many magical places she'd discovered while wandering through the forests. They felt lucky to know someone who most of the rest of humanity did not. And her status in their minds continued to be heightened by their earlier fantasies of her, their errant belief that she slept under the stars, foraged for food, drank from cold-rushing streams, did whatever she wanted, shunned civilization, and lived the uninhibited life they sometimes wished for themselves—free from family and civic obligations, liberated from the anxious need to grow up and be assimilated into society; and even though these romantic thoughts had no basis in reality, by the gift of association they still adhered to her. She seemed magical. And of course, they were also intrigued by the unseen yet ever-present fact that under her short hair, beneath the manly facial scar that she never talked about, beyond her passion for roaming through the woods and knowing the hiding places of bears, cougars, foxes, snakes, and badgers, along with her athleticism (she could easily outrun them both, even Ivan), and her boyish clothes, somewhere underneath it all, she wasn't a boy.

Many of his more disquieting thoughts about Hanh were civilized after August got to know her better, though now, after such a long absence, those old associations returned in their original costumes and he felt as though he were in the presence of the same rare creature. Hanh, he reflected, could exist nowhere else. She was a human feature of this strange area that he had moved away from, learned to be ashamed of, and now found endearing in a new way he couldn't fathom or explain.

"So, August," said Lester. "What are your thoughts about Forest Gate? Do you agree with Ivan?"

"Oh yes, on nearly everything," he replied. "It occurs to me, however, that when something like this happens in urban areas, we simply call it gentrification and don't think much about it."

"Except for the people who can no longer afford to live in those areas," said Ivan. "They think about it."

"Probably true," said August, failing again to make eye contact with Hanh.

"Forest Gate is a parasite," said Ivan.

"A similar thing happened during the Roman Empire," said Lester. "Some aristocrats who were no longer satisfied to remain in the designated political centers began to establish residences in rural areas. They of course needed servants in their homes and didn't want to work the land themselves, and a modified system of slavery evolved, which was later called serfdom. It lasted over a millennium in Europe."

"See, that's what I'm talking about," said Ivan, taking a quick gulp of cider. "It happened before, and it will again."

"It's always dangerous to have a historian in the room," said August.

Hanh walked away from the table, drew a glass of water from the faucet, drank a portion of it, returned and sat down.

Ivan's phone rang. After answering it he stood up, smiled apologetically, and went into the other room.

Hanh looked at her glass of water.

Lester drew out an additional ladle of stew and placed it in his bowl.

August took another drink of cider and his mouth pinched together.

"I'm afraid I have to leave," Ivan announced, coming up to the table and taking up his coat. "There's a problem with Jet Lag."

"I'm coming with you." August stood up.

"No need. Finish your meal."

"I should be with you," August complained.

"I'll take care of it, Gus. You stay. Hanh and Lester have been looking forward to seeing you. If I'm not back in an hour or two Lester can drive you over to my place."

"Glad to," said Lester.

August again protested, but Ivan made it seem it would be rude for him to leave.

"Let him go," said Lester quietly.

After the front door closed and the headlights of Ivan's truck could be seen moving through falling snow, Lester asked if August had been home yet to see his parents, and if so, how were they?

"I haven't had a chance to go over there yet," said August. "I just got back yesterday and was catching a bite to eat in Grange when I ran into Ivan. He invited me to spend a couple nights and, well, here I am."

"How long are you staying?"

"I don't know. For a while."

"Is everything all right, I mean between you and your parents?" asked Lester.

"Sure. Of course it is. Everything is fine."

"I haven't seen Jacob for a long time, I'm ashamed to say." Lester poured more cider. "Not since last spring. There was a time, and it doesn't seem that long ago, when Jacob and I used to see each other quite a lot.

I'm afraid getting old isn't kind to friendships. When you become less active, well, you don't see your friends as much. When you go over there please tell him I've been thinking about him."

"I will."

August remembered visiting Hanh after she stopped hiding from him. He, she, and Lester would spend time together. Sometimes they'd just talk, or rather Lester would talk and Hanh and August would listen, or they'd play a board game, or in some other way occupy space together before he and Hanh went off alone. She had insisted on this. Seeing Hanh always included spending time with Lester. As she once told August, Lester was all she had. "You have both parents, aunts and uncles, and a whole community that knows who you are and wishes you well. I have one old man and he's not going to be left out."

So, August had deep familiarity with Lester. He knew about the lives of his parents—especially his father—and many of his relatives, the countries the old veteran had been sent into as a young man, firefights he'd survived, men he served with, acts of bravery and cowardice he'd witnessed and performed, things he regretted and didn't regret, his favorite foods, and his inimical feelings about the politicians, industries, and social forces that instigated wars.

Finished with supper, they carried their remaining cider into the small living area and settled into more comfortable chairs. After a short time, Hanh got up, went into the kitchen and brought back pills for Lester to swallow. Then she returned to the kitchen, took off her scarf, rolled up her sleeves, and began washing dishes.

"I should help," said August.

"Stay where you are," Lester said. "I want to tell you a story you haven't heard before."

"Has Hanh heard it?"

"Many times, I'm afraid, but I don't remember telling you."

August rubbed his shoulders and settled into his chair.

"It happened on the coast of Nicaragua. As usual, the army was trying to keep us busy when there wasn't anything useful to do. Three of us were ordered to break off from the rest of the company, go several miles north, make camp on the beach and watch for movement on the water—patrol boats. George Samuelson from West Virginia, Brad Jackson from Kansas, and I hiked up there, scouted the area, set up our tents, phoned in our location, lit a fire, and were trying to fill the time. It was a beautiful place, I remember, warm and humid. When the sun went down it threw colors across the sky, and the water mirrored them. Soon, it grew darker and darker, clouds rolled in, and a couple hours later it was black as pitch. You couldn't even see the stars. George had a deck of playing cards and we were playing in the firelight, but it turned out that a half dozen of the cards were missing, so the game didn't last long. We had a radio but couldn't find anything in English. Then bugs found us, and we put out the fire, climbed into one tent, and busied ourselves with reading and writing letters from the light of a single government-issue kerosene lamp. George dozed off in the middle of his paperback, and I wasn't far from sleep myself. I kept closing my eyes for longer and longer periods, listening to the ocean beating against the shore. And then we heard scratching on the outside of the tent—more and more of it."

"Scratching?"

"When we folded back the flaps and went outside, the whole beach crawled. It was filled with newly hatched baby turtles, recently dug out of the sand. No bigger around than fifty-cent coins. They were attracted to the light inside our tent. All of them were coming toward us and it looked like the ground was moving. They scratched on the sides of the tent, trying to get in, climbing over each other, piling up, frantic as moths for the light.

"Very odd."

"Apparently it was normal for those turtles to hatch at night, a survival advantage because birds and other predators couldn't see them."

"Weren't they attracted to the water?"

"Sure, if they were close enough to it, but when the nests were buried a way off they had to rely on their instinct to move toward moonlight, which usually led them into the sea. On this particular night, however, the moon couldn't be seen."

"What did you do?"

"We scooped up as many as we could carry and took them to the water, where they sank in and disappeared. But it was hard to hold them and there were so many. The beach was covered with them and it was impossible to avoid stepping on 'em. After we turned the lamp off, they scurried around aimlessly. The beach looked like it was boiling."

"What happened?"

"After an hour the sky cleared, and the moon climbed above the horizon. Once they saw the new light—and it seemed they all saw it at once—they headed straight for the water. George and Brad and I went over and watched the little fellas moving into the dark ocean. The ground seemed to pour into the sea. They were returning to the womb of the world. What a sight."

"It must have been."

"I mean, at first they were confused. Their instincts were leading them astray, toward the wrong light. But after the moon came out, they knew. There was no question then. The light inside the tent could only fool them when it was the only light to choose from. When they saw the real thing, off they went."

"I'd like to see that myself someday."

"Unlikely, August—not those turtles at least. They died out, went extinct. Now they're only a piece of the historical record. It gets to you. When you are as old as I am you'll understand what I mean—all these glorious memories, and so few of them attach to anything that is still around."

"Their instincts couldn't save them," August remarked.

"True."

"Instincts can only be trusted when environmental conditions stay the same. With new circumstances, all bets are off."

"All bets are off anyway," Lester said. And then he remembered an afternoon when he and his father visited a relative in Illinois, in early November. "We took the interstate," he told August, and went on to explain how he and his father had come upon the scene of an accident; a truck driver had nodded off, lost control, and overturned in the median strip. The refrigerated trailer was lying on its side, the doors sprung open, frozen turkeys spilling out onto the grass. The unhurt driver had climbed out of the overturned cab and was writing something into a bound notebook. Cars pulled over on both sides of the highway and people were rushing out of their cars, snatching up frozen turkeys, and running back to their cars, sometimes coming a second time for more. Lester's father pulled over too.

But taking a turkey seemed unethical, so his father walked to the front of the truck and talked to the driver. "How much you want for one of them turkeys?" he asked.

"Thirty bucks," said the man. As Lester recalled, he was very tall with dark rimmed glasses and long curly hair; he wore tan cowboy boots with red leather soles and heels, and a suede coat with five-inch fringes along the bottom of the sleeves.

"That's three times what a turkey is worth," his father complained.

"No, it isn't. How often do you get a chance to buy a frozen turkey along the interstate?"

"But all those people are just taking them. You know, catch as catch can."

"That's stealing from the company that provides insurance for the truck. When they cook those turkeys and serve them, they'll taste stolen."

"I'll give you ten."

"Not enough. I'd settle for twenty, though."

"Still too much. I can get one for five dollars from that big guy over there with two under each arm."

"Sure, but then you'd be part of the theft."

"No, I'd be buying a turkey from someone along the interstate."

"From a thief."

"Okay, but for that matter how do I know this whole truckload isn't stolen?"

"I have the papers, for one thing."

"How do I know they're authentic?"

"I'll show them to you."

"Okay, let me see them."

"They're in the cab box. You can climb up there, jump down, and look for them if you like."

"Fifteen dollars is as high as I'll go."

"Okay, fifteen it is. But take a small one."

"Why?"

"Because fifteen isn't enough for a large one."

"I have a lot of people to feed."

"All the more reason. You'll have a lot of listeners to your story about buying a turkey along the interstate, and that's worth a lot. Your boy here can swear it's true. True and legal."

"Okay."

Lester said his father paid the man. They went to the back of the trailer and his father took one from inside.

"That's unbelievable," said August.

"I know it. But it's true. What's unbelievable about it?"

"It doesn't seem like it would ever happen."

"Why not?"

"Because no one would do what you say your father did—pay for something that was free for the taking."

"Are you saying it couldn't be true because you never heard something like that before?"

"It goes against human nature."

"And how do you know where human nature goes?"

"I don't. Look, all I'm saying is the story seems unbelievable. I'm not saying it didn't happen. It's also a little suspicious because it's about your father."

"What's wrong with that?"

"Stories about fathers are often embellished, intentionally and unintentionally."

"Why would anyone embellish a story about their father?"

"It's part of that old Father-God idea. Associations with your sire rub off on you. Saying your father was honest is a way of saying you are."

"I am."

"You are what?"

"Honest."

"I already know that, Lester."

"But you might not have known that about my father, which is why I told you the story."

Lester took another drink and August used the opportunity to look over again at Hanh, who had finished wiping down the counter. She hung the dishtowel on the handle of the oven.

"I'll take August back," she said.

"I can take him," said Lester.

"No, I'll take him."

"Maybe Ivan will still come," said August.

"He won't," said Hanh.

"Not this late," Lester agreed. "Ivan asked me to drive you back, and I want to."

"Well, you're not going to," said Hanh. "You don't see well enough to drive at night, unless you're right around here."

"I suppose that's true enough. Here, Hanh, before you go, will you add a splash of whiskey to this cider for me." Lester extended his mug toward her and she carried it off into the kitchen.

After she left the room, Lester adjusted his loose-fitting flannel shirt so the buttons running down the front fell in a straight line. He looked discomforted because Hanh had overruled him driving at night. Leaning toward August, he spoke in a low, cautious voice: "Listen to me, August. Come closer. Listen. It's good to see you again, but you need to be careful with Hanh. Things have changed here, and you need to be paying attention."

"Oh, sure," August whispered back. "Of course."

"Why does it sound like you're not taking this seriously?"

"I am. Believe me, I am. I'd never do anything to hurt her."

"I know you wouldn't, August. I'm just saying be careful."

"Of course."

Hanh returned from the kitchen with the mug. Bending over with the quick ease afforded by her diminutive frame, she set it on the table at Lester's right hand.

"Is there anything else you need before we leave?" she asked.

"Nope. Everything's as right as rain."

"Come on, August."

She still didn't look directly at him.

THE GLASS EYE

Snow fell slowly through the dark air, and at times the individual flakes seemed suspended, as though conscious choices were being made by weightless crystals to move toward ground instead of ascending back into the sky.

The surrounding trees balanced lines of accumulated snow on the upper part of their limbs, drooping from the added weight. Occasionally, the fragile balance didn't hold, and the lines of snow toppled over and plunged to the ground with soft, plopping sounds. Earlier tire marks and footprints had filled in.

The economical interior of Hanh's electric vehicle required they sit near to each other and August could smell the fabric in her parka. The engine made no sound, and except for a faint snow-crunching noise, the Kar seemed to float among the trees.

"The highway is behind us," remarked August.

"You haven't seen the inside of my home," said Hanh.

"True enough."

"Why did you come back, August?"

"My parents live here."

"Why did you really come back?"

"No particular reason."

"Ivan said you lost your lab job."

"I'll find another."

"He also said you were hurt by someone."

"Ivan told you that?"

"How else would I know?"

The vehicle's heater warmed up and August could now smell Hanh. Remembered associations moved through him like smoke up a chimney. At once, his memory set to work, gathering and sorting all the images, emotions, and thoughts related to the smell, rearranging the first layer of his mind like a card player looking at a new hand and separating by suit.

"Tell me about her," she said.

"No."

They rode the rest of the way in silence, flakes of snow flattening against the windshield, melting and streaming down the glass.

Hanh parked near the front of the house. They climbed out and walked through the snow. Stacked wood filled most of the porch. Hanh held the door open and turned on an inside light. August stepped in and was greeted by a room of heat with a round wood stove in the middle. He took off his coat.

"I like to be warm," said Hanh, putting both of their coats inside a closet. "This is the living room," she added.

"Very nice," said August.

He followed her through the small room and into an even smaller kitchen, then a study, bedroom, and bath. All of them were immaculate and sparsely decorated, with faint smells left over from fresh plaster, caulk, paint, and new wood.

"Very nice."

"You said that already."

August tried to discover an explanation for why the interior of the house seemed a little strange, and then noticed that each room had been furnished for a single occupant. Only one chair stood open by the table in the kitchen, and a lone chair rested in the living room. There was nowhere to sit in the bedroom except the narrow bed. One wooden chair stood under the desk in the study. Visitors had clearly not been considered, and because all the other homes August had been inside were furnished in anticipation of other people, the difference seemed striking. Oddly enough, it also had charm. It was easy to imagine each room satisfactorily occupied, like convent quarters, or a solitary den. August could picture himself taking up the available space in each room and completing the scene. The absence of extra chairs removed the anxiety of having to choose which to occupy, and it eliminated the open-ended question of who might fill the others. Once settled in, you wouldn't feel like you were waiting for someone else to arrive or sharing the room with seated ghosts. The economy of such a private life seemed as attractive as it was unusual.

"I'll make some tea," she said, and they went into the kitchen.

Hanh put a copper kettle on the two-burner stove and motioned for August to sit at the table. She pulled a folding chair from a narrow broom closet and sat on it across from him. Neither of them said anything.

There were no pictures on the walls. Plants of many sizes and shapes provided the only adornments, and they grew out of vases, pots, cups, jars, and painted buckets.

After the water boiled, Hanh poured it into a ceramic pot of dried leaves, and a short while later set a cup of tea in front of him.

August looked into Hanh's dark eyes. It seemed she'd forgiven him for his unannounced intrusion back into her life. She smiled and his good fortunes continued; the ocean of self-doubt he'd been drowning in suddenly seemed like a wading pool. Her influence over him seemed almost supernatural and he concluded that his psychic needs had a gender bias. Only women could reach inside him and straighten things up. The peace of mind secured through successfully relating to a woman didn't happen with other men, even with someone as genuinely thoughtful, admirable, and beloved as Ivan. Men proffered friendship, camaraderie, and even love; women promised deliverance.

"Tell me about her," she said, sipping her tea.

"I don't know what to say."

"Ivan said she came from a wealthy family."

"You might say that."

"What does that mean?"

Hanh heard something outside and crossed to the window. Though unhurried, her movements were still quick and focused, graceful and soundless. After briefly inspecting the area beyond the window, she returned to the table, silently perched on her chair and smiled in a reserved manner, as though to apologize for having her attention momentarily diverted.

"It would probably be more accurate to say that Amanda had everything," August said.

"Everything like what?"

"Brains, money, connections. Everything."

"Ivan said you told him you'd never get over her."

August looked away. Talking to a former lover about a more recent one clearly amounted to an exercise in obfuscation, and he wondered if Hanh appreciated how difficult she was making this. It wasn't exactly that he wanted to disguise his true feelings for Amanda; it was just that his true feelings for Amanda were honestly different when he was with Hanh, as though he were looking down on them from a significant elevation, and this seemed hard to account for and impossible to express.

"I think she was simply out of my class," he said. "And I don't think Ivan understands the full implications of that. I know he doesn't."

"Why doesn't he?"

"We're apparently different in that way. He's better suited to that kind of thing."

"What kind of thing?"

"Living without complications. He seems satisfied with being alone, dressing up every so often, going places where no one knows him, and picking up someone. He says he has simple needs."

"He told you that?"

"Yes."

"He did that once, August, and it didn't end very well."

"That's not what he said."

"Of course not. He admires you. Always has. Let me tell you what really happened. He went to this wedding reception where he didn't know anyone and took home a gal who turned out to be this homeless person who had broken into a vacation cottage when the owners were away, dolled herself up in their nice clothes, went to the wedding party where no one knew her, and brought Ivan back afterward. They were both arrested later that night."

"What happened then?"

"The homeless girl admitted what she'd done, and they let Ivan go. Thankfully she wasn't a minor."

"When was this?"

"A while back. You know, he fell apart after you left."

"That's not my fault."

"I didn't say it was. I just said he fell apart after you left."

"Today was a profound reminder of how inadequate I've always felt around Ivan—and you for that matter. His body works so damn well. The engineers who put the two of you together clearly had more experience than mine, and they gave you both more flexibility, speed, usable horsepower, more of everything."

"August, Ivan would do anything for you."

"I know. He's made an art form out of fidelity. When I met him yesterday, he was delivering chickens to save his grandfather a trip to town. He makes me feel like I'm ethically and morally bankrupt."

"He thinks you're immensely successful."

"That's a laugh."

"Not to him."

"I lost my job and was abandoned by my girlfriend."

"Ivan's sure you got a raw deal in both cases. He said you just didn't understand the hidden rules of the people you wanted to live around."

"Ivan hasn't done badly for himself. He lives on his own terms and even saved money from working on the pipeline, which I guess was quite profitable."

"He told you that?"

"Yes."

"And you believed him?"

"Of course."

"Lester and I never bring up the pipeline. For a long time, Ivan couldn't even talk about it. I think he saw someone get killed up there. Either that or he had to kill someone himself—that's what Lester thinks, and he's known a lot of people who've lived with bleeding consciences. Ivan stayed with his parents for over a year after he came back, and most of that time he didn't come out of the house."

"I didn't know anything about that. He seems fine now, though maybe a little more reactionary than I remember. For some reason Forest Gate really sets him off. Why is that?"

"He's been angry about that place ever since they built it," said Hanh. "Lester and I think he associates the people living there with the owners of the pipeline. Do you want to see it for yourself—the Gate?"

"What do you mean?"

"I can take you over there."

"From what I understand, no one can get in. As you already know, we met three of their security guards."

"I know a way in. Do you want to see it on the inside?"

"It's pretty late. Aren't you tired? We did a lot of work today."

"Ivan's right. Living in the city has changed you, August. There was a time when you'd never refuse a night walk through a forest of freshly fallen snow, into a forbidden place."

"Okay, let's go."

"I'll find you something less dark to wear," said Hanh.

Dressed in loose-fitting clothes, they closed the front door, stepped away from the house and crossed the creek into a stand of young oak trees, their trunks rising out of the ground like a field of cold, randomly placed pillars with elaborate tops.

Following Hanh up hills and along valleys provided a formidable challenge. She moved quickly, frequently changing directions to avoid briars, fallen trees, and open places where they might be seen from houses or vehicles along the road. He felt like a horse following a donkey along mountain paths. The blue-green moon glowed in the snow and August wondered if perhaps Hanh and Ivan were right in thinking urbanity had changed him. Most of his activities—all of them really—needed to find a home inside larger human activities involving more people and other schedules. It felt good to be away from the ever-present din of urban commerce, indulge in natural light, stand in the shadow of trees, listen to owls, inhale earthy smells, and walk through unspoiled snow.

"There," said Hanh, stopping and pointing with her arm and mitten. "That's the main entrance."

August came up beside her. Down the hill and across the road two massive columns stood connected by a heavy iron gate—a rebarbative structure that one might expect in a combat zone or an entrance into a basilica or prison. Across the top ran a lattice of wrought iron. The twisted metal spelled out Forest Gate.

"Looks impenetrable," said August.

"Nope," said Hanh. "There's a place we can get through. Come on."

August followed her along the winding ridge, then down onto the valley floor. They crossed the road and continued moving away from the entrance. To avoid the headlights of a passing car, they stepped behind a cottonwood. The vehicle slowed down, turned, paused, and moved inside the gate.

They trudged on. A quarter mile later, around the corner, a sharp ravine cut up the hillside and the security fence stretched across it at the top. Broken slabs of concrete from demolished highways and building foundations had been thrown into the gap to fill it.

Hanh climbed up among the jutting edges—some of them with the rusted ends of rebar poking out.

August came behind her. Near the top, with the fence above them, Hanh disappeared under several broken slabs of concrete, and about a minute later stood up on the other side of the fence.

August crawled under the slab and turned on the flashlight Hanh had given him. When the concrete had been dumped into the ravine, six or seven of the unwieldy shapes had wedged together in a way that allowed for a narrow passage, an opening here, then there. August crawled forward, turned, turned again, and later climbed up beside Hanh.

"See, that wasn't so hard," she said. "Come on."

Once again, he followed her uphill. After a short distance they began walking on a hard-surfaced trail through the trees. After several hundred yards, it led them to a wooden bench overlooking the valley. She brushed off the thin layer of snow and sat down.

August sat beside her. They stared at the lake in the distance below, and the homes encircling it. The water's surface reflected the moon along a broad, unbroken line, and dozens of lit windows and streetlamps burned along the shore. At the far end where the lake turned and spread into an adjacent valley, a tight cluster of pleasure boats rested on the water, neatly moored in a brightly illuminated marina.

The blinking light of a small helicopter moved through the sky, hardly making a sound. The hovering vehicle descended into the valley, floated over the lake like a dragonfly, crossed to the further shore and settled onto a helipad on the roof of one of the mansions. A shiver of pleasure moved through August. The glittering community seemed like a separate country, existing on the edge of time—a Disneyland of the professionally affluent.

"It's astonishing," he said, taking the compact binoculars away from his face and handing them to her. "Everyone's heard of those copters, but I've never seen one. They're reportedly lighter than drones, the synthetic materials they build them with are as expensive as the latest skins on the Pentagon's prototype jets, and the technology behind the soundless rotor-blades, well, it's next-level."

"Interesting," she said, without any apparent interest. Hanh looked through the lenses, focused, and watched a figure climb out of the copter, walk across the small helipad, and disappear into a doorway.

"It's like a fantasy world."

"I knew you'd like it," said Hanh. "You always admired wealth."

"Doesn't everyone?"

"Some more than others."

"It still seems strange that this place is here. I haven't been away that long. All this used to be hunting land."

"It also seems strange to the rest of us, and we've been living with it for several years."

"Do you know anyone down there?"

"No. Lester says they don't usually associate with locals."

"Locals," repeated August. "That's an ugly word."

"It's an even uglier idea. Do you see the house on the lake—to the left of the marina?"

"What about it?"

"It has a boxing ring inside with luxury seating. The owner hires professional fighters and privately advertises the matches; gamblers come from as far away as New York and California—invitation only, apparently. Twice a year, chauffeured cars line up along the access road and fill the marina parking lot; a dozen or more private jets land on the airfield. Additional security is brought in. Lester says it reminds him of when gladiators once fought for the pleasure of the Roman elite."

"Thanks for bringing me here, Hanh," August said, smiling to himself at the thought of Lester drawing analogies from history.

"Do you see that place leaning out over the water?"

"The one with the long, curving drive?"

"That's it. There was a lot of trouble there one night. Shots were fired and people were yelling and running around. Windows were broken out. The county police were called in and someone was finally dragged out of the house and driven away. Nothing about it was ever reported though."

"Sounds exciting."

"It was. And do you see that building in the middle of the hill, the one with the parking around it?"

"I see it."

"That's a theater. Three or four times a year they fly in off-Broadway players for one-night performances. It seats about three hundred. Afterward, there's a reception in the marina clubhouse, and it goes on until the following morning. Escorts are bused in to sit with the guests, serve drinks and, for stellar fees, provide complete services."

"It's really good to see you again, Hanh. And for whatever it's worth, whatever you used to have—that magnetic charisma—you have even more of it now."

"It's good to see you again too, August. But I need to say something, because you're apparently thinking about it. I couldn't sleep with you back then, you know, when we were both contemplating it, because if I had you wouldn't have left, and your heart was set on doing something with your life that you couldn't do here. If you'd stayed, you would have hated me for keeping you here."

"Impossible."

"You pulled back."

"I didn't want you to be hurt."

"I know that's what you told yourself, but you also wanted to leave. And I'm okay with that. I accepted it then and I accept it now. You don't have to feel guilty about what happened—and didn't happen—between us."

Far below, a security vehicle moved slowly along the access road, its searchlights reaching out on both sides. It briefly stopped beside a figure walking a dog and a slender trill of laughter rose out of the valley like the distant sound of wildfowl.

"Do you bring Ivan over here?"

"No."

"Why not?"

"I didn't know what he'd do. He resents this place and sometimes doesn't act rationally."

"Why do you come here yourself?"

"I need to know who's living around me."

"Like a proverbial fox."

"I suppose."

The SUV turned off the access road and slowly began climbing toward them, moving between homes that had been built into the hillside to take advantage of the southern exposure.

"Do you think I should have gone with Ivan after he got the call about Jet Lag?"

"He didn't want you to come. He used Jet Lag as an excuse to leave early. Sometimes, I think that's half the reason he keeps him."

"But someone called."

"I doubt it. Ivan sets his phone to ring when he wants to get away. He wonders if there's anything left between us, and he wanted to give us a chance to find out."

"Why does he care about that?"

"Can't you guess? He loves you, August. So he needs to know if he, well, if he and I would be getting in the way."

The patrol vehicle came around the last home on the hillside and turned onto the narrower road leading up toward them.

"Time to go," said Hanh.

They moved off the bench and back into the trees. After several hundred yards, they turned and watched the vehicle climb up out of the valley, eventually stopping near the bench they'd been sitting on. Steam came out of the SUV's grill and curled up through the luminous tunnels beaming from the headlights. A guard climbed out of the passenger side. He inspected the ground and surrounding area with a searchlight. Voices murmured indistinctly and the other security guard climbed out. Another light turned on.

"We need to get out of here," whispered Hanh.

"Right behind you."

They hurried down the other side of the hill, sometimes sliding and breaking their descent by grasping onto the trunks of sapling trees, their footsteps muffled by the freshly fallen snow.

After climbing out of the concrete-filled ravine, Hanh sprinted along the road, crossed to the other side, and headed up a tractor access to the field on the ridge.

August ran behind her across the plowed ground, wishing he could see better; and he worried about twisting an ankle in the dim light.

They climbed through several wire fences, clambered through a cattle gate, and ran into a thick vein of forest.

Back in Hanh's house, they stepped out of their boots and drank hot tea with bourbon in the kitchen. August explained his interest in discovering cancer cells with fabricated antibodies, and inducing programmed cell death.

Hanh looked at the clock. It was late.

After drinking his second cup, August stood from the table and walked to the door. "Are you going to take me back now?"

"No. I'll drive you back tomorrow morning after the snow melts. It's supposed to be a warm day. My car has very poor traction. You can sleep here. There's a Murphy in the study."

"Good enough."

They rinsed out the dishes and set them on the wooden drainer to dry.

A stationary air front settled over the room, accompanied by an awkward silence.

"Do you have a shower?"

"Of course. I'll get you some towels."

"After the shower, maybe I should walk back to Lester's."

"Sure, if you want."

One of Hanh's plants, August noticed, had been shaped into a spiral. It stood about four feet high in one corner of the living room, and the topiary reminded him of the double helix of deoxyribonucleic acid. He wondered if Hanh had intended the comparison and briefly thought about asking her. But he neither wished to know she'd anticipated someone forming the association, which implied something a little too predictable in himself and others, nor did he wish to know that she had not made the association and that he had overlooked a more obvious association, perhaps corkscrews or barbershop poles. He wondered if this was the reason many artists noticeably recoiled when asked to explain a particular work. If the comparisons were pleasing, then the piece "worked," and if the associations were unpleasant, then the viewer didn't "get it." It was also possible, of course, that she had not intended any associations whatsoever, but this seemed unlikely. Associations came whether you wanted them or not.

"As long as it's okay with you, I guess I'll stay here."

Hanh pulled a bed out of the wall in the study. It was already made. She checked the sheets, pulled a pillow out of a nearby cabinet and shoved it inside a clean pillowcase.

August showered and dressed in a T-shirt and sweatpants from a collection of Lester's old assorted clothes. He sat on the pullout bed and waited for Hanh to finish showering in the other room.

After she dressed, they poured more tea and bourbon, carried it into the living room and placed another log in her cast-iron firebox. Flames wrapped around the hardwood like yellow, red, and blue fingers around something sweet. Hanh clamped the stove door into place and the curved sides of the stove snapped from heat expansion. They finished the bourbon while looking at the fire.

"Well, goodnight then," she said, turning toward him.

"Goodnight," he repeated. They looked at each other. Then they stepped forward, hugged awkwardly, repeated, "Goodnight," drew apart, and walked away, Hanh into her bedroom and August into her study.

Lying on the bed, all August could think about was Hanh's wet black hair pressed into his chest, her narrow shoulder blades beneath his hands, the smell of her. Every cell in his body remembered her fine-grained essence. His mind tightly reorganized itself around the compelling problem of how the physical urgency he had at one time felt for Hanh could be so very much alive inside him now, when their personal circumstances were so different. Yes, he and Hanh had once been in love, or at least as close to love as either could imagine back then. But they'd both moved on, and there was no going back. She didn't want to go back, and neither did he, and what they both didn't want mattered. Choices had been made, roads taken, bridges burned. People were more than chemicals submitting to the immutable electron-sharing laws of chemistry. Conscious choices were available and there were risks to consider. And besides, those old feelings for Hanh that had revived in him with such alacrity might not have come alive in her at all, and he had good reason to fear her disapproval.

August climbed out of bed, crept into the darkened living room and sat on the floor next to the stove. It seemed this source of intense heat would understand his thoughts, and the rest of the room wrapped around him like an oversized coat.

Ten or fifteen minutes later, the door into Hanh's bedroom opened and she walked out carrying a red blanket. She did not turn on the light and sat next to him on the floor. "I worried you might need this," she said.

The round eye of borosilicate glass in the center of the stove door blazed from the visible heat on the other side, studying them.

They sat for a long time without speaking, staring straight ahead.

Then they spread out the blanket.

"I knew you were going to be trouble," said Hanh, and the length of her scar became outlined in the guttering light.

They reached for each other like drowning people for life preservers.

Soon, they were interlocked—in the grip of the three neuropeptides responsible for the sensory awareness of physical pleasure.

They moved in neuromuscular concert, oblivious to everything around them, releasing in each other higher and higher rewards, seeking a goal of such value that they dreaded failing to reach it. And as their passions mounted, their dilating eyes locked together and they gazed into the liquid center of existence, trusting in something as yet undiscovered to rescue them from their active hysteria and return them to the safety of their normal selves.

The silky pajama bottoms that Hanh and August had earlier stripped from Hanh's hips and carelessly thrown behind them lay bunched up against the stove door. In time, the thin fabric grew warmer and warmer, shrinking along the edges; smoke billowed into the air and the filmy fibers burst into flame, filling the room with bright yellow light and acrid smells. At first, August and Hanh paid no attention, and a little while later collapsed into the relief of each other's exhaustion. Then August got up, lifted the burning, silky material with the end of an iron poker and carried it outside, where it finished smoldering in the snow.

He returned the poker to its metal stand and lay on the red blanket beside Hanh. They contemplated their own dreamy attempts to withdraw from the grip of chemically induced instinctual behaviors and were reluctant to assume responsibility over their own thoughts. Like rapids survivors recently deposited on a sandy shore, they resisted climbing out of their shared canoe.

As they slowly adjusted to the smoke in the room, their minds gradually separated from each other. Individualized thoughts became more distinct. The sensation of returning to their earlier forms was accompanied by the satisfaction of having been recently renewed. Better bodies, it seemed, had been provided for them to return to, and August's muscles had either ceased aching or he simply stopped feeling them.

Unfortunately, with the return of their normal selves, they were soon aware of a plethora of reasons why they should never have allowed this to happen. There were no good explanations for their actions, no plausible justifications, and no excuses that didn't seem laughably ridiculous, and they argued about whose fault it was. Hanh blamed August because he'd made it seem like his girlfriend in Chicago had possessed some extraordinary advantages not available to the rest of womankind, which of course had to be proved wrong.

What girlfriend? August wondered. Then he remembered Amanda and blamed Hanh for unfairly exploiting his vulnerability and grief.

Though not exactly ashamed of allowing their naked reflexes to be openly shared with one another, they were nevertheless fearful that by doing so they had relinquished a secret power that could later be used against them.

But arguing quickly tired them both out and they went into Hanh's bedroom, crawled into her bed, and went to sleep.

Several hours later, the moon moved around the corner of the house and a shaft of greenish light silently entered the southern window.

They woke up like electrical circuits after an outage, turned to each other and hungrily embraced again. Like coals needing only a breath of air to rise into flame, their passions reignited. And this time, due to the somatic education they'd earlier acquired from each other, their movements were bolder and more purposeful. Hanh wanted to be on top, to take control of rhythm, speed, and angle of contact. After assuming a fox-howling position, her brain flooded with sensations of a different quality. Her less restrained vocalizations informed August of the physical changes taking place inside her and he attempted to participate with equal vigor. Then, the intensity of their writhing was matched only by its comparative brevity and concluded within several very frantic moments.

Afterward, they did not speak at all, and—still pressed together—slept as dreamlessly and still as death.

The patch of moonlight cast on the wooden floor moved east, narrowed, and disappeared.

August woke up alone, the room filled with midmorning light. He could still feel, or at least vividly remember, the imprint of Hanh's body pressing against him. He felt liberated, expansive, and slightly light-headed. Rescued from his former morose self, his existence once again made sense. His equations balanced. He found his clothes in the study, climbed into them, and wandered through the house, observing each domestic setting more carefully than before. In the kitchen, he poured a cup of tea from a waiting pot on the table and carried it into the small living room. The red blanket had been picked up and put somewhere out of sight.

Looking through the window in the front door, he saw Hanh sitting on the porch next to the mountain of stacked wood, wearing the parka from the night before and holding her cup of tea in her lap, staring into the morning. His first thought was to call her inside; but he kept watching. Melting snow fell from the roof in random drops, sometimes spilling over the edge in brief, clear spills, sparkled by sunlight. The trees growing along the stream also dripped and ran, their limbs dark in places. Patches of grass and leaves were clear of snow, wet. A pale blue sky had been hastily painted in with watercolors.

August sipped his tea and watched her. She seemed completely absorbed in the morning, her rapt concentration an object of beauty. He felt an aching love for her—an affection he couldn't remember feeling before, laced with loneliness, without the impulse to grasp and hold on.

He continued to watch her and gradually understood, again, that Hanh would probably never be entirely at home with anyone. An essential part of her would remain unknown to everyone. Hidden within her lived a troubling sorrow—a grief unlike any other—that must be left alone. Because of her early childhood, or perhaps simply because of whom she was, a part of Hanh remained in an attachment-free survival mode—anticipating the next approaching moment, numb to distraction. It explained the way she had sparsely furnished her home, set it up for only one occupant. Her default setting was social isolation. Unlike August, who depended on other people to constantly anchor his sense of self, she was more nearly self-sufficient. With other people, she performed. For her, the frantic intimacy they had shared the night before was left there. Its influence did not extend into the morning. She'd returned to the realm of silence where she normally lived. It was one of the reasons her relationship with nature remained so strong. For the succor she drew from it, nothing was asked in return, and loving her required accepting that. Including someone else in her life would remain a second language. Revealing herself would never come spontaneously. Making love to him—both times—was, for her, an ethical impulse, like picking up someone, driving him to a better part of town, and dropping him off.

The solitariness of Hanh conflicted with August's idea of a companion, someone with which to trace out the smallest wrinkles in their shared life. He longed to know, and be known by, a galaxy of mundane details.

Hanh could never endure such continuous examination.

August also understood that he'd always known this about her. She had always been more firmly attached to local realities as opposed to abstract ones. It was part of the reason he'd always seen moving away as unavoidable.

August imagined that she and Ivan might be well suited. Ivan could provide firewood for the rest of her life, but it would never earn him access to her most private thoughts. And Ivan was okay with that. He enjoyed chopping firewood. Like he said, he had grounded needs.

And then August felt immensely guilty and went back into the kitchen to refill his cup with more tea. The light coming through the windows bristled against the hard surfaces in a way that only morning light in a kitchen can, and he sat at the table to remain inside it.

He felt terrible about what he and Hanh had done.

What was it about human sexuality, he wondered, that involved such hand-wringing concern? Other activities weren't that way. Eating, exercising, bathing, taking a cooking class, working in sales, farming hydroponically, flying to Scotland, going to church, dressing in funny clothes, making appointments with doctors, debating international monetary policy, climbing trees, visiting relatives, singing in quartets, speaking foreign languages, repairing a refrigerator, reading books, buying crackers, bird watching, and donating to charity were all things to do that did not raise suspicions in others. But if any of those doings included sex, then questions with moral dimension quickly rushed to the fore. Why was that?

One possible explanation, August thought, was that capitalism had nearly succeeded in removing sex from the center of human concern and replaced it with commerce. Making money was promoted as good for the community and essential to the species, and sexual activity had almost been pushed aside. "Why are you working?" became the only question that could not be legitimately asked because work served as the starting line for legitimacy. Protestants had assisted in establishing this new center of human affairs; they married market paradigms to their longing for redemption, and interpreted the fruits of economic striving as signs of divine grace, assuring them of future entry into heaven.

It was a neat trick, August thought, and the new commercial center for human affairs held for more than three hundred years in the Western world, until weaknesses arose from having a supreme social value unsupported by biological compulsion or joy. Perhaps if the center had held a little longer, human physiology might have adapted and the algorithms for making money instead of making love would have become encrypted within the endocrine system, with orgasmic rewards released for clinching a sale or cashing a paycheck. Financial transactions would have triggered erotic excitement. People would have grown ecstatic with their wealth, kept it hidden, yet longed to reveal it to others. Glimpsing the corner of a hundred-dollar bill would set loose a fleet of pleasure-inducing antigens inside the brain. Adolescents would hang posters in their lockers of large numbers at the bottom of bank statements, and stare at them in pensive silence. Exchanging coins would provoke gratifying feelings of achieving intimacy, and if coins were exchanged in an especially skillful manner, the transaction would be accompanied by vocalizations. Wealthy women would wear expensive jewelry—not to draw attention to their beauty, but for their beauty to draw attention to the jewelry. Streaming ticker tape readouts of a strong, bullish market would be pornographic.

But before this happened, at least in the United States, the Vietnam War and other corporate-sponsored governmental acts exposed the levers of power required to keep economic arrangements at the pinnacle of social value, and people like Lester Mortal—who were asked to risk their lives and snuff out others to prop it up—noticed the absence of any direct biological benefits. Compliance with the market regime, they discovered, was not brought about through shared interests or mutually agreeable biochemical pleasuring, but rather through the coercive force of law and fear of punishment. And those making the laws, they noticed, were the same ones making out like bandits. So a cultural rebellion against the ruling order eventually included the elevation of women and the liberation of sexual expression, followed by a period of instability in which individuals were free to choose their own highest good, while society at large did not know how to proceed. Everyone, it seemed, longed for a civilization where sexual relationships could be freely enjoyed and family life could flourish without any entanglements, power struggles, or worries, but no one knew what an arrangement like that would actually look like.

None of this tangential thinking, however, explained how August could sleep with his best friend's lover.

He hated himself.

The front door opened and closed, and Hanh came in from outside. A small room of outdoor air surrounded her. "I can drive you back now," she said, setting her teacup in the sink.

August rose from the table.

August and Hanh rode most of the way without speaking. There were few other vehicles. The roads were wet, with puddles deep enough for moving tires to spray water.

August's rented car sat in front of Ivan's rented house, beside Ivan's pickup. She pulled in.

"You're right about something," she said, without looking at him.

"What's that?"

"You and Ivan are different."

"How?"

"He wants closeness; you want engagement."

"Those are the same."

"Not at all."

"What do you want?"

"To be wanted for a short time."

"Why are you telling me this?"

"It seems like something you should know."

They looked at each other with the sadness known only to people suited to each other in a physical way yet unable to stretch this compatibility over the other sectors of their lives.

He opened the door and climbed out. "Are you coming in?"

"No. Lester needs groceries, and he wants to take some potatoes over to a friend of his in Grange. They sometimes drink too much when they get together and I need to make sure that doesn't happen this time. And he has a doctor's consultation over some test results."

August closed the door and watched her drive away. Then he walked behind the house to check on Jet Lag. He found the donkey lying in the loafing shed, chewing fresh hay. His tank had been recently filled with three feet of water—clear all the way down. The animal turned his head, swiveled his long ears forward and looked at him with socket-eyed bemusement.

August went to the house and knocked on the back door. Ivan opened it.

"Come in," he said, standing out of the doorway, dressed in soiled green coveralls and rubber boots. There were several bruises on his face that weren't visible last night. "I saved some coffee. I know Lester and Hanh don't keep any around and if you're like me, you need a cup."

"Thanks, Ivan. I see Jet Lag is okay."

"He's fine. It was just a misunderstanding."

"About what?"

"Mostly about where my donkey can go without someone threatening me."

"And that was settled?"

"For now. Look, Gus, I need to take off. Mother called and Dad's behind at the shop. His best mechanic is sick and the work is piling in. The coffeepot's on the counter, and there's plenty to eat in the refrigerator. Make yourself at home."

"I should probably go see my parents," August said, pouring a cup into the same smudged mug he drank out of the preceding morning. "I might not be here when you get back. But thanks for everything. It's been good seeing you again. Like old times. I really appreciate it."

"Sure. Is everything all right?" asked Ivan, standing in the doorway.

"Fine. Everything's good. Why do you ask?"

"I don't know. Forget it. I'll catch up with you later. I mean, you're going to be around for a while."

"Sure thing. Sure thing. I'll give you a call in a couple days."

After Ivan left, August sat at the kitchen table and stared out the window. The ticking grandfather clock in the other room methodically positioned its occupying army in the silence, and August took off Ivan's clothes and changed into his own.

THE HOME PLACE

MIDAFTERNOON, AUGUST DROVE down his parents' driveway. Tree growth had narrowed the lane and pine limbs occasionally
brushed against the sides of his car. He parked in the gravel space his
father had leveled off to make it easier for visitors to turn around. Before
getting out, he waited to see if someone had heard him pull in, but no
faces appeared in the kitchen window.

Nothing stirred inside or outside his parents' house. It just stood
there mute, insensate.

He took his suitcases out of the trunk, carried them forward and
stood for a moment. The front door looked shabby, in need of repair,
a vertical crack running through its middle panel. The crack had been
there for as long as he could remember, and only now asked to be fixed.
Then the raw familiarity of the iron doorknob seemed to make it impossible to reach for, as though touching it might merge the present with
the past and leave no opening for the future.

Coming home, August reflected, amplified the importance of intol-
erably unique things, while at the same time nullifying them, and he
experienced a cavernous sense of loss. Everything around him longed
for his return to childhood, and he now understood what Lester meant
the night before: *All these glorious memories and so few of them attach that
is still around.*

Experimenting with the knob, the door opened, and he remembered
the many times his father had said locked doors in rural areas only protect
you from honest people.

He called for his mother and father.

Nothing.

August called again and received no answer.

Inside, he took off his shoes and walked in black socks across the
worn wooden floors.

There were several unwashed dishes in the sink—two forks, a knife
with a butter smudge along one side, and a spoon—but the rest of the
kitchen held its secrets more closely.

The furniture in the living room had aged and drifted further away from any known decorating style; the spaces between individual pieces seemed more cramped than he remembered, proving once again that memory plays havoc with dimensions.

Three books bunched together at one end of the cloth sofa, probably left there by his mother. Two of them had bookmarks poking out like flat tongues. All were thick books, speculating about the nature of space and time, written by female authors: a cosmological physicist, a phenomenologist, and a process theologian.

The open door to his parents' bedroom revealed a pair of his father's workpants tossed on top of the bed's lavender comforter, a leather belt loosely threaded through the loops. Lotions, coins, books, pill bottles, keys, a jumbled collection of framed photographs—half of them featuring August at different ages—hairbrushes, two wristwatches, pruning shears, pliers, two screwdrivers, a keyhole saw, a coffee cup, and a half-filled glass of water occupied the bureau top. A brown sweater and pair of navy-blue jogging pants with stripes appeared to be trying to climb out of an open bottom drawer. On the window ledge, a plump jade plant vigorously grew out of a gray ceramic pot.

At the end of the hallway, the door to his room was closed and he did not approach it.

Back in the living room, he wondered why his parents' house without them inside simultaneously seemed so empty and full. He vacillated between wanting to hurry his belongings back out to the car and picturing himself arranging his clothes inside familiar closets and drawers.

There was a time, of course, in which he couldn't imagine living anywhere else. Everything he'd wanted was here at the end of the lane between the pine trees, and his parents had orchestrated it all. They had cared for him like a newborn king, attended to every necessity and loved him without restraint. And they so successfully accomplished these parenting chores that a part of him—for the rest of his life—would dream, plan, search, and unconsciously yearn for a way to return to that joyful state of fulfilled dependency in which a kiss from his mother, or a ride on his father's shoulders, would silence all fear and outpace every expectation.

In later years, of course, his outlook had changed. The release of narrowly tailored hormones altered his metabolism, and a new layer of neocortical development reconfigured the ways he felt about his parents and his home. His moods shifted, and flashpoints appeared between him and his mother, and later, his father. He grew impatient with their plodding routines. They publicly embarrassed him just by being in public. He remembered these feelings now and felt a biting shame for having allowed them to lodge inside him.

All this, he now knew, was because of long-range biotic strategies begun when his human ancestors first began to differentiate from other primates. Over millions of years, the survival advantages of mating outside of natal groups had influenced *Homo sapiens* until most human offspring expressed the exogamic phenotypes necessary for leaving the group into which they had been born and seeking out a more diverse gene pool. Statistically significant numbers of adolescent primates painfully longed for something they could not find nearby. Their skin, voices, personalities, biorhythms, diets, social orientation, and habits changed. They became increasingly dissatisfied with themselves, their parents, their homes, and their surroundings. And their families became increasingly frustrated with being taken for granted, screamed at, hidden from, lied to, ignored, insulted, mocked, and scorned. When the final breakaway to more robust genomic pastures finally came, all major parties had been worn down to a frazzle of their former selves and were heartily in favor of offspring departure—even if, as in young fledglings, the flight feathers were not fully developed and the risk of leaving the nest entailed some obvious dangers.

August sat on the sofa next to his mother's books and thought about the irony of this phenomenon. To avoid the regressive alleles common to inbreeding depression, and to secure survival benefits for future generations, already-existing members of the species were internally provoked—from a relatively early age—to feel alienated from the people they loved and with whom, genetically, they held the most in common. Consequently, after hitting puberty, August could discover no similarities between himself and his father and mother, though each of his chromosomes had been directly copied from those living inside them, making them by far the most likely candidates for sympathetic and empathetic understanding. Their amino acids were identical. All of August's sensory apparatus, as well as his neural circuitry, had been directly fashioned from theirs. His eyes and tone of voice, he had often been told, were his father's; his mouth and facial expressions "just like your mother." He'd inherited his father's psoriasis and his mother's mold allergies; he moved like them, sounded like them, thought like them, and looked like them. Yet beginning at about the age of fourteen he'd emphatically dismissed the idea of seeking their advice or communicating with them about anything important. A wall of escalating intolerance grew up around him—inside his own home. The health of his future children depended upon his dissatisfaction with them and his longing for something, and someone, unknown.

He opened the side door and looked into the garage, where his parents' cars complacently waited for someone to drive them.

They *must* be around here, he thought, and then remembered Ivan saying that his father had purchased a vintage automobile and was devoting much of his recent retirement toward its restoration.

He discovered a full bottle of orange juice in the refrigerator and poured out a glass. On the front of the bottle, a small Post-it note contained four words in his mother's miniscule handwriting: "August, we're out back."

He followed the worn path through a hundred yards of rocks and prairie vegetation toward her garden on top of the knoll. For the last fifteen years, after retiring from two decades of Protestant preaching in a local church, she had spent so much time gardening that the chances of finding her anywhere else during warm days hardly rose above fifty percent. An inward-looking person, she came alive in the surrounding presence of outward-facing plants. And even when she wasn't working with a trowel, cultivating fork, or clippers, she enjoyed just sitting in her garden, staring into the distant valley and watching her thoughts walk away from her. On summer evenings when the sun performed its coat-of-many-colors vanishing act along the horizon, August had often found her there, seated upright, hands folded in her lap, her face turned in the same direction as the flower heads on every side of her, as though she were growing among them, made of the same heliotropic fibers. During winters, she sat near windows, poured through seed and garden catalogues, and corresponded with other housebound gardeners who saved seeds from hard-to-obtain varieties.

August had spent many years wondering what kind of spirituality or religion his mother nurtured in the privacy of her own mind. Unlike Hanh, for instance, who seemed to live inside an untended pantheistic world of already-consecrated nature, his mother seemed to sometimes experience something beyond, or in addition to, her natural surroundings, and then afterward she would enlarge her definition of nature to include these newly discovered frontiers. Especially after she'd stopped preaching, more and more of her time was devoted toward this expanding colonization of beyondness. For her, inward states of awareness often seemed more relevant (and real) than sensory impulses. It made her seem strange to many people, and even August sometimes experienced her as hopelessly eccentric. For instance, she sometimes claimed that an awareness of a divine presence was one of the most obvious things in her life, and that a wall of incomprehensibility separated her from anyone and everyone lacking this knowledge. She said she could talk to them, of course, appreciate them, and even love them, but she couldn't understand them. They seemed to suffer from a deficiency, she said, like people without a sense of humor.

His father was altogether different—an inorganic-materialist who enjoyed the sound of well-tuned machines and the company of mechanical things of all kinds. Wrenches, pliers, and measuring devices perpetually lived inside his pockets and even after his clothes had been bleached and hung out to dry, their pockets opened like bird mouths expecting to be filled. He wanted to know how things worked, and when they weren't working, he liked fixing them.

Before August reached the edge of his mother's sprawling garden, he heard talking. The words remained indistinguishable, but the cadence of human language was unmistakable. As he walked among plots of dried flowers, naked ornamental trees, and bushes, he saw his parents and at once understood why they were here. His father had been eager to finish his new restoration project, but when he brought the Model T home from the estate sale, gardening season was in full swing, and his wife, Winnie was spending most of her time out back. Not wanting to be away from her, he pulled the vintage vehicle near her garden, where he could work on it nearby. He erected scaffolding around the old car, covered it with a tarp to protect it from rain and dew, ran out an electric cord, and kept many of his tools there. He tinkered with the car through the summer and into the fall while his wife worked in various locations around him. Then, even after Winnie had put her garden to bed for the year, he continued to work there.

Now, not wanting to be stuck in the house or away from him, on warm afternoons Winnie followed him out.

His father had the front end of the Model T suspended from a three-sprocket chain hoist, the wheels three feet off the ground. Lying underneath, he was attempting to fit a new fiber brake band over the steel transmission drum.

His mother sat in the Model T, on the leather-upholstered front seat above him, talking about prayer. Sunshine slanted over the edge of the tarp, falling on her forest-green coat.

August stopped and listened.

"What I'm saying is that word-praying works best in song or some other form of incantation. Ancient people knew this, I think, and the older faiths are rife with singing and chanting. It's like riding a bicycle. You can't ride well if you must think about it, but after you learn the movements, your unconscious motor responses assume control. It's the same with prayer. Take the Jesus Prayer, which is nothing more than several short phrases spoken in an attitude of utmost sincerity: *Lord Jesus Christ, Son of God, have mercy on me, a sinner.* It's simple and direct, yet it contains everything needed for humble entreaty. The little prayer dates back to the Desert Fathers of the fourth century, and for hundreds of years its popularity was unrivaled, at least within Eastern and Oriental Orthodox Churches, where ceaseless praying was believed to be the most efficacious method for reaching God. It's true, the Western Church remained more resistant to the simple prayer, though it was sometimes employed in the devotional practices of a few isolated orders. Westerners found it hard to use. They couldn't give up, I suppose, their unspoken allegiance to the goddess worship they'd inherited from earlier agrarian cultures. They couldn't successfully imagine a divine being without fertilization powers, which they pictured through female figures. Prayers of supplication to the Madonna, and, more colloquially, to Mary, worked much better for them. Crying out to a male figure—especially in the role of son—violated deep-seated phychological protocols. It seemed unnatural to seek mercy from a man when in family life it was the mother who corrected, understood, and loved simultaneously. Within Western civilizations, males have almost exclusively represented judgmental figures, and judgment solidifies sin rather than releasing it. Mothers, however, have traditionally seen problems as temporary; they clean them up, and forgive in such a loving way that new beginnings seem possible. And the gender bias persists to this day; at least it does in me, which is why I fight against the Jesus Prayer whenever I use it, recoiling from the negative associations of the words, twisting myself inside. And of course, that's the whole point—the associations. Language becomes so easily corrupted from its sacred mission of pointing to, connecting with, and revealing, which are really the same things when you think about it. Seeing God in a rainstorm, something of men in women, something of trees in flowers, something of oceans in blowing grass, something of time in sand. Finding one thing in another makes knowing something possible. Yet when the words of the prayer are released in the right manner—like the refrain of a song that refuses to be still—a most wonderful outpouring of numinous joy and creaturely gratitude sometimes accompanies it. *Lord Jesus Christ, Son of God, have mercy on me, a sinner.* The prayer speaks through me as though someone else is saying it. Loneliness and yearning for peace are transformed through the realization that pleading is universal. The divine connects to all of us, maintaining our separate existences and at the same time cherishing the whole as a single unit. Are you having any success with your clamping?"

"Yes, I'm getting it. Can you hand down that metal bar on the seat next to you?"

"Which one?"

"The long one."

"Okay, here it comes. Why do you need it?"

"To release the spring tension in the transmission and begin threading the nuts on."

"No doubt an important procedure. Let me know if there's anything else I can do."

"I will. Do you think August will show up today?"

"I hope he does. It's been two days since the restaurant called and we went over and picked up the billfold he left in the booth."

"I worry about him."

"I know, Jacob. The boy moves through the world like he's stuck in a dream. He's been like that from the beginning. I wonder if he spent another night with Ivan?"

"It doesn't sound like it. Lester called this morning while you were in town. He said August, Ivan, and Hanh ate supper with him last night after making wood all day. They borrowed the splitter and an old saw from the shop. Lester had a borrowed trailer. Later, Ivan had to leave, and Hanh took August home with her."

"They spent the night together?"

"That's what Lester thinks. He said the snow was too deep for Hanh to drive him back. I guess her car lacks traction, probably because its weight is improperly distributed. Or it could also be her tire tread, or lack of any. Anyway, Lester walked over to check on them early this morning and found a pair of burned up pajama bottoms a little way from her front door."

"What do you think that means?"

"I don't know and neither did Lester."

"Did he see August?"

"No, he said he didn't go inside."

"Well, I don't like the idea of them spending the night together or burning pajamas."

"Why?"

"August can be so impulsive. And so can she. They haven't seen each other for a long time and things might be better if they went slowly."

"We never did."

"No, we didn't. You always took off whatever I wanted to wear."

"I never burned your pajamas."

"You would have if they'd gotten in your way. And you've gotten worse now that you're not working at the shop. There's no sense in buying sleepwear anymore."

"It's good to economize."

"I never thought Hanh and August were quite right for each other, and I still don't," said Winnie.

"Maybe not, but do you remember when she used to come around here looking for him, but was afraid to be seen?"

"Of course I do, Jacob. I'm not senile. I just wish August would come home. I'm making lasagna with spinach tonight and he likes that."

Several banging noises came up from beneath her, followed by a short silence.

"I hope you can appreciate how important this machine was to the history of this country, Winifred."

"I'm sure I don't."

"This vehicle changed everything. Before it came along, only rich people owned automobiles, all of them custom-built with individually machined parts. Henry Ford and his engineers designed a way to make the Ts on an assembly line with interchangeable pieces, one right after the other. It made them affordable. The old production manuals still exist, and the workers responsible for the job I'm doing right now were given only forty minutes to complete it, and that includes riveting the fabric pad to the metal brake band. For restoration purposes, some people now use strips of hickory soaked in hot oil and bent to conform to the drum curve, but that was an aftermarket adaptation. I thought it would be more satisfying to do it the way it was done in the factory during the 1920 manufacturing cycle."

"Makes sense to me," said Winnie.

"Holding these parts is like touching history. If the public had rejected this car, our country might have remained rural. Most people would have continued to use horses for transportation. Commuting forty or fifty miles to work would have remained inconceivable. This motor runs on gasoline, kerosene, and alcohol, and without its acceptance we would never have become dependent on refined oil. Interstate highways would never have been built. Farming would have remained labor intensive and rural areas wouldn't have become depleted."

"You might be right, Jacob, but I'm not sure we can know what would have happened if something important that did happen didn't."

"You often hear people complain that our civilization is too technologically driven, but there's something about new stuff that people can't resist. Steam engines, electricity, telephones, refrigerators, tractors, indoor toilets, trains, radios, televisions, outboard motors, airplanes, central heat, vacuum cleaners, air conditioners, tape recorders, microwaves, dishwashers, snowmobiles, computers, robots—it's almost like the acceptance of new technology is built into us."

"What a horrid thought."

August retreated twenty or thirty feet and called out to them.

"Over here," they yelled back.

The sight of her son caused Winnie's eyes to tear up.

August walked toward them. He said he was between jobs, and that the lease on his apartment had run out. He needed some time to complete a paper on cellular signaling that he hoped someday to publish and thought he might work on it here at home. Jacob crawled out from underneath the vehicle and enumerated the Model Ts prominent features along with the remaining areas that required work, and the circumstances through which he'd discovered the vehicle at the estate sale. He explained some of the plans he'd made and the parts he'd ordered.

Winnie climbed down from her elevated seat and was still rubbing tears away.

August said he'd help with the restoration.

His father kept smiling and nodding and said, "You can't work in those clothes."

"How did you get here?" his mother asked.

"I rented a car."

"From where?" asked his father.

"Green Line."

"Those are expensive. You can use one of ours while you're here. We'll take the rental back tomorrow. There's an exchange not far away."

"That's not necessary," said August.

"It is."

August noticed, or rather remembered, that the art of negotiation—so firmly entrenched in the middle class—had never taken root in his father, at least as far as August was concerned.

Just as August felt the old boundaries falling in place, defining the three of them within familiar parameters, he saw—for a fleeting nanosecond made possible by his long absence—his father and mother as simply a man and woman standing under a blue tarp, their hair beginning to gray. He saw them now and he envisioned them then, when a little less than thirty years ago their pheromones had whistled to each other and they'd fallen in love.

For his dad, it was his second time. His first wife had died young of pancreatic cancer. Propelled by the tragedy, he'd moved away from everything he had known, seeking to nurture his wound in the heavily wooded solitude of an unknown area. He bought an old house and opened a repair shop. August's mother—years younger than his father—had no prior experience with erotic love, but she thought about it all the time as she went about her duties as a new rural pastor. Because his repair shop and her church occupied space within the same village, it was probably inevitable that their paths would cross, though Jacob had no interest in religion and Winnie had no reason to enter his shop. So, they met by accident. Oceans apart, they had nothing in common except a persistent attraction to each other and the thrilling possibility that they might not be condemned to live the rest of their lives alone, subsisting on a low-joy diet of responsibilities and grief.

With no plan other than refusing to plan, Winnie immediately became pregnant. By the coin toss happenstance of genetic recombination, it was a boy. They hurriedly married so she would not lose her job and moved all her belongings into his house. With time and familiarity, their enjoyment of each other grew exponentially. Their inner darkness began to glow when they were together, and their baby grew up convinced they lived only for him. He believed he completed them, gave them reason to continue, motivation to breathe. He excelled in school to make them proud. Then, when he got older, he moved away. The man retired and the woman stopped preaching, and they fell deeper into each other, pulled by the gravity of sharing everything. By eating the same food and drinking the same water, their bodies became comprised of the same elements and they began to resemble each other, even to people who did not always picture them together. Before long, they thought nothing of participating in each other's waking thoughts, and talked of "we" as though their separate selves were two expressions of a shared phenomenon.

For a rare moment, August understood that the entire span of his life fit inside theirs with room to spare. They were far more than just his parents; his existence amounted to the accumulating interest from a single investment they'd made in each other—without touching the principle. Their storage rooms contained more than he could ever know. And then August lost the fleeting moment and he returned to relating to them in the manner in which they, and he, were accustomed.

"Hey, Mom, what's for supper?"

That evening, they played Scrabble. His parents sat on the sofa while August sat across from them on a chair with an orange upholstered seat. His mother won the first game, and during the discussion leading up to a second round, his father fell asleep, his head bowed, his left hand halfway in his pants' pocket and his right leg crossed over his left.

August couldn't remember his father falling asleep like this and his mother explained that Ivan's father, Blake, had called that morning and needed help with something at the shop. Jacob had been up early.

Still, August worried, and his attention was soon rerouted to years earlier when he had been sent to check on his Uncle Rusty and Aunt Maxine in their farmhouse. He had recently acquired a driver's license and was eager for the drive along rural roads where he could exercise his new skills.

A fresh covering of snow rested on everything, including the tops of fence posts along the fields and the woven strands of barbwire connecting them. The finely detailed scenery suggested a compulsive-bording-on-insane artist had been called in for the afternoon. Road crews apparently considered the amount of snow too small to bother with, and on some of the roads his tires left the first tracks, giving him a feeling of salience.

His aunt and uncle's squatty foursquare farmhouse stood off the highway in the middle of a wide expanse of white. Unblemished snow covered the yard. August pulled a short distance off the road and parked, not knowing where the hard surface of driveway ended and the grass began.

He tucked the green bean casserole his parents had sent along under his arm and trudged to the back door. He knocked, but received no answer. Reluctant to bang any harder, he let himself into the porch, where a dusting of snow had blown through the screens and thinly covered the painted wood floor along the west side.

On the inside door, he rapped at the window, waited, and tried again.

Stepping into the kitchen, he took off his shoes and called self-consciously, first using the terms Aunt Maxine and Uncle Rusty, and then trying Rusty and Maxine. He set the green bean casserole on the counter.

The house seemed unusually warm, even hot, and he remembered that he had this thought every time he came here. Comfortable temperatures meant something different to old people.

The kitchen smelled of cloves and garlic.

The faucet at the sink dripped hypnotically into an overflowing saucepan, its interior sides coated with a white, filmy substance that might have been oatmeal. August tightened the handle and stopped the drip.

He put the casserole in the refrigerator and explored the house.

In the living room, he was startled by the sight of his aunt curled up on the davenport, her head on an embroidered pillow, her legs and feet hidden by a yellow blanket. Nearby, his uncle, fully dressed in a heavy plaid shirt and gray slacks, sat in his leather reclining chair, his arms extended along the thick leather arms, his knotted fingers cupped over the front. His white head was cocked to the left. *I never take naps*, August remembered him declaring on several occasions.

They're both dead, August thought. His heart froze all the way to the ends of his fingers and a grizzly horror seized possession of the room. The silence seemed toxic. What would he tell his mother?—*Hi Mom, I came over and, guess what, Uncle Rusty and Aunt Maxine are both dead.*

Call an ambulance—give the people on the other end of the phone the address.

But he didn't know the address, only the name of the road.

Surely the name of the road was enough.

He pictured a cargo van with flashing lights screaming into the drive, swerving around his car and cutting deep, muddy trenches in the grass. First responders would leap out and rush toward the house with lifesaving serums, defibrillators, smelling salts, and gurneys. They'd burst through the door and come straight into the—

And then his love for his aunt and uncle attacked him and he began to die from heartbreak. How could lives be so easily snuffed out? Such an event should have caused an eruption in the earth. It seemed more than tragic. It was evil.

"August, how long have you been here?" asked his aunt, pulling the blanket away from her feet.

"Just got here."

"Why didn't you make some noise?"

"I don't know, thought maybe you needed the rest. Uncle Rusty always says he has a hard time sleeping during daylight hours."

"Oh, you know Rusty," she said, and patted her thin hair into place and pushed her feet into the pair of slippers waiting on the rug. "He says what he thinks ought to be true. Is your mother here?"

"No. She sent me over because your phone isn't working."

"One of us must have put it down wrong. Here, help me up. "

He did, and afterward he said, "I put a green bean casserole in the refrigerator."

"You didn't need to do that."

"Mom wanted you to have it."

Rusty and Maxine lived another three years after that, and died in the same nursing home room, in the same week.

But whenever August remembered the time he came upon them sleeping in the afternoon, spears of panic ran through him. The associative influence of his misperception couldn't be undone, and for the rest of his life, whenever he saw a ridge of snow along a wire, his heart froze.

"August, nothing is wrong with your father," said his mother. "He's tired. He didn't sleep much last night, or the night before."

"Why?"

"He was called over to Forest Gate to fix a heat exchanger. Someone was afraid of losing a solarium full of expensive plants."

Winnie leaned forward on the sofa and began to idly rearrange the lettered squares from the game they had just finished, pushing them into different combinations of words.

"And they called Dad?"

"No, their service manager called the Parks Supervisor of Thistlewaite County; he called Davis Plumbing and Heating, and Stephanie Davis gave them your father's number."

"Ivan hates that place."

"Davis Plumbing and Heating?"

"No, Forest Gate."

"Why?"

"I suppose he resents wealth and privilege."

"Then that boy—God love him—has some ridiculous prejudices."

"Mom, they wall themselves off from everyone, impose their own ordinances, and have their own private police force. There's a guy over there who has a fight ring in his house."

"Yes, and they have a landing strip, the best medical services in the state, a theater, and fresh meat, vegetables, and dairy products delivered right to their doors. Come on, August. How do you expect them to live? They're rich."

"Yes, and we're poor in comparison."

"There are advantages and disadvantages to both."

"Seems their advantages pretty much outweigh ours."

"For one thing, your father and I don't worry about malfunctioning heat exchangers ruining our exotic plants."

"You don't have either."

"That's what I mean. Every life comes with strings and how well you manage them is the only thing that matters."

"They use their wealth and influence to further benefit themselves."

"And the rest of us do the same thing as much as we can."

"I'm not sure you could ever convince Ivan of that."

"Maybe not, but you don't share his prejudices, do you?"

"I don't know. I haven't thought about it enough."

"Now I remember."

"What?"

"Ever since we started talking about Forest Gate my brain has been tickling me, and now I remember what it is. Someone over there is looking for a house sitter."

"Do you know someone at Forest Gate?"

"I garden for them."

"They hired you?"

"Isn't that what I just said?"

"You work for them?"

"Yes, August. I manage their gardens."

"And they need a house sitter?"

"They need someone to stay in their house while they're away, take care of the dog, water plants, and watch the place. They're very fussy about references and background checks and so forth, but I'm sure they'll approve of you because they know me. You could write that paper you were talking about. You'd like it there—anyone would."

"I'm not welcome here?"

"You are, but at your age home must seem like a museum of infancy to you."

"I want to work with dad on his Model T and spend more time with you."

"There's no rush. I don't think they're leaving for a couple weeks. We'll go over this week."

THE FISH ROOM

ON THE MORNING of October 13, a security guard walked out to meet them from the guardhouse attached to the iron entrance at Forest Gate. Winnie rolled down her window and the clean-shaven guard tipped his hat. "Good morning, Mrs. Helm. It's very nice to see you again. The Lux residence called and said you'd be coming. Is this your son?"

"This is August," said Winnie.

The guard leaned down and looked through the open window.

"Hi," said August.

"Hello, Dr. Helm. I understand you're a research scientist."

"Well, something resembling that."

"It's a privilege to meet you. I'm a great admirer of the work your mother does. Everyone appreciates the Lux gardens."

"You're too kind," said Winnie.

"On the contrary. Several of our residents who live on the other side of the lake always drive the long way around so they can pass your gardens on their way out or in."

"Phooey," said Winnie.

"Mrs. Helm, I still need to ask if on your person or inside your vehicle there are weapons of any kind, invasive plants or seeds, toxic chemicals, petroleum-based fertilizers, herbicides, pesticides, or other chemical agents."

"Nothing like that," said Winnie.

"I'm afraid our legal folks require a simple yes or no in our reports."

"No."

"And how long do you anticipate being here?"

"Maybe an hour, two at the outside. August is thinking of house-sitting at the Lux home and we're working out the details."

"Excellent. Well, enjoy your stay. If you should need any assistance, let us know."

"Thank you," said Winnie.

The guard stood aside, and the gate opened. Winnie drove in. Three other guards stood just inside.

At the first fork in the road, Winnie turned left and followed the lane into the southeast valley. The lots were large, between five and ten acres; all were professionally landscaped and meticulously maintained, with rock walls, stone walkways, and terraced yards. Many had coppices of old-growth maple and oak. Even near the lake, the more magnificent trees had been preserved and the roadways had been built around them, lending the community a sense of age.

"What's the story up there?" asked August, pointing to a building with round windows in the distance. It resembled the front of a luxury ship emerging from the hillside. Variously colored marble sculptures of dolphin, shark, and whale leaped out of the front yard.

"The owner owns a cruise line, and I guess she wanted everyone to remember that. She hosted a neighborhood party last summer with fireworks over the lake. One of the guests fell over her railing and broke his collarbone."

Each home was different, some with guest cottages, tennis courts, or swimming pools. A few flowed into the landscape. Others stood out in profiles of ostentation, with sprawling courtyards, fountains, heroic sculptures, and entrances resembling casinos.

Winnie steered downhill between ancient maples. As they drew near the water, a bevy of swans crossed the road, heading for the shoreline. Their curved necks undulated as they walked. At the end of the lane a multilevel home crouched beside the lake, the floors staggered over the water's surface.

Winnie pulled in front, and the nearest of four garage doors opened. She drove into the empty space and the door closed behind them. Three immaculate automobiles rested on the polished concrete surface to their left. They looked like an exhibit. Neither Winnie nor August recognized the makes or models.

A door to their right opened and a groomed Afghan bounded down three steps and into the garage. The hound rushed over to Winnie and inserted its slender face into her skirt and between her legs.

"She remembers you fondly, Mrs. Helm," said a casually dressed man, walking behind the dog. Well-built, at least six feet tall, five or six years older than August, he moved confidently, suggesting routine physical exertion. A straw-colored sweater with a knit collar drew attention to several prominent veins in his neck. August wished he'd taken his father's advice and not worn a dress shirt. The man deftly embraced Winnie, then snapped the fingers of his right hand, causing the dog (still trying to insert her nose and face between Winnie's legs) to retreat, furiously wagging a short, curved tail. "I hope they didn't hold you up coming in," he said.

"Not at all," said Winnie.

"Good. We have a new security chief and some of us think the guards—a couple of them anyway—are trying to impress her."

Then he turned toward August, smiled, and extended his right hand. "You must be August. I'm Thomas Lux. It's a pleasure to meet you."

"Hi, Mr. Lux," said August, offering his hand, which was abruptly seized, crushed, and released.

"Please call me Tom and come inside."

They followed him, and the longhaired hound pranced ahead.

August sorted through his first impressions of their host. Notwithstanding his crushing grip, his manner implied a desire to dispense with formalities; he communicated genuine affection for Winnie, and an eagerness to protect her from his pet's unwanted attentions. His welcome to August was uncomplicated, with appropriate eye contact; he avoided the coldness of looking away too soon and the privacy assault of lingering too long.

Yet he seemed like he was guarding something.

Inside, they walked along a hallway and into an entryway with two staircases curling up toward three separate levels arranged like drawers in a concave mahogany bureau. Looking into the labyrinth of railings and colored glasswork at the apex, August smiled. The child in him wished to dash up, explore the rooms, turn on all the fans and lights, ride the banisters, rifle through the closets, flush the toilets, look out the windows, run to the very top and enjoy the view from above, to take his shoes off and hurl them down.

Thomas Lux observed August, and the older man's likeability briefly flashed in his blue eyes and then withdrew.

August coughed lightly into his cupped hand, recovering his adult composure.

"I have an office just down here. We can go over your CV and talk about your references."

Thomas Lux headed through the archway between the two staircases. Oil paintings and multicolored prints hung on the walls, depict-
ing provocative scenes. In one, a cloven-hoofed male satyr with scales
and goatlike features stalked a young woman through a motley forest.
Despite his considerable size advantage, the satyr appeared wary, even
fearful, while the expression on the woman's face approached amusement. Another work depicted the son of man—a splendid black figure—ascending toward a golden throne, climbing through a lattice of
white demonic figures. His mother stopped to inspect this one. Thomas
waited for her. Winnie leaned into the picture, her face only inches
from the canvas.

"You two go ahead," she said, waving them away.

Thomas stood to the side of an open doorway and motioned for
August to go in.

"Some time ago, several of my relatives attended the University of
Chicago," he said. "One of them played football for the school before
they set aside their sports programs."

"That *was* quite a while ago," said August.

August paused before coming further into the room. From where
he stood, he could see several chairs, a heavy desk with filled bookcases
running along both sides ending in a wall of glass. Outside, the lake's
ruffled surface came level with the polished oak floor.

"Winnie!" a woman's voice sang out and was soon accompanied by
running footsteps. "Winnie! You're here! Why didn't someone tell me?"

Down the hallway, his mother turned, and a figure August could
only see out of the corner of his eye came into view. Two bare arms
wrapped around his mother's waist. "Do you like that painting, Winnie?
It's by a Haitian artist who was later executed by the Dominican rebels
that overthrew Aristide. You can have it."

"Oh no, April," said his mother, laughing self-consciously about
the attention she was receiving. "It belongs here."

"Not if you like it. I'll have it sent over today."

"No, no, no, our mice would chew it up."

"I'm sure the artist would highly approve of some creature devouring his art! What kind of mice do you have?"

"Many kinds, and they're all hungry."

"Do you have any with white feet? They've completely eradicated *Peromyscus leucopus* here because of those nasty spirochetes. I'd like to see one again. They were everywhere when I grew up, and they seemed like the perfect rodent. Oh, and did I tell you they're going to give us an award next summer—for your gardens? The committee would have given it to us at the end of last summer just after your dahlias opened up inside the chrysanthemum perimeter, but, Jeanne Whitaker, they gave it to her because she donated the rotating stage and upholstered seats for the theater and her cousin is on the committee. That lawyer Dillingham is one of the judges—with a first name something like Rex—and last Tuesday at the marina when we were arranging to put the boat up for winter, confidentially, I mean, he said they'd make it right next summer. Can I get you some tea? I have the kind you like, cinnamon, and I have a lot of it because Tom likes it too and Maurice found a new supplier with a superior line. Did you bring your son—the one who's been working with transmembrane signaling and wants to write a monograph? Where is he anyway?"

Winnie peeled away the two hands that were still clinging to her and stepped into the middle of the hallway, opening the view.

August stepped into the hall.

"April, that's my son, August. August, this is April Lux."

Standing behind and to the side of his mother, in a plain white shift with auburn hair gathered over her left shoulder, arms akimbo, one leg hastily tucked behind the other, stood one of the most attractively interesting creatures August had ever seen. Several inches shorter than his tall mother, her face opened into a quick smile, her deep-set hazel eyes radiating from black centers.

Even at twenty feet, she seemed very familiar, as though he knew her and knew her well. It was an unsettling feeling and he felt more than a little undone by it. When he tried to return her smile he felt his neck reddening, and he bit on his tongue to keep the warm sensation from expanding into his face.

April looked away, and it seemed to August that she had done this to save him from his own embarrassment.

"Nice of you to come," she said, and walked away. His mother gazed a final time into the painting and followed her.

"Come in," said Thomas, gesturing a second time toward the open door. His voice, August thought, seemed a little strained, the words clipped off with sharp, mitered corners.

August sat in one of the leather chairs in front of the desk while Thomas arranged himself behind it, repositioning the small computer screen, several notebooks, and a short stack of magazines. It seemed their placement were momentarily preventing him from beginning the interview, and as soon as he moved one item, the others fell out of alignment.

The shimmering surface of the lake at the end of the room gave August the impression of floating. He tried to read the titles of some of the books on the shelves. Many were directly, and indirectly, related to entomology. Popular identification guides were indiscriminately mixed in with more academic works on insects.

"I've spoken with the primary researcher you were recently working with in Chicago," said Tom. "And Dr. Grafton enthusiastically recommends you."

"I'm glad," August said thickly, his tongue hurting.

"Why aren't you still working there, Dr. Helm?"

"Please call me August. I've never liked titles and now with most doctorates clerking in hardware stores and waiting on tables, it seems especially pointless. The subsection of the grant that funded my project was discontinued."

"Why?"

"Budget cuts is what I heard."

"That's what Dr. Grafton also said. So nothing currently prevents you from staying here—full time—for the next month or two?"

"Nothing I know of . . . but I thought this was only for short while."

"Would you not be able to stay longer?"

"I suppose, I have no other plans."

"We understand you grew up in this area."

"That's correct."

"So you know the local people around here."

"Some of them. It's been eight years since I spent any real time here."

"I'm afraid we don't want anyone other than you in the house while we're gone, with the exception, I suppose, of your mother, who both April and I are quite fond of. And perhaps your father as well."

"That's understandable, I guess."

"We anticipate you may need to leave from time to time, but your ongoing visibility in the community will be important and it should be understood that someone is here."

"That seems reasonable. I'm looking forward to spending some time alone."

"And why is that?"

"Catch up on some things I've neglected and do some reading. Is the Afghan your only pet, Tom?"

"No. Hannah belongs to April and she also has an assortment of plants. They all mean a great deal to her and will require vigilant attention."

"I see. Are you interested in insects?" asked August, gesturing to the books on the shelves.

"Not at all. All insects are bugs to me. Can you tell me about what happened ten days ago—just over the hill from here?"

"I'm not sure what you're referring to."

"You and another man were cutting firewood, and some Gate guards spoke with you."

"Yes, I remember."

"What was the problem there?"

"Apparently we should have brought the better saws."

"Did you threaten a guard?"

"No."

"Did the man working with you threaten a guard?"

"Not that I recall."

"Like I said before, some of our guys can be overly protective. Our new security chief reported the incident and I understand she talked to you directly that day."

"Yes, I remember her."

"Whom were you working with?"

"An old veteran and friend of the family, Lester Mortal. He served in Vietnam, among other places, and there aren't many of those old guys around anymore."

"Have you ever been arrested?"

"No."

"Ever been bonded?"

"No."

"Do you own a firearm?"

"No."

"Do you know how to use one?"

"Not really."

"Do you smoke?"

"No."

"Drink?"

"A little."

"Drugs?"

"Not routinely."

"Ever feel resentment toward the upper class?"

"No, why do you ask?"

"I see you studied economic theory and cultural anthropology."

"Those were introductory courses. I had to meet social science requirements."

"And you took a class called History of Social Unrest?"

"Actually, it was better than it sounds."

"In what way?"

"Did you know that more poor people were killed during the French Revolution than rich?"

"Is that important?" asked Tom.

"It's both interesting and ironic. Can you tell me what happened here a couple months ago?"

"In the Gate?"

"Here, in this house. Someone was dragged out yelling at the top of his lungs. Shots were fired and windows broken. There were guards and local police everywhere. What was the problem?"

"How did you hear about that?"

"Someone told me."

"It was a misunderstanding."

"Resentment against the upper class?"

Tom laughed. "Okay, you got me on that one, August. It was a neighbor who decided he didn't want to be friends any longer. And for what it's worth, he was one of the first property owners at the Gate."

"What happened?"

"He apparently took offense at something April said, and he'd had too much to drink. Unfortunately, I wasn't here at the time. He had a pocket pistol and shot out some upstairs windows. At first, security was reluctant to become involved and April called in the local police."

"Where is he now?"

"Chicago, probably. That's where he stays most of the time when he's not at his home on the other side of the lake. He owns a number of businesses and his attorneys had him released before the initial paper-work was even completed."

"Any chance he'll come back while you're away?"

"I seriously doubt it. Come, let me show you around the house."

Tom's likeability had surfaced again, and he led August from room to room, beginning on the upper levels. As August suspected, they were all comfortably impressive.

By the time they were back on the ground floor, it had been agreed that August would stay in the house while Tom and April were away, and Tom explained, "Cleaners will come every other week, and we'll leave the name of the Gate management director and others to call if something breaks down. Feel free to take full advantage of the medical services at the clinic should you require them. The food service will send someone over to find out what you'd like to eat while you're here and you can arrange whatever dining schedule that most suits you. They're quite accommodating, and they also have dog food if you run out. Otherwise, you should have no other intrusions."

"Sounds fine."

"I hope you enjoy your time here."

"When are you planning to leave?"

"We were hoping to be gone within the next hour."

"Really?"

"I'm sorry, do you have a problem with that?"

"I wasn't expecting you to leave so soon. All the things I was intending to bring—changes of clothes and so forth—are at my parents' house. I suppose I could be back by two o'clock."

"Excellent, we'd appreciate it."

"If you don't mind answering, where are you and April going?"

"We'll be moving around a lot."

"In what direction?"

"I can't say."

Once again, Tom's eyes took on the character of an unheated garage. August felt himself bristling in response and assumed the tension could probably be traced back to the interest he had earlier shown in April.

August wondered how the behavioral rules for human mating could be explained to someone unfamiliar with them. Everyone, at least most adults, generally understood the cultural protocols, yet they were difficult to explicitly define. First, of course, monogamy was the law of the land, though "law" would be too strong of a word. Even in societies where third parties choose mating partners, rivalries persisted. But once matrimonial commitments between a couple had been formally or informally worked out, the two participants were free to indulge in—together—any and every sexual activity they desired, provided they kept these acts private. Others were expected to respect the couple's commitment to each other, and both were regarded as ineligible to receive outside sexual advances. In theory, well-meaning people in monogamous cultures stayed within these boundaries.

In practice, however, the boundaries were constantly changing and in the course of one lifetime, a man or woman could expect to form a number of loving partnerships with differing depths of involvement and commitment. As August had discovered with Amanda, relationships in modern societies were often elastic, tightening and loosening from one week to the next. Even when deeply in love and heavily invested in their own private drama, couples still enjoyed—as individuals—knowing they were attractive to others. People did not love each other in isolation, but in imitation, celebration, and anticipation of other loves. And most couples did not physically impose restrictions, nor erect walls to keep outsiders at bay; boundaries were encountered through the kind of social tensions that August and Tom were currently exchanging. August's response to meeting April—evinced through several easily-read physical cues—was being censored through Tom's stiffness.

"And where would you like for me to stay while I'm here—which room, I mean?"

"Oh, sorry, I meant to show you first off."

August followed Tom down into the basement level of the house, where they moved through several rooms devoted to electrical boxes, ductwork, water heater, and a generator, plus a game room with billiard and Ping-Pong tables. There was also one large bedroom.

"I didn't expect this," said August. "And I like it."

One of the walls in the bedroom was transparent, providing an underwater view of the lake. Fish of different sizes and shapes swam through plants and stone structures. It reminded August, on a minor scale, of the Shedd Aquarium in Chicago.

"This is the quietest room in the house," said Tom. "Outdoor noises never penetrate this far. April often comes down here to get away. It's a good place to sleep and read. A second bed is here, because the room is also a favorite with guests, and you can sleep in whichever you prefer. If you want to see more fish, push this button."

Tom pushed it.

Behind the window and from somewhere above, a variety of foods suitable for ectothermic digestion were released in the lake water. Fish of all varieties ate the falling pieces and this activity soon drew the attention of other fish, including several large bass and a northern pike that darted around for the best morsels.

"April has names for the larger ones. She says it's not good to feed them more than once a day. At night you can turn on the underwater lights, though April says you should only rarely do that because it disturbs their nocturnal habits and biorhythms."

"Yes, it would," said August. "It would throw off their oxygen intake schedule."

"That's exactly what April says, and when they're more active they nibble more on plants, which cuts down on the oxygen in the water."

"Not to mention possibly disrupting their reproductive cycles, which is common in fish-farming."

"That one there," Tom pointed. "I think April calls him Longfellow."

"This room will be fine," said August. "I'll see if I can find my mother now. I'll take her back and return before you need to leave."

"Very good."

"Where would you like me to park?"

"The same place you're parked now will be the most convenient. It's closest to the door leading into the house."

"Say, I'll need your cell numbers so I can reach you if something comes up."

"Something like what?"

"Perhaps a friend of your family will unexpectedly show up."

Tom looked at the fish. Several of the larger ones where chasing the others. "Sure," he said. "No problem. I'll add them to the sheet of other names and numbers."

"Thanks," said August.

Waiting for the gate to open and let them out, one of the guards came out of the guardhouse and spoke politely to Winnie, wishing her a pleasant afternoon.

On the drive back, his mother seemed both pleased and concerned that August would be staying at the Gate. And she was not surprised that April and Tom intended to leave within the hour.

"They're like that," she said. "Unpredictable and unsettled."

"How long have you known them?"

"A couple years."

"It's the nicest house I've ever been inside. What do they do to afford it?"

"I don't know," said Winnie. "It seems impolite to ask. I think inheritance must have something to do with it. And I knew you'd like the house."

"How long have they been married?"

"Who?"

"April and Tom."

"They're not married. Tom is April's older brother. The first year I knew her, he lived in Denver most of the time and only moved out here full-time a year ago. Before he was here, she lived alone."

"They're brother and sister?"

"Isn't that what I just said?"

"He seems protective."

"Some brothers are."

"April likes you, Mom."

"I'm fond of her as well. She's unusually bright and affectionate, and I love the gushing way she talks. A lot tries to come out of her at once. Her mind is always full. I couldn't help noticing your attraction to her. Neither could she."

"I didn't intend that."

"I know, but you touched every base short of drooling. She seemed a little alarmed."

"Do you think so? You should have warned me. She's attractive."

"Is that a refrain from a popular hymn?"

"No, she caught me off guard. You should have told me she was so—well, you should have told me."

"I haven't any understanding for what young people find attractive in each other."

"You were young once."

"Yes, but attraction is part biology and part culture, and I've lost track of the latter. I see now that the two of you might have things in common, but I still didn't expect you to have such a strong reaction to her."

"Why not?"

"I don't know. Your father and me, we were so different when we met, and well—" And then Winnie laughed.

"Why are you laughing?"

"I just wondered if maybe I was trying to match you up with April and didn't know it. Bodies are more clever than minds, especially mothers' bodies, and it wouldn't be the first time I did something without understanding why I was really doing it."

They rode in silence through a stretch of heavily wooded land. Winnie drove slower than usual, fearful of hitting a deer. With rutting season underway, it paid to be alert. Bucks and does had little concern for moving vehicles when they could smell each other.

"Mom, it seemed like I knew her. How old is she? How old is April Lux?"

"Twenty-seven."

"She looks younger."

"She isn't."

"Where did she go to school?"

"I don't know."

"Where did she live before she came to the Gate?"

"I don't know, and I really need to caution you about thinking of her in that way."

"Why?"

"There's something not exactly right with April."

"What do you mean?"

"I don't know, but a lot of trouble howls through that house. That's the impression I get."

"What kind of trouble?"

"Down deep, April is distressed."

"What about?"

"I don't know. I'm just saying be careful. She's not someone you can depend on. I honestly never considered that you might start having ideas about her. I just thought you'd enjoy staying in the house to finish your paper and, you know, reorganize your life. Really, she's not someone you can depend on."

Winnie turned into the long lane between the pines.

"I'm not interested in her money."

"That's not the kind of depending I mean."

"Look, Mom, did you ever meet someone who—right away—you knew you'd like to spend the rest of your life with?"

"August, this doesn't sound at all like you."

"I know. But did you? Did you ever want something so much that nothing else seemed to matter—nothing at all?"

"Aren't you concerned that what you call polypeptides might be leading you astray?"

"I've been thinking about that, and oddly enough, I agree with Ivan, or at least I agree with something Ivan said the other day. Physical attraction and manifestations of power are bigger than us, and we only live because of them. And if you can't believe your chemistry, what else can you trust?"

"Doesn't agreeing with Ivan ring some alarms in your head?"

"No. He's right about this."

"I don't want you to be hurt, August."

"That's not going to happen. And didn't you ever feel the way I do now?"

"Well, yes. I did, but when you get older you look back on those moments from a different angle." She pulled into the garage. "Do you have time to stay for lunch? We can call your father inside to join us."

"No, I need to get back. Tom said they wanted to leave right away. Are you sure it's going to be all right for me to keep your car this month? You won't need it?"

"I'm sure. Cars, motorcycles, golf carts, trucks, four-wheelers, and riding lawnmowers follow your father around like stray dogs looking for a new home. We're never short of vehicles around here. Money, yes; vehicles, no."

"Tom said you could come visit; a privilege he emphatically did not extend to anyone else. As I said, they like you. And I'll also drive over here every so often and check in, help Dad some more with the Model T."

An hour later, when he returned to the Lux home, one of the polished automobiles from inside the garage was idling in the turnaround. April Lux sat behind the tinted windows in the passenger's seat. Tom closed the trunk on a stack of luggage and handed August a bristling ring of keys.

"April just took the dog for a walk, so Hannah won't need to go out for a while. I've left a sheet of paper on the kitchen table with the security codes, passwords, numbers, and names, most of which you probably won't need."

"Thanks."

"I hope you enjoy your time here, August. Now, we really must be going."

"Good luck," said August.

Tom climbed into the car next to April, closed the door, and drove away.

August parked his mother's car in the garage and carried two suitcases into the house. The Afghan met him in the hallway and followed him into the kitchen, where he inspected the sheet of information. After assuring himself that Tom had added the personal numbers that he had promised, August stuck it to the front of the refrigerator with a blue, fish-shaped magnet. He found a glass, ran some tap water, and drank it sitting at the small breakfast table overlooking the backyard.

On the other side of the sliding glass doors, a cobblestone patio fed into a stone walkway that curled off into a mature stand of maple and oak. The dog flattened out under the table and fell into a deep sleep.

An immense silence seized the house. To combat it, August reviewed his memories of Amanda, his night with Hanh, the interview with Tom, meeting April, and talking to his mother while riding home to collect his things. The exercise proved as futile as heating a room with candles, and he gave in and contemplated the silence on its own terms.

He'd been looking forward to an extended time to himself to allow residual feelings about Amanda to unravel all the way, complete an academic paper in order to salvage something from his time in Dr. Grafton's lab, and think about what he wanted to do next—where and how he wanted to live. But now that the needed period of rehabilitation had begun, he felt overwhelmed, as though an impromptu exam had been announced. Part of this anxious feeling, he assured himself, was simply because of being alone. The emptiness of the house had revealed the insufficiency of his inner resources. He depended on others to furnish him with a sense of himself.

August felt the silence searching through him, hunting for weaknesses.

There was a knock on the front door.

EATING SNAKES

"Is April Lux here?" asked an elderly woman carrying an over-the-shoulder utility bag and two rectangular air filters. Willowy thin with facial lines leading every which way across her face, she seemed resilient and alert, her words forceful and crisp.

"Hello," August replied. "I'm afraid she just left and I'm house-sitting while she's away. Is there something I can help you with?"

Dressed in a black and blue combination of oxford cotton top and denim knee-length skirt with thick-soled brown shoes, she opened her utility bag, took out a white paper stub the size of a single-item receipt, and handed it to August. "Two of the air handlers need filter changing and there's a minor air leak in one of the upper north-facing windows, probably due to caulk, insulation, or casing shrinkage."

"Is this something I should attend to?" asked August, looking into the stub of paper and reading off several lines of digital code that resembled Russian.

"Of course not," she said, showing August her identification card. "I'll take care of it and be out of your way in a couple minutes. It's part of the upkeep agreement."

"And it needs to be done right now?"

"Of course. The grid prompt is already thirty-six hours old, well within maintenance parameters, but still. There was a slight delay in locating the matching filters."

"Come in."

August followed her into the basement furnace room (she already knew the way) and watched as she took a stepladder out of a small closet, then climbed up and swung open the metal sheeting on the bottom of two air handlers. After drawing out the old filters, she slid in the new ones and then reclosed the drop doors.

Upstairs in the north-facing guest bedroom, she inspected the windows, running an infrared leak probe along the wooden casing. After receiving a signal, she carefully pried open a piece of trim running along the frame, and squirted in five inches of foam insulation from a pressurized canister taken from her utility bag. Then she tapped the trim back in place, rechecked the perimeters, and went downstairs. August opened the door and she stepped though.

Outside, she walked over to an aluminum meter-box next to the garage door, inserted her ID card into an open slot and withdrew it, leaving a record that she had completed the work. Then she climbed back into her three-wheeled van and drove away.

August returned to the kitchen, found the coffee maker and located some coffee in the cabinet next to the refrigerator.

Another knock came and August noticed, again, that the Afghan did not bark as he accompanied him to the front door.

"Yeah, is April here?" asked a head-shaven man. He looked about ten years older than August, maybe forty, slightly built, delicate hands, his unbuttoned shirt hanging over his thin shoulders as if from a wooden hanger; his dilated eyes glistened.

"I'm sorry," said August, standing just inside the open door next to the Afghan. "She left with her brother a little while ago."

"When will she be back, sir?"

"They'll be away for at least a month."

"A month?"

"If you want, I can give her a message when she comes back."

"Where did she go?"

"To be honest, I don't know. I think they intend to move around a lot."

The man looked back at his blue pickup, then at the sky. He turned back to August. "Excuse me, sir, but are you sure April isn't here?"

"Yes, I am. Who are you?"

"The name is Backer, Roger Backer. I take care of the yard. Sir, I need to drain the gas out of her mower, you know, before winter, keep it from gumming up. And set the battery inside where it won't freeze."

"Of course," said August. "Go ahead."

"I'll need the shed key, sir."

"The shed key?"

"Yes, April keeps the shed locked. All of her equipment is state-of-the-art, if you know what I mean."

"Where's the shed?"

"Around back."

"I'll unlock it for you."

"Thank you, sir."

Around the house, a square, stone building waited with a bamboo garage door. A smaller, walk-in door stood at the side. August looked through the collection of keys given to him by Tom, found the only bronzed one matching the color of the lock, and opened the shed.

Roger Backer stepped inside and turned on the light. August followed. Lawn equipment and tools rested, hung and leaned in such an orderly way that it looked like a section of a garden and hardware store. Most of the implements appeared as though they'd just been purchased. August had never seen a shed like this, with finished cabinets, finished oak floor, three windows, and a sitting area with a porcelain sink. Roger unscrewed the mower's cap and peered into the tank.

"Just as I thought. This needs draining."

August and the Afghan watched as Roger found a pair of pliers, a funnel, and a gas can at the workbench. He pulled off the fuel line from the mower and drained a couple ounces into the can. After reattaching the line, he put the pliers and can and funnel back, wiping his hands on the front of his shirt.

"Aren't you going to run it?" asked August, "You know, clear out the injector."

"Yes, sir."

"Please don't call me sir. My name is August. I'm looking after the house while April and Tom are away."

"You're not in the family?"

"Nope. I grew up just a couple miles over the hill, outside the village of Words."

"Oh, I've been in Words before," said Roger, looking at August with a new, relaxed expression. He came several steps closer and asked, "Do you think you could loan me some money, August? I'm really short this month."

"I don't know. How much do you need?"

"Whatever you can spare will help. You know, for medication, for my mother. I'm taking care of her."

August opened his billfold and handed Roger several bills.

"Thanks," said Roger. "When did you say April would be back?"

"Not for at least a month."

"Too bad, I wanted to see her. I really did."

"I gathered that. If you'd like to leave a message for when she—"

"No, I just wanted to see her."

The mower instantly purred to life, ran a couple minutes, stammered, stuttered, and died.

"Well, that's done," said Roger, walking out of the shed.

"Weren't you going to put the battery in the garage?"

"Oh, right. Sure thing. I forgot that."

When this was finished, August locked up the shed and walked with Roger out to his truck. The older man hesitated before getting in.

"Any chance I could stay here tonight?"

"Sorry. This isn't my house."

"Yeah, but you're here. You could let me."

"I don't have the authority."

"Does that mean you don't have authority to let me stay, or you don't have the authority to prevent me from staying?"

"The former."

"Okay, okay, just thought I'd ask. Doesn't hurt to try. I'm leaving now."

"Good luck."

"Thanks."

August watched the truck disappear around the curve and listened as it continued over the rise.

Discomforted by the appearance and manner of the man, August returned inside and carried his suitcases into the basement bedroom. He unpacked, placing clothes and other belongings on the tops of bureaus, in drawers and closets. Five or six large fish silently patrolled the area behind the glass, moving dreamily through the greenish water without apparent exertion, as though propelled by psychokinetic activity. Their chosen paths, often repeated, seemed unusually purposeful, yet August could not imagine what the purpose might be. Seating himself on the bed nearest the fish, he studied them, trying to understand the behavior. Several smaller fish swam into the area. Their faster speeds were completely ignored by the larger fish.

Gradually, the presence of his recent visitor, Roger Backer, dissolved from his mind, and the dog barked at the top of the staircase.

Another knocking came from the front door.

Just on the other side of it stood a tall, narrow man with short, sandy hair and a pointed, graying goatee. A green double Windsor filled the shallow V-cut in his brownish orange sweater, and behind him sat a shiny blue golf cart of the kind August had earlier seen sitting in several driveways.

"Good afternoon," the man said, taking a clipboard with attached papers from under his arm and holding them in front of him in a practiced manner. His eyes were light gray, and he seemed dull, yet in an imposing way, perhaps in his early seventies. "I'm glad I caught you at home. I'm gathering signatures to oppose the motion introduced at last month's community board meeting. Have you heard about the proposal to change the garbage containers from the current green fifty-gallon receptacles to gray seventy-five-gallon containers?"

"No, I haven't, and I'm the wrong person to ask," said August. "I'm just house-sitting while April and Tom are away."

"Anyone can sign a nonbinding petition. It's purely advisory, calling attention to the number of members attending the last meeting not constituting a proper quorum, even when the authorized proxies were counted. Changes in association spending and contractual agreements should not have been considered or proposed in the absence of a quorum."

"I'm not an association member."

"I understand that, August, but you nevertheless have an opinion."

"How do you know my name?"

"I just talked to . . ." and the man looked down at the front sheet on the clipboard and continued, "Roger Backer. He signed. If it will help, I can show you a copy of the bylaws pertaining to procedure. I have them right here."

"Look, I really don't think—" August's protest was interrupted when the man outside the door was suddenly seized by a lengthy episode of spasmodic coughing. He briefly recovered several times, only to begin again.

"Let's get you a drink," said August. "Come in."

In the kitchen, after the man swallowed several ounces of water, the coughing subsided.

"May I sit down?" the older man asked in a weakened voice.

"Of course."

The doorbell rang and August wondered why his earlier visitors had not used it. When he answered the door, a strikingly handsome man in a tattered leather coat extended an open hand and said, "Hi. Is April here?"

August shook his hand and wondered if he'd ever seen such an attractive haircut before. The styling seemed closer to carefully considered ornamentation than trimmed growth, and because of it, the man seemed so extraordinarily handsome that he could almost be called pretty. August then wondered about his actual gender, but after thinking about it for several moments, he decided it didn't matter.

"No, she isn't."

"I'm Peter Robinson, her veterinarian. She brought Hannah into the clinic on Wednesday and we had run out of the leptospirosis vaccine. It came in this morning. I can give it to her now. Oh, Hannah, speak of the devil. Hi, girl."

The Afghan went out and wedged her nose between his legs.

"That's nice of you," said August. "Come in."

"Thanks. Is Tom around?"

"No, I'm afraid they're both away."

In the entryway, the veterinarian pulled on a pair of exam gloves, took a small vial out of his pocket, rubbed the rubber plug with an alcohol wipe, and filled a syringe. Kneeling on the floor next to the dog, he used a second wipe to clean a section of skin between the long, golden hairs behind the left shoulder blade, and made the injection.

"Afghans are sight hounds," he said, speaking around the plastic tip from the syringe in his teeth. "Their eyesight is unusually sensitive in registering tiny movements at a great distance, and they possess both speed and endurance. Some of their genetic markers run back to the very oldest recognizable breeds. About thirty percent of dolichocephalic canine are pure wolf."

"I'm not a great believer in the accuracy of genetic markers in tracing ancestry," said August.

"Neither am I," said the vet, standing up, his hair continuing to look magnificent. "Though I personally enjoy thinking about Hannah branching off from feral *Canis Lupus.*"

"Yes, it's a nice thought."

"When do you expect April back?"

"A month or two. I'm August, by the way, and I'm looking after the house while they're gone."

"You might want to tell her I stopped by."

"Sure. I'll do that."

"Would you like to sign a petition opposing the latest illegalities committed by the association chairman?" called the man in the sweater and tie from the kitchen, followed by several short, nearly inaudible coughs.

"Sure, I'll sign it," the vet returned, peeling off the exam gloves and stuffing them into his coat pocket. "What's it for?"

"Keeping the community board chairman accountable to his own charter."

"By all means."

In the kitchen, veterinarian Robinson introduced himself and signed his name on the petition.

August noticed him looking at the half-filled glass of water in front of the older man. August poured another glass of water and handed it to him. The vet drank down three-quarters of it immediately and kept holding the glass as though he intended to drink the rest later.

August joined them at the table.

"This is one fabulous house," said the vet, gazing at the galaxy of kitchenware hanging above them. "I've always wanted to be inside it. My brother is a chef in St. Louis and he would highly, highly approve of this kitchen."

"It seems adequate," said the man with the clipboard.

A new fraternity seemed to have formed from drinking water together. August regretted that he couldn't introduce them to each other, but he had never learned the older man's name. In the honored tradition of other highly preoccupied individuals that August had known, he assumed everyone knew him.

"Does April cook?" the vet asked.

"I don't really know," August answered, wishing he did, or at least wishing he could appear to know more about her than the other two. "It's my impression she and Tom obtain most of their meals through the local delivery service."

"That doesn't tell you anything about whether Tom or April cook," said the man with the clipboard. "The local food service will deliver a live goat as readily as precooked meals. Last summer I ordered gumbo and rattlesnake, not for myself, mind you, but to welcome some of my wife's southern relatives who were visiting at the time. They often boast about their snake-handling sons and persist in talking about other uncomfortable subjects with such relish that it never fails to silence everyone else. So I called the service to order them an appropriate meal, and an hour later Maurice called back and asked if I wanted the snake dressed out in the skin, filleted, or live."

"What did you answer?" asked the vet.

"To what?"

"How you wanted the snake."

"Broiled, of course. We were having it with gumbo."

"What did that cost?"

"I don't remember."

"Did they eat it?"

"Eat what?"

"The rattlesnake."

"Yes, of course. We all ate it, and it tasted nothing like chicken."

"Isn't rattlesnake eating against the law in Wisconsin?" asked August.

"Does that mean you can't eat Wisconsin rattlesnakes, or you can't eat rattlesnakes in Wisconsin?" asked the vet, smiling proudly over the narrow distinction.

"Either one."

"Literally, yes; legally, no," said the older man, who'd eaten it. "At my wife Alicia's insistence, I looked into the issue before I ordered. There was once a narrow departmental ruling about snake eating, but later administrations allowed it to expire without comment."

"When did you say April would be coming back?" asked the vet.

"I didn't. Tom told me a month or two."

"Okay, I remember you saying that now."

"It wasn't that long ago," remarked the older man, swallowing the last of his water, "when a woman like April Lux would not have been single for this long. Someone would have married her again."

"She's been married?" the vet and August asked at the same time.

"Twice married, as far as I know."

"Twice?" repeated August.

"That's my understanding. The first time, right after she graduated from high school, and again several years later. Her last husband still comes around here sometimes, a very decent sort of fellow. They seem to get along amicably, I mean, as far as divorced couples go. He had this house built before they were married, and then he gave it to her. He now spends most of his time in South America."

"You knew him?" asked August.

"Oh yes, Douglas Rothmore was a fine man, and one you could talk to. He was a litigation attorney whose family owned, and probably still owns, several blocks of downtown Dallas."

"She doesn't look old enough to have been married twice," said August, as though defending her.

"How true," said the vet, sipping water. "How true."

"Can I share something in strictest confidence with you two?" asked the man with the goatee.

"Sure," said the vet, his voice experimenting with an indefinite tone. He consulted his watch before taking another drink of water.

"Okay," said August.

"I'm currently experiencing a difficulty that I can't see a way out of, and I'd be glad for any insight either of you younger men might have."

"Fine," said August, relieved to have the conversation veering away from April. "When did this difficulty begin?'

"There, you've touched on the complexity right away. No one can confidently answer that question. Perhaps it started at the outset, when my wife Alicia was born several minutes before her fraternal twin Megan. In something like this, causation is a fungible concept. What seems fairly certain is that Megan resented Alicia's early tendency toward perfectionism, which established progressively higher expectations for her own behavior. Too often, Megan discovered she could not satisfy those expectations. To the point of hostility, she dismissed Alicia's accomplishments and triumphs by the same equal measure as other family members applauded them.

"There were other differences between them. Alicia has always been a morning person, for instance; Megan is more a night owl. But most of these dissimilarities are unimportant because on a more personal level, the twins remained very close—the only siblings from an alcoholic mother of Tibetan ancestry and a much older Irish father who carried so much water for the Prudential life insurance company that he spent very little time at home. And this closeness persisted even when the sisters were separated from each other. Alicia, I know for a fact, never stopped thinking about, and in some ways relating to, Megan, even in her absence."

"What happened to Megan?" asked the vet, drumming his fingers on the countertop and prompting August to notice that the informality granted by drinking water together at the kitchen table had made it harder for the handsome vet to leave the group and attend to the rest of his afternoon. Familiarity had both freed them to talk in a more relaxed way, and bound them together through the same unspoken rules.

"Megan attended several universities in California without ever graduating. She worked in Silicon Valley for several years, as an entry-level technician, and married an unemployed musician. Though she loved him deeply, he proved to be both cruel and abusive. After he died from health complications from his heroin addiction, Megan moved around a lot and never remarried. Years went by without my wife hearing from her, other than an occasional Christmas or postcard, always from different places. For decades, we didn't know where she was. Then, soon after Alicia was diagnosed with chronic lung disease, Megan showed up on our doorstep, and stayed with Alicia. And in the following years, every time Alicia's health took a serious plunge, Megan came out and stayed with us. On January 27 of last year, two summers after I retired and had our house built on the other side of the lake from here, Megan moved in with us full time."

"How did that work out?"

"It wasn't exactly my idea, but I agreed. We had the room, there's no denying that. And she pulls her own weight, along with continuing to be a big support to Alicia.

"About a year ago, there was a thunderstorm in the middle of the night, and it woke me up. I was lying in bed listening to distant thunder and watching the windows light up and go dark, hearing Alicia's rasping breath next to me. She always sleeps through thunderstorms, and everything else for that matter, because of her medications. After a little while I noticed someone else in the room, standing near the bay window. Every time the lightning flashed I could see this figure outlined against the wall. I saw it five or six times, always in the same place. And a while later, after a prolonged period of darkness—at the next flash—the figure had moved, and now stood closer to the bed, holding some object."

"Good God, man, what did you do?"

"I reached over and turned on the bedside lamp."

"Well?"

"There was no one there."

"So you had been mistaken?"

"Not really. After that night it became harder and harder to divest myself of the possibility that someone else—living or dead—came into our bedroom at night. I suppose for that reason I became more sensitive to disturbances, slept more fitfully, and woke up at the slightest noise.

"Several weeks later, I woke up around two o'clock in the morning and again sensed someone in the room. I had placed a small nightlight in an outlet near the bay window, and its orange light illuminated a figure walking in front of it, carrying a pitcher, going from plant to plant, and pouring in several ounces of water. I could hear the liquid sound. The third time the figure crossed in front of the nightlight, I recognized Megan in her nightgown. When finished with her watering, she left the room and as far as I know did not return that night.

"I was relieved. The activity seemed utterly benign compared to the wild imaginings I'd conjured up to explain the earlier experience during the thunderstorm. The following day, I did not mention it to either Megan or Alicia, and I've often wondered if this was where I went wrong. Perhaps if I'd talked to Alicia forthwith and explained—"

"Why didn't you?" asked the handsome vet.

"I'm not altogether sure. For one thing, Alicia is especially keen on her plants. Some of them have been with us since we moved from Ohio. Her illness has often confined her to the house, sometimes for months at a time, and her plants serve as ambassadors from a larger world. She talks to them while pruning them, tells them about her day. They're her friends, and it would greatly upset her to think she had not properly watered them—something she would likely resist admitting to herself even if it were true. And she would ardently resent anyone else taking care of them.

"Three nights later, it happened again. I woke up and the orange glow of the nightlight revealed the figure of Megan, barefoot in her nightgown, moving in a ghostly manner from plant to plant, pouring water out of a watering can with a long, narrow, curved spout. In the other hand, Megan carried a pint-sized mister, and by pushing down repeatedly on the plunger sticking out of its top, she sprayed the leaves, making soft, hissing sounds.

"This time there was no anxiety on my part. I even experienced a sleepy appreciation for Megan's efforts while Alicia and I slept, the way a patient might take comfort in the duties of the night nurse as she glides through a dark hospital room, checking monitors and medicine drips."

"Did you mention your appreciation to Megan?"

"No, I didn't, and again, looking back, I wonder if perhaps I should have. Talking to her might have been a way to divert the direction of future events, but I said nothing. Do you think I should have?"

"I honestly don't know."

"Why didn't you?" August asked.

"Because speaking to Megan about her nocturnal visits seemed to violate an agreement of reliance that Alicia and I have with each other. If I had said something to Megan without first talking to Alicia, then we would have shared a confidentiality that excluded Alicia, and she and I have always been open about everything. Neither of us likes to be surprised, and we have always kept each other fully informed about everything. There have been many times in our lives when we've had to trust each other absolutely, and neither of us has ever broken that trust. We depend upon it."

"That's commendable," said August, feeling a strange admiration and hesitant compassion for the older man.

"Thank you, but perhaps if our relationship had not been so tightly sewn, then things . . . but I'm getting ahead of myself. For the next couple weeks, Megan continued to come into our bedroom at night with her watering can and mister. I soon became concerned she might accidently collide with something and wake Alicia, and I placed another two nightlights around the room. Her movements were now visible everywhere except when watering and misting the hibiscus near the closet. There is no outlet in that corner. I also left the door into the hallway ajar, fearing that the opening and closing of it might startle Alicia."

"Ah, there it is," said the vet, standing up and refilling his glass from the sparkling-water faucet. "Now, I'm afraid, you're an accomplice."

"I see you have some legal training yourself."

"No, but I watch a lot of movies."

The older man waited for the vet to reseat himself at the table, and continued: "Like I said, this continued for a couple more weeks, until about five months ago. On this visit, after Megan had silently tended all the plants, she carefully placed the watering can and mister on the floor just to the side of the open door in the hallway and walked back into the center of the room. She stood for a long time next to Alicia's side of the bed, and then folded back a corner of the covering and crawled in beside her. Ours is a king-sized bed and I like to sleep near the north edge of it, a habit I acquired after many years of sleeping in hotel rooms. Alicia sleeps nearer to the middle, and there was ample room for her smaller sister to find a place to cover up and fall asleep."

"Megan fell asleep?"

"Yes, I could tell from her breathing."

"And Alicia didn't wake up?"

"Oh no, and I wouldn't have expected her to. Like I said, she sleeps very soundly, the dear."

"Was Megan there in the morning?"

"No. After sleeping next to her sister for two hours and forty-eight minutes, Megan climbed out of the bed, picked up her watering can and mister and disappeared down the hallway. The clock read eighteen minutes after five when she left."

"Did you speak to Alicia about this in the morning?"

"No. I was afraid—"

"Let me guess," interjected the vet. "You were afraid the narrative had become too involved, and by speaking of it you would have to admit you should have spoken of it earlier. She would see how you'd been withholding something from her."

"That's true. I said nothing, and two nights later the same pattern reemerged. After watering and spraying the plants, Megan set her watering can and mister to the side of the open door, peeled back a corner of the covers and crawled into bed next to Alicia. After sleeping about three hours this time, she got out of bed, collected her watering apparatuses, and slipped silently down the hall."

"Good God, man, what did you make of this?" demanded the vet.

"I didn't reach any definitive conclusion."

"But you must have thought about it."

"What was there to think about? They're twins born within minutes of each other. They had no doubt slept together many times while they were growing up. And now, for reasons that need not concern anyone but them, Megan apparently found comfort in sleeping next to her again. Perhaps it brought memories of their childhood. Perhaps she was lonely. Who can say?"

"Is this still going on?"

"Yes and no and not exactly."

"What happened?"

"Well, the pattern was repeated maybe a dozen times, into March as I recall, until about the middle of the month, when we had another thunderstorm. In any case, on this occasion, amid lightning bursts in the windows, Megan spent her usual ten or fifteen minutes watering the plants and hissing with the mister. After she set her sprayer and can out in the hallway, however, Alicia turned over in the bed, into the space that Megan customarily crawled into. Megan stood at the edge of the bed for some time, watching her sleep. Then she walked around to the foot of the bed and stood there for several minutes. After that, she glided out into the hallway, gathered her can and mister from the floor and disappeared.

"Three nights later, after Megan had silently finished caring for the plants, Alicia again turned over, into the space next to the edge of the bed. And once again, Megan simply left the bedroom, walking toward her own room at the end of the hall. Just before leaving, however, she pulled the bedroom door all the way shut, making an audible snap as the frame and closing mechanism clicked into place.

"The following day, the twins hardly spoke to each other. Megan ran errands in Madison, ate all of her meals there, attended a community play in the evening, and didn't return until after midnight.

"Two nights later, when Megan came in with her can and mister, she moved silently across the room, toward the closet in the opposite wall. There, she disappeared into the darkened corner and when she materialized again into the illumination of the nightlight, she had taken off her gown. Without clothing of any kind, she watered and misted the plants, moving from one to the next, pumping the hissing plunger and periodically tipping the can to pour. When she was done, she returned to the darkened corner, put her gown back on, collected her watering utensils and left the room."

"Go on," said the vet.

"Three nights later, the same thing happened again. Megan watered and misted the plants in her birthday suit and Alicia turned over into the space along the edge of the bed. This time, however, Megan did not leave the room right away. She stood at the foot of the bed for several minutes and then crawled forward, between Alicia and me. At the head of the bed, she turned around, drew her knees up to her chin and inserted her toes between the sheets. Then she slid her legs forward and, in this way, unfolded into the bed between us, naked and smelling of the lavender oil she'd added to the misting water. Within minutes, she had fallen asleep."

"Good God, man. What did you do?"

"I was still awake two or three hours later when she climbed out. At the foot of the bed she dropped the nightgown over her head, wiggled her hands through the armholes, and returned to her own room at the end of the hall."

"Surely you talked to them both then. I mean, for the love of God, these women are collaborating. Is it possible Alicia always knew what was going on—that you were mistaken in thinking she was asleep?"

"Impossible. I once sampled the medication she takes before going to bed and slept for sixteen hours."

"I've never heard of anything like this before. Never."

"That's part of the problem," said the older man with the goatee. "There are no guides, no precedents, at least not in my experience. No laws are being broken—at least none that are known to me."

"What happened?"

Yes, what happened, wondered August, noticing a disquieting similarity between the story being related and the night he'd recently spent with Hanh. On the latter occasion, he and Hanh had embraced before retiring to their separate rooms, and this negligible encounter lit an unseen fuse inside both of them, bringing imagined future events into play. It was the same with this story: Each beat anticipated the next.

THE FLAT WORM

"This went on for some time, and I became despondent," the older man continued. "And as my despondency grew, it became more apparent to my wife, and her sister. A heavy gloom settled over our household. Our meals together became sullen, our walks silent, we stopped playing cards together, stopped watching programs we customarily enjoyed, and we no longer discussed current events. And this lasted until May seventeenth. In the early hours of that particular morning, Megan came into the room more determined than usual, moving quickly and without the long pauses that I'd become accustomed to. She took off her nightgown and watered and sprayed the plants as though dispensing with an annoying chore. Then she slid naked between the sheets and after breathing deeply several times, she turned away from Alicia and manhandled me with such proficiency that whatever resistance I had to offer was quickly exhausted and I gave her my full compliance. Within a stiffened minute I was quietly and completely inserted inside her, experiencing a joy I'd not felt since before Alicia became seriously ill. Tears quietly ran from my eyes. And though we had to be very quiet, I confess I didn't last long. It didn't seem to matter to Megan, and afterward we fell soundly asleep."

"Good God."

"Since then, little has changed, though Megan now often sleeps until Alicia begins to stir in the morning before returning to her room. My stamina has greatly improved, I'm happy to report, and on some nights my sister-in-law and I perform our ritual for quite a while before falling asleep. Sometimes Megan turns over with pillows beneath her, the way Alicia liked to be taken when we were younger, and sometimes we're more casual, on our sides. The gloom that settled over the household has lifted, though I still privately entertain periods of melancholy when it can be safely contained within my own thoughts."

"And still—the three of you—haven't spoken of this?"

"No, and that's where I'd like any advice you fellows can give. See, I'm very uncomfortable with this and I don't know how to end it or improve it."

"Well, I most certainly have advice," said the vet. "And I'm not exaggerating when I say this story is at once the most immoral yet ethical tale I ever heard."

"Then you've grasped the kernel of the problem. But first, I'm afraid this water is running through me like a sieve. I wonder if I may visit your bathroom?"

"Of course," said August. "It's right around the corner."

The older man stood up from the table and shuffled around the corner.

August sat across from the vet and after a long silence asked, "What advice were you going to give?"

"I didn't really have any."

"But you said—"

"I thought I had something to say, and then it just went away."

"Were you surprised by his story?"

"Yes, but I shouldn't have been. I'm a veterinarian after all. I've been involved with breeding animals for years. Have you ever heard of a *Schistosoma mansoni*?"

"The parasite?"

"Yes, it's a flat worm that assumes different forms during its life cycle. In its infectious stage it's a cercaria. The microscopic organism has a forked tail and swims freely about in freshwater lakes and rivers. As it swims it searches for the unique mixture of fatty and amino acids emitted by human skin whenever people enter the water. The cercaria detects even the smallest traces, and by following them—with a little luck—it attaches to a human body. Once on board, the forked tail is no longer needed and is sloughed off. The cercaria then begins looking for a hair follicle and burrows down the follicle shaft until it reaches the hair root, which it recognizes in its own way as an entry point. The cercaria produces enzymes to digest the root and eats its way inside. It then morphs into a schistosomula, and as it adjusts to the warm environment, this immature larva proceeds to the nearest lymphatic node, enters the human blood stream, and starts feeding on red blood cells. Growing stronger, it migrates along the pulmonary vein, through the heart, all the way into the lungs. There, the schistosomula puts on its ultimate disguise by gathering nearby proteins from the host's lung tissue and attaching them to itself. Once in place, the protective film appears to the human immune system's parasite-seeking police as a piece of what the immune police are trying to protect. Invulnerable now, the organism moves to its final destination, the liver, where it embeds in the liver walls, consumes liver cells, and enlarges to its fully mature form, between twelve and twenty millimeters long. Then it begins looking for romance, following pheromone trails through the liver. After finding a suitable mate, the smaller female *mansoni* enters a gynaecophoric channel along the side of the male where, happily enveloped inside this love canal, she and he continuously copulate for the rest of their monogamous lives, which can last as long as thirty-five years. The female flat worm works with such efficiency that she can have sex and lay eggs at the same time. Some of these eggs find their way into the small intestines of the human host and are excreted through urine or feces. When the eggs reach a body of fresh water, they hatch, and the whole cycle begins again."

"Excellent example of adaptive engineering," said August.

"Excellent for them, not so good for us. *Schistosoma mansoni* infect over two hundred million people a year, often fatally. But the point I'm trying to make is that nature designs creatures for one activity: making others of its kind. So nothing should ever surprise us when people find ways to have sex. The impulse is so ubiquitous that it continues to seek expression in individuals even after there is no hope of reproductive success."

"I suppose. And it's also important to remember—at least for me—that social customs are adapted to biological urges, not the other way around."

"Well spoken," said the vet.

The Afghan barked and the doorbell rang.

"I'll get that," said August, walking out of the kitchen.

Outside stood two women, one with a slightly larger bone structure but more than a little resemblance to the smaller one.

"Sorry to bother you, but is Albert Russet here? We saw his golf cart and thought he should be coming home by now. He's been gathering signatures for most of the afternoon. I'm Alicia Russet and this is my sister, Megan."

"Does this Albert Russet wear sweaters and have a small beard?"

"Yes, and his beard is turning gray."

"He's inside," August said, finding it hard to make eye contact with either of them. "Albert is inside," he repeated.

"Would you send him out here," said Alicia, her pale voice matching an equally pale complexion. Her skin seemed papery, puffy, especially around her deep brown eyes. Her hands and wrists were swollen, and though she looked unwell in many ways, she also seemed as though at one time she might have been regal-looking. She stood with dignity, proud and straight, inside a long gray coat with a belt buckled around her thick waist. Next to her, the smaller and healthier woman inspected the front of the house as though appraising its value. Her skin glowed and her eyes burned dark brown—the same eyes as her sister's. She wore a sleeveless sweater, and when Hannah attempted to insert her snout into Megan's red-and-brown skirt, her backward-skipping avoidance maneuvers revealed a spryness that many sixty-year-olds no longer retained.

"Get away now," she laughed. "Get away. Oh, oh, I hate dogs."

"Lie down," barked Alicia, and the dog immediately sank onto the driveway and stayed there.

"Albert!" August called. "You'd better come out here."

The handsome vet reached the open door first and looked at the two women as though they had just flown in from space.

"Hello," said Alicia in an aloof manner.

Then the older man with the goatee joined them and walked outside.

August and the veterinarian watched as Albert, Megan, and Alicia climbed into the two golf carts and motored away.

August offered to make coffee.

"No thanks, I better be going," his guest said. "Nice meeting you, August."

"Thanks again for vaccinating the dog."

"You're welcome. When did you say April was coming back? Never mind, I remember now."

"I'll mention you came by."

After he drove away, August closed the front door and stood in the entryway. To fill the unoccupied space in his mind, he climbed the staircase and began to explore.

The upstairs library, like the downstairs office, had books on entomology, liberally interspersed with law books. Two smaller tables were strewn with maps. A fully stocked bar extended out of the bookcase, the cut glassware and canisters dusted and shining. A bay window with several comfortable chairs took advantage of the view overlooking the rolling lawn and rising, curving lane. The landscape reminded August of the open pastures in his childhood—grasslands ornamented with trees. Between the two chairs, a mounted spotting scope rose out of a swing-arm on the connecting table. August sat in one of the chairs, looked outside, and let his mind wander. The sun had fallen into the last quadrant of the afternoon sky, throwing shadows.

An indeterminate time later, in the distance, he saw a lone figure walking along the edge of the lane toward the house. He pulled over the spotting scope and stared through its polished lenses. As the image squeezed into focus, he experienced a stab of guilty pleasure. Even her eyelashes came into view. It felt like spying.

Her expression suggested both unease and resolve, like someone deciding to walk to her destination after missing a bus. Her stylish plaid-and-pleated dress came down within an inch or two of her knees; forest-green knee-high socks rose out of brown leather high-top walking shoes. A gray woolen cap hid most of her black hair and her slender frame carried her along in an almost artful manner. One thing for certain: she knew how to dress. Every piece of her outfit was pleased for the opportunity to be on her.

Her overall bearing seemed somehow too mature for such young skin and muscle tone.

As she neared the house, her expression narrowed.

August stepped out of the front door.

"Hello," he said.

The woman walked up to him and stopped—so close that August partially backed into the open doorway.

"I need to talk to April Lux, right now," she said. Her eyes dared to be looked into; her voice was strong, with no accent. She had been blessed with a semidark complexion resembling old copper. Without the spotting scope between them, her presence seemed even more distinct, and August thought this was probably due to subliminal communications—pheromones, heat exchanges, infinitesimal facial changes, and ambient reflections that the spotting lenses could not capture. Her gray cap suited her so well he assumed it must have been designed specifically to sit on top of her head.

"Sorry, April isn't here."

"Unacceptable," she said, pursing her plentiful lips. "I must talk to her. Tell her to come out here."

"That's simply not possible."

"Where is she?"

"She and Tom left on a road trip this afternoon. They don't intend to be back for at least a month."

"Where'd they go?"

"I don't know."

"Don't lie to me."

"I'm not."

"Give me her number," she said, taking a phone out of her pocket.

"I'm sorry, I can't do that. Is there something else I can possibily help you with?"

"All right, you can tell me if April Lux is still sleeping with my husband."

"Oh, boy," said August, sitting down on the polished stone step and taking hold of the Afghan's collar. "I'm simply the wrong guy to ask. My name's August Helm. I'm house-sitting while they're away. This morning was the first time I'd met either of them. My mother gardens here sometimes, and I suppose that's why they hired me. But I'm simply the wrong guy to ask."

Her large eyes did not blink, and she shot back, "I don't care who you are or why you're here. I need to talk to April, and I need to talk to her *right now*. I can't live with this any longer. Do you have any idea what this feels like?"

"No, I don't. Like I said, I'm just looking after the house."

"She's really not here?"

"No, she isn't," said August, standing up again. "Come inside. Please. I'll make some tea."

"I don't want any of April's damn tea."

"Then I'll replace it tomorrow with some of my own. Come in."

"I should go back home."

"Come in. It's a long walk back."

"How do you know?"

"I assume you live here at the Gate."

"You know who I am, don't you?" she asked.

"No, I don't. Like I said, I'm just house-sitting."

"I'm Chopra Scarborough. Everyone calls me Chopie, and I'm married to Dennis Scarborough. I assume you've heard of him."

"Nope."

"Dennis shot out some windows here a while back."

"I think I heard something about that, but no names were associated with it."

"Well, now you have one: Dennis Scarborough."

"Come in."

August seated Chopra Scarborough at the kitchen table, found some tea in the cupboard, and set a pot of water on the industrial-sized gas stove.

When he sat across from her, she said, "I've been thinking about coming over here for months. Today, my courage finally caught up to me. I need to know if April's still sleeping with Dennis."

Chopie removed her wool hat and set it on the tabletop, releasing a copious volume of coal-back hair, which framed her face in velveteen.

"I might have said the wrong thing a little while ago," said August, "when I said I didn't know how you felt. It wasn't that long ago when I felt like you do now, angry and sick with jealousy."

"Impossible."

"Why?"

"Are you married?"

"No."

"Have you ever been married?"

"No."

"Are you a woman?"

"No."

"Have you ever been angry enough to not care if you killed your-self or someone else but thought you ought to do one or the other and maybe both?"

"Yes."

"Still, you can't possibly know what I feel."

"Feelings aren't unique, Chopie. All emotional states result from the cultural associations we form around the activity of only nine neu-ropeptides, which are pretty much identically shared among us. For the most part we're all roughly navigating by the same set of biological coordinates. And if that weren't true, then language, psychotherapy, psychotropic medication, compassion, empathy, and frankly recipro-cated love would be impossible."

"Are you a damn scientist?"

"Yes, damned and currently unemployed."

"I thought you were a professional house sitter."

"Hold that thought while I get the teapot."

As August poured boiling water into two mugs, he remembered the sheet of information left behind by Tom and currently posted on the refrigerator. Chopie noticed it at the same time, jumped to her feet, and snatched it.

August set the teapot down.

Chopra dialed her phone.

After fifteen seconds she dialed the other number, waited, and returned the phone to her pocket.

"Those numbers were disconnected," she said, flicking the piece of paper away from her.

August tried them on his phone with the same result.

"Well," he said, sighing. "So much for contacting them."

"You know her first husband killed himself within a year of their marriage," said Chopie.

"No, I didn't."

"They married right after high school, and he shot himself before finishing his first year at the university. He had a football scholarship and killed himself before the end of the season."

"Where'd you hear that?"

"April's second husband told Dennis."

"Her second husband," repeated August. "The guy who left her this house?"

"That's the one—Doug Rothmore."

"Why would he tell your husband that?"

"How would I know?"

"Why did your husband tell you?"

"We were fighting about April. I suppose he thought it would score a point for the Dennis team."

"Why did he commit suicide?"

"I don't know. Maybe because that bitch April is rotten to the core."

"There are other cures for less than perfect marriages."

"Are there?"

"Sure. Separation and divorce come to mind."

Chopie scowled for a short while and said, "I'd rather be dead than divorced."

"You can't be serious."

"This is a nice kitchen. Not at as nice as mine, but nice enough."

"Let's take our tea into the office down the hall. It looks over the lake and we can watch the sunset."

"Okay, Mr. August."

In the office, they pulled two burgundy chairs close to the wall of glass and sat sipping tea. The reflection of colored sky on the surface of the restless water gave the impression of liquid incandescence.

"Before today, I'd never seen a room like this before," said August. "You know, water level with the floor."

"We have a better view at our place, but this is okay. Dennis had first choice of sites when they developed this area."

"How did that happen?"

"Dennis gets what he wants."

"Why did you say you'd rather be dead than divorced?"

"Because I would."

"You love your husband that much?"

"Hell no. But if we break up, I'll be left with nothing. Dennis made certain of that."

"Do you have family you could go back to?"

"No, Dennis wanted it that way. No escape. That was the agreement from years ago in Bangkok. He wanted more than a wife to be seen in public with; he'd already had two of those, and both had disappointed him. Like many aggressive men, his sex drive interferes with the rest of his life if he can't attend to it, so this time he made conditions."

"You're from Thailand?"

"Yes. Dennis saw me in a nightclub. He was in Bangkok with some other men buying cocaine and taking over a technology company."

"You were single at the time?"

"Of course. Escort girls are not allowed to marry, be sick, gain weight, get knocked up, or age."

August took a sip of tea and frowned.

Chopie continued. "Dennis wanted someone to keep his house and flatter business partners, and yet never stop servicing him like a street urchin rented by the hour. His first wives apparently discovered a higher plateau of dignity after they married him and he didn't want that to happen again. I was fifteen; he was thirty-five. He bought me from the agency and settled the terms of indenture from when my parents had sold me into the trade. And he made certain that if I ever left him, or failed to perform, well, he'd ruin me."

"Jesus."

"I don't ever intend to go back to living like that."

"You wouldn't need to. That was a long time ago."

"I mean living without money, you fool. Once you become accustomed to having it, the idea of not having it is unacceptable."

"Money's not that important to me," said August.

"You really are an ignorant rube. Where'd April find you, anyway?"

"Through my mother, the gardener."

"Oh right, you said that earlier."

"I hope you're wrong about April and your husband."

"I'm not. I mean, it might not be April, but he's seeing someone. I can feel it."

"Feelings often deceive."

"Not mine. Not about this. From the age of eleven, staying alive and being attractive were the same. I know when someone wants me as surely as your mother's plants know when the sun shines. Dennis slept with April last summer—after the horrid neighbor in her horrid ship-captain uniform gave a horrid party in her horrid house that is supposed to look like one of her horrid boats—and since then Dennis hasn't had the same interest in me. It's happened before, but never for this long."

"I still think you're wrong."

"I'm not. Women have desire radar, and with practice, it's nearly foolproof. We know when we look good to someone, and when we don't. Right now, I can feel your attraction. Every time my voice changes in pitch or I move, you react. Don't get me wrong, most heterosexual men do, but you respond more than most. For some reason you're not particularly interested in my breasts, though I can assure you—they're perfect. No, it's my thighs that draw you out and upward, and I wonder why. When I pat them like this, let's see what happens. Oh yes, saliva just gathered in your throat and your nostrils flared like little trumpets. And that animal vein in your neck stood out and your ear tips darkened. Your eyes are going glassy. You're trying to stop showing what's happening to you, but you can't, and it makes you angry. You don't have to be embarrassed, though. Currently, Thai women are considered some of the most beautiful in the world. Add to that my natural self-confidence, innate intelligence, and ability to purchase the most expensive and flattering clothes, cosmetics . . . you're simply reacting to all of that as well as ideal waist to hip ratios. What if I pat the tops of my thighs like this, with both hands, so you can hear the contact? Yes? Oh, you like that even better, yet it's such an innocent action, the way your mother might have called you over to her. Uh oh. Wrong thing to say, I guess, because now I can smell you oiling up. And my hands; you keep looking at them. Is it my complexion, or the painted nails? I'm different from women you've recently known, and I alarm you in other ways too. You're afraid, I can tell. If I were to take off all you clothes right now, you wouldn't even know what you wanted me to do with you. All your secrets would spill out of you. And if they didn't come right away, I could milk them out. And for some reason it excites you to have a woman talking this way, not pretending to be coy, or girlish, and you're trying to keep from imagining what it would be like to have everything you ever wanted, in a house you don't belong in, and with a woman you could never in your wildest dreams afford."

August turned away from her and looked into the sunset.

"Dear boy, stop it. I understand you're in love with April and your interest in me is pure reflex. Your conscience would never allow you to open to me. I know that. You're a good boy and have always been. I'm just pointing out how easy it is to read you."

"You can't possibly know anything about me!" snapped August.

Chopra Scarborough laughed in a short, rapid giggle, crossed her legs under her plaid dress and picked up her cup of tea. "You're a delight, Mr. August. Outside, when you met me at the door, when I first mentioned April, you looked like you'd been shot with a pistol. Your whole body stiffened with guard duty. Your jaw clenched. Your eyes narrowed, your breathing grew shallow, your voice changed, and you began playing the role of protector. You invited me inside, not because you wanted to comfort me—which you also graciously did, and I appreciate it—but to learn whatever I could tell you about April. You're in love with her, but you know almost nothing about her. When the telephone numbers they left for you didn't work, you felt betrayed. A short time later you wanted to leave the kitchen, to get away from the place where you learned of their betrayal. You want to know what I know about her. That's what the tea and sunset was all about. By making me comfortable you hoped I'd be willing to tell you more."

"It's embarrassing to be so obvious."

"Sorry, but my life has trained me. You have no idea what I've seen, in the trade."

"Like what?"

"Like you, Mr. August, most people have constant sexual urges but manage to push them down and go about the rest of their lives. They're incessantly hungry, but well trained to eat only at certain times. They wash their hands first, comb their hair, put on clean shirts, and sit politely at the table. They don't fidget or make faces; they take small portions and are careful not to spill. But there are others who can't. They try, but they can't. They never forget about their cravings long enough to concentrate on anything else, and because of this they always imagine someone finding out about them. Their recurrent nightmares—when they aren't about sex—are about being hunted."

"Would this characterize your husband, Dennis?"

"God no. Dennis is efficient, organized, and focused. He succeeds in nearly everything he attempts. He's a more forceful version of you. It's easy to make him happy. You would be just like him if you had more money and could give yourself permission to go after what you really wanted. No, I'm talking about these poor folks who can hardly tie their own shoes because of their obsessions. They never get enough, no matter what they do—or what you do for them—or how many times they do it."

"Tell me all you know about April Lux."

"I already told you," she replied, settling her cup into the saucer. "Her first husband shot himself inside their first year and her second husband divorced her at about the same time he gave her this property, less than three years after they were married. That's all I know. She's apparently a very successful fundraiser for charities of all kinds, but she seldom attends Gate events. I've met her a few times and she never impressed me one way or another. She's much like you are—lost in the world of her own damned thoughts. But be forewarned, Mr. August, if she's sleeping with Dennis and won't give him up—I'll kill her."

"You can't be serious. You wouldn't do that, Chopie."

"Oh, I won't do it myself. I'll hire someone."

"I think you're wrong about April and your husband. A man wouldn't shoot up the home of a woman he was sleeping with."

"No, no, dear boy, the question is why a man would shoot up a woman's home if he *wasn't* sleeping with her."

"From what I've heard, your husband was nearly blind drunk and trying to kill April as she ran through the rooms trying to get away from him. Look, can I drive you home?"

"I'd rather walk. It's good for the gluteus maximus."

"Do you mind if the dog and I accompany you?"

"That would be nice, thank you. But first, since you don't seem to be able to keep your eyes from returning like compass needles to my thighs, would you like me to come over and sit on your lap . . . so you know what that feels like? I promise I won't pull up my skirt or take down my panties. And you can keep your hands in your pockets if you want."

"Thanks for the offer, but no thanks."

"Are you sure?"

"I am. Besides, what would your husband think?"

"Are you kidding? There's nothing Dennis would like better than for me to tell him about sitting on your lap. He'll bellow at me like a wounded bull, hurling every vulgar expression he can remember, with spit flying out of his mouth. He'll strip me down to my heels, turn me over the back of our couch, and have at it. Really, he loves that game, or rather he used to love it, and me, until April got hold of him."

"If it's all the same to you, I'd rather not play any role in motivating that activity."

"Suit yourself, Mr. August. It was only a suggestion. Now, I should probably leave. It's a little over three-quarters of a mile back to my house and I need to get back in case Dennis calls tonight. He can tell where I am when I answer, and he doesn't like me being away from home when he's gone."

August had the Afghan on a retractable leash, and he and Chopra walked along the edge of the lake. Mist gathered in the air. Lights in the marina reflected across the water in yellow lines erratically broken by waves. A dark necklace of geese floated through them. August thought about how vibrations of differing wavelengths, directed from varied angles of agitation between air and water, were entering his eyes. Through a photovoltaic process, these vibrations were converted into the biological stimuli needed to travel along the optic nerve and enter his brain, where thousands of associative electrochemical interactions gave rise to conscious impressions. The air temperature, scent of watery vegetation, stirring breeze, hazy moon, and faintly audible murmur of waves overlapping each other encouraged an almost transcendent gladness inside him, which he projected into the natural scene, and imagined it to be orchestrating his mood.

Chopra preferred to walk quickly, August noticed, and her steps were light, nearly soundless. Yet she politely waited whenever the dog stopped to explore interesting smells.

A parliament of owls chortled in a ghostly manner somewhere along the ridge and August sank even deeper into dreamlike tranquility.

"So, you grew up around here," she commented.

"I did."

"What was that like?"

"I don't think growing up can be compared to anything else. It isn't like anything else. It's too subjective. What was it like where you grew up?"

"It wasn't like here. I mean, it was dirt poor, but not this kind of poverty. This area around the Gate frightens me. The people seem so . . ."

"So what?"

"Isolated and uncivilized. You see them along the road, standing on broken sidewalks in dismal towns. You wonder if the men even speak a known language, and the women all look like they're either ill or carrying knives."

"I assure you your impressions are entirely wrong. If you simply give them a chance..."

"I have no intention of doing that."

"That's your loss. Is that your home up ahead?"

"How did you know?"

"Just guessed. You certainly have a wonderful view. Those lights set in the rocks are dramatic."

"Nice of you to notice."

They climbed the incline along the curving cobblestone drive and stood in front of the massive oak door. Built to appear like an extension of the rock abutment around it, the entrance made a formidable impression, as though ancient craftsmen had carved the structure out of the native limestone; its windows seemed to look into the earth itself.

"I'd ask you in," said Chopra, "but if your profile isn't in the system the buzzers go off and the badges come."

"I understand. Is Dennis here?"

"No. He mostly stays in our Chicago place. That's where most of his businesses are. In the copter, he can make the trip in less than an hour. If he takes the bullet to Madison and picks up the Lamborghini, it takes an additional half hour."

"Well, good night."

"Good night."

August watched her go in, and the door closed behind her.

Lights came on inside.

August studied the arabesques in the rock wall and began walking back.

DOGS PLAY

AT REGULAR INTERVALS along the lake, painted wooden benches had been placed near the water.

About halfway around a woman sat waiting, holding on to the leash of a black Labrador. When August and the Afghan neared, she stood up and her dog lunged against its tether.

"I hope you don't mind," she said, dressed in a thickly knitted black sweater and gray wool slacks.

She was attractive in a very interesting way, with an effortless smile. August had no idea how old she was. Like many young people who had not yet lived through the tale-telling depreciations of middle age, he did not readily recognize them in others and could only roughly guess her age at somewhere between forty and sixty. Also, her standing height (an inch or two taller than his own) seemed remarkable, and this also made it more difficult to reach an opinion about her age. The skylight clarified her long, gray hair and August liked her immediately; she reminded him of several humanities professors he'd known at the university—older women whose quick, acerbic wit he'd often admired from a safe distance. "I saw you go by earlier and hoped you'd be willing to let our dogs play together. Missy cherishes her playtime. She sulked all afternoon because April didn't bring Hannah over at the usual time."

"Sure, they can play," said August. "Can we just let them off-leash?"

"Don't worry, they always come back."

When the dogs were unsnapped they stood close together, stiff-legged, necks arched, ears back, staring out of the corners of their eyes. Then at some unknown signal, they bolted across the lane and up the hill, growling, snarling, and snapping at each other. Careening between trees, they disappeared over the crest-top.

"I'm Skylar, by the way, and that's my house with the glass lanterns along the overhang."

"Hello. I'm August Helm and I'm—"

"You're house-sitting for April. Most of us already know who you are."

"Surely not," said August, incredulous at the idea of being known.

"It's a small community. Our security people are the biggest gossips—it's true—but that doesn't exonerate the rest of us. We keep informed."

The dogs came racing downhill, joyously panting and yipping at each other. After rushing past, they continued along the edge of the lake, leaping, biting, bumping, and splashing water.

"They seem to enjoy each other," observed August.

"Dogs are exceedingly social," said Skylar. "At least they were before we bred them out of their packs and into our homes. Nevertheless, the older responses often come back when they're together."

"Spoken like a confirmed animal lover," August said.

"You're not?"

"Oh, I am, I am, though I'm a little out of practice. A long time ago I even had a pet bat."

"Aren't they repositories of viral contagions?"

"Their immune systems are less prone to inflammation, and for that reason they don't react to many of the same viruses we do, but my mother made sure my pet and I were safely inoculated against each other. I kept him for years."

"People who don't like animals seem only half human to me. Say, what did you think of Chopra Scarborough?"

"Well, to use a phrase my father occasionally employs, she's something."

"Everyone likes Chopie."

"Everyone?"

"It's the safest response. She's not someone to get on the wrong end of."

"No, I don't suppose. Charisma usually comes with teeth. What can you tell me about her husband?"

"Dennis is universally disliked, and he seems to go out of his way to cultivate additional contempt. Everyone avoids him when he's here—which is seldom—and he lets Chopie handle most of the public relationships. Sort of like a skunk sending out a mink."

"Very colloquial. Are you from around here?"

"Not really, but I've picked up some rural jargon from my partner, Janet. She grew up on a northern Wisconsin farm. Now, she's CEO of an agricultural concern in St. Louis and I'm the bored little wife in the vacation home."

"I see," said August, wondering in what way "little" could refer to someone taller than himself, then deciding that the outmoded "little wife" had been used for its ironic relief, not literal comparison of physical sizes. "Where are you originally from?" he asked, watching the rushing chaos of the dogs heading back toward them.

"Originally?"

"You know, before you came to the Gate."

"I lived most of my life out east, mostly in New York."

"Then you're a long ways from home."

"Not really. I always felt like a stranger, even in my own family. The only real home I've ever known is Janet."

"Nicely put. I'm envious."

Skylar watched the dogs roughhousing, and said, "I understand you grew up somewhere around here before you went into biochem."

"That's right."

"Must not have been very easy for you."

"Why do you say that?"

"I mean, making the transition. It seems like a very rough area here—the local people."

"In what way?"

"Sorry if I offended you. Maybe it's the pervasive poverty, and I'll admit I'm getting a little more used to it after the many times I've driven through it. Months ago I even stopped in a local grocery store in one of the small towns. It wasn't quite as bad as I imagined it might be from the security index mapping on Safe Stopping, where much of this surrounding area is listed PWC—proceed with caution. But the little store was fairly clean, and the people were actually nice, in their own way. I mean, nothing really went wrong except some inappropriate language, overcharging at checkout, and bagging my produce in the wrong sacks. But frankly I don't like being stared at, or worrying if someone will key my car in the lot, or jump me for not smiling politely at a crude remark. Janet sometimes wonders if we should have moved here—built this place, I mean. She worries about our car breaking down on these winding roads and she always makes sure to gas up before she enters the area so we won't have to stop. She's talking about buying a small aircraft. About half the Gaters have them. What do you think?"

"I'm the wrong person to ask."

"Why?"

"I cherish this region and I've only flown once in my life."

"That doesn't disqualify you from having an opinion."

"Like I said, I grew up not far from here and I frankly can't imagine being afraid of the area, though I suppose it would be different if you had no experience with the people. Like everywhere else, what you expect from them influences the way they respond to you."

"Sure, but expectations run both ways, and people in rural, insular communities seldom meet overly tall, gray-haired lesbians looking for esoteric salad ingredients, and it's anybody's guess how they might react to encountering one."

"Point taken," said August. "But I don't think lesbians are rare in rural communities; I suspect the fear on both sides is more a factor of disparities in wealth. Having a lot of disposable income is more uncommon around here than tall lesbians wanting the fixings for a tasty tossed salad. Problems between people come from not understanding the rules the others play by. In my case, I grew up in a place where loyalty and general acceptance of most people in the neighborhood was taken for granted, and I went to a place where loyalty and acceptance were conditional and expensive. It was a trade I made in exchange for aquiring the skills I wanted, but it was still a trade."

The dogs had expended their social exuberance and lay down next to each other near the water's edge, licking the fragrant lake water from their lower extremities.

"They seem content," observed August.

"Strenuous exercise relieves some of the complex tensions that canines experience living in a confined human environment. That's one of the reasons it's important they have their playtime."

August looked toward the Lux house in the distance and saw lights burning inside two windows. His pulse rate increased. There were no lights on when he left.

"I'd better be going," he said, nervously.

"Will you bring Hannah back tomorrow?"

"Sure. What time did April usually come?"

"In the morning, around ten o'clock?"

"If possible, I'll be here."

"Missy and I will look for you."

August turned toward the distant burning windows again, hesitated, and spoke awkwardly. "Before going, may I ask you several rather untoward questions?"

"You may, but I might not answer."

"How long have you known April Lux?"

"About three years."

"What do you think of her?"

"She's a responsible dog owner."

"That's not what I mean."

"You'll have to be more specific, August. I have many thoughts about April."

"Is she trustworthy?"

"I believe Hannah trusts her, and that's important because a dog's life is structured through its owners' routines; the more orderly, the better. I noticed right away that April understood Missy—the first time they met—and recognized her unique features and appreciated her complex personality. Far too many people, I'm afraid, do not really care anything about dogs; rather, they like owning them, and those they don't own, they have no interest in."

"Do you believe April would make a trustworthy friend?"

"What kind of friend?"

"A friend in love with her."

"The rules for normal civility don't apply to people in love."

"Trust extends between you and Janet?"

"Of course, but we've been together a long time. Why do you keep staring off across the lake? Are you worried about something, August?"

"No, no, not really, but I should be going. It's been most wonderful meeting you and Missy and I look forward to seeing both of you tomorrow."

"Why the interest in April's trustworthiness?"

"I have high interest in the subject."

"Trust?"

"No, April. Look, I really must go back now. A house sitter shouldn't be away for very long. I'll see you again tomorrow."

"Until then."

SHAMPOO

AFTER WALKING BACK, August looked through several windows, hoping to catch a glimpse of whoever might be inside. Then he checked inside the garage before entering the house, wondering if Tom and April's car might be there.

It wasn't, and he poured some dry food in the dog bowl. While Hannah ate, he punched numbers into the security pad and went inside.

He walked down the hall and into the entryway. Above, light from the second-floor library spilled onto the landing. Climbing up, he stopped frequently to listen. After entering the empty room, August noticed that the spotting scope on the table-mounted swing arm had been moved. There were no other signs of recent occupancy, and after looking through the adjacent rooms, he returned to the ground floor.

Running water could be heard in the kitchen, and he went there. The room was mostly dark, but August saw the outline of someone sitting at the table. He found the light and turned it on.

"You're back," said Ivan, standing up. His hair and beard were uncombed, and he was dressed in the same coveralls and denim jacket August had last seen him in.

"Ivan. What are you doing here?"

"Thought I'd better come over and make sure you were all right. Hanh apparently talked to your mother, and she told me you were here."

"How'd you get though security?"

"I pestered Hanh until she showed me the way."

"Is she here?"

"No, she had things to do."

"I saw the house's lights from across the lake," said August, still trying to adjust to Ivan's presence.

"I turned them on to get your attention. I probably shouldn't stay too long."

"How'd you get inside the house?"

"I know a guy who installs security systems. These high-end units come in three different wiring schemes, he says. The one on this house can be disarmed by holding a cow magnet to the right side of the pad when you enter a code—any five-digit number with two sixes will work."

"Did anyone see you?"

"Of course not."

"I'm not supposed to have anyone else here."

"You want me to leave?"

"No. I'm glad you're here. This day has been strange. There's so much I need to talk about, but let's see if we can find something to eat first. I'm starving."

The refrigerator had nothing inside it but juice, fruit, and lettuce, but the upright freezer held a glacial bonanza, including choice cuts of Kobe beef, two-pound tubs of North Sea brown shrimp, a slab of unsliced bacon, truffles, a holiday-sized turkey, seven quail, and several large Chinook.

"Let's go with the fish," said Ivan. "Do you have any idea how much these would cost in a restaurant or store, if you could find them? These red beauties will soon belong in museums. And shrooms, of course, we have to have some of those. Too bad my grandfather isn't here. He'd go wild."

"There's a bag of Kennebecs under the island sink."

"Let's bake, since we have to broil the fish anyway. And we'll need pepper, salt, garlic, parsley, sage, thyme, lemon, or lime. Orange peel will work too. Pickles would also be good, and a little mayonnaise wouldn't hurt, and a cheese topping for the potatoes."

"I'll thaw out one of these fish and build a fruit salad," said August.

"Whoa, they have saffron," said Ivan, rifling through the spice cabinet.

In less than an hour, they were eating at the kitchen table and drinking wine from a bottle found in the pantry.

"When did you come over today?" asked Ivan.

"Around one o'clock—that's when they left."

"Who?"

"April Lux and her brother Tom."

"Tell me about them."

"Not much to tell."

"How old are they?"

"She's our age, or a couple years younger. Tom's four or five years older, and he seems nice enough, but he's hard to read because he's wound pretty tight."

"How'd they end up with this swell place?"

"April's second husband gave it to her. Part of the divorce, I guess."

"How long were they married?"

"A couple years. Her first husband shot himself."

"I wonder where she got this salmon?"

"The Gate apparently has a gung-ho food service. A guy I met this afternoon said they provided rattlesnake for him."

"I thought eating rattlesnake was against the law."

"Apparently it isn't."

"People shouldn't eat snakes."

"Why?"

"They just shouldn't. Did the guards give you any trouble when you came in? You know, from the other day cutting wood?"

"No. I'm apparently in the inner circle now. One of them called me Doctor."

"Funny how working for the same folks makes everyone family. I suppose that's the great hope of capitalism: after there's only one company left, we'll all be wearing the same uniforms. What's this about being attracted to April?"

"I never said that."

"It was pretty obvious. I thought you weren't going to let that happen to you."

"It happened anyway."

"How?"

"I heard her voice, and then I saw her."

"That's it?"

"Yup."

"You're hopeless."

"I know it. I know it. And now we need to talk about Hanh."

Ivan hesitated for a moment. "Okay, but in order to do that we need something stronger to drink."

"There a bar in the upstairs library."

"Let's go, Doctor Gus."

August heard the Afghan scratching at the garage door, and he let her in.

"This is Hannah, Ivan, and Hannah, this is Ivan."

"Nice dog, narrow head, racing features," said Ivan.

In the upstairs library, they sat in chairs at the bay window. To see out, they turned off all the lights, and drank bourbon from heavy, cut glasses. Along the lane below, yard lamps spaced at regular intervals cast light cones through the gathered mist and onto the ground.

"So, what's been happening here?" asked Ivan.

"This woman came over today, hoping to settle a score with April for sleeping with her husband."

"What did you do?"

"I told her April wasn't here."

"What happened then?"

"She said she was afraid of living in poverty, and saw no difference between death and being poor. And this area around the Gate—where you live, and our parents raised us—it frightens her. And I get the impression it frightens many others here. They're apprehensive of the area and people like you and me."

"You mean like me, not you. I'm sure they like you well enough."

"They're anxious about the lower class, even if they grew up inside it."

"That's what wealth does to people," said Ivan.

"But people are people. The social rules should generally apply to everyone."

"But they don't, Gus. Marx spent most of his life trying to point this out. With enough money, you can change the rules."

"No, you can't. Rules are rules and laws are laws."

"What was this gal like—the one afraid of poverty?"

"Cute as a button, with enough charm to start forest fires."

"What's her husband like?"

"Never saw him. Apparently he's older and very unpopular around here."

"How'd he get her?"

"He bought her from an escort service in Thailand."

"*See.*"

"See what?"

"When you can buy beautiful women and handsome men then the unspoken social contract that governs the rest of us is broken in pieces. The rest of us—in order to have friends and attract lovers— have to actually be decent, likeable people, Otherwise, no one wants to be around us. But when you can buy friends and loves, then you can avoid the natural law. Unpopularity no longer means what it does for everyone else. Money does that."

"Interesting."

"Imagine you're a thief, coward, liar, or criminal. Those things usually turn everyone against you, Gus—everyone except other thieves, cowards, liars, and criminals. But with enough wealth people look up to you no matter what. They're envious of the money, and since it's your money, they envy you. The law gets turned inside out."

"Sounds like you've thought about this."

"Or say you're a weakling, easily intimidated. According to natural law, you carefully choose where you go and avoid threatening situations. But when you can buy stronger men, their strength is yours. Then, even when you're weak, you go wherever you want. You can bully others, smack them around, and people will fear you. When purchased, the power of others is yours. It's you. You have their strength. The laws the rest of us follow don't apply."

August smiled, enjoying the bourbon and company. It had always been this way with Ivan. Listening to him had a calming effect.

"And let's say you're naturally stupid, always unable to find the right words. Whatever ideas you have are selfish and shallow, and no one listens to you. Whenever you tell people what you think, you're laughed at. But when you can buy people smarter than you, their intelligence is yours. They lend grace to your unpopular opinions; they make your stupid thoughts seem reasonable; you can now proudly attend public meetings and forums, sit at the round table, and listen as your ambassadors talk for you. Their rhetorical skills resonate, and if they don't resonate you can spend a little more and hire more qualified people—people who demand the recognition of others, who seem to argue for truth, virtue and justice—no matter what they're talking about. I mean, they're still selfish and crass ideas, but the people speaking for you make them sound almost holy. And because they're being paid, most of your hired talkers believe they're advocating their own positions, which makes them seem even more sincere. When the voting comes, your proposals win out. Legislation is written to benefit you and people celebrate your cultural influence. With money, you've succeeded, and because the money is yours, you've done it yourself. You're desirable; you're strong; you're smart."

"What you say seems a little extreme," August said. "People may respect a liar or a coward because of his money, but they still know he's a lying coward. And someone might be able to buy an attractive woman or man, but only one that has already decided that they're for sale."

"You're wrong, Gus. And that gal you were talking to who fears being poor . . . she knows it. Whatever you can buy becomes you. Once someone gets accustomed to having nature's laws no longer apply to them, they're uneasy around ordinary people and afraid to live without the immunity that comes from wealth."

"I honestly don't mind people adapting to whatever conveniences they can afford," said August. "But why can't they remember who they used to be? This woman I talked to today, she survived slavery as a child, if you can imagine such horror. After that, you'd think nothing would ever frighten her, but she's afraid of the people in small towns around here."

"Hanh would say she's replaced one form of slavery with another."

"You and Hanh have talked about this?"

"Sure, when Hanh's in the right mood we talk about everything."

A silence slid into the room, and August banished it.

"Why didn't you tell me that you and Hanh, were, well, very close?"

"I tried."

"Well, you didn't try very hard."

The brooding silence annexed the darkness around them, and August again noted sexuality's intrusion into every aspect of his life.

"It was my fault," said Ivan. "I should never have left you two alone that night. I can see that now. But I needed to know if you and Hanh . . . well, I just needed to know."

"You should have told me. Really, you should have told me."

"I tried."

"Hanh loves you. I found that out."

"I hope so," replied Ivan, pouring another inch of bourbon into his glass. "We're good together, Hanh and I, though we both need a lot of personal space."

"I'm sorry, Ivan."

"Cripes, don't apologize, Gus. Never apologize. Whatever happened is between you and her. I won't deny it affects me; it does. But it's still between you and Hanh. I know you care for each other. God, I understand that better than anyone. I've loved you both since I was a little kid."

August felt like hugging him, but didn't. Instead, he revisited the brief memory of April Lux standing in the hallway, her hands on her hips. And the thrilled assurance returned—the promise that he'd found the answer to every question that could be asked. April Lux was the key to all the rooms he would ever need to unlock.

Ivan handed the bourbon to August and he poured.

"So, the time you worked on the pipeline," said August. "Anything else you want to tell me about that?"

Ivan walked to the dark window, touching the glass with his left hand, looking out.

August waited.

"Did someone say something to you?" Ivan asked.

"Yes."

Ivan turned away from the window and looked at August, then raised his gaze through the darkened room and into the indirect light on the landing.

"One night there was a party," he said, and stopped, as though those few words explained more than he intended to say—the way a single detail can rally all the other parts of the event to it. Ivan continued staring into the light in the hall, as though drawing strength from its framed luminosity, and he began again—this time from further back.

"There were over eight hundred people working on the pipeline, Gus, I mean if you counted everyone, and between twenty and thirty welders. Some had been with the company for years, were skilled at holding a reduction arc and accustomed to living on the road; they tended to hang out with the foremen and equipment operators. The rest of us were young, raw, and from all over. A few were like me—from rural areas where local economies had bottomed out. Some were escaping relationships that had gone bad, others hiding from collection agencies; several guys had families waiting by the mailbox for a piece of their paycheck; a couple of ex-servicemen hoped to find a permanent home inside an industry nearly as regimented as the military; six men had been recruited from Middle Eastern oil regions and promised citizenship tracks; three substance abusers were bravely trying to stay clean; a few other guys never talked about themselves at all, and the rest of us assumed they were avoiding arrest. And there were two women welders, one from Little Rock, the other from Brazil.

"The foremen kept moving us around, assigning us different areas, and it didn't take long to become acquainted with all the welders. There were a few dustups, but for the most part everyone found a way to get along.

"After working for a year and a half we got used to having a party when a new pumping station had been completed. These celebrations weren't much more than streamed-in movies and heavy drinking, followed by a day off, but they were popular. On this particular night, about half the local crew showed up to watch a sci-fi movie in 3D with plenty of pornography. We ate popcorn and salted peanuts and drank alcohol.

"The next morning in the cafeteria, someone said the two women welders had not returned to their trailer. They went off-site sometime in the evening, taking one of the R-Corp runabouts. We were in the middle of British Columbia at the time, with no towns of any size within fifty miles, so we wondered where they had gone. Most of the local people in the area had been against building the pipeline, and there was some low-level hostility toward pipeline workers, even when we spent money in the small towns.

"Then someone came in, dished up some breakfast, complained about the cold eggs and hard toast and reported that a runabout had been found near the equipment shed. Several of us went to check, but it wasn't the one they'd taken out.

"Early that afternoon, I borrowed a four-wheeler from one of the foremen and went out to explore the surrounding forest. I kept to the trails, and then went overland toward the river—miles away from camp. Coming down into a deep valley, I crossed some tracks recently made by a heavy vehicle and followed them. I guess I wasn't paying enough attention, because I hit a rock and was thrown over the handlebars, busting the front axle and spraining my ankle. There was no phone service, of course. Abandoning the four-wheeler, I limped toward the river, hoping I wouldn't have to follow it all the way back before someone came along, but the chances of that were slim.

"With the help of a makeshift crutch, I hobbled about a mile when I smelled smoke. I went toward it, thinking there might be a house or cabin nearby. The underbrush grew thicker and thicker—the kind of gloomy weeds that grow in shade—and then I stepped into a small clearing with two oaks and some large, leafy bushes near the center. Smoke was coming from the other side of the trees and as I approached, I saw two corpses on the ground. Both women were naked and mutilated, with missing fingers and breasts. There was blood all over them and their mouths were taped."

"Jesus, Ivan."

"Quiet, Gus. Let me finish this. There was a shovel a little way from the disfigured bodies, a freshly dug hole, and a fire on the other side of a hawthorn bush. I couldn't turn away, as though looking at those corpses long enough would somehow tell me why this happened. Or maybe I just wanted to return to the world I lived in before walking into the clearing, and since the sight of them had taken me out of that world, I thought maybe they could take me back. My mind was dead and I felt sick, numb.

"Then I heard a noise, it grew louder and resembled talking, and out of nowhere two men stepped from the surrounding forest. I recognized both. They were Bret Logan and Slack Peters, R-Corp roustabouts who set up and tear down the temporary camps along the pipeline, and sometimes operate machinery. They had just showered and changed clothes somewhere. Their hair was still wet. At first, they didn't notice me, and I suppose for that reason I'm alive today. From where they were, I was mostly behind the hawthorn bush. If they'd seen me right off, it would have been all over. They were both powerful men—each with about thirty pounds on me. And I couldn't run because of my ankle. On equal terms, against either one of them I didn't stand much of a chance. Against both, well, it didn't look good. They tossed their bloodied clothes and shoes into the fire and watched the flames working into the stained fabric. Slack laughed at something Bret said and poked the fire with a long stick. They continued talking. We were separated by about ten or twelve yards, and they still hadn't seen me. They kept talking, and at one point they turned away and handed a pint bottle back and forth.

"Right or wrong, I placed all my faith in a police training manual I once read. It said deliberate actions were always quicker than reflexes, even though it seemed counter-intuitive. I grabbed the shovel and went at them. Bret's reaction was a little slow after he saw me, and he caught the shovel blade in the side of his neck. He went down, fighting to stop the blood flow. By then, Slack had his knife out and came at me. We circled each other and my left hand and both arms were soon bleeding like leaking faucets. I threw a shovelful of coals from the fire at him, and he lunged at the wrong time and caught the spade point in his left eye. He grabbed his eye and fell. Then I jabbed him again and both he and Bret bled out."

Ivan's voice was shaking, and August stood up and went toward him.

"No, let me finish," said Ivan, pushing August away. "I need to say it all."

August sat back down.

"I found their pickup and drove it back to the base camp. The foremen called in heavyweights. After the medics had bandaged my arms and hands and put an ice wrap on my ankle, three company executives, a security expert, and two lawyers helicoptered in. We all drove out to the clearing, which turned out to be only a couple hundred yards from a nature trail where the women's runabout was parked. The lawyers recorded everything I told them, took pictures, made measurements, put the shovel in a bag, wrote things down, and talked a lot on the company phones in the SUVs. This time, looking at the corpses, I did throw up. One of the older lawyers took me aside and explained how thankful the company was. R-Corp women had disappeared before, he said.

"'This has happened before?' I asked in disbelief.

"'Three times in the last five years,' they answered. 'We didn't know who was doing it. Once, they didn't even attempt to bury the bodies.'

"The lawyers explained how my part was over. I was a hero, they said. Everything would be taken care of. I'd be protected, my name withheld. They'd move me to a different site with a better clinic, where I could see specialists, take a couple weeks off, heal my ankle. And I shouldn't talk about what happened, they said. The families, of course, would be notified.

"'How about the authorities?' I asked.

"'We'll take care of that,' said the security expert. 'R-Corp has a much better forensic department than any of the local law enforcement branches. We'll take care of everything. If anyone other than Bret Logan and Slack Peters were here, or knew about this, we'll find them. You've been through enough, Ivan. You're a hero now, and you don't deserve to be harassed by incompetent officials or media fools wanting to know how you feel.'

"'You're going to cover it up,' I said.

"The older lawyer stepped in closer. 'Mr. Bookchester, if these were your sisters, daughters, or wives, would you rather hear they'd died like this, or that they perished—instantly—in an equipment accident? If state agencies become involved, the insurance remunerations to the families will be challenged, possibly with success. They won't receive a dime.'

"We then went back to the base camp, and I was sent from one work site to the next without any specific assignment, and I never lit another torch. After a month, they paid out my contract, plus a termination bonus, with an additional bonus for signing noncompetition and nondisparagement agreements, which meant I wasn't to talk about the circumstances of leaving the company—ever. Then they put me on a plane in Vancouver, and I headed home."

August stood up again. "Those men were monsters, Ivan."

"It doesn't help to call them that, Gus. And I'm not finished with what I have to tell you. There's something I left out."

His voice changed slightly, and he now spoke as though his words were escaping from a trap. "When I was behind the hawthorn bush as the two men were tossing their bloodied clothes in the fire, I could

sometimes hear what they were saying. They were discussing shampoo. They had just washed their hair and one man was saying how the
shampoo he'd used was going to dry out his scalp and leave his hair
unmanageable. His hair would lie flat, he said, and not look right. The
other man dismissed the complaint. He liked the shampoo and enjoyed
its fruity smell, and he named two other brands that were also good for
oily hair. Sometimes, he said, you could find them on sale."

"Good God," said August.

"I know it. Some nights I wake up and remember every word. After
those guys finished what they'd been doing, they *talked about shampoo.*
Doesn't that pretty much cancel out even the smallest possibility that in
some hidden corner of the human soul there might be a small, redemp-
tive value? I mean, how can any kindness or man-made discovery or
lifetime achievement ever make up for those two guys talking about
buying shampoo on sale? It's a stain on us that won't ever come clean—
all of us. How can you explain it?"

"There's no explaining it."

"How can it be true, Gus? How can something so awful occur?
How can people who look like us, talk like us, dress like us, move like
us, eat the same foods we do . . . how can they do something like that?"

"I don't know. I doubt if horror ever makes sense."

"But isn't there a reason for everything—even if we don't know
what it is? There has to be. At the most fundamental level we're nothing
but a gazillion little energy strings lurching from one adjacent quantum
space to another, so doesn't that mean if you could understand everything, put it all together, it would explain even talking about shampoo?"

"Nothing will ever adequately explain it," August said. "Most
men—not all, but most—are born with a latent desire for women, a
time-release urge to be involved with them in some way. Yet prior to
birth, there's always the possibility that radiation-induced mutagenesis
will randomly alter the genetic encoding for future desire, and as desire
bio-mechanisms mature, stochastic disruptions in endocrine expression
and early neuronal imprinting will sometimes warp the expression of
the normative sexual impulse. And sometimes the environment itself
will switch off the genes responsible for serotonin production, with dev-
astating consequences for socialization. All it really takes is a single

differently edited gene to radically change hormone exposure. Lowered stimulus-response thresholds in a few critical areas can alter perception patterns and influence behavior."

"It shouldn't be humanly possible for anyone—at any time and for whatever reason—to do the things those men did."

"I'm really sorry for what happened to you. I am. But sources of potential deviation are innumerable, and we'll always have abnormal people among us, especially since normal is biologically meaningless. Our form of sexual reproduction ensures genetic indeterminacy. We imagine humans as consistent across the board, but we aren't. There are significant differences between individuals."

"I killed them both, Gus. And the second one . . . he looked up at me . . . I could have let him live. Instead, I jabbed him with the shovel again. I could have let him live."

"Good you didn't, I say."

"Shit, Gus. There's nothing good about any of this."

"Maybe not. Playing a frontline role in natural selection is more responsibility than most of us can accept. I'm just sorry it was you."

They were both quiet.

"Look at it this way," suggested August. "If I'd stumbled into that clearing instead of you, I'd be dead and those two guys would be looking for more victims. On some very basic level you were the right person in the right place at the right time, doing the right thing."

"I've wanted to tell someone for a long time. I really hope you don't mind me unloading all this on you."

"You should have told me as soon as I got here—first thing."

"I wanted to, but I didn't know, well, I didn't know for sure if you were really still you."

August stood up and they hugged until they became uncomfortable, and then they poured more whiskey.

"Have you ever heard of NK cells?" asked August.

"No. Why?"

"NK cells are cytotoxic lymphocytes—part of our immune system. They detect foreign bacteria, diseases, and harmful toxins. And they eliminate them. All other immunizing agents, or macrophages, rely on antigens displayed on the surface of infected cells to trigger a response.

Not NKs. They sense certain kinds of tumors and infections without antigen signaling. It makes NKs fast-acting, indispensable in maintaining healthy organisms."

"What does NK stand for?"

"Natural killers. They've evolved to eliminate whatever becomes corrupted. Just think of yourself as part of a wider social immune system, an effector cell—ones that actually make the corrective changes that—"

"I get the point, Gus. I get it. And I'm glad I told you. It feels better to have someone else know."

"Well, I can't say it's good to know, but I'm honored you told me, and I'm honored to be your friend."

"Damn, Gus, I'm glad you came back."

Lights flashed across the darkened window outside. A vehicle moved slowly over the rise, its headlights tunneling through the fog. The twin beams followed the curving lane toward the house. After a short distance, they stopped moving.

Then the headlights shut off.

"Someone's sitting out there in the dark," said Ivan.

"Maybe security," suggested August.

"I'll go check."

"No, I'll go. You're not supposed to be here, remember."

"Oh, right."

August went downstairs. He checked the time: 11:45.

When he opened the front door, Hannah squeezed through first.

INSECTS

AUGUST WALKED UP the drive. The fecund smell of the lake prowled through the misty air—the sweetened edge of rottenness. He could not make out the vehicle parked in the distance. The night tightened around him, and Hannah grew impatient with his slow pace. She ran ahead, disappearing into the fog. August wondered about calling her back, then decided against it.

He thought about the torment that Ivan had carried inside him after stumbling into the clearing in British Columbia—his hopeless search for answers to the problem of evil. People of conscience had been staring into that blinding irrationality from time immemorial. As Lester Mortal once said, "Human history is an ever-widening path of terror." Despite universal anthems to the sanctity of human existence and the many wonders of the bipedal ape, crimes against humanity filled the Book of Life from its preface onward. As soon as the first ancestral female with a sufficiently wide pelvis began giving birth to offspring with thirty-percent larger skulls filled with bumpy lobes of ganglia, her brainy children began professing the highest moral principles while cutting each other's throats. The bigbrainers anointed themselves Earth's rulers with the divine ability to understand the same natural forces out of which their own existence had miraculously sprung, and at once began destroying that divine spark in each other. And while they often pretended to know nothing of their own bestiality, in truth, they celebrated it. When awakened by an unidentified sound in the night, the sapient imagination did not instinctually envision poisonous snakes, bears, tigers, or other wild creatures. Rather, the imagined horrors were pictured in the form of fellow men.

Man's chief predator was Man.

August listened to the sound of the soles of his shoes on the lane and wondered if his species would survive much longer. The so-called higher brain's irrepressible tendency to impose idiosyncratic beliefs onto an otherwise objective world perhaps erected a bridge too far for long-term survival. Images, emotions, and sensations associated with actual occurrences could be dialed in merely through iterative thought; while this greatly enhanced the ability to picture the future and prepare for contingencies, it also allowed for more sinister calculations. In the human mind, there seemed no way to prevent the same biochemical machinery that fueled the urge to understand the basic principles of life from also providing secretarial services to the desire for power.

August gradually became aware of the sound of other footsteps.

His senses quickened.

About fifty yards away, a male figure walked into the illumination of a fog-filled light cone. Slight in build, nearly attenuated, the stranger moved in a relaxed and shambling manner, his hands shoved inside loose-fitting pants pockets. The Afghan walked closely beside him, from time to time looking up, as though to affirm something between them. After ten or twelve steps, the figure and the dog both moved out of the light and were again swallowed by the milky mist.

Convinced he'd never seen the man before, August continued ahead.

They met in the middle of the next light cone.

"Hello," August said. "May I help you?"

The man seemed about fifteen years older than August, maybe more. His bespoke coat and trousers were a muted gray, reserved yet stylish, and he had brown, tousled hair. He stroked Hannah along her back and sides, and the Afghan leaned affectionately against his leg.

"Probably not," he said, his smiling manner denying the mist's somber authority. "Thanks for asking, though. Who are you?"

"August Helm. I'm looking after April's place while she's away."

"Excellent. Then let me apologize, August, for not calling ahead. I'm Doug Rothmore, April's former husband. I was in the area and needed to pick up some things at the house."

The older man spoke as though he had treasured August's company for a long time.

"So, you parked a quarter mile away?"

Doug laughed. "I admit I wanted to avoid notice—slip inside the house, find what I needed, and quietly leave without disturbing anyone. It's late."

"April didn't know you were coming?"

"No, she didn't. How is she?"

"What do you mean?"

"I hope she's in good health. I assume you're a friend of hers."

"Yes, well, I hope to be someday . . . a friend, that is . . . I only recently met her through my mother, who manages the gardens here."

"Oh, so you're the garden lady's son?" he replied warmly, as though some vital connection had been established between them.

The title of "garden lady's son" took August by surprise, and he hardly recognized himself inside of it. He paused. "I don't usually think of my mother—or myself for that matter—in those terms."

"No offense, August. Really. I'm a firm admirer of your mother."

"I'm glad to hear that. I suppose it's not really demeaning to refer to someone by a recognized skill or occupation, though when it's your mother it's only natural, I think, to be a little sensitive and—"

"I completely understand. I should have said I'm a devoted fan of Winnie Helm and have the highest regard for her many talents. She's immeasurably enhanced the loveliness of this place, and for years has been a consistent blessing to April."

"Thanks. I'll tell her you said so."

His companion's easy confidence implied a truly adventurous spirit, August thought, as well as an expensive education, and privilege running so deep and wide that the gilded edges of aristocratic arrogance had long ago been sloughed off.

They walked toward the house, the dog in between them, the surrounding mist isolating them from the wider environment.

"How long's April been away?"

"She left this morning with her brother."

"When's she coming back?"

"Frankly, I don't really know."

"Where'd they go?"

"Don't know that either. And there's no way to find out. The numbers they left aren't functional."

"Have other people been looking for her?"

"You could say that."

"I see."

"What? What do you see?" August asked.

"April has a magnetic, almost capturing personality, as I'm sure you've noticed. Her brother Tom tries to protect her, and from time to time they escape into anonymity together. I suppose you might say she's sought after so much she's forced into hiding."

"Why is that?"

"I don't know."

"I thought you were married to her."

"That doesn't mean I understood the secrets of her extraordinary likeability."

"Where'd you first meet her?"

"I saw her across the room at a fundraiser in Boulder, Colorado. She'd planned the event. The entertainment and cuisine perfectly suited the cause. I thought she was simply delightful."

"You thought she was delightful?"

"Yes, isn't that what I just said?"

"I guess it is. Sorry. I'm just trying to understand her as well as I can. What do you mean by delightful?"

"I mean what others mean when they use the term. She seemed unusually talented, personable, and intelligent. The way she brought different people together and engaged them in meaningful ways, well, it impressed me a lot. I remember at one point early in the event, someone challenged her proposal to sponsor grassroots, educational projects for young girls in sub-Saharan African countries. A rather large, bearded man with a deep, authoritative voice said that educating girls in third world countries was both labor intensive and enormously expensive, and not the most effective way to combat the gender discrimination found in rural areas. Studies proved, he said, that simply placing televisions in the homes of rural villagers, and letting the young women watch soap operas while their husbands were at work, inspired women to the same levels of independent thinking as providing them with a costly education, and it was less disruptive to community life."

"How did she respond?"

"Her amicable tone never changed. She smiled, thanked the man for adding to the discussion, and praised the two researchers who had first studied the status of young women in developing countries before and after the introduction of daytime television. April even referred to the scholars by their first names and celebrated their creative method-ology. She then pointed out that inspiring poor, isolated women toward greater independence through the idolization of television celebrities had little practical value in securing them brighter, healthier, and more satisfying futures. Fantasizing about a different life may offer a welcome escape from oppressive circumstances, she said, but knowing how to read, write a letter, make change, process information, avoid transmit-ted diseases, fill out government forms, locate inoculation centers, make a budget, open a bank account, read a map, and teach other women these skills was revolutionary. 'And we're here tonight,' said April, 'not only to encourage our sisters to dream, but to climb out of bed in the morning with the skills needed to solve the real problems in their lives.'"

"Sounds pretty persuasive," said August.

"The applause was deafening, and the fund drive far exceeded expectations. I do remember wondering—a couple days later—whether the man challenging her had been planted."

"So, you weren't stunned by how appealing she was, I mean, physically?"

"I think I said she was attractive."

"Yes, but did you ever think, *I* simply *must have her?*"

"That seems a little vulgar, August, if you'll forgive me for saying so."

"Oh, I agree. But honestly, isn't that the problem we have, as men, I mean our instincts are, in themselves, unforgivable. Don't many, many women appear to us, rightly or wrongly, in the shape of our imagined pleasure? They seem like something to devour. I can't believe you're completely immune to those kinds of thoughts."

"No, not entirely. But . . . I changed."

"You changed?"

"I got older. Mostly April changed me—that's what I think."

"You divorced her."

"Staying married wouldn't have been fair to her."

"Why not?"

"Like I said, I changed."

"I'm not following this, I'm afraid," said August.

"Then once again, I apologize. I talk too freely, especially when I've been away from other people, as I have."

"Away?"

"Well, not exactly *away*—just away from people who talk about the kind of things must other people talk about. I joined a team of entomologists in South America. They're dedicated and talented, but most of them seldom talk, except about insects."

"What are they, and you, studying?"

"Right now, we're looking into *Wolbachia*."

"Bacteria in insects?"

"I see you're familiar with it."

"*Wolbachia* is one of the oldest reproductive parasites that we're currently aware of. The different strains of it are sometimes, though rarely, used to guesstimate genome age. And there's speculation that an early form of *Wolbachia* could possibly have served as a mitochondrial prototype."

"I'm glad you've heard of it. *Wolbachia* currently infects nearly fifty percent of insects worldwide and eighty percent of insects in tropical zones. Because invertebrates have no adaptive immune systems, they're defenseless against the newest mutations."

"Sounds like an epidemic," August said.

"Rising temperatures have created advantageous conditions for *Wolbachia*. In recent decades, we've lost thousands of insect species. Many of the remaining ones have been infected so long that when they're treated with antibiotics and freed of the bacteria, they don't survive. *Wolbachia* inhibits reproduction and feminizes offspring, but without it many insects no longer reproduce at all. The bacteria form a symbiosis with its host, and there are now several isolated insect species with no active male chromosomes at all. They're all female."

"That doesn't seem possible."

"It's happening. When the female ovum divides, during the second phase of meiosis, which is . . ."

"I know what meiosis is."

"As the gamete divides, the division is interrupted by the bacteria. The unfertilized ovum remains intact, with the two sets of chromosomes needed for conception."

"It still doesn't seem possible. Apomixis and parthenogenesis have been going in bees and aphids for a long time, but there are still males."

"I know, but some insects are now reproducing through *Wolbachia*-assisted female cloning. After hundreds of millions of years, nature is headed in a different direction. Females can clone because only females contribute both Y and X chromosomes to offspring."

"Those are your books in the libraries inside?"

"Yes. I'm here to pick up some notebooks I left behind. I've been fascinated by arthropods for as long as I can remember—since I was a child playing in our backyard in Texas. As you probably know, August, over half of all living things are insects—over half—and most of them have been around three thousand times longer than us. The bugs of today—their ancestors survived massive climate fluctuations, glaciers, drifting continents, changing atmospheric conditions, asteroid collisions, and centuries-long volcanic eruptions. We live on a settled planet of insects; humans are just recent interlopers."

"Point taken. I think everyone admires the fortitude and organization of insects."

"Perhaps, but I'm afraid much of the hardiness we attribute to invertebrates may have been misplaced. By even the most conservative estimates, we've lost over half of them—most in the last thirty years. Many losses are due to extinctions—species that can no longer be found anywhere. The majority, however, are from extirpations—local extinctions, where a certain beetle, for instance, that once thrived throughout a wide region, can only be found in isolated, confined areas. And the problem is compounded when you consider that insects are our most efficient processors of protein, which they covert from plant cells. Losing them endangers all protein-dependent birds, reptiles, and mammals, including us. And they're disappearing."

"A pity," said August.

"And the pity runs even deeper when you consider all the lost opportunities to learn from these creatures. For instance, the often-lauded organizational abilities of ants and bees: How can we ever hope to study them in a thorough and methodical manner when their populations are constantly threatened? Exposure to a single chemical irritant can completely alter the self-determining information channels that feed into complex group behaviors."

"I'm sure you're right."

"In the case of *Reticulitermes flavipes*—a species of termite—there are three differentiated castes: workers, soldiers, and reproductive agents. The relative size of each caste is regulated through changes in hormone production and hormone absorption rates, responding to changing environmental factors. So, when needed, more termite larva develop into workers than soldiers. Since our own species is splintering into groups that very much resemble castes, with different skills, work habits, diets, vocabulary, and energy consumption, you'd think it might be good to know how polyphenism works in termites. Can humans maintain caste-like distinctions and somehow avoid the violent reactions that some termite castes experience when they encounter members of another caste?"

"I think most people agree that insects are very important."

"Good, because if our estimation of life doesn't include them, it can't be a serious one. Take, for example, approach-avoidance reactions triggered by pheromones acting at a distance—developed in insects over millions and millions of years—without these reactions, we would not be able to consciously feel anything at all. The many dimensions of our current sentience were made possible by the work, and lives, of bugs."

"I thought you were an attorney."

"I was. My sister, brothers, and I represented the family firm in Dallas."

"No longer?"

"That kind of work ceased to appeal to me after I met April. It made no sense to keep living like that. Studying insects was all I ever really wanted to do."

"I don't imagine your family was very happy about your decision."

"That's an understatement. But I couldn't bear to keep spending all my daylight hours in a temperature-controlled building with eighty other office workers, and my family eventually accepted the choice I made. They didn't like it, but they accepted it. Perhaps it was easier for them to release me because I was the youngest—the most immune to the siren call of familial duty. Also, they were not unhappy to divide up my share of our grandfather's inheritance."

"You renounced your patrimony?"

"That sounds more high-minded than it was. The bequeathal never felt like it belonged to me in the first place. Other than being born, I'd done nothing to deserve it, and when I wanted to do something with my life that the family considered frivolous, even disloyal, it seemed reasonable to give the inheritance back, or at least most of it. Besides, I already had more than I needed."

"I understand you gave this house to April."

"You know a lot about me, August. How long did you say you'd been here?"

"I'll admit my first day has been something of a crash course."

"In any case, you are correct. I had the house built for April and I still believe it suits her. She loves this place and I always intended for her to have it. As for me, I wanted to spend most of my time outdoors studying insects. And besides, winters in Wisconsin are too cold."

"I still don't understand how you could leave April."

"Let me try to explain it in another way, if you'll hear me out."

"I certainly will."

"Imagine that tomorrow the postman delivers an official letter, instructing you to show up at a designated location for a physical examination prior to your induction into the army."

"That's implausible. Compulsory draft legislation would never be enacted in our current political climate."

"I'm only asking you to imagine it, August."

"Okay."

"After passing the physical exam, you're ordered to a training camp in Tennessee, and then sent to fight against rebels in the mountains of Peru."

"Why Peru?"

"You don't know why you've been sent to Peru—other than what the government tells you. You're just following orders."

"Okay."

"So, there you are, living with your combat unit in heavily forested mountains, perspiring, watching for snakes, sleeping poorly, keeping your eyes peeled for an enemy you know nothing about and couldn't speak to if you met, and trying to stay alive.

"Weeks and months go by and you begin to form relationships with some of the men and women in your battalion. You work, eat, sleep, drink, and dream together. Though none of you want to be living in Peru, or fighting rebels, you make the best of your situation and before long find yourself caring very much about the people in your unit. Their approval has value to you. As you learn more about their families, the trials they faced growing up, and the unique quirks that set them apart from other people, your fondness for them grows. A tribal bond forms, knitted together by shared fears, joys, longing, boredom, and sadness. You love them—not all of them, of course, but many. They're almost like family, and you'd do anything to protect them.

"And then your government makes a deal with the rebel forces. The dispute that precipitated the conflict is resolved. The war ends. Helicopters will soon arrive and fly you to an urban base, where you'll stay for a week and then go home. The option of staying with your new family—the people you've come to love—isn't available. Your government is no longer at war, and you are no longer needed. The question is: What do you do?"

"Do about what?"

"Those family-like relationships were by-products of being forced into doing something you didn't really want to do. You were drafted and sent to a remote location with others who also followed orders. It wasn't your choice to be there, but things happened, important things, the kinds of things that trigger the deepest levels of commitment. Then all of a sudden, you're freed to return to the life you were living before the government set you down in another country. So . . . what do you do?"

"I don't know. Go home? Isn't that what soldiers do?"

"That's my point."

"What point is that?"

"Choices. We think we make important decisions, but do we? We grow up in families we don't choose and adapt to situations and circumstances beyond our control. And then, on the basis of what we've inherited and learned to accept, we think we're free, self-determining agents."

"You could say the same thing about going away to college or moving to a different state or—"

"I know. That's what I'm trying to point out. Nearly every situation we find ourselves in has been, in one way or another, forced upon us. Our experiences rush at us; we don't invent them. Yet our lives still seem meaningful—at least most of the time."

"Are you saying you and April simply grew apart?"

"It would be more accurate to say the circumstances that drew us together changed, and we adapted to those changes. Does that make sense?"

"Not in the least."

"Then I again apologize. Why are the most important things always the hardest to explain?"

August thought Doug Rothmore was unlike anyone he'd ever met, making him impossible to understand. He appeared to have nothing to hide, nothing to gain from impressing August or anyone else, no agenda to protect, hide, or promote. There seemed no boundaries to their conversation because nothing would offend him, and he evinced a congenial emptiness that August had never encountered before.

Their walk through the mist was rapidly drawing to an end and the house loomed up in front of them.

"I hope you don't mind me asking this," said August, "but weren't you in love with April?"

"Oh, God, yes. You've met her, haven't you?"

"Of course."

"Then you surely understand how someone might love her. I still do and can't imagine ever not loving her. I'd do anything for her—anything."

"How can you bear to be away from her?"

"Like I said before, it wouldn't be fair to her. It wouldn't be fair to me either, but mostly to her. It's like I was saying: when the government ends the war you were drafted into, there's nothing left but to go home."

"I really don't understand."

"No, probably not. When you become better acquainted with April you'll comprehend more than I can ever tell you."

"Is it true her first husband committed suicide?"

"Sadly, yes, poor devil."

"What happened?"

"I guess he couldn't live with himself any longer."

"Why?"

"I doubt anyone knows why. Suicides present us with greater mysteries than murders, as far as I'm concerned. Unfortunate psycho-chemistry, I guess."

August opened the front door, and they went inside.

The Afghan came too, sticking close to Doug.

"You'd better stay here tonight." August said. "It's late."

"Thanks, but I have to leave after I find those notations."

"As you know, there's plenty of room, and it's after midnight. The fog could get heavier."

"I need to get back to O'Hare for a flight."

August accompanied him down the hallway and into the study where Doug opened drawers and rifled through cabinets.

"Can I at least make you a cup of coffee?" asked August.

"Sure, that would be nice."

In the kitchen, August assembled the machine and made coffee. A little later, he heard Doug on the stairs and August went into the entryway to watch him climb to the upper level and go inside April's bedroom, followed by the dog.

By the time he came down, the coffee was brewed and August had poured two cups.

"Did you find everything you needed?"

"I did, thank you."

"Like I said before, you're welcome to spend the night."

"No, I need to leave."

Doug's tired gaze wandered from place to place around the kitchen, and August wondered what it must seem like—to Doug—for a stranger to offer him a cup of coffee and an invitation to spend the night inside the house he'd built and lived in with April. He also wondered why Doug had gone into her bedroom.

After drinking the coffee, Doug shook hands with August, went out the front door, and ambled away from the house.

August prevented the dog from joining him by holding her collar. He stood in the doorway and watched his latest visitor's thin form disappear into the fog.

"Everything all right, Gus?" asked Ivan, materializing behind him, petting the dog.

"I guess so," said August.

"Who was that?"

"April's ex—the guy who built this house. He picked up some old notebooks."

"I smell coffee. Is there any left?"

"Plenty."

Sitting at the kitchen table, August asked Ivan why someone might say it wasn't fair to stay married to someone else.

"Maybe he's gay or found someone he liked better."

"I don't think so," said August, staring into his coffee. "I've never met anyone like him."

"In what way?"

"He's empty . . . in a good way. It's like he found what he was look-ing for a long time ago and is now—well, he's just living."

"What do you make of that?"

"I don't know."

They drank coffee without talking. The compressor in the refriger-ator snapped on and the unidirectional sound of the humming motor filled the room with invisible vibrating cotton fiber.

"You never really told me about living in Chicago," Ivan said.

"I don't know what to say. Urban life changes you, but you end up not noticing how. Chicago's spread out. It's many places all tossed together. I don't know what to say."

"That's okay. Never mind. I'd better be getting back. I promised to help Nate and Beulah build a chicken run today."

"Thanks for coming over."

"I'll be back."

August walked with Ivan to the front door and watched him disap-pear into the fog, the same way Doug had.

Fighting the urge to call him back, August sat on the front step and put his arm around the Afghan. Beneath the soft, long fur, Hannah's breathing expanded and contracted her rib cage, and August wondered what it seemed like to her to have Doug—someone who had once been an integral part of her life—suddenly walk back into it and just as sud-denly leave again. How did animals cope with such inconstancy?

An unseen flock of birds flew overhead, their wings sounding like people in sweaters slapping their chests. When he could no longer hear them, August went inside.

He washed the coffee cups in the copper sink, dried them, put them away, and filled the coffee machine for tomorrow morning.

He checked the dog's bowl, where a layer of irregular pieces of dog food still covered the bottom.

The impulse to go upstairs and enter April's bedroom rose in his mind and was defeated by a quick rinsing of shame.

He went downstairs to lie down.

Before reaching the stairwell, however, he heard knocking on the front door.

WHITTLING

EARLIER THAT DAY, Hanh took Lester to meet with his doctor at the Grange Clinic, located on the edge of town in a single-level building with a steep staircase and a switchback wooden ramp leading up to the front door. Built for overflow from overcrowded rural hospitals, the heavily used facility looked older than it was. Lester avoided the steps and took the longer walk up the ramp.

They went in together, read wrinkled magazines in the cramped lobby, followed a nurse down a narrow hall and into a beige room frenetically lit by two florescent tubes.

Lester sat nearest the door in a new pair of denim overalls and a white shirt. As though preserving body heat, he crossed his legs and folded his arms. Hanh settled in next to him, her slender hips occupying about half the chair's seating area, the toes of her sneakers just reaching the floor.

When the doctor came in—a young, neatly bearded man with a pressed lab coat, holding a manila folder of lab reports—he sat on the stool, and swiveled to face them. From this low elevation he explained that Lester's recent test results had confirmed what earlier studies only suggested: liver cirrhosis, end-stage.

Partly due to the incongruity of a stranger informing him of something vitally important about *his own body*, and partly due to the nature of the information itself, an eternal moment opened up inside the sterile room.

"I see," said Lester, receiving the fatal news without uncrossing his legs or unfolding his arms. He looked at Hanh and smiled reassuringly.

The smile immediately began to haunt her, and after driving him home and settling him into his chair with a beta-blocking pill, a warm mug of milk, and an egg sandwich, it continued to vex her. Hours later, after returning to her own home and drinking three cups of tea half filled with bourbon, it began to melt her insides.

She woke up around midnight, thinking about it.

The doctor had waved the checkered flag at the end of Lester's life, and while staring into the face of his own immanent death, the old man's natural impulse had been to reassure her that everything was okay. He didn't want her to worry. Lester had given her a protective, loving smile, mirrored through hundreds of remembered smiles, back to the first time she'd seen it in the mountain forests of Vietnam.

Lester Helm had promised a dying army buddy—Hanh's grandfather, whom she had never met—to check on his son's family in Vietnam. When Lester finally made it over to the remote area, seven- or eight-year-old Hanh (she didn't know her exact age) was the only remaining member of the family. Her parents, grandmother, and most of the small mountain community had died years before.

After searching most of the day, Lester found Hanh living like a half-feral cat on the edges of the disease-ravaged village, begging for food, foraging, stealing, and sleeping wherever she could. As the surviving villagers explained, she didn't talk, but they were certain she understood Vietnamese and English. Her parents spoke both languages, as did her grandmother. A landmine, they explained, had carved out the scar running down her face and neck, detonated by another child walking through the field beside her.

Lester explained to Hanh that he was a friend of her grandfather's. He asked her to come with him to the United States. He'd take care of her, he said, and they would make a new life together. Sitting down, he carefully explained that his own life recently had dead-ended. Well, not exactly recently, but he'd recently noticed that it had, and he needed to start over. They would start over together—make a go of it. He'd stopped taking drugs and had mostly quit drinking, he said. He'd find them a little place of their own in the United States. Everything would be all right. A new day would dawn.

Young Hanh gawped at him from a safe distance away and didn't trust him. People lied. And though all people were different, those who hurt you used the same language as those who did not. From their talking you couldn't tell them apart. So she didn't believe anything Lester said. Why would a stranger help you—just because he had served in an army with her grandfather? It didn't make sense. Only blood could be trusted, and even then you'd better be careful. Everyone, now or later, wanted something you didn't want to give.

Day after day, Lester came to visit at her shelter of branches, bark, and tin beside the drainage canal. Some mornings he brought rice, dried fish, fruit, and other foods, and on other days he brought carbonated drinks, sandals, clothes, insect netting, blankets, soap, an occasional chocolate bar, and trinkets.

He came the same time every day.

He moved and spoke slowly.

He never tried to come near her or touch her in any way.

The more he came, the less he talked, until there were hardly any words coming out of him. And this suited Hanh, who had abandoned talking altogether after walking through the abandoned field two years before, when her companion was blown into gelatinous pieces. Though the event had not injured her ability to talk, it had completely removed all motivation for doing so. When the person beside you could explode at any minute, what was the point?

Sometimes she would sit a comfortable distance away and watch Lester carve small animal figures from pieces of soft wood. He seemed to take great pleasure in doing this, whittling out monkeys, horses, dogs, cats, or cows. Once, he made a bear. When finished, he'd turn the figures over and over, concentrating like a jeweler, taking off a nip here and there; then he'd unpeel the thinnest blade from his knife and bore a hole through the body of the carving. He'd insert a length of leather string and tie a knot to hang from a limb. Then he'd leave it for her.

After watching this process for a week or more, Hanh became increasingly agitated when he neared the completion of a carving, until she finally rushed forward and snatched the fresh woodcarving out of his hands before he could make a hole in it.

Lester smiled, put the knife back in his pocket, and returned to the village.

Then he came the following day and began carving another.

He continued to smile in a reassuring way, and the more he smiled, the more he seemed to—possibly—convey something that couldn't lie, deceive, or corrupt. Something inside him seemed to know her, to believe in a part of her that she barely knew herself. By smiling, he communicated something immune to her insecurities—something that stayed still while everything around it lurched and quivered.

He patiently coaxed her to set her fears aside, to look beyond the primal directives: survive the moment, drink safe water, avoid injury and capture, and secure nutrition. The inducement to look away from these urgencies long enough to imagine a future of her own making could be found in Lester's smile. And it slowly drew her in.

She became increasingly familiar with his shape, movements, and smells. And she grew cautiously fond of his company, treasured the food and other presents and, over time, felt comforted by his presence. Her trust accumulated until she took a bigger risk and sat next to him while he carved.

That smile began to live inside her, even when he wasn't there. It served as the opening between her earlier and later life; it was the reason for accompanying him to the United States, and the most tangible explanation for everything else that came later. Whatever faith she eventually found in the world could be followed directly back to it. And while everyone must find her own path to escape along, she had found hers in Lester.

And a little more than two decades later, Hanh didn't know if she could live without that smile. Lester Mortal had found something in her to love and that had changed everything. He had been an avatar to her, even after his frailties had accumulated and his idiosyncratic habits had found ways to annoy her more than any other mammal on earth did.

And now he seemed even more unnatural, because it was surely beyond human to think of her in his own fiery moment of need—when his own death notice had just been pronounced by a doctor seated on a chair with wheels. No creature depending on water and oxygen should be able to do that, she thought. And while that kind of caring may indeed be the universal magic conjured out of proteins that August kept looking for in his textbooks and test tubes—the elusive, hard to identify, harder to understand, yet ever-present element-in-action that made all life possible—she had first experienced it through the frail form of Lester Mortal, and, for her, he was its source.

Of course, she had known for a long time that Lester was going to die. She'd been staring into that stop sign for most of her life. He was more than fifty years older than she. She'd seen it coming from a long way off, but she still wasn't prepared.

What would happen when he died? As his body decomposed in the ground, would his love feed the plants too?

As these thoughts continued to plague her, she knocked on the door where August was house-sitting.

When the door opened, she asked, "Where's Ivan?"

"He left fifteen minutes ago," said August.

Hanh walked into the house wearing a blue windbreaker. Inside, she took the hood down, shook her head as though clearing her thoughts, and paced around the entryway.

"So this is where you're staying," she said in a disinterested way.

Then she headed down the hallway, briefly turning on lights and looking into the rooms.

August followed her.

"Hanh, what is it?" he asked.

"Where's Ivan?"

"He went back home, I think."

She continued down the hall, through the entryway and into the kitchen. She stood next to the window, looking into the mist-filled backyard.

August stood beside her and remained quiet.

When distressed, Hanh didn't like to talk. She'd been like that for as long as he could remember; she often wanted company, but had neither the desire nor aptitude for discussing whatever troubled her.

Possibly because of his own inclination to talk ceaselessly about almost everything, August admired Hanh's approach to managing her psychological budget.

"I have something to show you," said August, and she followed him down into the basement bedroom with the underwater view into the lake.

He turned on the submerged lights so she could better see the fish.

Hanh moved near the glass wall, staring intently. Several varieties of aquatic life gathered in front of her, then drifted away and resumed their mindless floating about. After five or ten minutes she turned off the submerged light, sat on the nearest bed, and continued watching the shadowy shapes.

"Fish never sleep," said August, sitting beside her. "At least that's what many people believe. They're cold-blooded. Even when they're dormant, their brains never register the deep rhythms we associate with regenerative sleep, which makes them perfect for guarding over our unconsciousness."

Hanh turned to him. "August, can you please leave me alone? And is it okay if I rest here a little while?"

"Sure, sure. No problem. If you need anything I'll be upstairs."

August walked to the door and watched Hanh curl up on the bed, facing the glass.

Upstairs, he walked aimlessly in and out of rooms on the first floor. What he should think about wasn't clear, and he felt like someone in need of the unknown.

He wished he knew what was upsetting Hanh, but if someone doesn't tell you what's wrong, how can you know? That's what language was for. Bees and other insects danced to communicate vital data, but humans used speech, and until they did information could not be shared.

Taking a walk along the lake seemed like a good idea, but when he went outdoors he met Ivan walking toward him out of the fog.

"Is Hanh here?" he asked.

"She's sleeping in the basement," said August.

"How is she?"

"Agitated."

"When I couldn't find her at home, I checked with Lester. He said she'd taken him to a doctor's appointment that afternoon. When I asked him about his test results, he shrugged and said they weren't important because he'd already lived longer than he should, and I thought Hanh might have come over here."

Downstairs, Hanh had heard the front door close and come upstairs.

Ivan walked over to her. She looked at him and tears filled her eyes.

Ivan put his arms around her, and she did not resist him.

"Come on," he said. "That old goat will live at least another ten years. He isn't even a hundred yet. His body has mended more broken bones, sloughed off more toxic chemicals, healed more bullet holes, survived more terrible food, and digested more cheap beer than science would ever believe. And he'll outlive anything a doctor might tell him—if for no other reason than to prove the science wrong. Come on, let's get you back home."

"Where were you?" asked Hanh. "I was looking for you."

"And I was looking for you. Come on, let's take you home."

"Let me get my coat," she said. "I left it downstairs."

After she went down, Ivan explained to August that Lester would worry until she returned.

"Of course."

"Say, Gus, could I take that last salmon in the freezer? I forgot about it earlier. You have no idea how much my grandfather would like that fish."

"Sure, take it," said August.

"Thanks. I'll tell him it's from you."

After Ivan disappeared into the mist with Hanh and the frozen Chinook, August returned to the basement bedroom.

Crawling into bed and turning out the lights, he stared at the murky shapes moving behind the glass. Recollections drifted in and out of his mind and he clutched the thin thread of memory until it snapped.

Before tonight, he'd never seen Hanh cry.

CARJACKING

AUGUST WOKE UP in the middle of the night and became acquainted with an impression of someone else in the house. The adjoining space seemed occupied by another member of his species, and his suspicion seemed corroborated by the dead silence.

While dressing, he wondered how such an intuition was possible. Perhaps it had something to do with what Doug Rothmore had said about the evolution of pheromones in insects. Perhaps he'd inhaled an ectohormone and it triggered an emotional twinge in his brain—not strong enough to register as an odor, yet enough to give him a notion of unease. It seemed a reasonable theory. Animals and other social creatures used pheromones to mark territorial boundaries and warn others away, and such a signal might indeed be experienced as a wary sensation concerning the immediate area.

Thinking further into the problem, the subject of chemically induced preconscious notions flowered into several related possibilities: Encountering random pheromones could also explain frequently changing moods. You could be thinking about one thing and then inhale an emotion-inducing molecule, sending your thoughts flying off in completely different directions.

He climbed the staircase.

Upstairs, everything seemed exceptionally dark and quiet until phone prompts sounded in every room of the house.

"Hello," he answered, speaking into the empty air. "This is the residence of April Lux, August Helm speaking."

"August, it's April. Could you come pick me up?"

"Sure. Where are you?"

"Where am I?" she whispered to an unknown listener, followed by muffled talking.

"I'm in a little town named Luster, August. Do you know where it is?"

"Of course. It's less than an hour away."

"Good. I'm inside a lovely little home on Main Street, on the edge of a grocery store parking lot, and it's—"

August could hear more off-line talking, then April's voice returned.

"Sorry, I made a mistake. I guess it's not a grocery store—not anymore. The family who owned it for seventeen years sold it last spring to another family, and now, in addition to groceries, they also sell garden supplies, second-hand clothing, and used furniture." There was more indistinct talking off-line. "And jewelry," she added. "They also sell locally made jewelry. Look, August, can you come right away? The house is on the main street, you can't miss it." More indistinct talking. "And the store also sells fishing supplies, and bait. Please come quickly. It's the last place on the block and there is a porch in front with a light on. The number is 423. I apologize about the late hour, and I really hope I didn't wake you."

"I'll be right over."

On the road to Luster, the mist from earlier had mostly dispersed, except in valleys. He drove at the upper edge of the posted speed limit. The downcast headlights of his mother's car did not illuminate very far ahead—opening up new vistas of visibility only briefly before rushing into them.

His heart, he noticed, beat faster than usual.

A small herd of deer stood in an open field, and when his headlights swept past them their eyes glowed greenish yellow.

The town of Luster was small, empty and sparsely lit, with several hundred houses haphazardly positioned around a tight cluster of stores guarded by towering grain bins.

Soon after driving into the village and turning west, he saw a house on the edge of a parking lot appear, a yellow bug-light throwing porch-post shadows into the road. All the other houses and buildings he could see were dark, the traffic nonexistent.

August parked on the street and walked up onto the porch, the old, spongy boards rubbery under his shoes.

Looking through the window in the unpainted front door, he could see into a small living room of faded furniture and beyond to an even smaller kitchen, where an older couple in housecoats sat on wooden chairs at a wooden table. They both leaned forward, talking, laughing, moving their hands, and never looking away from the other end of the table, blocked from August's view. Seized by the moment's momentum, they seemed desperate to explain and entertain.

August rapped on the windowpane. The couple turned without interest toward the sound and went back to talking and gesturing even more earnestly.

August knocked again and the couple stood up from the table. Then April Lux walked from behind the section of wall hiding her from August's view, her movements hesitant yet alert, like a fawn moving into a clearing. Her presence seemed magnified by her self-consciousness, and the couple in housecoats hovered close to her as she walked toward the door. The woman carried a plate of cake wedges and urged her to take one.

Seeing her again set loose the same cascade of neural attraction that August had experienced when he'd seen her the first time. The distinctive configuration of light rays bouncing off her and striking his retina excited every positive reaction his endocrine system could provide, riveting his attention all the way down to microcellular levels. And though this rapid escalation of impending desire was strictly taking place inside him and nowhere else—without any intention or even awareness on her part—August couldn't keep from attributing all his feelings for April to April. She and she alone made him feel this way. He categorically discounted the millions of years of gene selection, mutation, and ancestral mating preferences that had gone into providing him with a general outline of what to look for, as well as the thirty years in which his formative experiences had predisposed his centers of perception to value certain physiognomies, grooming styles, and attitudes in women, but no, as far as his conscious life was concerned, his instincts were unquestionable, and even if he'd wanted to question them, what interior faculty could be depended upon to conduct the interrogation? He was the end product of millions of years of evolution and several decades of environmental influences, and within the first instant of seeing her, the matter was settled. April Lux was the most valuable female on the planet and any observer who didn't agree with him simply wasn't seeing her correctly. And he could feel his brain making a memory, time-binding the moment to carry with him for the rest of his life.

April drew her dark blue coat together in front. Reaching into her pockets, she drew out a pair of wool gloves, slid her hands into them, shook her head to refuse another piece of cake, blushed and smiled ambitiously.

August could feel her discomfort. There was no easy way to graciously leave the company of people who wanted you to stay.

Neither the old man or woman moved to open the door, so August turned the knob and pushed it in. As soon as the space opened, April stepped onto the porch beside him.

"Thank you again," she said, turning back to the couple in housecoats. "Thanks for taking me in. You've been unexpectedly kind. And thanks for the cake."

"You're more than welcome, little lady," said the man. "Come again, anytime. Come again, anytime."

"Come again, anytime," echoed the woman. "Come again."

August and April walked to the car. April slid into the passenger's seat and pulled the door closed.

"Where's your brother?" he asked, climbing behind the wheel.

"In Milwaukee with friends. They're going up north for a week of hockey matches. I hope I didn't wake you up."

"You didn't. How did you get here? Where's your car?"

"Some teenagers stole it."

"What?"

"I decided to come back home. I have no interest in hockey and after I left my brother, traveling didn't appeal to me. I took the scenic route and actually enjoyed the drive. Not far from here a young woman was walking along the road, no older than sixteen, I'd say. She waved and I pulled over to pick her up. She only had a short way to go, she said, and directed me to make a few out-of-the-way turns. She wanted to be let out in front of what looked like an abandoned house. As soon as I stopped, however, two young men jumped from behind trees, waving weapons and yelling at me to get out of the car. One of them stood in front of the hood, pointing his weapon through the windshield. They kept yelling and yelling and wouldn't stop. "Get out of the car, lady. Get out of the car. Get out of the car."

"What did you do?"

"I told them I'd drive them anywhere they wanted to go, but that taking my car was an extremely bad idea. They wouldn't listen and just kept yelling and pointing their weapons in my face."

"What kind of weapons?"

"You know, guns—revolvers with loaded cylinders that go around when the hammers are cocked. What difference does it make what kind of weapons they were? I couldn't reason with them. Maybe they'd been drinking or taking drugs, I don't know. They were nearly incoherent."

"So, they took your car?"

"I tried to talk them out of it, but they wouldn't listen."

"What did you do?"

"I got out of the car and the three of them drove away in it—with my phone and handbag, not to mention luggage in the trunk. Then I walked into town, which took quite a while, and looked for a light burning somewhere. When I found one, I knocked on the front door. Mrs. Hastert had apparently gotten out of bed to find something to settle her stomach, and she invited me in. Then her husband George got up and they fed me milk and cake and told me all about themselves. Apparently, they don't get a lot of company."

"Did you ask them to call the police?"

"I didn't want to alarm them. I mean, it's their neighborhood, so I made up a story about going for a walk and getting lost in an unfamiliar area."

"Should we call the police now?"

"That's not necessary. All my cars have security systems. My brother insists on that. If the weight and movements of the driver don't match the pre-sets, GPS signals are relayed to the nearest patrol stations. Also, the tank was getting low. If they stop for gas the engine won't start again and the doors will lock."

"For someone who was just carjacked, you don't seem that upset."

"This has happened before. The cars are always returned. Insurance pays for any damages. I just wish I'd talked them out of it. Years of unnecessary grief for themselves could have been avoided by simply changing their minds, and it's partly my fault. I keep buying the kind of cars that other people want to drive."

Inside the house, the man and woman peered out of the front door, watching them.

"We better leave. Take me home."

August drove out of town.

They rode for several miles without talking. April stared at shapes flashing through the dark landscape. August tried to drive in a calm and professional manner as he experienced rising anxiety. April's presence was having a catalytic effect on his endocrine system, and his emotions hurried forward without any concern for his overall well-being.

"Your ex stopped by," he said.

"Doug?"

"He left a couple hours ago. Charming fellow."

"What did he want?"

"Notebooks. He apologized for not calling ahead. Said he didn't want to disturb anyone."

"He came for his bug books?"

"Yes."

"Was he alone?"

"Yes."

"How was he? I mean, how did he seem?"

"Healthy and in good humor. I tried to talk him into staying the night, but he didn't want to miss his flight."

"He was never good about calling ahead."

"Why's that?"

"Just the way he is. His agendas never really include anyone else."

"Apparently, they don't even include his family anymore."

"What do you mean?"

"He said he left the family business in Texas and never looked back."

"Doug told you that?"

"Isn't it true?"

"Yes, though I'm a little surprised he told you. I've always hoped I didn't have too much to do with that."

"Why would you have?"

April drew away from the window, and August could feel her studying him with the intensity of a psychic sun.

"I met Doug at a fundraiser—well, several fundraisers, actually. We kept running into each other, and before long his family invited me onto the board of a charity foundation sponsored through their business."

"They must have thought highly of your abilities."

"I guess so. I'd been putting together fundraisers for five or six years by then. They wanted me to work full-time for their foundation, offering grants and low-interest loans to small, eco-friendly companies."

"Did you?"

"Yes, but after several months I began to question if there was adequate separation between the family business and the charity."

"What do you mean?"

"The foundation raised money from other sources, but it never seemed entirely independent from the firm. Funds seemed to flow both ways. When I pointed this out, Doug was sure I was mistaken."

"I assume you weren't."

"I'd worked with many NGOs and learned to distrust high administrative costs and out-of-house accounting. Doug said he'd look into it, and when he confronted his brother and sister—well, I understand they weren't happy."

"What happened?"

"I never knew. Doug and I were married by then and I simply resigned my position on the board and went back to freelance fundraising. Six months later Doug resigned from his position in the firm, backed away from the family, and jumped with both feet into entomology, which had always been his first love."

"And he never told you the details?"

"No. Like I said, his agenda is always full."

August came to a stop sign and waited for a pair of headlights to clear the intersection from the right. After they did, brake lights came on. The patrol car swerved onto the right-hand shoulder of the highway, made a U-turn, and came back. With the car's overhead lights flashing, a tall, lean officer climbed out and walked over to the car, his long strides purposeful and quick.

August rolled down the window and fumbled for his billfold, but the officer continued around to the passenger's side.

"Sorry to hold you up, Ms. Lux," he said respectfully, leaning against the roof of the car with one arm and tipping his hat with the other. "I thought you'd want to know your vehicle has been recovered, along with your phone and handbag."

"Where?"

"In a Mauston gas station near the interstate, about an hour from here."

"What shape is it in?"

"Both side windows were smashed, but for the most part it looks pretty good. At least that's the report. The two young men inside were apprehended before they could climb through the broken glass."

"No one was hurt?"

"Not really. One of the boys got a little cut up, but nothing serious. The handguns under the seats were not loaded."

"I'm relieved, and I appreciate your letting me know."

"My pleasure," he said, still using the same deferential tone. "I can guarantee that those two won't be bothering anyone for a long time. They both have prior violations. Real troublemakers. There's some concern that one of the carjackers got away, however."

"Really?"

"The nozzle from the refueling hose was still sticking into the tank of your car. There must have been a third person working the pump while the other two waited inside."

"Did the attendant at the station see anyone else?"

"The pumps are fully automated."

"I see. Well, once again, I appreciate you letting me know."

"You're welcome, Ms. Lux, and where would you like the vehicle delivered?"

"There's a body shop in Grange," said April. "They've done work for me in the past and I'm sure they can replace the glass and fix anything else that was damaged. I'm afraid I don't remember the name of the owners though."

"Perhaps you mean Holt's Auto? They have the computers to work on those kinds of cars. Charles and Glen Holt."

"Yes, that's it."

"Fine. I'll see it's taken there and that someone leaves Charlie and Glen a note with your number on it. They'll send someone over with your luggage, bag, and phone."

"Thank you ever so much, Officer Jackson."

"My pleasure," he smiled, "And please call me Stanley." He tipped his hat again and went back to his patrol car.

August turned right and carefully drove along the highway.

April shifted in her seat, as though settling into a space that had been preordained for her to occupy.

"I told you they'd recover it," she said, the triumph relaxing her voice into slightly lower registers.

"How did that policeman know you were in this car?"

"Gate security probably told them I was not at home, and that my house sitter had recently left in his mother's car; also, I have a chip in my shoulder."

"A chip?"

"It was recommended, and my lawyers signed off on the idea. The police claimed they could better protect me this way."

"So, you're constantly under surveillance?"

"No, I can deactivate the chip whenever I want. In fact, I only turned it on after those kids jacked my car. I can nix the signal now if it makes you nervous."

"That's not necessary. Sounds pretty sophisticated."

"I suppose. It also monitors chem levels in the blood and reports spikes and other abnormalities to my phone."

August drove around a tight corner in the road, passed a slow-moving pickup truck carrying three old mattresses, and turned his high beams back on. A pair of animal eyes briefly glowed by the side of the road, and then disappeared.

"So, what other threats did you experience in the past?"

"I'd rather not talk about it."

"Okay, but why didn't you tell the officer about the other carjacker—the young woman you picked up? Wasn't she in the car with the others, and isn't it likely she was the one pumping gas?"

"Is that what you would have done—told him about her?"

"I don't know."

"Well, I didn't know what to say either. Perhaps she was coerced in some way. Isn't it enough that two kids will lose some of the best years of their lives for a very stupid mistake?"

August drove in silence. Of course, there was also the likelihood that the young woman had planned everything. Perhaps she'd coerced participation out of the two males with the promise of sex or the threat of refusing it in the future. The possibility couldn't be ruled out. As

August's philandering boss in Chicago had pointed out, the entire supply and demand system of economic exchange rested on the bedrock
of brokered sex—servicing a constantly renewing need. Sexual motivation could never be underestimated. Whether openly acknowledged
or not, the Law of Carnal Desire wrote itself into nearly every human
transaction. At least according to Dr. Grafton, better sex was the
inspiration behind the invention of money and the ever-hungry root of
most criminal activity, as well as good deeds. Even the existence of the
much-acclaimed freedom of will could only be explained by insisting
that free will benefitted successful reproduction more than a mindless
biological algorithm working toward the same end would.

August felt an unstable excitement growing inside him. April—by
simply breathing—was introducing a sublime urgency into his thoughts.
A psychological drawbridge lowered, allowing an army of agitated joys
inside. The way she talked, the way she thought, the way she moved, the
way she looked, the way she smelled, the way she held her hands in her
lap, her clothes. She had an unusual presence. Compelling mysteries
surrounded her.

She seemed both above him in position and beyond him in experience, and this greatly increased her appeal. These assets had also been
present in Amanda Clark in Chicago (though to a lesser degree), but
he'd dismissed them in deference to a naive belief in an essential, class-
less, egalitarian society. His more recent experiences had educated him,
and he now noticed every gilded thread, each gesture, noncommittal
smile, qualified statement, and sigh of entitled impatience that betrayed
feeling secure at the front of the line.

August felt like a lower element on the periodic table in contact
with a higher one. His core identity—the person he was and thought
himself to be—would be changed if the electron bonding between
them were allowed to go forward. She would alter him.

"I know what you're thinking," she said, staring out the window
again at fleeting shapes along the road.

"No, you don't."

"You think the girl I picked up along the road might have led the
younger men astray with her cunning, feminine ways."

"Seems unlikely, but, yes, it did occur to me."

"I could feel you thinking it."

"Okay, how does that work?"

"It's something most people would consider, given the conversation we'd just had. After I explained why I didn't tell the policeman about the girl, it's only natural to wonder about the opposite possibility."

"Did you know the policeman from before?"

"I think so. I don't remember. Why?"

"He wanted you to call him by his first name."

"True, but I'm afraid I've forgotten it already."

"Stanley."

"Of course, now I remember."

At the Gate entrance, August stopped and spoke through his open window to the two guards standing in front. They immediately noticed April and hurried around to the other side of the car, wanting to know about the carjacking. She assured them she had not been harmed and explained that her car had already been recovered. Repeated condolences were offered, along with comments condemning the regrettable lack of moral instruction provided for young people in schools, the absence of teacher-led prayer, and suggestions for how the local police might crack down harder on law-breaking.

"We also had a bit of excitement here," one of the guards said.

"In what way?" April asked.

"Oh, nothing to worry about. Earlier in the evening the new infrared field scanner picked up two temperature signatures that did not correspond to any of the owners or their guests. Two intruders had somehow found their way inside."

"Who were they?"

"We don't know. One was about one hundred ninety pounds, over six feet tall, and beside him moved a child or very small adult, under one hundred pounds."

"And you caught them?"

"No, but there was something curious about the larger figure: he carried a block of ice."

"Ice?"

"The readout showed a frozen oblong about two feet long under his right arm, the temperature of frozen water."

As AUGUST DROVE over the rise leading up to April's house, a light greeted him from out of the dark distance.

"Did you leave on an upstairs light?" April asked.

August couldn't remember anything other than his hasty departure.

"That's my bedroom," she said.

August parked in front of the house and April climbed out of the car and stared up at the lit window.

"Is someone inside?" she asked.

"I don't think so. Wait here. I'll go in and check."

"And if there's an intruder, what will you do that I couldn't do myself?"

"Okay, let's go in together."

"Nix that idea. This is why we have security guards. They have training."

"Surely that's not necessary. I'll go. It won't take long."

"I hate this."

"What?"

"Worrying about who might be in my own house."

"I'll look around and be right back."

August unlocked the front door, and as soon as it opened the Afghan ran outside and greeted April with bounding and barking. As though responding to a prearranged agreement with her pet, April clapped her hands and ran around in circles, calling the dog's name over and over, encouraging more barking and bounding.

Inside, August moved through the house, turning on lights, walking into rooms, looking in closets. He readied himself to act quickly if needed, but he also worried that he might find Ivan or Hanh, or both, and wondered how he would explain them to April.

Thankfully, he found no one, but the patio door off the kitchen was unlocked and slightly ajar, which he decided not to tell April about. Putting the concern out of his mind, he set the lock and went around to the front of the house.

She was no longer standing next to the car, and after a short while he found her and the dog walking along the edge of the lake.

"Coast is clear," he said. "Apparently your ex left the light on after briefly visiting your bedroom—which he did prior to leaving."

"Fine. Thanks for checking."

"Forget it."

They looked across the lake, where moonlight, and yard lights from the marina streaked over the surface of the water in long, wavering ribbons. The subtle, not-unpleasant smell of wet and rotting vegetation floated in the air, joined by several loud declarations of wildness by nearby whippoorwills.

"Let's go inside. You've had a long day."

"You don't need to look after me, August. I do that all by myself."

"Of course."

April buttoned the top button on her coat and sat down on a painted wooden bench. After hesitating for several minutes, and without asking permission, August sat beside her.

"I know I've only been gone one day," she said, "but did you at least have a chance to start the monograph you wanted to write?"

"Not exactly."

"Does that mean no?"

"I succeeded in thinking about the subject and narrowing the topic significantly, which was an important step."

"Tell me."

"It's not in the least bit interesting to someone who isn't already interested."

"Let me be the judge of that. I need something else racing around in my head to compete with the memory of those boys hollering and pointing guns in my face. So, go ahead, tell me."

"Okay." August shifted his position, careful to not actually move any closer or in any other way encroach upon what she might perceive as her personal space. He adjusted his voice to match what he imagined might be the sound of a confident yet modest speaker. "Imagine a human cell as a self-contained living organism that moves from place to place, communicates with other cells, expels toxins, absorbs oxygen and burns sugars to produce the energy needed to, at the appropriate times, make thousands of different proteins from genetically inherited instructions."

"I think I already know that much," said April.

"Hoped you might." Her comment seemed benign, signaling that she might be engaged with what he was saying, at least so far. Clearly, however, she did not wish to be lectured or to play a purely passive role.

He continued: "Imagine this cell's time of usefulness has ended. The organelles inside it are wearing out and beginning to compromise the local homeostasis. For the sake of the larger organism, the cell needs to self-destruct. To accomplish this, it must first synthesize the amino acids necessary to build proteins called cytokines, then release them into the extracellular environment, and later absorb the same cytokines through designated receptors on its surface. Then, after the cell's cytokines are drawn inside the cell—and only then—does the degradation and decomposition begin, leading to self-annihilation. This cellular action of sending out self-destruct instructions is called autocrine signaling."

"Fascinating."

"I'm glad you think so," August said, grateful for her quick, furtive look in his direction, and a smile that could not quite be seen but easily imagined in the dim light. An edge of psychic strength flexed inside him, renewing his courage. "I keep thinking about this and comparing it to our conscious lives, or at least to mine . . . and please try to overlook my unplanned leaps into universality. I invariably turn very small, personal thoughts into unwarranted generalizations. So, even though the cell manufactures cytokines internally—makes them from scratch, as my mother might say—it still must release them from its body so they can be experienced through external receptors on the cell's outer surface. It's analogous to our lives, or at least to mine: I keep looking for something outside me to make the impressions I want to feel inside."

"You're not thinking of self-destructing, I hope," she said.

"No, no, no, not at all, but it works in the same way. We don't believe anything unless is comes from outside us. Internal phenomenon is categorically undervalued. Take joy, for example. I want to be happy. Otherwise, my life seems pointless and I feel like a failure, a burden to my parents and friends, a waste of natural resources. I need to feel joy, but I want this happy feeling to come from something, or someone, other than myself, even though all that matters—as far as joy is concerned—are the biochemical processes taking place inside me and what they make available for other biochemical processes. Without those internal interactions nothing can be real to me or for me."

"I hope I'm not oversimplifying this, August, but aren't you simply saying you want something good to happen to you?"

The sound of his name in her mouth infused him with adrenaline. "Yes, that's where joy and happiness always seem to originate—out there. See, I already have all the chemistry needed for perfect bliss. The biomechanics are inside me, but it doesn't work without outside stimulation. I'm like a player piano waiting for something, or someone, to turn my cylinders and release the music. The exaltation we experience through the most glorious happenings we can possibly imagine—the best things we can ever hope to feel—must already be inside us, and if they're not there we'll never experience them."

Somewhere on the other side of the lake, a barn owl shrieked. Neither April nor August were familiar with the sound. And when the shriek was answered by a similar shriek from a different direction, they both assumed, in the privacy of their own thoughts, that some interspecies communication had taken place, but did not picture the communicators wearing either feathers or fur.

"When I was young," August continued, "I often wondered about Christian paradise—that transcendent region imagined to follow upon human death as a transactional reward for God-fearing behavior. It's something my mother frequently talked about, and between the ages of four and seven I devoted a lot of thought to the subject."

"And where did those thoughts lead you?" she asked.

"Well, even heaven would be humdrum if those individuals who had been saved by grace and blessed by going there didn't already have paradisiac responses built into them. I mean, beholding the face of God wouldn't be at all rapturous if you didn't already have an appropriately jubilant response just waiting to be triggered."

"So, our experiences are preordained by the specific concoction of chemical reactions that have been preset to go off inside us?"

"No, not the experiences themselves, no, but our responses to them are, and that's all that matters. Our responses are already here, fashioned and adapted through the lives of our ancestors. From the ground up, we're built to experience certain qualities in response to certain stimuli. We are powered by them like batteries power new toys."

"I imagine substance abusers understand this in some way," said April.

A shooting star streaked quickly through a small piece of clear sky, making no sound and leaving no impression.

"They may not understand it," said August, "but they clearly take an active role in tickling the responses they want out of their own bio-chemistry. They ingest agonists to induce their receptors to respond as though they were reacting to naturally occurring serotonin, dopamine, and other reward-enhancing neuroendocrine peptides. Such short-circuiting doesn't work in the long run, as we know, but at least addicts are trying to take responsibility for their own situations, in a somewhat irresponsible way. What makes these substances so insidious is their ability to induce the feeling of being loved—the prime elixir of life itself—in many of those who inject them. I suppose masturbation also qualifies as a solitary remedy to an organic tension primarily designed to lead us into relational experiences with other real people."

"Okay," April said. "Our bodies and minds evolved to qualitatively interact with the environment, seek protection, food, and perpetuate genes in the same way parasites live and regenerate within hosts, and consequently everything's interconnected and dependent upon a larger whole. What's wrong with that?"

"Nothing, I guess. I'm just telling you about the trap I keep walking into in my mind. And of course, there are people who aren't nearly as bothered about these biological snares as I am. My mother and father, for instance, and my friend Ivan—they aren't waiting around for something to come along and play their music. They fit in nicely with their surroundings, their environment. They're already complete, or least they seem that way to me, and compared to them I feel only half-finished. It's like attending a party where everyone else merrily dances to the invigorating rhythm provided by the band, and all I can do is wonder who invented the steps and what ultimate purpose they serve."

"You're looking at other people from the outside. On the inside we're all waiting for something, or someone, to fire our neurons in just the right way. Everyone instinctually knows, I think, that at any given moment we can only be as happy as our brains will allow. But what's wrong with just accepting that our instincts and sensations adequately represent both us and the world around us?"

"Adequately?"

"The sensations we receive give us a reasonable picture of the world, and the emotions we feel in response to them provide us with a fairly reliable history of the accumulated associations we've formed around those stimulations."

"But that's just another way of not seeing the trap I'm talking about—the one we can't avoid, and the one we spend our lives denying is even there."

April looked at the water at the edge of the lake and frowned.

"I'll try once again to describe it," said August, "and if I can't make you see what I'm talking about, then we'll simply go on to other things. A couple days ago I tried to explain this to Ivan, and he didn't get it either. I told him that our ancestors had circumscribed the lives we live for us. The things we want and the ways we go about obtaining them have been prescribed through genetically timed and chemically induced desires. What we often think of as endless possibilities stretching from cradle to grave are the narrow paths our progenitors made while plodding around inside the cages that they themselves had been bequeathed."

"What did he say?"

"He said our biological cages make it possible for us to have a life— any life—so we should just enjoy them and paint the bars whatever colors we want."

"Is it all right to disagree with both of you?" asked April.

"Of course."

"While it's important to know—deep down—that desires, instinctual reactions, dispositions, physical potentialities, and even longevity are inherited, it's more important to take responsibility for what we consciously do with them. It's willful ignorance to give feelings and inclinations the first and last word over our actions. It's like someone defending murder by saying, 'She made me mad,' or justifying war crimes by claiming, 'I followed orders.' Someone may be prone to experiencing fear, for instance, but how she decides to act is much more relevant in assessing her character. Yes, we inherit a sketchy template of emotional predispositions and are culturally indoctrinated into conventional ways of looking at the world. But we aren't compelled to accept either. And if this weren't true then a timid and sickly child like Theodore Roosevelt would never have become a formidable leader; women would never have obtained suffrage; the Shaker society could never have given up procreating; Quaker, Buddhist, Mennonite, and Amish societies could not shun violence. We are not entirely captive to the rough programming we're born with."

"I still don't think you can deny that we live in biological and cultural cages."

"Fine. All I'm saying is we do a lot more than paint bars. Sure, there are parameters that come with vertebrate living, but we participate in designing our own prisons. And the proof of this resides in human societies diverging in how they govern and are governed. In this particular society, we don't—at least at this time—physically restrain our girls before they reach puberty and surgically remove the prepuce from their clitoris, nor do we customarily perform any other number of genital mutilations that are practiced in some other societies. And I only cite that example because I will be compelled to address that topic at an upcoming teleconference. In fact, there are no areas of conscious behavior over which we do not exercise some freedom of thought and movement, and the choices we make, individually and collectively, directly influence and even prescribe the quality of both our individual and collective existences. So, whether the cage we're born to live in has an open door depends on how we build it. We all participate in making choices—every minute of every day, including now."

"Perhaps. But let's consider my mother, for instance—"

"Stop right there. I hope you're not going to start criticizing your parents. I really hate that."

"What do you mean?"

"Maybe I spoke too soon, but I keep noticing that once people get a chance to talk about themselves—which is what we're doing—many blame their mothers or fathers for something. I know people in their eighties and nineties who haven't forgiven or even tried to understand perceived parental injustices from their infancy. It peeves me—obsessing over the only parts of their lives that are impossible to change."

"I'm not criticizing my mother or father," August said, wondering why April made this accusation. He suddenly worried she might harbor some deep-seated instabilities herself, obsessions, or dangerous personality disorders. Of course the comment could also have been an associative leap, revealing her willingness to wander off into other unfenced conversational fields, but who could know? At the very least, a caution flag had been thrown in his mind.

"Well, good," she said.

"And I agree with you, mostly. Parents come in for a lot of unnecessary condemnation. How was your childhood?"

"Just fine. And yours?"

"Yeah, me too—great childhood," he said, noticing with some regret that they had just shut the door on April's earlier life, a topic he was keen to investigate.

"I often wonder," said August, "how we can even think about the meaning of life when all we ever know with certainty is what feels good and what doesn't."

"Is that what you intend to write your paper about?"

A short distance away, a fish broke through the lake's surface in pursuit of a floating scrap of vegetation, making a small splash. The sound temporarily shattered the illusion of privacy surrounding them, and their attention swept outward. August noticed that his center of awareness quickly returned to their bench, while hers remained scanning distant perimeters, as though expecting, or seeking out, further disruptions.

"Just the transcription factors—a few of the molecular exchanges involved in signal transduction mechanisms," he said.

"You mean without any analogous comparisons to your own conscious experience?"

"Correct."

"Can I ask you something I've always wondered about?"

"Sure."

"In an evolutionary sense, how did what feels good get worked out?"

"What?"

"You were just saying that we're organized through the biological phenomenon inside us, and it conditions us to experience pleasure and pain and a whole greenhouse of other emotions in response to different stimuli. What I've always wondered is how all that got sorted out."

"Some people think there are only eight distinct emotional qualities originating in the amygdala. All the rest come from different combinations of the eight, like mixing loneliness with familiarity to yield nostalgia."

"You're not understanding me."

"Probably not, but please don't give up on me yet."

"Why does an apple taste like an apple?"

"Because it's an apple, I guess. It's all about ligands and receptors."

"But some apples taste really, really good. You take a bite, and along with tartness, crispness, sweetness, coolness, and juiciness, you get treated to a blast of indulgent satisfaction, an impression of goodness. 'Wow, that's a really good apple,' you think. What I'm asking is where that good part comes from."

"Joy and satisfaction come from the cerebral activity within pleasure centers. Through activating the reinforcement centers in the brain. When synapses cascade in those areas with the appropriate neurotransmitters, we feel good; when even more neurotransmitters are involved, we feel *even better.*"

"Come on, that's just playing games. Pointing at a location in the brain doesn't explain the mystery. It doesn't explain anything. What does increased blood flow, protein uptake, synapses, ion gradients, and receptor molecules have to do with feeling good? Are some specific molecules themselves good? Do *they* feel good when they transmit across synapses, and are they feeling good before they make the gap dash, or only during? I've thought about this question a lot, August. Why does feeling good feel good?"

Once again, he experienced a rush of joy at hearing her vocalize his name. He considered saying her name in response, fitting it into a sentence, but feared he could not pronounce it without his voice shaking.

"Then where does goodness come from?"

"It must come from our pleasure centers—beta-endorphins, serotonin, and dopamine."

"But how does feeling good come out of protein fragments? Chemical events are physical; emotions aren't. You can't see emotions or touch them or point to where they are."

"Yes, but emotions correlate—directly—with physical changes at specific locations. Nothing else makes sense. When people lose the reinforcement centers in their brains—which evolved to reward certain behavior—they lose pleasure."

The eastern horizon began to glow from the scattered light of an unseen sun. In response, a few random bird peeps, chirps, and twitters erupted unpredictably, from unknown places. The stochastic sounds increased as the milky light grew. August could hardly believe how much he enjoyed the conversation. She somehow understood his deepest thoughts and was able to dance with them.

"Of course," she said, "but how does something physical relate, or translate, into something nonphysical?"

"Sentience is epiphenomenal. Its causes are indirect and can't be predicted from the factors out of which it arises. It just happens."

"Well, *just* isn't just."

August laughed with abandon. "I love when someone exploits the meaning of simple words. It's like turning an orange inside out."

"So, you enjoy talking to me?" she asked, changing her position on the bench. She looked at him in a way that might be interpreted as coy, sisterly, cynical, flirtatious, or simply curious, depending upon which feeling was making the interpretation. He didn't know her well enough to intuit how she meant the question, and then he felt the tension relax between them, replaced by a new freedom, and he felt empowered to interpret her question however he wished. She had somehow granted him the liberty of thinking whatever he wanted about her intentions. A thin breath of acceptance passed between them and he experienced it like the first crack of light in locked basement.

"Yes, very much."

A pair of headlights moved along the distant shore, advancing slowly, and April's attention leaped toward it. As she watched she seemed increasingly agitated. He felt her draw together as she stood up, and she walked toward the house.

"I need to go in," she said.

August and the dog caught up to her.

"I know this didn't work out like I planned," she announced. "I was only gone for a day. I just couldn't bear the thought of sleeping in hotels or driving around any longer. I'll pay you the full amount, however, so there's no hard feelings."

"That isn't necessary. I'll just pack up my things and go. It's no problem. Besides, I've enjoyed getting to know you and meeting the people who stopped over here while you were gone."

"Do you mean Doug?"

"Yes, and the guy who put your lawnmower away for the winter, and the woman who replaced your furnace filters and caulked a slow leak in the upstairs window, an extremely handsome veterinarian who gave Hannah an injection, and the neighbor gathering signatures for a petition, and his wife and sister-in-law, and a woman with a bitter grievance."

"Tell me about that last one."

"She was an unforgettable person of rather indeterminate age. Her shortened name was Chopie. She lives on the other side of the lake in a stone home that looks very much like a small castle with a helipad on the roof."

"What did she want?"

"She wanted you to stop sleeping with her husband."

"What did you tell her?"

"I told her she was probably mistaken."

"What did she say?"

"She said she wasn't."

They walked the rest of the way in silence. Inside the house, the overhead lights seemed too harsh, clashing with the crepuscular semidarkness they'd become accustomed to. August closed the front door and the warmth of the house hugged him like an old friend. He realized he'd been cold for the last hour. April took off her coat, hung it in the closet, turned off the overheads and snapped on a small shaded lamp. He tried not to stare at her. She seemed like a freshly hatched butterfly without her coat— glowing in the soft light of the lamp.

"I'll just go down and get my stuff," he said, turning toward the stairway.

"Wait," April said. "I mean, if what you said earlier was true, that you don't have anything better to do . . . maybe you could stay the rest of the week. At least until my brother gets back." Traces of anxiety had entered her voice.

"Okay, maybe there's something I could help with."

"Do you do windows?"

"Windows?"

"Yes, they need to be washed."

"Sure, I do windows."

"Good. Last month the cleaning crew said they would no longer perform any tasks with ladders."

"I'm good with ladders up to maybe twenty feet."

"Then I'll see you in five or six hours, after we've both had some sleep. But before you go downstairs, can I ask you something?"

"Sure. Anything."

"And you'll answer honestly?"

"Of course. Why wouldn't I?"

"I can feel you want something from me, August. I felt it the first time I saw you, and I still feel it. What is it?"

He repeated the question, hoping it would re-present itself in a way that would be easier to answer: "What do I want from you?"

"Yes. What do you want from me?"

"I'd rather not say."

"Why not?"

"It doesn't show me in the best light."

"Just tell the truth."

"Right now, the truth seems compromising."

"You must tell me or we simply can't go on any further. You'll have to leave."

"I want as much of you as you'll let me have, April. And I want to know why you came back after only one day."

"Your mother often talked about you, and after meeting you, I was curious."

"What about your brother?"

"He really likes hockey. A lot."

DIVINE MADNESS

AFTER SAYING GOODNIGHT to April, August went downstairs
to the guest bedroom with the glass wall and visible, freshwater fish.
But after climbing into bed and closing his eyes, he discovered that
a blissfully frenzied disquiet continued to accelerate his breathing
and bolster his heartbeat. Falling asleep was out of the question. He
couldn't remember ever experiencing such lack of control over his own
ideation processes, and to tame the divine madness, he speculated about
where such dictatorial feelings might have first originated within the
long evolutionary story. How far back could compulsive fixations on a
single individual of the same species be traced? Although he enjoyed
only a casual familiarity with evolutionary biology, he felt confident in
assuming that his ambition to always be near April—his desire to trade
his solitary existence for a lifetime of shared experiences with her—
was a relatively modern development and could only be understood by
his most recent progenitors, whose bodies had synthesized the specific
peptides that made loving focus possible.

Of course, some of the more generalized emotions he experienced concerning April were no doubt available in the prehistorical
world as well, and August's long-ago ancestors would, he acknowledged, have immediately understood the raw physical attraction she
induced in him. That part had existed for millions and millions of
years. Sentient creatures of all kinds and at many stages of maturity
could surely relate to the limbic layers of his affective attraction—
those most deeply wired primal impulses. Creatures with separate
male and female gametes had been experiencing urges to integrate
their gametes ever since sexual reproduction had branched away from
the asexual habits of plants and fungi.

But plant, insect, fish, snake, frog, and herd sex generally did not
allow for a great deal of discrimination between procreating partners, he speculated, and millions of generations of relatively mindless genetic experimentation had no doubt played out before gan-
glion capacity increased enough to make conscious, selective choices

possible. Organisms simply mated—thoughtlessly—with whoever came along with the appropriate equipment. Eventually, however, individual hominids (female, according to the most recent archeological evidence that August knew about) became aware of their own sexuality and sought out (or held out for) the most appealing partners before engaging. During estrous cycles, they became choosy about their partners. Males competed for their attention, naturally, and due to the competition—over time—relative male body-size increased. The largest and strongest males invariably established mating rules in their own favor, and the social practices relating to them became more formalized, ritualistic—even compulsory. And when estrous cycles evolved into menstrual cycles, and having sex became an every-waking-moment concern to males rather than having their mating impulses called into existence by sporadically appearing, arousal-inducing pheromones, social accommodations became even more consciously centered around reproduction. For that reason, most early human communities were organized through hierarchies of power, with the males collecting as many women as they could afford and defend.

But with larger populations and more complex social structures, these winner-take-all systems began to break down, and within many societies monogamy, or pair bonding, proved as beneficial to the survival of human offspring as it had among many other species of mammals and birds. And accompanying these evolutionary changes, the neuroendocrine proteins responsible for human mothers bonding with their children gradually migrated into the relationships between mating couples themselves. Males discovered as many endearing features in their mating partners as mothers found in their children, and affectionate attraction became a prominent component of the reproductive process, and an equally important factor in community organization and offspring rearing. And the divine madness inspired in August by April found its vertiginous origins here.

August then decided that when he told April that everything about her appealed to him, what he really meant to convey to her was that his internal production of oxytocin and other genetically inherited, socially

bonding neuropeptides increased in response to the unique visual stimulation he experienced from the way she looked and moved; in addition,
his olfactory responses to how she smelled, and the auditory sensations
he received from hearing her voice ricocheted though the limbic layers
of gray matter and stimulated his endocrine system; and finally, the
resemblances shared by her chosen vocal expressions and his own way
of speaking completed the circle of chemically bonded assurances of
future good fortune. And the more his cellular responses delighted
in her, the more the frequency and potency of his cerebral pleasures
increased, creating a positive feedback loop. The more he saw of her,
the more he liked her.

Somewhere near the end of these ruminations, August fell asleep.

The following morning, he made coffee and toast in the kitchen
and waited for April to come downstairs. When she did, he poured
the caffeine and buttered the toast and told her that on the previous
day he'd committed to meeting a neighbor named Skylar for a canine
playdate at ten o'clock—about an hour from then.

April smiled sleepily and said she'd like to come along, but only
after having more coffee and another piece of toast. "Skylar," she said,
refilling her cup, "has made housing, feeding, grooming, and exercising
her pet into a performing art."

"Yes, she's serious about her responsibilities," agreed August,
dropping more slices of bread into the toaster. He was relieved that
the mutual closeness they'd established on the previous night had not
evaporated during their brief absence from each other, and though
direct eye contact still proved a little too challenging to prolong, for
the most part, they quickly recovered a similar plateau of timid comfort and tentative trust.

After breakfast, April hurried upstairs to change and returned
wearing ironed denim pants, a hand-knitted brown sweater with
corded designs running along the sleeves, and bright-yellow canvas
high-tops.

They left the house with the Afghan and walked along the lake.

The sun burned out of a clear blue sky and seemed to be system-
atically melting the blueness of space into the lake. August left his
jacket unzipped in front, and April did not bother to take her gloves

out. On the end of the leash, Hannah strained forward, yanking on April's outstretched arm. Several cars moved slowly along the road above them, headed in opposite directions. August wished he could watch April more directly—stare at her as she walked beside him. Her proportions seemed to change in his mind whenever he wasn't looking directly at her.

Following an abrupt change in the direction of her interest, Hannah lunged to the other side of the paved path to investigate an aroma near the water's edge, and in response April switched the leash to her other hand.

"I can take her if you like," said August.

"No, I've got her."

Hannah slowly exhausted her curiosity in the odors and continued.

In the far distance, Skylar and her dog, Missy, came into view. April waved.

Skylar waved back and made several exaggerated, dance-like movements.

"Should we let Hannah off-leash so she can run to meet them?" asked August.

April shook her head. "Skylar decides when to turn them loose."

"Why her?"

"It's just the way we usually do it."

The wind shifted, and the ruffled surface of the lake assumed a more granular appearance. He decided against asking any more questions. A tightly organized flock of small birds raced toward a pine tree and completely vanished among the blue-gray needles.

April added, "Skylar has a better feeling for our security personnel—a more instinctive understanding for when it's acceptable to ignore the leash ordinance."

The Afghan looked up, saw Skylar and her dog for the first time, and lunged ahead, pulling against the leash.

"Heel," said April, and the narrow, long-haired dog immediately fell to walking just behind and to her side.

"I was wondering," said August. "The other night when Doug came for his notebooks, it seemed that Hannah and he . . . I just wondered if maybe she was his dog—first . . . and then yours."

"You're right. Doug brought her into our relationship and, later, left her with me. Did he say something about Hannah?"

"No, it was just an impression I had."

Ahead of them, Skylar stopped walking and let her dog off the leash.

April responded by releasing Hannah. The dogs covered the distance between them within seconds; they play-fought and smelled each other until their owners reached them, and then—like the night before—ran along the edge of the lake, snapping and snarling.

The three *Homo sapiens* greeted each other less demonstratively, with brief, formal hugs, fleeting eye contact, and small, intentional smiles.

Skylar's lined denim jacket covered the upper half of her one-piece baize jumpsuit while two-tone, low-cut duck boots housed her feet. In the direct sunlight, August noticed her abundant hair was not the gray it had appeared in last night's moonlight, but rather a blonde so pale it might even look white under most lighting conditions. She was also younger than he'd assumed—by at least five years.

Skylar seemed relieved that April had come, and August also guessed—by the way the two women greeted each other—that April had changed clothes in anticipation of what Skylar might wear. Standing together, they looked like a page out of a three-year-old outdoor clothing catalogue, and August momentarily wondered how important they were to each other.

April said she needed to participate in an afternoon conference call and should be home within an hour to prepare for it. Skylar set the alarm on her wristwatch.

In the distance, a tight cluster of six joggers in bright, formfitting clothes ran steadily toward them from the marina side of the lake. To remove the dogs from the temptation of badgering them, Skylar drew a thin metal whistle out of her coat, silently blew into it, and began walking up the grassy slope leading to the upper hiking trails. Hannah, Missy, April, and August followed.

At the summit of the first hill, while the dogs randomly chased squirrels up trees, Skylar said she wanted to continue an earlier discussion that she and April had begun the week before. She invited August to join them on a painted bench overlooking the wooded ravine.

"If I remember," said April, "we were talking about the Consenting Adults concept and wondering how strictly the term should be interpreted."

"Excellent topic," said August, breathing greedily because of their recent uphill walking speed. "I imagine it depends on the context—whether you're in a rape trial or talking to someone on an adjacent barstool at closing time."

"The legal context doesn't interest me," said Skylar, folding her hands together on her lap. "Laws governing private behaviors vary, depending on the country or state. Even the existing statutes outlawing, say, incest between consenting first cousins, or sodomy, or adultery aren't usually enforced unless the prosecuting attorney has a political ax to grind. And like most other reasonably minded people, I think such laws obviously violate our innate freedom of association and expression."

"Okay, so what's left?"

"What's left is everything falling under the informal understanding of Consenting Adults—the agreement that supposedly takes place between grown-ups every time before they have sex—the mutual go-ahead pact that sanctions everything that comes later . . . that prevents one participant from later crying, 'I didn't agree to *that*.'"

"What Skylar was saying," explained April, "is that social contracts are assumed to exist every time people have licit sex. Because the contract is often unspoken, what happens when people later don't agree on what's consented to? I personally think the underlying issue is how to best minimize the risk of being blamed for bad sex."

"It surely depends on the situation," said August.

Skylar leaned forward and turned toward him. "Let's say the individual seated next to you on the barstool at closing time seems like a good candidate. You've seen them around. They're nice, relatively clean, and fun to be with. You're attracted to them, and they seem attracted to you. The chemistry is working. They dress well, have good teeth and a reasonable smile. You appreciate their sense of humor and they rarely laugh at their own jokes. They seem fairly well educated, and their world outlook matches up pretty well with your own. Assuming this is all you know about them, when they take that last swallow, put a tip down on the bar and ask if you'd like to come over to their apartment, should you go?"

"Definitely not," said August.

"What else would you need to know?" asked April, looking at him.

"Plenty. Is this person secretly married, or a member of a mob family? Are vaccinations up to date? Are other people waiting at the apartment? Hidden cameras? How about STDs?"

"But people can't reasonably expect to know that much about each other—not right away," complained Skylar. "It's a risk we usually take—in the beginning of a relationship especially. You have to assume important things will be revealed—voluntarily. If someone is married, or underage, or infected, or involved with jealous gangsters, or pornography, they should disclose this, and if they don't, they're in breach of the contract."

"But that's the point, isn't it?" said August, standing up.

The two dogs raced past him and headed downhill, running noisily through the thin covering of dry leaves.

"Outside of outright prostitution—where there really is a contract for services—there's always a risk. Even when you know the other person pretty well, it's hard to know what they—at any particular time— actually hope to get out of it. What is it they really want to do to you, or have done to them? I guess what I'm saying is if you don't know who you're about to have sex with almost as well as you know your immediate family members, with whom you should never have sex under any circumstances, then you shouldn't have it. Sex without absolute commitment invariably ends in distress."

"That's the conclusion Skylar and I reached the other day," said April, standing up on the bench so she could keep Hannah in view. "Having sex always involves an element of risk, including for couples who have been together for a long time. Bad sex is always possible, even when both partners are trying to avoid it. And for that reason it should only be chanced with someone, or some ones, you're loyal to."

August sat back down on the bench and zipped up the front of his jacket. "I suppose that's true," he agreed. "Whenever expectations are involved, there's always risk. Sexual disappointment, embarrassment, and distress are strangers to no one."

"I'm surprised you say that," said Skylar, leaning back on the bench, locking her fingers behind her head, and smiling in a superior way.

"Maybe I'm just prejudiced, but I never thought men had these problems. Don't guys always get off—even when your partner is frightened, drunk, or comatose? That's why the consenting part always falls on women . . . as well as the blame."

"You're right," laughed August. "That statement is not just prejudicial; it's misandrist."

"Stop it, you two." April sat down on the bench. "August has a point because consenting adults agree to accept some risk, and the risk is roughly proportional to how well you know the person you're sharing the risk with. And Skylar is correct in saying that—generally speaking—men shoulder less of the moral, ethical, and practical consequences associated with having sex, which is a way of saying they risk less."

Skylar's wristwatch made noises and she turned the alarm off. The three stood up from the bench and, after the silent whistle was blown, the two dogs at the bottom of the ravine raced toward them.

After scheduling a next visit with Skylar, April clipped Hannah onto her leash and she and August took the winding trail back to April's home. Soon, the dogs were out of sight of each other.

August and April walked without talking, listening to their feet scattering leaves. The sunshine falling among the bare trees printed shadow-limbs along the forest floor. Beams of glancing light lit up April's hair until it seemed to radiate amber. After about ten minutes, the roof of her house came into view, light bouncing off the solar panels. Beginning to walk downhill, August asked,

"Do you always talk about such challenging topics?"

"Not usually."

"Was today's subject for my benefit then?"

"I don't think so. If you like, I can give you my own interpretation."

"Please."

"Skylar's partner, Janet, comes home after a fortnight or more away in the city—like she did last night—and Sky, well, her thirst for an intense, even savage level of intimacy has been building, because she's mostly alone here, her days filled with routine chores. But Janet, she's exhausted, and her relational budget is maxed out; she wants low-key, domestic downtime."

"A prescription for frustration," said August.

"It's not that they don't love each other," continued April, "or that they're not equally committed. They're both acting in good faith; it's more a matter of poor timing. One of them wants a lot of something the other has only a little of to give. Sky doesn't want to talk about this directly, of course, but she's still upset and even a little distressed, and she talks around the edges of it. It's a compliment that she allowed you in."

"That's a generous way of looking at it."

"What other way is there?"

"Hey, I understand and even sympathize. She's frustrated and maybe even a little embittered because there's shame in being rebuffed for coming on too aggressively. She imagines resetting the scoreboard with someone she doesn't know—getting revenge. She insists chances need to be taken with people we don't know. She's playing the movie in her head—thinking it over. I get that. I'm just saying it's our responsibility to understand we're all in the same situation because nature put us here—men, women, and all genders in between."

"August, I'm just explaining why the conversation went in the direction it did."

"And I appreciate that, but it doesn't explain why you assumed such a defensive posture—trying to shut down the conversation before it could really open up. There is a whole lot more to be said on the subject."

"And you forget I'd already had this conversation with Sky. I was afraid you might encourage her to take chances, but when you didn't there wasn't any reason to continue. We both underlined the dangers of profligate behavior, which was the advice I thought she needed to hear."

That afternoon, August cleaned all the windows on the north and west sides of the house, and the following day he did the windows on the east and south, only encountering one mishap when he leaned too far out on the ladder and fell eight feet. Luckily, this happened lakeside and his fall was broken by four feet of water.

They shared meals catered in by the food service. Otherwise, April spent most of her days in her upstairs study with the door closed, following up with donor consultants, NGO representatives, and fellow fundraisers about a possible campaign to prevent female genital mutilation. Opinions openly collided on the subject, and many believed that even the best-intentioned efforts to reduce clitoridectomy, infibulation and other forms of clitoral cutting were doomed. Earlier campaigns had already succeeded—after long and expensive efforts—in outlawing the practices in a few targeted countries, but the laws were nearly impossible to enforce because the traditions and attitudes giving rise to the procedures persisted. Families carried them out, hoping to ensure the marriageability of their girls; in some cases, the girls themselves wanted to be cut because their friends had been. The crimes were performed by grandmothers and in some cases mothers—women who had been mutilated themselves at an early age. Currently, there were about three hundred million survivors of clitoral cutting, and almost all of them still believed in the need for such obscene measures, and eagerly participated in their continuation.

"Something should be done!" other conference participants loudly insisted. They advocated cash payments to families who refrained from maiming their daughters—verified through routine physical examinations, beginning at around the age of four or five.

Activists from other social organizations believed gender discrimination practices could not be separated from the subjugation of women in general and would only end through education.

Several younger strategists voiced the idea of distributing smart phones among indigenous community members. Better communication and ready access to frequently updated information, they believed, would eventually resolve the problem. Continued exposure to modernity would—over time—end the old ways.

After two days of talking, no consensus had been reached. April despaired over the prospect of further conversation and became more than a little depressed. While she knew as well as any other reasonable adult that much human suffering could not be avoided, at least the suffering issuing out of inhuman human traditions should be easy to correct. When it wasn't, and ignorance proved as willfully tenacious as earthquakes, lightning strikes, and the infirmities of old age, she felt aggrieved.

VISITORS

WHEN AUGUST ANNOUNCED during breakfast that he needed
to leave for a short time to visit Lester Mortal, April asked, "Who is
Lester Mortal?"

"He's an old friend, a nonagenarian veteran who now claims all
military conflicts arising out of nationalistic reasoning are occasions
for voluntary insanity. A lifetime bachelor, he adopted a Vietnamese
child who became one of my dearest friends. When I was growing up,
Lester Mortal was a pillar in my life. His influence on how I thought
about the world, and myself, rivaled my parents'. He recently received
a diagnosis of late stage liver failure. His house is a couple miles from
here and I really should visit him. I want to make sure he understands
how important he has been to me. He probably already knows, and if
he doesn't know it obviously won't do any good to tell him, but I still
want to."

"Would it be all right if I came along?"

"Why?"

"I need to get out of the house, and it might be nice to go somewhere with you. Lester Mortal sounds like someone I'd like to meet."

"Not too sure that's a good idea. He can be a little reactionary,
depending on his mood."

"All the better."

"Sometimes he just sits there and won't say anything. And there are
days you need to already be firmly committed to liking Lester Mortal
because nothing he does or says is likely to win you over."

"Sorry, I'm not dissuaded."

"It's not uncommon for him to be inappropriately abrupt. His
aging has dissolved many of the social inhibitions that keep most
people in line."

"Then I'll feel right at home. You need to let me come."

"His prejudices run pretty deep."

"Good, so do mine."

"Did I mention he lives in a small, ugly shack?"

"Not going to work on me, August."

"I'm just giving you fair warning. Lester joined the armed service before he graduated from high school, and over the next several decades he fought in more battles than he can even remember now. And during that time, he became accustomed to the company of other men. He learned how to read them—how to relate to them. He's a man's man."

"What does this have to do with me coming with you?"

"It was like a second childhood."

"What was?"

"Lester's time in the military—it amplified the experience that many males have growing up. See, before our endocrine systems kick in, boys spend most of our time with other boys. We socialize each other. Then, when our emotional lives become more complicated and volatile—around the fifth grade—we experience those physical and mental changes within an already established boy culture. When our need for more acceptance and status all of a sudden includes members of the other—well, with girls—this really complicates everything, because female endocrine systems generally begin expressing hormones years earlier than boys; so many girls are way ahead when it comes to competing for attention and advantage. They've had practice in negotiating their base instincts."

"I'm just barely following where you're going with this."

"Sorry, I'm trying to say that when boys are stressing out with new levels of competition among each other—fighting, longing for more physical strength and self-confidence—they're also talking about girls, who they know very little about. And they're frightened of them, or at least some of them are. I'm saying Lester Mortal learned very well how to get along and even shine brightly among other men, but he went out of his way to avoid having anything to do with women, and this had absolutely nothing to do with homosexuality."

"And?"

"Except for his adopted daughter, Hanh—who is his one successful relationship to humanity's other half—Lester has a nearly mythic fear and hatred of women. He won't admit it, of course, but he does. My mother used to go over to his place from time to time with a casserole or pie for him and Hanh. She never found anyone at home and would leave whatever she brought inside the door. But when my father went over—for whatever reason—he'd be gone all afternoon, talking with Lester."

"Now I can't wait to meet him."

"Well, I guess it's all right if you come, as long as you remember I don't think you should."

"Noted. We can take my electric Cort. It's a two-seater—brand-new, quick, silent, and very fun to drive. It needs to be driven."

"I think we should go in my mother's car. The roads get pretty rough over there and Lester's driveway is rutty."

"The Gate's auto service will send someone over if the Cort gets dirty."

"I'd still feel better taking the older vehicle. No one will want to steal it from us for one thing, and Lester will recognize it."

"Fair enough. Can Hannah come?"

"Of course."

"What should I wear?"

"Exactly what you have on."

"No, I've been wearing this all day. I'll find something and be right down."

She bounded upstairs. August watched until her lithe form hurried out of sight. Then he changed out of window-cleaning clothes, found his keys, and cleaned out the back seat of the car for the Afghan.

"You're overdressed," he said when she came outside.

"I'm not."

"And you put on makeup."

"Trust me, your friend will appreciate it."

"How do you know that? You've never met him."

"If he's breathing, he'll appreciate it. Makeup helps me look better than I am. Should we bring a gift? Bachelors are generally low on food and napkins."

"Not this one, but something appropriate might be nice."

"I think I've got just the thing."

She hurried into the house and a noticeable time later returned with her dog, a jar of pickled herring, and a box of fancy crackers. She ushered the Afghan into the back seat and carefully closed the door to avoid pinching her tail. Climbing into the front passenger's side, she carefully arranged herself in the available space. The seat belt slashed across her breasts like a baldric for a ceremonial sword.

"He'll like the herring," August said.

On the way over, August noticed that one corner of the sky contained a compact assortment of cumulous clouds that roughly resembled a pile of white, overstuffed pillows. It seemed odd because the rest of the sky remained clear blue. He turned off the main highway and onto one of Wisconsin's remaining gravel roads. The crackling sound of rocks thrown up by the tires and striking the underside of the car—well remembered from his childhood—resembled popping corn in a thin metal pan.

Lester's long driveway looked bad. As the car lurched over and through the more dramatic furrows, April clung to her seat and door handle. They continued through a grove of naked filbert trees and past Lester's outlaying sheds, hutches, fenced garden, a shapeless greenhouse of cobbled together windshields and car doors, and an abandoned outhouse, until they saw the unpainted house and a pale stream of smoke rising noiselessly out of a metal chimney.

August parked in front. Hannah bounded out of the back seat and ran around, sampling smells.

Lester Mortal stepped out of his front door in red wool socks, the suspenders of a faded pair of overalls looped over his red-and-black plaid shirt, and holding a yellowed paperback parted at about the middle. He raised his left hand in a tired but friendly wave and smiled. Clean-shaven and uncombed, his white hair flamed in all directions. He stared at April as she came out of the car.

"Hello, Lester," August called.

"Hello yourself," the old veteran replied in a nearly airless voice. He continued to stare.

"I'd like you to meet April Lux, Lester. April, this is Lester Mortal."

"Nice to meet you." April extended her hand and Lester pinched it briefly with the ends of his fingers before letting it go.

"Come in," he said, standing away from the open door and exposing the cramped interior.

"We brought herring and crackers," announced August.

"Good, open them up. I have a bottle of red wine and some Swiss cheese to go with them."

"I heard about your doctor's report," August said. "Surely you're not still drinking wine."

"Why shouldn't I?"

"Because your liver is failing and drinking alcohol leaves insoluble fatty deposits in liver tissue."

"I'm ninety-six."

"All the more reason."

"When you're ninety-six, reasons stop having a lot to do with you."

"Is it all right to leave my dog outside?" asked April. "She likes to explore but won't go very far away. And she's perfectly harmless."

"Sure, let her go wherever she wants. An Afghan?"

"Purebred."

"Don't see too many of those around here."

Inside, Lester tore open a package of cheese and with a butcher knife cut off a dozen or more domino-sized pieces. August pried the cork out of the wine bottle. April emptied the herring into a plastic bowl, set the bowl in the middle of a plate and arranged a circle of crackers around it.

They sat at the little wooden kitchen table. Lester continued to stare at April while they talked, ate, and sipped wine out of jam jars.

"This is the warmest autumn I can remember," Lester said, his voice still airless. "By rights, we should have a foot of snow by now."

"I remember you telling me about a winter when ice formed on the top of five feet of snow," August said.

"True, and temperatures that year were unusually cold. The five feet of snow got so hard you could walk on the top of it. People like me who burned wood had to go out many times to cut down trees and drag them home. In May, after the snow melted, there were stumps all over the woods that rose out of the ground to about head level. It looked like someone had come along and cut them off while standing on a ladder."

"Do you have napkins?"

"No, but we can tear off paper towels."

"Do you intend to keep living out here, or are you perhaps thinking about moving into town?" August asked.

"I'm staying here."

"Is that wise?"

"I owe a lot to this place."

"What does that mean?"

"I was a certain kind of person when I moved out here, and I changed. I like the new me better."

"This favored version of yourself could also live closer to medical facilities, more reliable electricity transmission, taxi cabs, grocery stores, pharmacies, libraries, fire stations, and other people."

"No, he couldn't. Look, August, I appreciate your concern, I really do, but I'm fine with everything. I am. My life—right here—gives me all I expect from it."

"But people are concerned about you living alone."

"Hanh and Ivan stop over, more than they need to, and they provide me with all the necessities. And did you hear about the people looking for Ivan?"

"What people?"

"No one knows who they are. There are three of them, and they're not from anywhere around here. They came all the way out here. Day before yesterday, and again this morning."

"What do they want with Ivan?"

"They don't say. Something about the time he worked on that pipeline."

"Where's Ivan now?"

"I don't know. I think he's avoiding them. Hanh said someone's sitting in a car in Ivan's driveway, waiting for him to come home."

"Did you talk to them when they came out here?"

"Twice."

"What did they look like?"

"Middle-aged white people who have never been in the armed services. Southern accents. Educated, but not very. Shaved, combed hair. Fairly clean clothes, not new. Five-year-old automobile—a diesel burner with not much rust. Arkansas plates. Two men and a woman."

"Could they have been lawyers or police?"

"I don't know. What do lawyers and police look like when they're not in their work clothes?"

"What did they say, exactly?"

"They asked if I knew Ivan Bookchester—the one who worked on the R-Corp pipeline several years ago. I said I did, and they asked if I knew where he was. I said I didn't. They asked if I knew how to find him; I said I didn't. They asked for the names of his friends and relatives, and I said I wasn't sure he had any. Then they gave me a number to call if I saw him. Written on a piece of paper. Before they left, they asked for directions to a modestly priced restaurant."

"Did you ask why they were looking for him?"

"All they said was that it was important."

"Were they friendly or unfriendly?"

"Neither."

"How did they seem to you?"

"Earnest."

"And you really don't know where Ivan is?"

"I haven't seen or heard from him for three or four days."

"Maybe I should go over and talk with whoever is sitting in Ivan's driveway, get him to tell me what they're doing here."

"Won't work, August. Hanh already tried that, and Ivan's mother confronted them before that, and before that your own mother badgered them to tell her who they were and what they wanted, but they wouldn't say."

A long silence sloughed through the house and August and April ate more herring and crackers.

"If you want," April began, "I can find out who they are."

"How?"

"I know someone who can tell us."

"Who?"

"Someone who occasionally works for me."

"How would he find out?" asked Lester, staring fiercely at April.

"I'm not sure how she'll do it, but she's resourceful. The people you want to know about don't sound very difficult to pin down. They're clearly not lawyers, police, or professionals of any sort. They're low income, unaccustomed to searching for anyone, and not trying to avoid notice. They're hesitant to say what they're after, though unwilling to make an excuse for why they're here, and rather clumsy in presenting themselves. My guess is they're not working for anyone else and are all in the same family."

"How would this person . . . how would she find out who they are?" asked Lester, repeating the question with the appropriate pronoun.

"I know little about how she works. She might not need anything more than the license plate number on the car in your friend's driveway, which she can probably recover through satellite imaging. Or she may speak to whoever is in the car, capture a picture of them, record their voice, or leave with a hair or fingerprint. Almost any piece of information can be matched up. She works with data banks as big as office buildings."

"Sounds expensive."

"Not so much."

"And she can do this by when?" asked Lester.

"Tomorrow afternoon, unless she's out of her office, and then her daughter will do it."

"And just where do you get all your damn money?"

"Lester!" exclaimed August. "What kind of question is that?"

The old veteran turned toward August and spoke as though they were alone.

"Hiring someone like she's talking about can't be cheap. And I assume this is who you've been staying with over at the Gate. Houses over there are worth an English king's ransom and this woman can't even be thirty. She's no older than you or Ivan. I mean, she looks really good, sure, but where does her money come from? People don't just come around and write you checks because you look like a model in a magazine."

August grimaced and closed his eyes, and April replied with amusement, "No offense taken, really. Relax, August. Mr. Mortal, my income comes from a number of sources. I received compensation after the death of my first husband, from his estate, and my second husband was quite generous in drawing up the terms of our divorce. I also make a decent living through my fundraising, but the largest part of my income comes from my mother, a businesswoman in New Zealand. She gave me a Swivol before I left home."

"I don't know what that is," said Lester.

"Sorry, I thought you'd recognize the term. Swivols are named for Carmen Northrop Swivol, an international speculator, currently living in Brussels. She discovered a successful formula for using quantum algorithms in digital investing. Entry-level Swivols begin at around one million dollars. My mother bought me a Swivol 001-17, and since then I've received quarterly dividends while paying back a few points to Swivol, Inc. It's without risk, insured through an international consortium of banking agencies, and as regular as an atomic clock. You can't touch the original investment because the recursive formulas only work properly with fixed amounts to reinvest in derivative markets—sometimes at blinding speed, I'm told—and the only way to get back your original purchase price is to terminate the contract. And of course there are big penalties for that. Swivols are nontransferable, so they can't be stolen, or given away for that matter. And there are many other advantages too tedious to go into."

"How do entry-level Swivols differ from higher levels?"

"The more money you spend for a Swivol, the higher the payout. With larger funds to move into and out of markets, there are better returns. The guaranteed percentages are proprietary, of course, but I've heard upper levels run between twelve and fifteen percent, maybe even higher."

"A twelve to fifteen percent annual return on the Swivol purchase price?"

"Yes, but you have to remember that top-tier Swivols are expensive, ten and eleven figures. Larger investments make larger footprints in the markets."

"And they guarantee those higher returns as well?"

"Oh, yes. I suppose it's reasonable to assume that not all quantum-to-digital investment programs make money for the Swivol Company, but the ones that lose money are offset by others."

"So," said Lester, with a look of disgust on his face, "once you're a Swivol owner, you are more or less guaranteed to remain rich."

"Pretty much."

"Like you are."

"I suppose," said April, smiling, "though I don't think of myself as rich."

"No?"

"Not really, except sometimes in a quasi-religious way, when I feel lucky to be alive, blessed with knowing an abundance of good people, and being a hapless recipient of excellent health. I suppose it's a matter of perspective, though. Maybe I'm higher-middle income, but not rich. I know many rich people—I'm a fundraiser after all—and I have little in common with most of them. And if the truth be told, Swivols are very conservative fiscal properties; most truly wealthy folks find twelve to fifteen ROI insufficient."

"Insufficient for what?" asked Lester.

"Ambitious needs. My Swivol works for me, though, because I'm happy not having to think about investing or financing."

The old veteran fell silent, overtaken by an infantry of memories— none of which he intended to share. He lowered his gaze to the tabletop and absently passed his right hand through his silky white hair. Taking a sip of wine, he swallowed slowly and set the jam jar back down on the tabletop. Then he raised his eyes and looked again at April.

"And you could have this information about who's looking for Ivan by tomorrow afternoon?"

"I most certainly will."

"That's good," said Lester, smiling. He relaxed inside his loose-fitting clothes, speared a lump of pickled herring with a wooden toothpick. "Then can I expect to see you and August again tomorrow?"

"That's up to August. He's driving."

"Sure, we'll come back tomorrow."

Outside, April and August looked for Hannah, and April told August he had been right about the makeup. They found the dog a short distance away chewing on a decomposing squirrel.

Back in the car, August did not want to immediately return to April's home. Instead, he drove north to swing by Ivan's house.

There was an automobile sitting in Ivan's drive, a dark blue sedan with someone inside it; the motor was not running. Ivan's pickup was nowhere to be seen.

August drove past and parked along the road a short distance later.

"Ivan Bookchester," April began. "I assume he's a friend of yours and Mr. Mortal's."

"Ivan and I grew up together. Nothing separated us, and there were times when the only place I recognized myself was with Ivan."

"What separates you now?"

"Our lives went in different directions."

"You seem unhappy about that."

"I suppose I am, but hanging on to the past is a mistake."

"I know; the more you hold, the faster it recedes."

"You sound familiar with the problem."

"Oh, yes."

August opened his car door and placed a foot outside.

"Where are you going?"

"Ivan keeps a donkey in a shed behind the house; I'm going to make sure he's been fed and watered."

"I'm coming."

"Okay. But leave the dog here."

They moved diagonally through the weed field next to the road and crawled under a fence. Keeping out of the line of sight from the front drive, they entered the loafing shed behind the house. Inside, August turned on the overhead light.

The donkey lay in a fresh spreading of straw, contentedly chewing green, leafy strands of hay from several fresh slices in the feed box. The water barrel had been filled to the top.

"Someone was just here," April observed.

"Looks like it," echoed August.

"Did you know that burros are one of the earth's most resilient mammals?" April asked.

"I think I heard something like that from Ivan."

"Well, he's right. A burro can lose thirty-five percent of its body mass through water loss, and completely recover after drinking for only six minutes. If humans lose just nine percent, we're toast."

"How do you happen to know this?"

"I once fundraised for canyon wildlife and one of our presenters talked about burro habitat. He said they were originally brought here from Spain. They live to ripe old ages, he claimed, and they have an uncanny ability to sniff out scarce food and make efficient use of nutrients. Because burros had unusual strength for their size, they were set to work in mines and employed by prospectors looking for gold; due to their inherent hardiness, many of the shaggy four-footers outlived both the mines and the miners, and then went feral."

"What's the difference between a burro and donkey?" August asked.

"I think donkeys are domesticated burros."

"Ivan named this one Jet Lag."

She knelt beside the long-eared animal and ran a hand through his short, bristled mane, scratching behind his ears. "He sure is cute."

"Ivan says Jet Lag likes to spend time with the goats down the road." August noticed that April had torn her dress in several places in crossing the weed field and crawling under the fence, and there were burrs clinging to her clothes. She looked wonderfully disheveled.

"Anything is probably better than being alone. What's that phrase: similar biological systems integrate?"

"Yes, something like that, but I don't know how similar goats and donkeys really are."

"Compatibility is all that counts. Anyway, someone was clearly here, probably within the last hour; do you think your friend Ivan might be close by?"

"It's possible. But if he wanted us to find him, he'd be here. One thing about Ivan, he usually knows more about you than you know about him."

"Do you think he's in the house and just not answering the door?"

"We can check. The back door can't be seen from the front driveway, and he never locks it."

"Let's see if he's home."

The back door opened on the first try, but there were no signs of anyone inside. It also didn't look like anyone had been there lately. All the lights were off and the windows closed. The thermostat had been turned down to fifty degrees. Beds were made. The refrigerator held nothing but commodities like ketchup, mustard and pickles. No milk, salad, leftovers, meat, cheese, or anything else that would spoil. The sinks were dry and the wind-up clock in the living room wasn't running.

They went through every room in the house, even the dirt-floored basement, and ended up in the living room.

April settled into one of the overstuffed chairs, neatly fitting herself into its leather pocket and folding her legs under her. The knife-closing movement of her lower limbs surprised August. It seemed out of character for her to assume such a relaxed attitude inside a stranger's house while unknown and possibly threatening individuals waited in the driveway.

"You seem mildly alarmed about these people looking for Ivan," she said. "Why is that?"

"I don't mean to seem alarmed."

"No, I'm sure you don't. But what are you afraid they might be after?"

"I thought you knew someone who could possibly find that out for us."

"I do, and she's working on it. I texted her before we left Mr. Mortal's house."

"I just wonder how Ivan is getting along. His pipeline experience involved some unpleasantries that I hope he can avoid having to revisit."

"What sort of unpleasantries?"

"I'd rather not be more specific."

"Why?"

"I don't think Ivan would want us, or me, talking about it."

After winding the clock's spring and repositioning its hands, August sat across from April in a similar leather chair. Outside, the sun fell into the horizon, hurling long shadows through the colored air. The house grew darker and darker. "I stayed here when I first came back from Chicago," he said, as though answering a question that had not been asked.

"Older houses are sort of nice," April commented, disinterestedly. "They seem authentic in a collapsed sort of way, and charming so long as you ignore the fusty smells, dripping water pipes, and bugs. How many days did you stay here?"

"Just one night."

"Did you sleep well?"

"Well enough."

"You're looking at me in that way again."

"What way?"

"Like you want something."

"I'm glad you brought that up again. It's not just *you* I anticipate good things from; it's *us*. I want us to find a home inside each other."

"What kind of home would that be?"

"A place where we fully become ourselves. I know I feel that way."

"What way?"

"Centered, focused and whole when I'm with you; adrift when I'm not."

"You hardly know anything about me, August. And I know very little about you."

"True, and correcting that situation will take the rest of our lives. At least I hope so. Look, I'm sorry if Lester offended you . . ."

"He didn't. You gave a fairly good description of him before we left, and he turned out to be as interesting and unpredictable as I'd hoped. I understand what a strong impression he must have made upon you growing up. There's nothing off-the-shelf about that man, though I fear his health is severely compromised."

"You liked him?"

"If I hadn't, I wouldn't have agreed to see him again tomorrow. Tell me about Hanh."

"She's his adopted daughter, the one I mentioned before, one of my closest friends."

"Along with Ivan," she added.

"Yes, along with Ivan."

"Do you and Ivan both sleep with her?"

"Why would you think that?"

"There's something in the way you talk about her, and the way you talk about Ivan, and the way Mr. Mortal talked about the three of you. Also, when you first heard me mention Hanh's name it occurred to me your thoughts momentarily flew off in that direction."

"Mind reading again?"

"I prefer to call it thought-sharing."

"Interesting," August said. A narrow room of panic tunneled open in his mind, and then slowly, thankfully, closed up again.

"So do you?"

"Do I what?"

"Do you and Ivan sleep with Hanh? No one would blame either of you. She's an impossibly cute little thing, moves like a soccer player, has a beautiful complexion, lovely dark eyes, with hair as black as a crow. She wears her facial scar proudly, and it gives her an almost otherworldly aloofness."

"How do you know all this?"

"I had my digerati friend look into you before you came over with your mother to ask about house-sitting. I also had the house surveillance files from the day I was away, and it looked like Hanh slept for a couple hours in the fish room downstairs while you talked to Ivan upstairs. So, do you?"

"You have surveillance files?"

"Yes, though the audio feed isn't currently functioning."

"I guess I didn't expect that. When did you look at them?"

"The night we got back. If you'd known your movements were being recorded, would it have made a difference?"

"I suppose not."

"Are you and Ivan sleeping with Hanh?"

"I really don't know how to answer that, April."

"I thought you wanted us to know everything about each other."

"I do. But it seems too soon to share histories of intimacy, until— well, maybe until after we're having sex ourselves."

"Is that what you imagine we're going to do, August? Is that the reason you're interested in me? Do you imagine I'll be the one opening your music box, turning your cylinders, and playing your music?"

"No, no, not at all. Well, not exactly. Okay, I do think about it from time to time, and, yes, I imagine you and I might possibly reach a giddy level of intimacy together, but my attraction and appreciation for you is a whole lot more comprehensive than that . . . a lot more. For one thing, I've never known anyone I could talk with like you. Never. My thoughts seem released, freed, even empowered."

"You say that as though you should be congratulated for having such broad-based interests in me. But for the sake of discussion, let's say that you, or I, or both of us, are only interested in seeing how sex might turn out between us—do you think that would be wrong?"

"Oh no, it wouldn't be wrong, no, not wrong exactly; but it's also true I've had some fairly regrettable experiences with purely sensual agendas—"

"Are you now thinking of your time with Amanda Clark in Chicago?"

"How in the world do you know anything about Amanda?"

"People should stop being surprised by other people knowing about them. Everything you do leaves a record, and we now have technology to recover it. I wasn't going to let just anyone stay in my house. And just because I'm very fond of your mother doesn't mean I should automatically extend that trust to you."

"No, I suppose not."

"You're not going to tell me if you and Ivan are sleeping with Hanh?"

"I feel threatened by that question, so, no, I'm not."

"Then I apologize for reading you wrong. I sensed, apparently mistakenly, that you wanted to cover a lot of ground between us in a hurry."

"Actually, I do."

"Did you think knowing each other was only going to involve you knowing about me?"

"No, of course not. It's just that four days ago, after I first met you, I didn't expect to be sitting in Ivan's house talking to you about the kinds of things we're now talking about. And concerning Ivan and me and Hanh, I'm certainly not comfortable enough to talk about either of them, not yet. Why are you laughing?"

"I was remembering when I used to feel the same, when it seemed unfair that events came at me faster than I could process."

"So why are you laughing?"

"Because that seems so naive now. I haven't had the luxury to think all the way through anything in years. It's the modern way. It's quaint you haven't had to accept that. The things happening to me always seem to arrive in a late stage of pregnancy. For instance, I certainly never saw you coming."

"What do you mean?"

"I wasn't ready for you."

"Nor I for you," August agreed.

"Things like this happen too often," April said. "My heart leads me into impossibly dense thickets, and here I am in a ripped dress with stickers jabbing my thighs, my hands covered with donkey fur, inside an old, crumbling house smelling like unwashed clothes, in the dark, unable to turn lights on because someone we don't know is sitting in the driveway in an automobile with Arkansas license plates, looking for the owner of the house, a friend of yours—who I've never personally met—for reasons you won't explain to me. It's insane. I should never have taken a chance with you. It doesn't make sense. Every time I follow my instincts, they lead me astray. But they're all we have to depend on—instincts, I mean."

"I can't believe you feel that way!" August exclaimed, leaning forward in his chair. "That's exactly how I felt before I met you. My instincts betrayed me every time."

"Why do you think they aren't betraying you now?"

"Before you, I kept making other people into something I wanted them to be."

"Why am I different?"

"The person I wanted to turn people into is you. I don't need us to have sex. We're already gendered reflections. I don't mean we're the same, but you are who I might be if somehow, during gestation, I hadn't come out on the male end of the curve."

"I don't see how you can possibly know that."

"And I can't tell you because it's a purely subjective fact. But it's still a fact. When I'm with you, April, I know. I know in the same way I know what I feel."

"We don't need to sleep together?"

"No. Well, not really. I mean, of course in a biological sense it's nearly a forgone conclusion—given our shared affinities. It will probably happen, I mean, if you want it to. Do you have objections? It's okay if you do, of course…but do you?"

April laughed. "You're hopeless. To be completely honest, I've been ready since the donkey shed, but I have things I must tell you . . . about me, things that will alter everything."

"I can't believe that, but I've sensed there was something about you I didn't know . . . yet needed to."

"I've been wanting to tell you, but I keep losing courage."

"Tell me."

"And you'll listen without interrupting?"

"Yes, yes, of course."

Outdoors, headlights turned off the road and moved up the driveway, bursting through the windows and sweeping through the room in a spray of illumination, bringing April and August out of their chairs, breathing heavily. From the living room windows they watched as the headlights drew alongside the parked car and were then extinguished. Doors opened and three darkened figures stood in the starlight, talking. Then they walked toward the house.

"Do you think they'll come inside?" April asked.

"Let's get out of here," whispered August.

A frame-rattling knock on the front door came as August and April walked through the backyard toward the donkey's shed. They crawled under the fence, slogged through the weed field, climbed out of the ditch and into the car.

About a mile down the road August realized he was driving too fast and eased off the accelerator. He felt exhilarated, and his nearness to April seemed alive.

VIOLATED

AT THE FRONT gate, two security personnel rushed out of the guardhouse and spoke to April in the flat, unhurried speech that professionals often employ when conveying concern. There was recent trouble, they explained, at April's house—within the last hour. Local law enforcement had been called in and three county patrol cars were already over there, working with Gate Security.

When April and August arrived at the house, seven vehicles rested on her front yard, with several doors left open. Every window in the house was lit from inside.

Three guards escorted them across the yard, the same elite team who weeks before had confronted August and Ivan over using outdated chain saws, and after a vigorous internal struggle, August succeeded in not thinking about the coincidence of encountering the same grouping.

"The person who did this wore a mask," the security chief explained, looping both thumbs inside her thick black utility belt, ignoring August, and speaking in authoritative monotone to April. "The house surveillance log shows an intruder entering through the garage shouldering a blunt object, with a paint can hanging from his left arm. He remains inside the premises for a little less than four minutes, indiscriminately smashing things and painting on doors and walls. The intruder's appearance and movements are consistent with a white male in his early twenties, approximately five-eight and weighing between one hundred and forty and one hundred and fifty pounds, dark brown hair and brown eyes, which can be seen through the holes in his ski mask."

"Do you know who it was?" asked April.

"As I said, the vandal wore a mask. We're currently reviewing entry and exit records for the last few weeks, looking for matches to the general profile. It's of course early, but at this point we don't have a reasonable candidate."

"I just don't understand how something like this can happen," said April.

"Nor do we," responded the chief. "Our protocols serve as a model for single, restricted access enclave population security, and we were recently cited in *Protection Magazine* as the best in the country. Officers arrived here in under six minutes."

"I didn't mean to imply—" began April.

"We assume whoever did this had a ride waiting or fled into the wooded area behind your house. Officers are currently searching adjacent properties. And so far, we're not aware of the whereabouts of your registered Afghan."

"She's with us," said April, "in the back seat of the car."

"That's fortunate."

The security chief's eyes glistened with reflected light as she turned to verify the animal in the vehicle behind them. "It's also probably fortunate you weren't home, Ms. Lux."

"I would have been with her," August said.

His comment was ignored, and the younger male security guard—the tall, sharp-faced officer who days ago had shoved August and later decided against shoving Ivan—said, "If your brother Tom had been here, Ms. Lux, things might have been a lot different."

April asked the chief, "Could the vandal have been flown in to avoid being photographed at the guardhouse?"

"It's theoretically possible, Ms. Lux, but highly improbable," she replied. "Visitors skyporting into the Gate face a higher level of inspection than those entering by the front entrance, and Gate owners themselves, as you know, were thoroughly vetted before they purchased lake properties. All owners are highly reputable."

"Dennis Scarborough is not reputable by anyone's standard."

"We're cognizant of the misunderstandings you've had with that individual, and for that reason I understand exactly where you're coming from, Ms. Lux. But Dennis Scarborough has many more profitable ways to spend his time, and it makes no sense for him to bother himself with such a crime."

"It wasn't a misunderstanding—he threatened me with a loaded pistol and shot out several windows."

"Yes, we fully understand your interpretation of events on that evening, though the matter was thoroughly resolved by a local court."

"It wasn't resolved at all. The judge refused to hear the case on procedural grounds."

"You were well compensated for the damage to your property, Ms. Lux."

"Yes, through a third party. Dennis Scarborough's an insult to decency itself."

"He has also, for the past month, exclusively resided at his Chicago residence. We checked. No, Ms. Lux, the defilement of your home tonight was carried out by a marginal, relatively young, low-intelligence individual."

Inside, shattered glass lay spewed across the polished wooden floor. Larger glass shards littered the hallway, where most of the framed paintings had been smashed. Glass tabletops, cabinet fronts, lamps, and other lighting fixtures were damaged beyond repair.

Uniformed police taped off the area, and government technicians measured and searched for traces of evidence, their movements accompanied by the cracking and crunching noises of the soles of their shoes walking on glass. The carved banister that curled upstairs had been splintered in three places. Broad strokes of paint marred the walls. Dripping red letters on April's upstairs bedroom door spelled DIe BItCH; a longer phrase ran from left to right across the balcony, KILL THE WHOR, ending after the author either failed to consult a spell-checker, ran out of paint, or thought his text would be clear enough without the last letter. A single noun, DEaTH, sneered from the inside of the front door.

"This is unacceptable," whispered April. She and August stood together and stared from place to place, only distantly registering the voice of the security chief as she reassured April of the efforts currently being undertaken to discover the identify of the person responsible. Then April stood closer to August, touching his arm, as though to draw comfort from his animal nature.

On the upstairs balcony, Thistlewaite County Deputy Officer Stanley Jackson (who had personally reported the recovery of April's stolen automobile four days ago on the road outside of Luster) noted that the owner of the house had arrived. He descended two and three steps at a time, interrupted the security chief, took off his hat, and offered his sincere condolences to April. He'd come as soon as the call came in, he said, and all the resources at his command had been dedicated to finding the person who had done this. Nothing would stop him, he assured her, in discovering and apprehending the vandal.

"Thank you, Officer Jackson," said April.

"Call me Stanley, Ms. Lux, please."

"Are other parts of my house also damaged?"

"Not that we can tell," said Stanley, his eyes often returning to April's torn and stained dress. "The destruction is pretty much confined to what you see."

"How about the basement?"

"Nothing serious there. It looks like he briefly went downstairs and took a swing at the wall separating the basement and lake, but the transparent material was so resilient that he returned upstairs where his efforts were more effectual. This guy clearly wanted to inflict maximum damage quickly."

"There's another possibility," August felt compelled to point out. "The unknown individual may have considered the volume of water in the lake, the relative depth of the basement room he was standing in, and the hydrodynamic events likely to follow from even the smallest puncture in the transparent polymer membrane responsible for holding back hundreds and hundreds of thousands of gallons of pressurized water, and he might have reconsidered the advisability of breaking through the barrier."

Looking around her again, April uttered an irrational laugh of despair, and asked, "Why would someone do this?"

"Hard to say," sighed Officer Stanley.

"He might have wanted to get back at you for something—either real or imagined," said the security chief. "And he also might have done it for no reason at all. For certain lower life forms, breaking things, expressing vulgarities, and defacing private property are goals in themselves."

"The speed in carrying out the wreckage suggests he planned this," said Officer Stanley. "He was likely aware of the local response time, and at the last second slipped between the closing fingers of the security team. And it's also possible there was more than one person involved."

August and April continued watching as the twelve or fifteen people in the room began putting away their equipment, as though responding to a silent command. Within minutes, the room had been cleared except for Deputy Stanley and the three Gate guards, and then they also walked out of the house, climbed into their vehicles, and drove away.

August disappeared into the garage, returned with a broom, and began pushing lanes of glass fragments into larger and larger piles.

April changed clothes and found another broom. They succeeded in clearing the floors and staircase, amassing several heaps of debris. The glass shards were transferred to garbage bags and set against the inside garage wall. Leaving their brooms beside the bags, they returned to stare at the dripping red letters on the doors and walls.

"Stain killer," said August. "To prevent bleed-through we'll need to apply stain killer before repainting."

April agreed and remarked that the floor would require refinishing to take the nicks and scrapes out of the wood. "What a nuisance."

"Will your homeowners insurance cover any of this?"

"It will cover all of it, but still, what a horrible thing for someone to do."

"How soon can we get some stain killer?"

"There's one-hour delivery to Gate owners. I'll order a few cans. While we're waiting, let's have a drink."

The alcohol inhibited the excitatory neurotransmitters in their central nervous systems and further dampened brain activity by enhancing the effect of naturally occurring gamma-aminobutiric acid. August and April noticed falling levels of anxiety, lagging response times, boundary fuzziness, heightened congeniality, and wider associative pattern formation—looseness of thought. Because they encountered these changes simultaneously, they experienced them as shared experiences, and felt closer together.

Even in rooms where the vandalism was not visible, the house seemed alive, quivering with impending violence. They turned out the lights in the main entryway and upstairs hallway, hoping to minimize the hostile spirits emanating out of the red letters, but the darkness provided an even more fertile environment for suspicions of still-active malicious intent.

April remembered hearing that sealed chambers were some-times built into ancient Assyrian temples for the purpose of divine communication. No one—not even priests—came into these door-less, walled-off rooms and the only objects contained therein were inscribed clay tablets, confidential reports from the king to his patron god—a prototype, no doubt, for what would later be called top secret or classified material. Written language (in this case, cuneiform) was thought to have magical properties and writing someone's name in some way brought the individual (or god) under your spell. Current-day people who left messages in restrooms no doubt appealed to a similar variety of magical thinking.

"I've never believed in closure," April said, resuming her seat in the upstairs library.

"Tell me more," said August, who sat to April's left, where he had two views of her—a facial profile, and a reflection from the window overlooking the darkened lawn. They held his attention in different ways and he looked back and forth between them.

"I don't believe the repercussions of one event can be ended by another," she continued. "When something like this happens, it keeps happening. Even if Officer Stanley discovers the person who did it, and even if that person is imprisoned for the rest of his life, and all the breakage is repaired, the floors refinished, the walls and doors repainted, new furniture moved in, the workers paid—the ugly fact of it having happened will still be there, influencing the present moment."

"Do you dismiss the idea of opposing forces, the Newtonian third rule that every action has an opposite reaction?"

"On the contrary, I'm confirming old Newty. I'm reacting, and I'll go on reacting, afraid something like this will happen again, perhaps when I'm here alone. I'm wishing for better security, police-state inspec-tions of all strangers within ten miles, mean dogs stalking around my house; I want my annoying but very tough brother back from his hockey games; I need guns and stinging sprays, cattle prods, better electronic surveillance, knives, and poison gas to protect me. And it doesn't matter if the person responsible receives adequate punishment. It doesn't mat-ter because the way I feel about people has shifted. My chemistry has reoriented, and I'll go on living under its hateful prescription."

The subject appealed to August, and he hurried into it: "My friend Ivan would agree with you, I think. He once said humans could never make up for what some humans have already done."

"Are you referring to what happened when your friend worked on the pipeline?"

"Yes."

"I thought we weren't going to talk about that."

"I only brought it up to say that your idea enjoys wide circulation."

"We create the future without realizing we're doing it, one act of kindness and one delinquency at a time."

"Do you really believe Dennis Scarborough was responsible for this?"

"Yes. I think he coerced, convinced, or simply hired someone to do it."

"Why would he?"

"The security chief says Dennis has many more productive ways to spend his time, but she ignores an important observation: arranging this vandalism would bring him spasms of pleasure. The man loves his animosity."

"That's not what his wife thinks, or at least that's not what she says she thinks, which is that you've become the object of his desire."

"Well, she's got the object part right. Chopie probably hates me too, I know that, but it's hard to imagine her carrying through on much of anything. She's more like a brightly colored moth than the burrowing weasel she's married to."

"I sometimes wonder what moths and weasels think about us using them to illustrate our psychological states."

"Perhaps they use us as well, as examples of planet-destroying nincompoops."

"Perhaps," laughed August, taking another drink, and repeating the word to hear it again: "Nincompoops."

Through the windows, they watched headlights come over the rise and approach the house.

When the knock came, they went downstairs and received a plain paper bag with three cans of spray-on stain killer and a receipt.

"Do you know how to use this product?" asked the uniformed delivery woman, adjusting her hat and smiling.

"I think so," April said.

"Please remember to allow a full six hours drying time between the first and second application. Otherwise, adherence may suffer, and you might encounter bleed-through, or even wrinkling."

"We'll try to remember."

"For best results, before beginning to spray, a full minute of shaking is recommended—a full minute, even if the little metal agitation ball rattles freely against the inside of the can after shaking for only fifteen or twenty seconds. Some professionals strongly advise two minutes of shaking, so the one-minute minimum should be interpreted as unconditional."

"Good to know."

"And it's important to remember to vigorously shake for ten or fifteen seconds after each application interruption, and to shake occasionally during longer periods of continuous spraying to keep the mixture inside the can from separating out. And just before storage, it is recommended that you invert the can and spray for several seconds until only clear propellant comes out to prevent the nozzle from clogging."

"Sage advice, I'm sure," August said.

"Is there anything else you need, Ms. Lux?"

"Not that I can think of."

"Goodnight then, Ms. Lux, and thank you for calling on us."

An hour later, August and April finished spraying over the red lettering, obscuring the hateful words with feather-edged blotches of whitish-blue stain killer. The house smelled of chemical drying agents and they both felt absolutely exhausted, physically and emotionally.

April shut herself inside her bedroom and August went down into the basement.

Before falling asleep, he watched fish on the other side of the transparent wall. They seemed to exist in a world of graceful fluidity, moving from place to place without any apparent effort. Their elongated shapes were soothing to contemplate, their changes in direction and speed apparently accomplished without any expenditure of deliberate decision-making, as though swimming patterns had been choreographed beforehand and rigorously practiced. He wondered if soaring eagles looking down on urban pedestrian and vehicular traffic might have the same impression: the appearance of executive micromanagement brought about by a multitude of individual decisions and random chance. A similar problem of scale could also be found in the activity of human cells, wherein each tiny organism performed delimited functions within a specified environment, unaware that its actions were supported by and supporting of a larger organism. ·

Still entertaining these thoughts, August crawled into the bed furthest away from the fish and was just falling asleep when a soft-knuckle knock came at the door; it opened, and April, covered from chin to feet in a terrycloth bathrobe, crossed the room. "I don't mean to disturb you," she whispered into the low, greenish light, "but I needed to watch the fish." She climbed onto the other bed, curled up on it, and faced the transparent wall.

Looking over the top of his sheet and bedspread, August thought about going over and sitting beside her, perhaps wrapping around her; he then wondered about several things he might say, or whisper, when he joined her. A strong yet short-lived twinge of anticipatory excitement visited him, blending into a recollection of how it felt to press against terrycloth. Then he wondered if climbing out of his bed and walking over might be interpreted as an infringement on her private space, because this was her house, after all, so coming to his bedroom in a bathrobe shouldn't necessarily be seen as amorous invitation; perhaps she just wanted to watch fish. The contrasting content of these thoughts soon became onerous and he tried to have greater confidence in believing that April was attracted to him and that her entering the room and curling up on the adjacent bed was a deliberate signal of her desire for him to join her. But if this were true, why had she worn such an all-concealing bathrobe? And then he remembered that she had said they needed to have a talk before anything of a sexual nature happened between them, and he wondered what that talk might consist of, and then realized that his wakefulness had seriously begun to ebb. It was easier to think with his eyes closed, and easier to remember than think, and he pictured April curling up in the old leather chair in Ivan's living room, pulling her legs up under her. Soon, he felt a familiar vertigo occasioned by millions of serotonin and melatonin molecules entering his lower brain and he fell asleep.

Hours later, he woke up and the greenish-amber light pouring in from lakeside was enhanced by sunlight pounding against the unseen surface of the water. She was gone and the bedroom door had been reclosed.

HOT BISCUITS

THE FOLLOWING AFTERNOON April and August parked in the rutty drive before Lester Mortal's home. They'd called beforehand, and the old man was standing in his front yard in a beige work coat. He came toward them and let the Afghan out of the back seat.

"Hello, Mr. Mortal," said April, a file folder of papers under her left arm.

"Call me Lester, April."

"Were you waiting for us?" August asked.

"No, I was just getting some air. Come in. I'm glad you came."

Inside, Hanh wore a high-collared black-and-red outfit that drew attention to her complexion and hair. She set four cups of hot tea on the kitchen table but didn't speak.

"Hanh, this is April Lux," August said. "April, this is Hanh."

They greeted each other with quick, similar smiles.

"I'm a new friend of August's," April explained, trying not to look at Hanh's facial scar.

"I know who you are," said Hanh. She smiled again to reaffirm her goodwill and perhaps to again show her evenly spaced, white teeth. "I hope you don't mind me being here. Lester said you might have information about the people looking for Ivan."

"I've been looking forward to meeting you."

"All of you, please sit down," said Lester.

With his back toward the kitchen, August sat to April's left, directly across from Hanh, with Lester across from April. The smell of coffee lounged in the air, as though a pot had been brewed in the last hour; something was baking in the oven, and its yeasty fragrance grew stronger with each passing minute. Perhaps because of the oven, or the sunlight barnstorming through two nearby windows, the room seemed unusually warm.

August had not anticipated Hanh being here, and her presence ramped up his anxieties about integrating his past life into his hoped-for future with April. He worried Hanh might make a scene or say something untoward or critical. He also feared April might not have uncovered any useful information, which would embarrass both of them, or that whatever information she'd discovered might be presented in an overly formal manner, perhaps interpreted as condescending by Hanh or Lester, who would neither appreciate nor understand that formalism did not necessarily indicate a haughty personality, but rather came from years of committee work. He also wondered if April might once again have overdressed, not so much in her choice of light brown slacks with sharply creased pleats, white-on-white canvas shoes, and a dark green button-up blouse with elbow-length puffy sleeves, but because the designs and fabrics made them appear overly costly and a little too fashionable. He worried what Lester and Hanh might think of her, especially since Lester had only yesterday criticized her for looking like someone recently escaped from a magazine.

April squared the file folder on the table in front of her, opened it, and passed around sheets of paper with bulleted items running from top to bottom.

In a relaxed voice, she talked through the report: "As you can see, the Arkansas-registered vehicle belongs to Edgar Pierce and his wife, Alice, who work respectively as a car-parts salesman and medical aide in Little Rock. Both are midway into their fifties, regular members of the First Baptist Church, with no criminal records; they are active in their local community and vote in state and federal elections.

"Their son, Samuel, twenty-five years old, lives with them and works part-time at a convenience store; he does not own his own automobile, and much of his spare time, and some work time, is spent video gaming online. The Pierces have extended family all around Little Rock, and their lineage in Arkansas goes back four generations. All three have attended at least one year of community college; they do not owe back taxes, and their credit ratings are average to above-average. Edgar owns two registered small-caliber long guns and a larger bore bolt-action rifle suitable for hunting moose or bear. He belongs to a men's sporting club mostly comprised of other Baptist church members.

"Edgar and Alice had one daughter, Hester, younger than her brother Sam by two years and four months. She died in an industrial accident while employed as a welder for a US fuel interest named

R-Corp, September 2, 2024, in British Columbia. The company was building a pipeline along the Pacific coastline when a five-hundred-gallon propane tank exploded, destroying a metal-sided utility shed.

"Three others died along with Hester: another young welder named Ruth Orland, and two older, middle-aged men, Bret Logan and Steven Peters, site managers responsible for transporting, setting up, and tearing down temporary work camps along the pipeline. Mr. Peters was apparently also known as Slack, and related to—though once removed—one of the R-Corp owners.

"About a year ago the Pierce couple began making information requests concerning their daughter's death. R-Corp ignored the requests and the family filed a formal complaint with US authorities, which, along with a Canadian agency, had investigated the explosion. After receiving no response to their complaint, the Pierce family bombarded R-Corp and the US and Canadian governments with several months of emails and phone calls, demanding more information about the explosion and the death of their daughter, whose body, they claimed, had not been turned over to them for two months following the accident. And when they finally received their daughter's body, a medical examiner hired by the family found no evidence of burning.

"Edgar and Alice are currently on unpaid vacations, and it is not known what arrangement their son may have made with his employer to accompany them. They left Arkansas nine days ago and began driving northwest, leaving a trail of credit card purchases for gasoline, three-party meals and motel lodgings. In Seattle, they visited the R-Corp headquarters, and then drove into British Columbia, where they stayed two days. Then they drove directly here and are currently staying at a budget motel called Lights Out in Grange."

When April stopped talking, the memory of her speaking boiled and simmered in the room. Lester and Hanh looked away from their papers, then returned to them and parked their eyes safely back on the bulleted lines, reading them over and over.

April continued: "Since leaving Seattle, they have texted relatives and friends in Little Rock, and the communications explain how Edgar, Alice, and Sam hope Ivan can provide details about Hester's death. Several former R-Corp employees apparently told them that if they want to know what happened to Hester they have to talk to Ivan, who was transferred out of the area after her death and left the company a short time later after signing a nondisclosure agreement."

August waited for Lester or Hanh to say something, but they remained staring into their papers.

"Do you have any questions?" asked April.

Hanh didn't move or say anything.

"For the life of me I can't think of any questions," said Lester uncomfortably. "You covered all of the bases, I'd say."

"Hanh, do you have any questions?"

"I think the biscuits are done," she said, and rushed away from the table.

"That dog of yours sure likes to run around outdoors," Lester said, looking through the windows into the side yard. "What kind of animal did you say he was, April?"

"She's an Afghan."

"That's right. I remember now. An Afghan. Don't see many of that breed around here."

"Lester, do you know where Ivan is?" August asked.

The old man didn't speak. Then a tired smile briefly visited his face, as though placed there by a delinquent thought, and August knew why he'd experienced so much tension since coming into the house.

Ivan was here.

Lester's face resumed its earlier impassiveness and he returned to looking out the window.

August stood up. "Where is he?"

Hanh moved hot biscuits from the baking sheet to a porcelain plate, her hands covered with quilted oven mitts. "Who?" she asked.

"Ivan."

Looking, or at least trying to look like he had been walking by the house and decided to come inside, Ivan came into the kitchen from the small living room. Since the last time August had seen him, he'd shaved off his beard and cut his hair, which made him look quite different above the shoulders; the rest of him remained unquestionably the same as a week or two before.

"Hey, everyone," he said.

"Why were you hiding?" August asked.

"Gus, just because you didn't know I was here doesn't mean I was hiding. Is this April Lux? Hi, April, I'm Ivan, Ivan Bookchester, Gus's oldest and best friend from way back before there were even laws; well, there were laws back then, I guess, but you get the idea."

"I'm pleased to meet you," said April, half rising out of her chair and shaking his hand. "I've heard a lot about you."

"And I've heard a lot about you, a lot. And if you don't mind me saying so, you validate every claim Gus made for you."

When no one else spoke, April, who still felt in some way responsible for facilitating discussion, said: "So, Ivan, did you know Hester Pierce, and do you have any information to pass on to her family?"

"Yes, I knew her, or at least I worked with her a number of times, sat in lunch line with her once or twice. I didn't really know anyone there very well. I mean, there were a lot of welders, and about a third of them didn't speak English."

"And you knew about the accident?"

"The accident?"

"Yes, the exploding propane tank described in the company report—the one they say destroyed a utility shed and killed Hester and three others."

"Oh sure, the accident."

As soon as the platter of biscuits arrived with a tub of butter and jar of jam, Ivan turned his attention to drawing another chair up to the table and eating.

"You never said anything to us about a fatal accident," said Hanh.

"Didn't I?"

"No, you didn't," Lester said, defending Hanh. "What's this about?"

Ivan nibbled his biscuit and looked trapped.

"You never said anything about a fatal accident," Hanh said again, her voice slightly more accusatory.

Ivan swallowed and noticed the sky had clouded over outdoors; a northeastern wind blew dried leaves through the yard.

Also noticing the changing conditions outdoors, Lester wished he could leave, take a walk with April's dog, feel the wind push against his face, climb to a place where he could see a distant horizon, stare into moving clouds and experience being old in a more elemental way. Yes, he'd been worried about what these people from Arkansas wanted with Ivan. But after learning they were coming to terms with the death of a loved one, his interest receded. He well knew how difficult it was to hang onto cherished ideas about the world while at the same time acknowledging the meaningless death of young people, but he'd lately begun to see the more general problem of mortality as something best to simply accept. Most of the important figures from his life had passed over to the other side, and now seemed to wait for him to rejoin them in some yet-to-be experienced revival of past-but-still-relevant events.

April pulled open a hot biscuit and carefully smeared small amounts of butter and jam onto the flaky disks' soft, steamy insides. She marveled at the delicious smell and felt a pang of hopeless envy overtake her. People who successfully baked were practitioners of an unlicensed magic that she could only wonder about. Stealing a look at Hanh, she noted how her dark eyes moved in an almost proprietary manner around the table, watching as biscuits were taken from the platter and consumed. As her eyes moved, they seemed inhabited by a calm that for several long seconds threatened April's core until she recognized it as a reflection of her own jealous insecurities about whatever might still be alive between Hanh and August. After coming to this realization, April ate the second half of her biscuit, ushered several crumbs from the table onto the paper napkin on her lap, carefully thought about eating another, and decided against it.

Hanh wished she and Ivan were alone so she could yell at him. There was no justification for withholding information about his past from her. She and Ivan were connected in a way that was *supposed* to mean that she and he knew all vital information points about each other. No undisclosed surprises should exist. That's the way it was meant to be. Word-dependent creatures depended upon voluntary disclosures and autobiographical storytelling, and it was maddening to have a knotty event from Ivan's past begin to untie itself in the presence of August and Lester, while she knew nothing of it. Nothing. She'd been caught off guard. And on top of that, August's lack of affect upon hearing April's report suggested that he must have already known something about the untimely death of the two young women and two older men, and though what he knew may have come from April's hired cyberdetective prior to coming over to Lester's, it was more likely to have come from Ivan himself. She also noticed that Lester's attention had veered away from realities at hand and was slowly but determinedly heading off—again—into that netherworld of the way life used to be. As a bottomless sadness gathered under her, she noticed April steal a second look in her direction. Hanh's resentment flared up like a lit match, but its flame couldn't be sustained for very long because April—who Hanh guessed to be several years younger than herself and who clearly enjoyed her biscuit and was trying to keep from eating a second one—seemed nice enough, was sincerely deferential to Lester, and impeccably suited to the part of August that Hanh could never relate to. She enjoyed how April's wavy auburn hair fell over her shoulders and thought the pleating on the front of her slacks was especially attractive, though a person had to be tall for that kind of thing to really work for them.

August worried about Ivan, who was currently monopolizing the jam jar, devouring one biscuit after another, and avoiding eye contact. He seemed unusually tired and a little vulnerable without his beard, possibly because of the unusual paleness of his face and neck. When a windowpane rattled in the adjacent room—referencing a change in wind direction—Ivan anxiously turned toward the sound, and August wondered what he might be thinking.

"If you all don't mind, I think I'll take a walk," Lester said.

"You haven't eaten your biscuit," Hanh complained.

"I'll finish when I get back. Thanks, April, for taking the time to do this, and is it okay if your dog accompanies me? I won't be gone long."

"Of course. Hannah loves walks."

"I'll be back before you know it."

"Which way are you going?" asked Hanh.

"North. I'll go north."

Lester walked away from the table, pulled his scarf off the bent nail near the door, and tied it around his neck. Choosing the coat with lining, he slid his arms through the sleeves and pinched together the metal snaps along the front; halfway up, he noticed a misalignment, popped the already closed snaps open, and started again. He covered the top of his head with a fur-lined hat and stepped outdoors.

Hannah met Lester in the middle of the yard, and they stood together looking at each other, as though agreeing on how fast to walk and how long to be gone.

Both dog and man turned as the sedan with Arkansas plates came into view; the vehicle bumped and slid along the lane and stopped near them. Three people climbed out. The younger man petted Hannah. Lester talked to them, shook his head, adjusted his hat, shrugged, gestured toward the house with one of his gloved hands, and walked away with the Afghan, moving east.

Inside, watching through the windows, August, Hanh, April, and Ivan saw the three family members come toward the front door.

"I can send them away," August offered.

"No, let them in." Ivan hard-swallowed his last biscuit and stood up from the table. "I need to get this over with."

"You look exhausted," August pointed out. "We can set a time to meet with them tomorrow, or the next day."

"Don't want that, Gus. Let 'em in, Hanh."

The older couple at the door remembered Hanh's name from meeting her before and apologized about interrupting her afternoon. "We don't mean to make a nuisance of ourselves," said the woman, smiling in a forced manner. She and her husband were nearly identical in size, with similar light brown eyes. They seemed fatigued yet resolute, in matching green zippered jackets that fit them haphazardly, as though shopping clerks with shortened attention spans had recently dressed them. Their son, more carefully put together, wore fairly new hiking boots, jeans and a leather coat. He seemed protective of his parents yet determined to stay in the background. "We're still looking for Ivan Bookchester, and Mr. Mortal told us he might be here. Is he? We're hoping to talk to him."

"Please come inside," said Hanh.

They entered and stood close together, casting furtive glances at the others and inspecting the small space.

Hanh introduced them. "This is April Lux, August Helm, and Ivan Bookchester."

"You're Ivan Bookchester?" asked Mr. Pierce, stepping forward. "It's good to finally meet you. My name's Edgar Pierce. This is my wife, Alice, and my son, Samuel."

"I heard someone had been asking about me," said Ivan. "I've been away."

"We were hoping to talk to you in private," Mr. Pierce said.

"We can talk here," said Ivan, making it clear that the other people in the room would be included in whatever conversation there would be. He cleared his throat to steady his voice.

"Were you a welder with R-Corp when they built the line through British Columbia three years ago?"

"I was."

"Did you know our daughter, Hester?" asked Mrs. Pierce, drawing a photograph out of an inside pocket. She held it toward Ivan and when he didn't take it, she nudged it closer, as if it were alive.

Ivan glanced at the picture and said he remembered her. "I didn't know her well, but I knew her. We worked together a couple times."

"We're hoping you can tell us how she died," Mrs. Piece said, looking at Ivan expectantly.

Ivan froze.

When he didn't speak, August asked everyone to sit down.

The Pierce family took the chairs nearest the door. Sam shoved his hands deeply into the front pockets of his leather jacket, his legs stretched out in front. His parents sat stiffly upright. Ivan and April took up positions on either side of August, and Hanh, still standing, asked if anyone needed something to drink, like a glass of water.

No one did, and Mrs. Pierce held out the picture again, sliding it onto Ivan's lap, who was seated to her left.

Ivan kept his arms folded in front of him and looked down at the picture. He did not pick it up.

"We just want to know what happened," Mr. Pierce said, and August noticed he hadn't shaved that morning. "It's always hard to lose someone, God knows that, but when you're unsure about what happened, well, it's harder still. They said you could tell us."

"That isn't quite true, Edgar," Mrs. Pierce corrected, with patient resignation. "We were told that Ivan Bookchester *might* know."

The couple stared at each other.

"It seems such a long time ago," said Ivan.

"Not to us," said Mrs. Pierce. "That's why we need you to tell us. Not knowing keeps everything raw."

Ivan smiled weakly and said, "I remember her as a fun person to be around. She had a way of making everyone feel better, and that talent was especially appreciated because much of what we did was pretty monotonous."

"Oh, yes, you did know Hester," gushed Mrs. Pierce. "I can see that. She was always able to—"

"Can you tell us how she died?" Mr. Pierce almost shouted, refusing to be drawn away from their agenda. "What exactly happened? The details? That's what we're here for, and as soon as we learn the facts then we can go back home."

"There's no need to go and lose your temper," said Mrs. Pierce. "I'm sorry, Ivan. This has been hard on us."

"Look, I don't know what I can tell you," Ivan said, looking again into the picture on his lap. "The company had me sign a nondisclosure agreement."

"We know," said Mr. Pierce. "We know that. They told us. But we thought it might still be possible . . . for you to tell us the truth."

"The truth," repeated Ivan. He handed the picture back to Mrs. Pierce, leaned forward in his chair, rested his elbows on his thighs, interlocked his fingers, and appeared to be almost ready to say something.

Before he spoke, April shifted in her chair and said, "Perhaps it isn't my place to say anything, but I think it would expedite matters a great deal if you, Mister and Missus Pierce, could tell Ivan what you already know about your daughter's death. This is difficult for everyone, but if you will explain to Ivan what you already know, make clear to him the questions you have, then perhaps he can supply some of the missing parts without actually violating the agreement he signed."

Ivan glanced at April, releasing a guarded expression of gratitude.

"I guess there was an accident," began Mrs. Pierce. "A propane tank exploded inside a utility shed, we were told—"

"Right there. Right there," interrupted Mr. Pierce, jabbing a fore-finger into the air, as though pressing an unseen Stop button. "*That's what we were told.* That's what we were told, but propane tank explosions are extremely rare. They almost never happen, and I do mean never. I've worked with propane my whole life, and so have several of my cousins. The tanks never blow up. There's no oxygen in there to burn the fuel, and there's a pressure valve to keep the liquefied gas from exceeding combustion limits. To get a tank to explode you'd have to increase the pressure faster than the release valve can let it out, and frankly that's just never going to happen except during a building fire, and no one said anything about a building fire."

"I'm just explaining what we were told, Edgar," said his wife.

"I know what we were told, but it's all lies. It's nonsense. That's why we're here. The fucking company is lying. When we got her body back from those lying bastards there were almost no burn marks anywhere on her. That's what the examiner said. She was all hacked up, her fingers and toes were gone, and her breasts, for crying out loud, but almost no burns, no propane residue, nothing consistent with an explosion. That's what the examiner said, nothing consistent with a lethal explosion. And they wouldn't let our medical examiner see the other bodies—the other people who supposedly died in the so-called propane tank explosion. It's all a bunch of damn lies."

"Edgar, you don't need to raise your voice."

"Leave him be, Mom," Samuel Pierce said, shoving his hands deeper into the pockets of his coat. "This isn't something you just talk normal about."

"That's because Hester wasn't in the utility shed when it blew," Ivan said.

"What are you saying?" asked Mr. and Mrs. Pierce.

"She wasn't inside the shed and neither was I," Ivan said calmly. "We were both behind the shed, standing to the back of one of the transport trucks. Between Hester and I and the shed stood a mountain of rock that had earlier been busted up and pushed together by the doz-ers. When the shed blew—"

"Stop right there," shouted Mr. Pierce. "Are you repeating to us the lie that a propane tank exploded?"

"It wasn't that simple," said Ivan, turning his head to look directly at Mr. Pierce. "And you're right: propane tanks almost never explode. But in this case the tank's pressure valve and the line running to the heaters along the wall had been leaking gas into the closed shed for weeks. Oxygen in the air had plenty of time to mix with it, neutralizing the chemical odorant. So, when Ruth, Slack, and Bret rolled open the door and came in the shed looking for a couple runabouts, they didn't notice anything. Bret apparently lit up a cigarette and that was that. There were two explosions really, one when the vaporized gas in the shed ignited, and a second when the pressurized propane remaining in the tank blew. The second followed so closely it seemed like only one explosion. The sides of tank peeled off like fruit rinds and were later found one hundred yards away."

"But you and Hester were outside," April said firmly. "You said the two of you weren't even in the shed."

"Yes, and the explosion blew a hailstorm of rock down on Hester and me, or I should say it would have brought the rock down on both of us if Hester hadn't pushed me to the other side of the truck. She saved my life, but unfortunately wasn't able to save her own. The rock and shed pieces battered her unmercifully, cut her up like a hundred knives, killed her quick, I mean, it buried her in seconds."

A stalking silence moved through the small house, and Mrs. Pierce took the picture of her daughter out of her coat again. She looked at it and put it back in her pocket.

"She saved my life," Ivan repeated, lowering his head. "I'm thankful for that, will be for the rest of my life, and I'm sorry for her death. If I'd been standing where she was, and she where I was, everything would have been different."

"She pushed you?" asked Mr. Pierce.

"She knocked me to the other side of the truck. First there was the blast and immediately after that Hester shot forward, pushing me from behind. Sure, maybe it was partly the blast that threw her into me, but I think she did it on her own. And I'll go on thinking that. The transporter shielded me, saved my life. They still had to dig me out, but I didn't die, and if I'd been standing where Hester was instead . . . well, I wouldn't be here."

"No one blames you," said Sam. "You were just lucky."

Another silence opened up, and it seemed able to draw away thoughts and feelings, making it easier to breathe, easier to exist, and everyone in the room accepted its authority and waited inside its solace for as long as they could.

"It just wasn't adding up," said Mrs. Pierce.

"The company lawyers said you'd be compensated," Ivan said. "They told us there'd be insurance payments to the family."

"I detest that word," said Mr. Pierce.

"Insurance?"

"Well, that word too." Mr. Pierce laughed a short, unexpected laugh that sounded like a cough and did not prompt anyone else to laugh or smile. "The word 'compensated' really rattles my cage. After over a year they cut us a check, enough to bury her and set up a gravestone, but not enough to hire attorneys to sue them. There's no excuse for a leaking propane valve and fuel line, not from a company licensed to build a pipeline."

"Ivan, we heard you suffered some injuries as well," said Mrs. Pierce.

He waved this comment aside. "Nothing Band-Aids and a few stitches couldn't cover."

Hanh walked into the kitchen and began putting the leftover biscuits and napkins away.

"Do you have any more questions?" April asked.

They didn't, at least not then.

As though responding to an unseen signal, everyone stood up. The Pierce family surrounded Ivan, exchanging short, awkward statements. Ivan gestured and talked, demonstrating where he and Hester had been standing in relation to the truck, the shed, and the mountain of stone.

August watched Ivan, noticing him grow more uncomfortable.

Standing next to August, April asked, "What's wrong?"

"Probably nothing."

"Tell me, August."

"Ivan told them what he thought they wanted to hear," August whispered.

"What's the matter with that?"

"Anything short of the truth is temporary."

"Yes, but people *are* temporary."

Hanh saw the Afghan hound walk across the front yard, unaccompanied. She hurried through the crowded living room and went outdoors.

Ivan put on his coat and went after her, taking Hanh's blue, hooded coat from the peg on the wall.

The others stayed inside. August explained to the family that Ivan and Hanh had gone to check on Lester Mortal—the old man they had met when they first arrived.

April let Hannah inside and put down some water for her in the kitchen.

Outside, Hanh and Ivan stood together at the edge of the yard, looking into the surrounding trees and brush. Leaves rattled across the ground and a few sparse, thin clouds moved rapidly across the steel-gray sky.

"He was headed east when we last saw him," Ivan said, placing the coat over Hanh's shoulders. "Any idea where he might have gone?"

The wind made the air seem colder than it was, and Ivan buttoned the top button on his shirt.

"Not really," Hanh replied, tossing on her coat, zipping up the front. "Wherever he is, he's probably fine. It just seems odd for the dog to come back without him."

"She's not his dog."

"I know that, Ivan," Hanh snapped. She waited several seconds, and then added, "He tires quickly, so he shouldn't be far away."

"Hey, Lester!" yelled Ivan.

"That won't do any good. He doesn't have his hearing aids in."

"He can't be far away."

"We should split up, look in different directions."

"If it's all the same, I'd rather stay with you," Ivan said.

"Why?"

"Just because."

They moved through the brush and trees, picking their way around rocks and thick stands of pine until Hanh decided they should change directions.

"There's a place along the ridge where he sometimes goes."

"The overhang?"

"Why didn't you tell me about those people who died on the pipeline?"

"I wanted to."

"Why didn't you?"

"It seemed like something you'd never need to know. I mean, knowing it wasn't doing anything for me."

"Don't ever do that again."

"Do what?"

"Not tell me something."

"How do I know what you need to know?"

"Always tell me everything."

After walking uphill for a half mile, they saw the old man at the edge of a collection of hardwoods, sitting on the ground, leaning against an ash, his legs stretched out in front. He appeared to be sleeping.

Hanh turned to Ivan and said, "I'm going back now. He doesn't like me keeping tabs on him. He calls it fussing."

"I'll bring him back," Ivan said.

When Ivan reached Lester, he spoke loudly. "Hey, Les."

The old man opened his eyes and looked up.

"What's the matter?" he asked. "Why are you here?"

"The dog came back without you."

"She got bored when I stopped moving and was under no obligation to stay with me. She's not my dog."

"Were you sleeping?"

"I might have nodded off. This seemed like a good place. I've sat here a lot of times. There's a good view. When I couldn't get back on my feet, I thought I'd rest before I tried again."

Ivan helped him up and they walked back together. The wind stopped blowing. Three unidentifiable birds flew overhead, moving rapidly toward an unknown destination.

"Is that family from Arkansas still around?"

"They were when I left."

"What did you finally tell them, Ivan?"

"I said their daughter died in an accident."

"How did they take it?"

"I think it's what they wanted to hear. The company had given them a report and they were looking for a reason to believe it."

"Did you tell them the truth?"

"Not really."

"You think it would have been harder for them to hear what actually happened?"

"Harder to hear and harder for me to say."

The wind returned, noisily stirring the needles in the nearby pine copse, and several dogs could be heard barking in the distance. There was also a low, deadening, industrial sound, like a truck shifting gears, but it could not be specifically identified.

"How do you feel about it now?"

"About what?"

"Telling that family something other than the truth."

"I don't feel exactly good about it, if that's what you mean. But the occasion seemed to call for it—don't you think?"

"I don't know what happened."

"What really happened is their daughter was raped and tortured to death along with another woman, and the two men who did it were killed."

"Who killed them?"

"I did."

"Is that why the company let you go early?"

"Yes."

"And you don't think this family would want to know that?"

"Knowing it hasn't done much for me, and if there was some way to unknow it, I would."

"How did you manage to kill them?"

"With a shovel."

"Why didn't you tell me about this a long time ago?"

"It's hard to explain."

"Try. But let's rest for a couple seconds while you do. I can't walk very far without getting tired."

Lester eased down onto the swollen root of a fallen tree, adjusted his hat, and shoved his fingers deeper into his gloves; Ivan sat beside him. The sky darkened as shadows mixed with air.

"I shouldn't have to explain it to you, Lester. It's always there, waiting to twist whatever I'm thinking. And when you're lucky enough to forget about it for an hour or a day—it comes back. It's like a disease without a name. Once you know, really know, what monstrosities people are capable of—that you, yourself, are capable of—it changes everything. Even the most beautiful events—while you're experiencing them—can turn ugly. Good things seem unreal; what is always real is that someone could hurt you, really hurt you, or someone you care about, at any time of day and for no reason at all."

"People are vicious," said Lester. "People are vicious. History reveals it. The Roman Empire celebrated butchery for over four hundred years, entertaining its public with organized carnage. They called it games. It was hugely popular, with the wealthiest citizens sitting in the shaded balconies while everyone else packed into the cheap seats. Mercenary troops went all over the world to capture future victims. There was an insatiable demand for large animals and slaughter-ready people. For four hundred years the citizens of Rome—generation after generation of fathers, mothers, grandparents, children—filed into the coliseums, ate salty foods, and cheered as thousands upon thousands of tigers, lions, elephants, gorillas, and people were killed for the spectacle of watching them die. It's bred into us, Ivan—killing and killers."

"Those two guys did it because it pleased them."

"That's what I'm saying. No one forced the Romans into coliseums. They wanted in on the fun. Most of the large animals in Europe were hunted to extinction and died while crowds cheered. It didn't end until the Goths eventually overran Rome, cancelled the Western Empire, and did away with the games. And the Romans called the Goths barbarians."

"Stop talking about Romans, Lester. Do you think it was wrong to not tell the Pierce family what really happened to their daughter?"

"They should know the truth."

"Why?"

"That's my opinion."

"Why?"

"Because there are some things you can lie about, and life goes on. Other lies injure everyone."

"I don't think I have it in me to tell them the truth."

"Then do whatever you want."

"But you think I should tell them?"

"They can't begin to heal until they know."

"They'll never get over it. There is no meaning in her death."

"There is, and they drove out here looking for it. They need to know what took her life to understand how broken they are. They need to know what did it to them. Then, for the rest of their lives they can know that every decision they make, everything they do, is because of what happened. But they can't do that if they don't know the truth."

"The men who killed her are dead. There's nothing left for anyone to do."

Lester waved his hand in the air as though brushing aside flying insects.

"People have to stop pretending that murder, torture, terrorism, genocidal wars, animal cruelty, and other atrocities deviate from our nature. They don't. You can't begin to fight back unless you see that."

The clouds thickened with more layers of moist air, and the sky ran from a deep, rusting gray in the east toward a bumpy sea of dark, muddy green.

FEMICIDE

WHEN LESTER AND Ivan arrived back at Lester's home, the light had nearly drained from the sky, leaving an uneven purple smudge along the western horizon. The Pierce family car still sat in the front yard, and there were several violent gashes in the muddy drive. Deep, greasy trenches running toward the road—tire-furrows left by a larger vehicle.

Inside, the Pierce family, Hanh, August, and April sat around the small kitchen table drinking iced tea and eating barbequed chicken wings, cornbread, deviled eggs, and deep-fried onion rings. Hanh filled two plates and carried them to Ivan and Lester. She explained that April had called the Gate's food service and ordered the snacks. On the way out, the delivery truck had experienced a little trouble with the driveway, she said.

"I'm surprised they came all the way out here," Lester remarked. Hanh led him into the living room and settled him into his chair.

"April talked them into it somehow," whispered Hanh. "I think she was trying to impress August. What took you so long to get back?"

"We walked slowly."

"These wings aren't spicy enough," Ivan complained, after eating three.

Lester took a bite of cornbread, drank a little water, and fell asleep in his chair. Hanh had one of Lester's medications at her house, and she went to retrieve it after promising to return in less than an hour.

The Pierces thanked April for the food and began putting on their coats. If they checked out of the motel right now, they wouldn't have to pay for an extra night.

Ivan privately asked August and April if they would assist him, or at least stand beside him, as he explained to the family how their daughter had really died.

"You should have just told them in the first place," August said.

"I don't like this," April said. "What are you going to tell them?"

"Exactly what happened."

"Your integrity will be questioned."

"I know . . . but if I were them, I'd want to know."

"Are you sure?"

"I think so."

"Should we wake Lester up?" August asked.

"No. His heart's in the right place but it's going to be hard enough without hearing about Romans."

As the Pierce family was going out the door, Ivan called them back. He had something to tell them, he said, but when they came inside and closed the door, he couldn't find the words to begin.

"What is it?" Alice asked, her eyes studying Ivan with a narrow, newly discovered suspicion.

"It's just that, well . . . there's more . . . or, not exactly more . . . but. . ." Ivan's voice progressively weakened, and finally gave out completely.

"What is it?" Edgar asked, agitation climbing into his voice.

"I didn't tell you the truth," Ivan explained, looking at the floor. "There's more to this, and I apologize for that."

"Spit it out," Sam snarled.

Ivan looked directly at him: "It was a free weekend. Your sister went off somewhere with her roommate, Ruth. They checked out a utility vehicle sometime around seven p.m. and were not seen for the rest of the night. At breakfast there was a lot of talk about them being gone. Midmorning, R-Corp sent out a couple low-level security people to look. They tried to track their phones. Helicopters were later called in. They were still missing in the middle of the afternoon and I took out a four-wheeler. There were many trails they could have taken and it was easy enough to get lost. We were in middle of nowhere."

Mrs. Pierce's expression had frozen, and she gripped Edgar's upper arm as though to maintain balance.

Sam took off his hat, held it for several moments, and put it back on his head, pulling the brim down to eye level.

As his audience's apprehensions rose, Ivan discovered more difficulty in finding the appropriate words, and, after finding them, speaking. It seemed almost as if the events he needed to relate could be retroactively prevented by not relating them. As long as the truth remained unspoken, the ambush could be postponed.

Ivan also learned what many other carriers of bad news often discovered: the seeds of responsibility for dreadful acts are somehow planted—like false evidence—inside the knowing of those acts. Little wonder that emperors often executed envoys bringing unwelcome reports. King David killed the courier who informed him of his son's death, because until he heard the news, his son lived.

Ivan wondered if they would believe him. He'd lied before, so why would they believe him now? Besides, what decent person could ever believe the story he had to tell?

Madness must feel like this, he thought, and he glanced over at August, frantic for some assistance.

"What are you saying?" Edgar demanded.

"They were dead," August said. "They were both dead when Ivan found them."

"Who were dead?"

"Hester and Ruth," Ivan said.

"How?"

"Slack Peters and Bret Logan killed them, killed them both."

"How do you know this?"

"Because I found them there—in the clearing next to the fire and the dug grave. I saw them lying there. A short time later Slack and Bret returned with their bloodstained clothes, and I killed them with a shovel."

"You're lying," Sam shouted, coming forward.

April stepped in front of Ivan. "Calm down," she said. "It's in the reports."

She opened the file folder she'd been holding and passed around copies of R-Corp documents, stamped Restricted.

"How did you get these?" asked Alice, leafing through the pages.

"My tech pulled them through two cipher drips, out of a back door to the company's encrypted archives. The first report summarizes a longer communication between R-Corp's forensic investigator and the head of its security division. Everything is there, including four autopsy reports and the legal team's decision to attribute the deaths to an explosion, and to terminate Ivan's employment with a muting package. The other document describes similarities between the deaths of Hester and Ruth with other mutilation murders during the preceding decade, possibly carried out by the same men."

The family sank into chairs to read the reports, and then reread them.

Ivan felt the despair in the room like water pressing against him.

Sam let go of the pages he was holding, and they fanned out against the floor. He started to weep, then stopped.

April picked up the discarded sheets of paper and returned them to the file folder.

Alice continued staring into the printed lines like a trapped animal looking into an advancing fire.

"They lied to us, and we can sue them," Edgar said, his voice slightly louder than a murmur. "With these reports—"

"I'm afraid not," April said. "You'd be arrested. Immediately. Just having these reports is a serious felony, to say nothing of showing them to a lawyer or anyone else. Thanks to conservative courts, corporate property laws have severely tightened over the last few years, and I must collect all the copies after you're finished reading them. I can't take the chance. None of us can. The current enforcement regimen for proprietary violation is impossible to stand against. All federal courts and almost all state courts would back them up."

"Why didn't you show us these when we first came here?" Sam demanded from April. "Why did you repeat the company's lie?"

"My tech warned me against showing the restricted reports to anyone. Just having these papers is dodgy. We could get in a lot of trouble—especially Ivan—because of the binding agreement. It would have been much safer to not show them to you. But when Ivan decided to tell you what really happened, I changed my mind, because you had a right to know. I did not mean to cause any additional harm, and now that I have, I'm sorry."

"You lied to us."

"At first, yes, that's true. I had hoped the company's statement would fly."

"Why should we believe you now?"

"You've seen the reports, but what you believe is up to you. Ivan, August, and I have no stake in this. You came here looking for the truth; at first, we went along with the company lie. Then Ivan decided he couldn't live with that, and August and I support Ivan."

"I don't understand. If the company didn't want anyone to know what really happened, why wouldn't they simply destroy the reports?"

"That's not the way these companies work," said April. "They don't destroy data; they manage it. Destroying data is risky. Someone might turn up with it in the future, or claim to have it, or have a different version of it, and they would be vulnerable. To prevent that, they maintain all records. It's a little like Germany during the Second World War; even though they were committing crimes against humanity, they couldn't refrain from account keeping."

"R-Corp went out of their way to protect the reputations of the monsters who did this," Samuel said. "Why would they do that?"

"They didn't care one way or another about the men who did this," April said. "All they cared about was protecting themselves against future penalties, lawsuits, revenue losses, and plummeting stock values. The negative publicity would have potentially gone on for years."

"How far did their lies go? Is there any chance those two men are still walking around somewhere, alive?"

"No, they're dead," said Ivan.

"I wish they were still alive, so I could find them," said Sam.

"That wouldn't bring Hester back," said Alice.

"No, but I'd feel a whole lot better."

"It didn't make me feel any better to kill them," Ivan remarked, mostly to himself.

"Maybe not, but I wouldn't kill them with a shovel. I'd use a pair of pliers."

Ivan experienced relief for Lester's absence. If the old veteran were not currently asleep, he might be saying that the desire to hurt someone—or watch someone else doing it—was always looking for an excuse to come out. And even if there was some truth in Lester's argument that intentional violence could not be justified by invoking the three time-honored justifications—punishing wrongdoing, expressing righteous anger, and administering vengeance—Ivan was glad the old man was not pointing this out right now.

"I *knew* something like this happened to her," Edgar said. "From the time we first heard about her death, I *knew* it. I always knew it."

"So did I," Sam said. "I never believed R-Corp. I always knew it was a lie. In my own way, I could feel it."

August wanted to contribute something, but he couldn't think of anything good to say. He didn't believe people could know about things they had no evidence for, or see into the future. When one's worst fears were realized it often felt like some malevolent prophecy had been fulfilled, or that a past evil had been resurrected, and if there were high expectations for favorable outcomes, then an unfortunate turn of events seemed like cosmic injustice. But when unexpectedly agreeable outcomes were experienced, people seldom attributed them to the unseen working of benevolent forces. They tended to just accept them. Agencies of darkness were assumed to involve more behind-the-scenes maneuvering than forces of light, and it always seemed more convincing to claim unwanted things were ready to happen than to portend impending good fortune. Disheveled men in beards seldom stood on cold, windy street corners proclaiming happy days for everyone listening. Likewise, when beloved family members narrowly escaped life-threatening circumstances, people seldom exclaimed, "Oh, of course, of course, I knew they'd be fine." But after learning of a recent tragedy, people would often remark, "I had a feeling something like this would happen." Perhaps such comments were a way of denying psychological power to the element of surprise. *I may be hurt but at least I wasn't blindsided.* As a general rule, natural selection had conditioned creatures to pay more attention to fear than hope. An organism could possibly survive without sanguinity, but not without a functioning impulse to fight and/or run away.

The Pierce family continued to ask questions and Ivan kept answering them as well as he could.

Over the next hour, their questions became more speculative, more difficult to answer. "Why would those men do something like that?" "Was it all about sex in some perverted way?" "Isn't it always about sex in the end?" "What else can explain it?" "Surely there were suspicions about these men? Didn't someone check these guys out before they were hired?"

Pauses between questions and answers began to take up more and more oxygen in the room.

April gathered up the reports and replaced them in her file folder. To fill the persisting silence, she said, "For whatever it's worth, every year there are, worldwide, over one hundred thousand cases of femicide—the killing of women by men, primarily for being women. In addition to stranger-driven crimes, many, many more women are beaten, maimed, disfigured, or killed by their own families, neighbors, friends, and lovers. The crimes are so prevalent that one out of every four women can realistically anticipate being violently assaulted in her lifetime. And not all violence against women comes from men. In rapidly developing countries, when ultrasound technologies first become available and pregnant women learn the gender of their fetuses, they often abort the females. Some do it to keep from losing their husbands; others do it to preserve scarce resources for male children. Violence against women and girls has been endemic since the beginning of organized agriculture, and will no doubt continue until social impulses toward equality, fairness, and indiscriminate compassion eventually grow stronger than the urge to dominate and reproduce."

No eye contact was made for several minutes.

Then Edgar stepped forward and extended his hand toward Ivan. "Well, I guess we learned what we came here for, Ivan. I'm not sure I can bring myself to thank you, but we're going to leave now. You're a stand-up guy, even if it took you a while to find your feet."

"I'm really sorry for what happened," Ivan said, shaking his hand. "I really am."

"Son, none of us asked for this, and you did what you needed to do; now we must do what we must."

"What's that?" Ivan asked.

"Go home."

The Pierce family went outside.

Ivan and August followed them outdoors and watched them leave, their car spitting up mud and deepening the ruts in the drive.

The night tightened around them, and they listened to the automobile pulling onto the road and accelerating on gravel. The abrasive sound grew more and more distant, and as though in direct response, Ivan felt palpable relief—a weighted shadow detaching from his body and dissolving in the darkness, leaving him thirty-five pounds lighter and five years younger.

August turned toward Ivan and said, "Someone broke into April's home, busted it up as well as they could in a short time, and painted invectives on the walls."

"When was this?"

"Sometime yesterday. We found it after we got back last night."

"Who did it?"

"The intruder wore a mask. April thinks she knows who hired him—a local homeowner with a grievance—but all the surveillance video shows is a guy somewhere between my size and yours, in a mask with a hoodie pulled up over his head . . . a white guy in his early twenties."

"Why didn't you call me?"

"You were in hiding, remember? We even drove over to your place looking for you, checked on Jet Lag to be sure he'd been fed."

"I snuck over every day to feed him and visit for a bit."

"That's what we discovered."

"Why did this guy hire someone to trash her house, and what does he have against her?"

"She didn't say."

"Hanh and I will help clean up."

"We already did that . . . and applied stain killer."

"What color was the paint?"

"Red."

"Probably should have two coats—stain killer, I mean. Hanh and I can help with that. We'll have the walls painted before you know it."

"We got it covered."

"Just the same. This is serious, and I need to do something for April. I owe her. Did you know she had those reports?"

"She didn't say anything about them."

"Is she really interested in you?"

"What do you mean?"

"You know what I mean, Gus. Is April Lux interested in you in the way women occasionally get interested when they want to have sex?"

"I think. I certainly hope so."

"Something about her seems unapproachable."

"Why?"

"She's intimidating."

"I don't share that opinion, but I understand how someone might possibly feel that way."

"I didn't mean it as a criticism; in fact, the opposite of that. Did you call the police about the vandalism?"

"Her property alarm triggered Gate security and they also called in local law. They were there before we arrived, taking pictures and stepping on broken glass. April says the floors will have to be redone."

"I'll come back with you and take a look around. It might not be safe to stay there."

"We stayed there last night."

"Are you sure it wasn't a woman?"

"The police thought the shape and movement of the figure on the video were more likely male than female."

"I still think I should come back with you. For one thing, I'd make sure all the windows are locked. The guy who broke in might have left a way to get in later. Also, are you sure there isn't someone hiding inside the house right now? Maybe he's in there."

"I don't think so, Ivan. The police looked already and security cameras are everywhere. There are pictures of him leaving through the back door—off the kitchen."

April and her dog stepped out of the house, the file folder tucked firmly under her left arm. Her hair seemed almost red in the odd light, and both Ivan and August kept staring at it. She also looked tired and ready to leave.

"I'll call you tomorrow," August said, walking toward the car. "And I'll make sure all the windows are locked."

Ivan thanked April for her help, and April asked Ivan to give her best wishes to Lester Mortal when he woke up. "I've grown quite fond of the old soldier."

"I'll make sure he knows that, but I wish you'd let me come back with you to make sure it's safe to stay there. Gus explained about the vandalism and it worries me."

"Thanks for your concern, Ivan, but I'm sure the security people have covered everything. It's been a long day, especially for you. We all need some space."

She ushered her dog onto the back seat.

"Well, thanks again for your help."

"You're sincerely welcome." She climbed into the car beside August.

August started the engine and they slogged down the muddy drive to the road.

"You didn't mention having those restricted reports this morning," August said. "Why didn't you say something about them on the drive over?"

April stared into the path of illumination streaming out of the headlights and falling onto the road ahead, and it seemed a little like they were standing still as the roadway ran beneath them like a treadmill. "I wasn't sure myself what I wanted to do with the reports."

"You first helped Ivan lie, and later helped him tell the truth."

"I thought that's what you wanted me to do—help Ivan. He changed his mind about what he wanted to tell the family, and I stayed with him. You said he was important to you."

"I'm not criticizing you; I just didn't anticipate how much help you'd provide."

Two Gate guards waved them through, and at the end of April's drive they sat for a short while before getting out of the car, the lights and the engine shut off. When the windshield began to fog over, they got out.

Inside, the red paint had penetrated through the stain killer and the vandal's words were once again visible, now in pink.

"This is depressing," August said, hanging up their coats. While inhaling a quart of closet air, he noticed a tightening in his chest, and assumed this was because of muscle tension precipitated by the bleeding words.

SNOW

STARTLED BY A dream that ended violently, Lester Mortal jerked awake in his bed. He opened his eyes, surveyed the bedroom, and waited for his nearly audible heart to level off.

The house seemed extraordinarily quiet. It was still dark beyond the east-facing window and he closed his eyes and tried to fall back to sleep. Rearranging himself on the mattress, he made a renewed effort to conjure up a benign state of unconsciousness and failed. He blamed this on the many poverties of aging: just as people's names randomly disappeared from his memory, he was also, apparently, forgetting how to stay asleep at night and how to remain awake during the day. His life was fragmenting into moments of lucidity within a domestic ocean of uncertainty, and he thought about this on his passage to the bathroom.

After relieving his anxious bladder, he washed his hands with soap and tepid water and dried them with the fresh yellow towel that Hanh set out the day before. The floor felt glacial under his feet and he took down the robe hanging from the back of the bathroom door. He gathered the soft fabric in front of him and looped the limp belt at his waist. Holding the edge of the sink for balance, he inched his feet into cloth-lined slippers and could not remember if he'd placed a log in the stove before going to bed. The geography of his short-term memory included several unexplored regions, and many recent activities left no trails to follow back from the future. Perhaps his brain had grown so old and inflexible that some experiences were no longer recorded in new protein chains, and past events simply vanished like unheard sounds in a forest.

He shuffled off into the cool, dark living room and opened the stove door. Annoyed with being disturbed, the iron hinges shrieked.

Inside, the fire had fizzled down to a lumpy layer of dark ash. When stirred with the poker, a few small coals blinked to red life and he sprinkled handfuls of white pine bark and wood chips on top of them. Then he added dry branches and an assortment of smaller logs—taken from the wood box Hanh had filled that afternoon.

Nothing happened at first; then rolling smoke gathered at the top of the firebox, exhaling plumes of gas into the room. Then a single flame poked up inside the carcass of branches, followed by several more fragile yet eager blades of light. The eruptions spread, and a bright, lurching fire soon hurled its nimble colors into the room, flickering against the wall. Lester eased into the nearby chair and waited for new warmth to embrace him, and inside this anticipation of comfort, he relaxed.

The interior of the small house breathed several times and audibly sighed.

A movement caught his eye. He closed the stove to make the out-of-doors more visible and leaned closer to the window. Out there, a hundred thousand shredded snowflakes drifted aimlessly into the yard, and two mature deer stepped noiselessly, ritualistically through the falling snow. It seemed like the opening scene of a ballet—reserved for private viewing only—and he imagined an unseen orchestra preparing to play, the director gripping the baton, both hands above her head.

As he observed the scene beyond the window his thoughts gathered into a familiar, wordless reverie. His better self woke up. The deer took several steps on taut, stalk-thin legs; they lifted their heads and cautiously tasted the air. Somehow, the alchemy of their untamed alertness joined sacred beauty to open fear.

Lester yearned to be part of the creatures' unapproachable otherness, to simultaneously experience them through an objective distance and yet to know them from the inside—to *be* them. His desire intensified through the impossibility of its immediate fulfillment, as well as its eventual guarantee. He and they shared a mortal community, driven by the same biotic gears. Deer and people could wonder about each other as much as they wanted, but only if their mutual separations held. At some irrevocable yet unfixed future time, their personal, twitching lives would cease. Natural forces would dissolve their individual autonomies and reduce them to common elements. Their forms would decompose—converted by water, minerals, enzymes, and microorganisms into the ingredients for other living things. In and through the infinite impossibility of time and the indomitable reordering of physical reality, their spirits would scatter and join, and someday they would know, and eventually be, the other.

The new, falling snow mostly melted after reaching the warm ground, yet collected on tree branches, fence posts, and the deer; they carried the new white layer without effort or concern.

In the same noiseless manner that they'd first entered Lester's frame of view, the wild animals moved beyond it. After they were gone, Lester felt emptied. He tried to hold onto the sense of brushing against the edge of something divine—a brief disclosure within a holy space— but the feeling could not be sustained.

He watched the snow falling into his yard for a little longer, turned away from the window, and reopened the stove. Heat and light rushed out and the weightless, dancing shapes again frolicked silently against the wall.

Settling deeper into his chair, Lester contemplated the fire. The pulsing flames loosened his thoughts. Because he was not paying attention to whatever impelled one recollection to merge into another, it seemed as though he roamed aimlessly through the past—a traveler without an itinerary. Those met along the way— friends, relatives, neighbors, public figures, junior versions of himself, people he'd only known momentarily—wanted nothing from him beyond recognition, and he asked nothing from them other than to momentarily share their stage. Most, of course, were now dead, but the knowledge of their deaths was not included in the scenes he remembered. His memories were impervious to suspicion, fully alive, yet not really living.

The fire inside the stove burned brighter and hotter, and to encourage even more heat and light he put in another log and adjusted its position with the poker until a uniform row of flames curled around the woody surface like the long, fiery tines of a garden rake.

He moved his chair back several feet and settled into it.

Once, almost ninety years ago, at the age of five or six, Lester went for a walk around the block with his father. They weren't gone very long and nothing extraordinary happened, but Lester often remembered the outing and now entered the recollection with a quiet satisfaction reserved for only his most treasured mnemonic souvenirs. He wondered if his fondness was an outgrowth of the many times was he'd revisited it, or if the revisiting itself was prompted by the fondness.

The remembrance began with a narrow sense of familiarity and a quick glimpse of its events. Then, by relaxing into the memory's central feeling, its more subliminal parts were marshaled into chronological order. And the more he indulged the mood, the more details emerged. Within a short time, Lester had rediscovered his childhood. He was small again, led from one moment to the next by a need to experience everything, unable to divide the urgency of the present into important events and those that could be safely ignored. The agency of his attention could not be governed and he tried to process all the new sensations that surrounded him as though trying to drink from a fire hose.

After supper, his father asked if he wanted to take a walk, "To help our food settle."

Lester was simultaneously elated and wary. He loved his father with a worshipful intensity that never stopped hoping for opportunities to occupy the center of his notice, but because this so rarely happened, and his father's time was so seldom shared, an unexpected invitation to take a walk filled Lester with a mild foreboding. He wondered if there was some hidden agenda, like weeding the garden, sorting trash into piles next to the front porch, or raking up grass clippings. Settling food seemed an unlikely motivation for a walk; it lacked the banal purposefulness of most adult behavior, and even if there was perhaps some digestive truth lurking within the statement, what about the hundreds of meals that had never gotten a chance to settle inside his father's stomach in the past? What about those?

It was summer. There were no coats, hats, scarves, boots, or gloves involved in leaving the house. The back door creaked open and banged shut, and out of the corner of his eye, the neighbor's orange cat darted behind the shed.

After they were outside, Lester relaxed. His father walked out of the yard and started down the sidewalk, keeping to the right-hand side of the rectangular concrete squares so there was room for Lester to walk beside him.

The evening glowed from the inside, and shadows fastened to the bottom of solid things and looked like holes with sharp edges. Telephone and electrical lines were strung overhead, straight in one direction, sagging along another, and a line of dark birds with moderately long beaks quickly gathered on a single wire, spacing their lumpy shapes with near-geometrical precision. Once in place, they fidgeted, jerking their heads, ruffling their feathers, glancing into space. Cars with and without burning headlights moved along distant streets—their hulking bodies making grinding, crushing noises. Something jingled in his father's pants pocket. Change, Lester thought. Or keys. Lester wished he had change or keys in one of his pockets and wondered, if he did, if would they rattle in the same way. Maybe his pockets weren't roomy enough. The evenly spaced birds above him on the wire exploded in a muffled roar and hightailed it out of sight because of some unrevealed emergency.

After twelve or thirteen normal walking steps beside his father, Lester became assaulted by a nearly fatal boredom, and to correct for this he began walking robot-stiff, as though his legs were made of solid metal pillars; then he hopped on one foot; then he avoided straight-across sidewalk cracks, and, later, all sidewalk cracks; next, he walked backwards, jumped, and moved his arms in circles.

They didn't go very far before a neighbor greeted them. His father stopped, adjusted his shoulders, and crossed the street to the neighbor and the neighbor's sedan. Lester let his father get most of the way across the street and then dashed over and ended up next to him after a short skid. The rusty, beige sedan was still shiny in a few places and Lester looked at his reflection in the glossy paint. His memory didn't know why the neighbor was standing in his driveway or what he talked about with his father, but the feeling of the encounter remained very strong. There were no dangers, or threats, presented by the neighbor. No alarms went off. His father effortlessly slipped out of his Dad uniform and into a more public edition of himself—part citizen, part local celebrity, part next-door entertainer. The neighbor respected his father and was pleased to be talking to him. And this respect carried over into how Lester himself was greeted—as an extension of his father. Lester was his son, and because of that, Lester was somebody. The neighbor extended his open hand and Lester shook it, despite not liking to shake adult hands because of the gigantic size and height differences. The inequalities of bulk always seemed to reduce the greeting ritual into a mocking display of adult power.

A short time later he and his father returned to the other side of the street to resume their walk around the block, and his father momentarily placed his hand on Lester's shoulder. The contact seemed both protective and affectionate, and the feeling of his father's hand on his shoulder lingered for a while after it was removed. More birds rallied on the wires.

They continued down the sidewalk, turned left at the corner, and walked until his father stopped, reached down, and picked up a scruffy-looking penny that had fallen into the strip of grass between the curb and sidewalk. After rubbing it between his fingers and examining both sides of the coin, his father handed it to him and Lester put it in his pocket, feeling like he'd witnessed a magical act. His father's abilities to succeed in the world seemed almost superhuman, and while Lester stared into the fire and the heat seeped into his clothes, he indulged in feeling a reverent awe for his father—an adoration that had been planted in his young mind and out of which most of his other values and ambitions later branched off. His father's early influence over Lester was so profound that it threatened to define everything else about him— the choices he'd made, his reasons for making them, and the ways he thought about himself. Early impressions of his father—rightly or wrongly—served as the owner's manual for the rest of his life. The love he'd experienced for, and from, his father—over ninety years ago—still governed him through a silent, benign imperative.

Lester then thought about Hanh. He wondered about checking on her to make sure she was all right, but he didn't want to call in the middle of the night.

I'll drive over there, he decided. Can't sleep anyway. If her lights are out and the house seems quiet, I'll just come back. Don't need to knock or go inside.

Lester closed the stove door and shuffled away into the bedroom where he changed clothes. At the front door, he put on his heavy coat, gloves, hat, and scarf, and stepped outdoors. Big, ragged snowflakes fell on him, some brushing against his face and melting in bursts of wetness. A profound stillness accompanied the downfall, as though everything outdoors tried to hear the snow landing on the ground but couldn't.

He stood in the yard and thought about the deer. "I'm here," he said. "I'm here."

Inside his truck, he inserted the ignition key, twisted it, and engaged a single mechanical snap from the engine's starter. A second attempt prompted another similar sound like a mousetrap springing shut.

He climbed out of the truck, closed the door, and stood in the front yard while the snow landed on him.

He wondered about walking to Hanh's house. It seemed a sensible thing to do. The night was deliciously dark, the snow spilling out of an overhead void, reminding him of other winters in other places. A kind of peace surrounded his thoughts. She wasn't that far away—probably less than a half mile—and by the time he returned home he would be ready for several hours of deep, dreamless sleep.

Besides, he felt more alive outdoors.

After walking for five or ten minutes, Lester noticed the snow was falling more vigorously. Individual flakes were smaller, but there were more of them; they no longer seemed to float or glide through the air. They now hurried toward the earth with blind determination—straight down—and were beginning to cover the ground—at first leaving a splotchy mix of dark and light sections, then eventually filling in the dark ones. The air thickened and Lester began having difficulty seeing more than several yards in front of him. Some irony could be found in a blackout of too much white stuff, but it nevertheless seemed somewhat serious.

Though intimately familiar with every feature along the way, his familiarity came mostly from driving along the lane rather than walking, and at slower speeds familiar sights looked different. He remembered August once said that looking through a microscope rendered even the most everyday objects unrecognizable. It was hard to keep to the winding lane through the trees, and several times he had to backtrack to recover the correct path.

Several inches of snow accumulated on the ground, and it seemed he'd been walking for a long time. He held his watch close to his face, but there was not enough light to see the hands. The night also seemed a lot colder, and he tugged his coat together as snuggly as he could, pulled his hat down further over his ears, and wound the scarf more tightly around his neck.

The snow fell and Lester continued walking into it. Placing one foot in front of the other, he strode on, leaning into the white teeth of the storm.

The snow grew deeper and the stillness hypnotized him.

Lester's awareness of his surroundings began to narrow. There were elongated moments in which he no longer remembered where he was going, or why he was going there. Systemic fatigue crowded out other sensations.

On the plus side, he no longer felt cold. The darkness extended in all directions and his sense of who, and what, he was—his identity—only contained scraps of biological reference, the fragile intuition of a rapidly beating heart and the slogging movement of numb hands, legs, and feet. Yet every so often he experienced a sudden, intense sense of well-being, an impression of a gentle space opening up, an energy, perhaps even an accompanying presence that he had never encountered before, existing alongside yet-beyond him, in another dimension. But when he tried to reflect on this new energy—even to consider whether it was truly new—he found he could not make it the center of his thoughts. He was too tired.

Hanh had left her porch light burning, but when this light first began to penetrate Lester's darkness, it didn't seem like light at all, only another variation on the theme of whiteout blackness. As he plodded forward, the illumination became more pronounced; it seemed somehow softer and increasingly interesting to his left, and he sloughed off in that direction.

After he discovered Hanh's porch light—a single bulb inside a lantern-like fixture on the side of the house, mounted above the front door, protected by the overhanging roof—Lester smelled the medicinal qualities of wood smoke.

The porch floor was a wall of stacked firewood, and the ledge too high for him to step up on. He discovered Ivan's truck with its snow-blade bolted to the front, covered with snow, parked to the side of the little house. Ivan had obviously come over to clear her drive in the morning, and they were no doubt sleeping inside, insulated by the thick layer of snow on the roof. Lester tried to open Ivan's truck door, but it would not budge.

There was a metal chair sitting in the front yard, and after colliding with it, Lester sat down. The energy-presence he'd experienced earlier returned. The smell of wood smoke returned, and an immense relief crept into his mind; he closed his eyes to capture it more fully. He thought about his father; he thought about Hanh, and Ivan. He felt safe. Living wasn't that difficult. The one thing worth knowing—the singularity of life—was to identify what you most loved and follow it. After you persevered long enough, others would join. He'd made it through the snow and conquered the cold. After he regained his strength, he would climb up on the porch. He'd go inside and eat breakfast with Hanh and Ivan. After that, Ivan could drive him back. And tomorrow he intended to . . . well, he didn't know what he'd do tomorrow, but right now it felt good to just sit. The snow continued to fall.

Four hours later, at first light, Ivan came out of the house. The air was still and silent. It had stopped snowing. He found Lester frozen under a mound of white, his earlier tracks covered by three inches of new fall.

Snow lay over everything. The only blemish on the surface was a thin, irregular trail left by deer. The tracks came out of the narrow lane, up to Lester, then headed north.

Ivan brushed off the snow, carried the surprisingly weightless body over to the truck, and placed him inside. After clearing the windshield, he climbed behind the wheel, started the engine, raised the blade several inches, adjusted the tilt, and headed down the lane. Though deep, the white stuff pushed easily, and a humped, uneven snow-dam mounded up on one side. Once, at a bump in the lane, Lester's frozen form fell over, and Ivan settled him upright. He thought about telling Hanh that he'd found Lester at home in his bed but couldn't make up his mind if he should.

LINKS AND LINKAGE

No one was particularly surprised when August's mother assumed responsibility for planning Lester Mortal's memorial service. Hanh did not easily interact with most people, and she strenuously resisted the obligation of making the necessary arrangements. The anguish she experienced over Lester's death seemed too personal to share with anyone.

Lester knew this about her, of course, and he'd written a page of suggestions for what might happen after his death, which he'd left in an easy-to-find sheaf of personal papers. Under the heading of "Thoughts About Dying and So On," near the top, Lester wrote that he hoped August Helm's mother, Mrs. Winifred Helm, would take charge of all preparations related to his interment.

Winnie welcomed the responsibility. She had decades of experience in helping people take leave of loved ones, and she believed in the need for family and friends to openly celebrate the life of someone who had recently stopped living. An individual's death, she thought, was an occasion too momentous for people to suffer alone. Grief management, she believed, was one of the more positive benefits that a religion could proffer: time-honored ways to say goodbye, and language suggestions for saying it.

Winnie sometimes acknowledged—to herself and those near at hand—that her thoughts about funerals and leave-taking had gradually softened through the years. She'd become more comfortable with the epistemological inconsistencies that many people demonstrated when someone close to them passed away. In the beginning of her ministry, it had discomforted her that people should be so wobbly. She was especially bothered by those who habitually wore realism on their sleeves, eschewed spirituality and metaphysical thinking of all varieties, scoffed at wishful thinking, and firmly rejected "fanciful" explanations, but when their own mother or father or daughter or son or brother or wife or husband died, their devotion to firmly established materialistic principles suddenly went up in ontological smoke. Deceased loved ones were pictured entering a paradisiac sphere of existence wherein molecular decay had no purchase over them, a realm of timeless tranquility and peace. Then weeks later, these same people who had so recently pictured their deceased family members living with the angels, would gradually drift back to their earlier attitudes about the inviolate order of the physical universe as seamlessly as returning from a recent vacation. When Winnie was a young preacher, it had seemed to her barbaric to borrow the hard-won beliefs that others struggled to establish and maintain, to use them for a short time, and then abandon them.

But as Winnie grew older, many of her edges had worn off. Beliefs should serve people, she eventually decided, and not the other way around. Ways of thinking about existence, the afterworld or underworld, did not need to be consistent; they needed to be helpful. And if they weren't, then new beliefs were required. Like tools, the healthy mind kept different beliefs in separate drawers for different occasions.

When someone died, those left behind often faced debilitating emotions. Intense anguish pushed them beyond the usual considerations of everyday life, and they would wonder about things that were not openly talked about in polite society—like the limits of sentience. Did subjective experience expire when oxygen ceased flowing into the brain, or did the capacity for experience simply oscillate along different orbits? Did an individual's identity somehow endure beyond the decomposition of their eukaryotic cells? Should a pervasive fondness for someone no longer living still have relevance to the living? Was remembered love real?

Humans, Winnie concluded, were not properly equipped to think about these things. As her son August often pointed out, natural selection tended to favor individuals who did not waste much time on grieving. After someone died, it was necessary for those still living to adjust, and allow the fact that certain death waited for everyone to recede back into its hiding place . . . and get on with life.

The ability to plan proved essential to successful living. People used their experiences in the here and now to benefit them in the future, and while it was permissible to briefly linger in the past, gaze backward at unresolved sorrows, tensions, and regrets, it was essential to keep moving—to make survival plans. There was wood to chop and water to carry. Dwelling on the past for too long should be avoided.

But memorial services, Winnie thought, were times when normal, forward-looking practicalities could be set aside—when the inevitability of a permanently cancelled tomorrow could be allowed to float up to a conscious level. On these occasions, communities needed to come together, crowd into shared spaces, and think about the implications of remaining alive while others died. The great chain of life could be seen more clearly after a link had recently been removed.

With multiple generations crowded into pews or sitting on folding chairs with inadequate back support, dressed in uncomfortable clothes, balancing paper plates of shared food, the reality of a constantly breaking yet continually rejoining biological continuum didn't seem so worrisome. When you saw tears in someone else's eyes, your own seemed less important. And when only a few people showed up for a ceremony, the overwhelming significance of one-on-one connections became even more evident. The linkage counted more than the links themselves.

Lester had wanted his body cremated and Winnie arranged for this through a funeral home in Grange. However, the old soldier did not leave instructions for how he wished to have his ashes disposed of, and Winnie very carefully asked Hanh if she had any ideas. They were waiting for Winnie's husband, Jacob, to come over and drain the water pipes in preparation for closing Lester's house up for the winter. Hanh was sitting across from Winnie at Lester's kitchen table and staring outdoors. In a voice that seemed a little like a growl, Hanh explained that she did not wish to make any decisions about the ashes—or think about them in any other way—until some future time when she might consider them with less emotional distress.

"That makes sense," said Winnie. And she knew she should probably say no more on the subject, but she couldn't refrain from mentioning an article she had recently read in an ecologically friendly magazine about disposing of cremains by placing them inside helium-filled balloons and letting the balloons rise, detonating them, and scattering the ashes from an altitude of four or five miles in the air. As dramatically satisfying as this method of disposal was, the article explained, it was actually less desirable—from a clean-planet standpoint—than simply burying them.

"Why?" asked Hanh, without interest. She continued to stare out the window, sipping from a warm cup of tea yet never actually tasting it.

Winnie continued: "The high temperatures inside cremation furnaces remove all carbon-based materials—all of them—so only heavy metals and a few minerals are left behind. If everyone had his or her ashes spread into the atmosphere, it would become another source of pollution, not unlike volcanic ash. The earth's soil is much better than the open air at neutralizing minerals and metals. And the helium balloons advertised as biodegradable, in many cases simply aren't."

"I haven't made up my mind on what to do with the ashes," said Hanh.

"That's fine. It doesn't have to be decided immediately. Where would you like the service? The funeral home has adequate space, of course, but we'll need to act quickly in reserving the building."

"Funeral homes are out of the question."

"Okay, then April Lux has offered her home."

"She doesn't have enough chairs. Lester's friends need a lot of chairs."

"April says additional seating can be provided through a rental agency, which she has already contacted."

"There are vulgarities on the walls in her house—vile, red words. People will see them."

"They're hidden now. April's brother Tom came back, and he and August repainted."

"New paint stinks."

"The paint they used is odorless. I was over there earlier today, and I couldn't smell anything."

"The gate security guards checking them in would offend Lester's friends. And besides, many of those old guys can't drive and don't have cars. Most are living in nursing homes."

"April says she can get passes for everyone—no questions and no searches. And she knows of a local transportation service that will chauffeur both ways. She'll pay for it. Some of the Gate security members and a couple of local police officers also volunteered to help out. They said they wanted to do something for the remaining Vietnam War veterans."

"Lester hated the Gate."

"Why?"

"The land they appropriated at one time had wild ginseng and good mushrooming. He hunted there for years. And the people who live there now aren't from around here."

"Neither was Lester," said Winnie. "And by any reasonable standard, you and I are also outsiders."

"Look, Winifred, I really can't deal with this now."

Jacob's car pulled up in front of the house. He climbed out.

"I've changed my mind," said Hanh.

Winnie opened the front door and Jacob stepped inside, stomping his boots on the rubber mat. He nodded in Hanh's direction, and she nodded back.

"I don't want the pipes bled anymore," Hanh said.

"Why?" asked Jacob.

"I'm going to stay here."

"Why?" asked Winnie.

"It feels closer to him."

"If that's what you want," said Jacob. "What about your own house?"

"We don't have to worry about that. It has backup heat."

"I'll stay with you," said Winnie.

"I'd rather you didn't."

Jacob shoved his hands into his pockets, as though to protect them from the tension in the room.

"Snow's quickly melting," he announced, as though the sunny skies, warm air, and water running everywhere—which had begun early that morning and continued throughout the day—had somehow escaped notice by everyone but him. "It will all be gone in a couple hours. I don't remember ever seeing weather as radical as this. It's hard to know if you're coming or going."

"I want the service held here," announced Hanh. "This is where he lived."

"It's tiny," complained Winnie. "I'm afraid more people will want to come than the space can accommodate."

"If people think it's too crowded, they don't need to come, and if they come and don't like it, they can leave. This is where Lester lived and this is where his service should be."

Winnie and Jacob looked at each other.

"It will take days and days to get ready," said Winnie, and then added, "or as ready as it can be made."

"I'd like to be alone now," said Hanh.

"Sure. Jacob and I . . . we'll go, then. I'll put the obituary we wrote up this morning in the paper."

"Good. Thank you, Winifred."

"Is it all right if Jacob and I come back early tomorrow morning? We can help spruce up the place, and maybe bring a few more people to help. And more chairs."

Hanh returned to the window and remained silent.

"Ivan said he was coming over," said Winnie. "We can wait until he's here."

"He isn't coming."

"I'm sure he told me he was."

"I told him not to."

"Well, okay . . . is there anything we can do for you before we leave?"

"No."

"Are you sure?"

"Yes."

"Well, then, we'll be going."

Jacob and Winnie left, and Hanh continued sitting at the kitchen table, staring out the window.

After several hours, most of the light had drained out of the sky, and as the darkness outside grew, the window began to mirror her own image back to her. Still, she remained at the table.

LIVING'S BOOKENDS

HANH COULDN'T REMEMBER ever feeling more alone, and this alarmed her.

Lester's death had unraveled something in her world and she struggled to discover any comforting thoughts, anywhere.

Who was she?

Throughout most of her life, Hanh had blamed her sense of social dislocation on her grandparents, the stormy commingling of a young Vietnamese woman hardly older than a girl living in the Central Highlands and working on a Chinese-owned flower plantation within walking distance from her village, and a US soldier only a year or two older than a boy, serving in a country he could not have spelled or located on a map prior to receiving a notice from his local draft board. On a steamy evening between two torrential downpours, while other US soldiers searched for Vietcong, dropped bombs, and sprayed neurotoxic defoliants, her father led her mother into a private corner of the floral warehouse, and surrounded by the dizzying aroma of a million gassy blooms, joyfully, thoughtlessly, and successfully impregnated her. All the lies, suspicions, and fears of the Second Indochina War had conspired through that one moment of frenzied pleasure to create Hanh's father, who, of course, had passed them on to Hanh.

In 1975 the US withdrew its last remaining troops from South Vietnam, leaving behind over two million dead Vietnamese. After the Americans pulled out—straightaway—North Vietnamese forces moved into Saigon and overran the South. The country's limited resources were carefully allocated, and priorities included rebuilding shipping harbors and population centers. Rural areas made do with less.

The well providing water for Hanh's family and the rest of the small village became contaminated. Hanh's entire family died, and a short time later she began living like an animal, scavenging and stealing. Mere survival replaced other concerns, and she moved from moment to moment by tightly clutching a slender, grim focus. Questions of who she was, or where she belonged, did not receive enough oxygen to be real to her.

Lester Mortal eventually found her, and she came to understand that his primary motivation was not to fulfill a promise made to her dying grandfather, nor to act on a singular, selfless impulse, but rather to redirect his own life—to take a new direction and reconcile the more than sixty years he had already lived with the remaining years he hoped to live. To save himself he needed her to let him take care of her.

And for Hanh, things had turned out pretty well. She never disputed that—to herself or anyone else. Her levels of contentment varied, of course, but they were generally fairly high. She enjoyed living on the edge of the forest in her little house, keeping bees, tending her hazelnut orchard, gathering wild ginseng, and marketing gourmet honey, filberts, and roots. The quantities she sold were relatively small, but she took pleasure in maintaining high standards and finding attractive ways to package and advertise her products. The majority of her customers lived in China and renewed their orders annually with an almost calendrical regularity.

She attended conferences on the latest beekeeping and nut-roasting innovations, but no personal relationships resulted from these gatherings. Sharing an interest in apiculture and horticulture did not provide the necessary social glue for friendships, at least not for Hanh.

She remained suspicious of people who grounded themselves through claiming a shared identity that she could never feel. Clearly, the psychological sweetmeat responsible for persuading people that they were part of a specific group did not persuade Hanh. Either her emotional repository lacked the necessary hormones, or her versions of them simply weren't convincing. The warm and safe feelings people enjoyed by belonging to groups felt to Hanh like aversion therapy. Her only feelings of togetherness came directly from one-on-one interactions with individuals. For example, a bond existed between she and August's mother. Hanh had grown accustomed to the many tonal ranges in Winnie's voice, the way she moved and smelled, the things she usually wanted to talk about, the foods she preferred, the kinds of jokes she laughed at, the clothes she wore; Hanh could anticipate how Winnie would likely interpret and react to different situations—not always, but with reasonable accuracy. And for the most part, Hanh understood how to get along with her. She recognized when Winnie was happy, sad, anxious, fatigued, or remorseful. If Winnie wanted something from her, or wanted to be left alone, Hanh knew it. A genuine fondness, even love, had grown up between them, and these feelings greatly comforted Hanh. But she didn't feel she belonged to Winnie, or she to her.

Depending on her mood, Hanh sometimes took refuge in thinking that she had strong, anachronistic tendencies. The modern brain's aptitude for bonding to aggregate populations was a relatively recent phenomenon, but in earlier times the world had been overwhelmingly populated with people like her. Throughout most of human evolution, the size of self-regulating societies had been limited by the number of people a single individual could know and maintain meaningful relationships with—somewhere between one hundred and one hundred and forty people. Larger groups lacked cohesion and struggled with consensus building.

All that had changed rather abruptly with the advent of language development and the spread of organized agriculture. Within word-oriented and grain-storing societies, separate social classes emerged: priests, warriors, accountants, scribes, nurses, royalty, and peasants. And like the divisions of labor within ant colonies, these more complex social structures allowed for much larger groups. It was no longer necessary to know everyone within a community as long as individuals could intimately relate to a few other individuals performing similar functions. Clans burgeoned into tribes; tribes into nations; nations into empires.

None of this would have been comprehensible to someone in hunting and gathering societies, she reflected. People living in small, nomadic groups—from cradle to grave—knew everything about the people they lived among. Individuals didn't even think of themselves as individuals. They could not picture living apart from the group and trying to explain to a hunter-gatherer how modern loyalties were not restricted to *known people* would be impossible.

Hanh reflected that the people living around her right now were expected to feel an affinity to and solidarity with millions of others whom they had never met. To identify as an American, for instance, meant extending her trust and sympathy to countless others on the assumption that they shared similar beliefs and abided by similar laws. But, of course, experience invariably proved they didn't; beliefs, attitudes, and values widely varied.

Trusting others did not come easily to her, and loyalty was something she extended on a short-term basis.

Yet, at Lester's insistence, she'd become a US citizen. He had sworn that citizenship would guarantee her the right to certain protections and freedoms, even though he deeply mistrusted the people responsible for maintaining those same protections and defending the same freedoms—a conflict he struggled with throughout his adult life and never really resolved.

"Living somewhere is always risky," Lester had once said.

Hanh owned property, voted, paid taxes; she had a Wisconsin driver's license in her wallet and a US passport in a cupboard drawer. But these things had almost nothing to do with who she was and everything to do with who Lester Mortal had been. She was here because Lester brought her. He'd wanted to live here, and she'd come along, and everything else followed from that. Everything about her was contingent upon something that had earlier happened—to her—and now contingency itself had lost its signal reference point.

Lester died and severed her connection to, well, everything.

After sitting for hours staring into her reflection in the darkened window, Hanh wondered why the house remained so uncharacteristically warm. She'd built a fire when she first came but hadn't put in any additional wood. She glanced at the wall clock and was astonished to see it was after midnight.

When she opened the front door, a wall of moist, July-like air greeted her from the darkness beyond, accompanied by the rapid, chortling sounds of several young barred owls halfway up a conifer tree. *Summertime out there.* The contrast with several days earlier—when Lester froze to death—seemed to mock her grief, as though meteorological forces had conspired to reveal the arbitrary nature of even the most heartbreaking events. A person could now, apparently, sit in a lawn chair in front of his daughter's house and freeze all his major organs, or wait a day or two and go boating.

Not wanting to return inside, she stepped through the front door and into the yard . . . and immediately felt a little better. The outdoors wrapped around her and arrested her with a panoramic performance of night. The wet-fresh air assaulted her senses, and she looked up into light years of open black space filled with shiny galactic bodies so unfathomably far away they seemed smaller than safety pin perforations in black plastic. The unbounded universe smiled at her.

Inhaling deeply, Hanh remembered that she usually felt better out-of-doors. Though not a panacea, a great many inner ills could be improved by simply going outside. She felt less vulnerable here. Social alienation lost much of its credibility in the face of an unobstructed sky.

Hanh felt connected to nature at large, and her irrevocable membership in the wider world gave her a warrant for lateral thought that did not fully exist inside homes or in the company of most other people. Lester had either known this about her or had shared her fondness for untended rural areas, or both.

Then, just as quickly as she felt rescued from her own self-annihilating thoughts, the burrowing sadness of Lester's death found her again, and she was reminded that she would never again be whole.

Lester had so thoroughly acquainted her with himself his values, ideals, and attitudes had begun to seem like they were hers. His love for her had such a profound influence over the quality of her interior life that even when she remained unaware of it—which was, regrettably, much of the time—its benign influence continued to work in her. But with Lester gone, even those things she most wanted to believe in felt threatened. Dignity, courage, beauty, truth, kindness, bravery, forgiveness, mercy, and compassion—how could she ever sufficiently honor these principles by herself? She wasn't big enough.

Like now, the chattering owls in the nearby tree acknowledged Hanh's presence by speaking in muted burbling sounds so ripe with uninhibited, demented merriment that she could not discover an adequate response. But if Lester were here, he might talk back to them, imitate their hooting warble, or simply laugh about sharing the outdoors with such blithely chattering folks; if Lester were still alive, he'd find a way to celebrate a phenomenon that began inside eggs, matured in less than a year, found full-time employment working night shift in pest control, and now spoke coded gibberish in run-on sentences.

Lester loved owls.

As though reacting to her private thoughts, the two birds stepped out of the nearby tree, opened their wings and soundlessly glided overhead, casting flat, wraithlike shapes ripping over the uneven, skylit ground. As she watched, Hanh's brain provided her with a memory of Lester explaining how owls moved soundlessly through the air because, compared with other bipeds, their body mass weighed less; a larger proportion of their feathers and bones were hollow. In addition to nearly defying gravity, they also came equipped with asymmetrical hearing and could pinpoint the source-position of the faintest rustling sounds on the ground below. They could see in ultra low-light conditions due to oversize, round, hyperopic, binocular eyes rigidly set inside tunnel sockets, and to compensate for the fixed immobility of their eyes, a generous number of neck vertebrae allowed their heads to swivel 270 degrees in both directions without restricting blood flow.

It was easy to understand how all these adaptive features had contributed to the continuation of over two hundred species in the nocturnal order of Strigiformes; harder to explain was how dimorphism (female owls are larger than males) added to their ongoing success, though several attempts had been proffered. During mating season female owls viciously repelled the advances of unwanted males, sometimes with crippling or lethal results. Perhaps smaller, quicker males were more likely to escape and, over time, these males passed on their skills (and size) to male offspring. Also, males were the primary caregivers in raising owlets; females did most of the hunting, and perhaps male caregivers gave more attention—and better food—to female owlets.

While alive, Lester had made these observations about owls so frequently that Hanh had come to dread hearing them. And in later years, when the old veteran couldn't remember what he'd recently told anyone, he sometimes delivered his collection of factoids—complete with all the solemnity and hand gestures of an eight-year-old importing a vital discovery—whenever an owl popped into his mind. Just last week, Hanh learned of the weightlessness of owls and the ferocity of mating females . . . twice in a single afternoon.

As the two shadows raced silently across the ground, she despaired. Her former impatience over Lester's failing memory and deteriorating social skills were turned, by the chemistry of death, into pure grief.

The wind shifted, delivering even warmer air.

Without closing the front door, Hanh walked away from the house, going south, finding her way among darkened trees. Her footsteps were almost silent on the wet ground. The aroma of soggy leaves and damp humus filled her nostrils. Unseasonably humid air radiated sounds throughout the valley's widening corridor and the night seemed vibrant and alive. She heard dogs barking in the distance, a vehicle moving along a faraway road, water dripping, the time-delayed hum of an unseen jet engine, and the muffled sound of birds perched in wet trees, shaking moisture out of feathers. She heard thunder, a sound that had been absent for many months. It was odd to hear thunder without cloud cover.

She took a meandering path to the top of the hill, then down the other side. A half-lit moon entered the easternmost quadrant of the sky. She heard a fox bark—a single, harsh, vowel-less sound.

Coming upon the blacktop road, she walked along it for several miles.

The wet macadam glowed jet black and glistened in places with reflected light. There was no traffic of any kind.

As Hanh walked, boxlike farmhouses loomed into view at random intervals, set off from the road at the end of driveways. Most of the dwellings had one or two lit windows. Despite the late hour, some people were apparently unable, or unwilling, to sleep—nudged into wakefulness by the unusually warm temperatures and distant thunder. In the available light, she could make out shapes of men and women standing outside their homes, in sleepwear, sitting on open porches, leaning against sheds, drinking from steaming mugs. In the dark space beneath a low-hanging carport, she saw the flickering tip of a cigarette, held by an unseen hand and smoked by an unseen mouth. Later, two faces faintly glowed from the greenish light of phone screens.

Most people took no notice of her. Some stared into the sky; others looked off into the distance, as though expecting the arrival of invading hordes from over the horizon.

Hanh felt them too—the spirits of human and prehuman ancestors fleeing habitat erosion, fire, infestation, flooding, famine, and war, searching for places they could keep their children alive, moving in herds, driven by the sharpened point of certainty: *Leave or die.* Whenever weather patterns strayed far from normal, the restless spirits of past migrations began moving again, and the animals that inherited their genotypes could feel them.

Twice, Hanh thought she heard someone on the road behind her, timing their steps to match her own, but when she stopped to concentrate on the sounds, she no longer heard them. At a pasture adjoining the roadway, she stepped over a waterlogged ditch, slid through two strands of barbed wire and threaded her way between a half dozen draft horses milling around a round bale feeder. The weighty animals seemed equally agitated by the strange weather, and warily regarded her through globe-like, bright black eyes. One gelding backed away, drew back his ears, and flared his nostrils.

Hanh continued across wet, short-cropped grass toward the next valley. After jumping a channel of runoff, she continued across the remaining pasture. At the timberline, she ducked through another fence and backed up against a hickory trunk, looking behind her. She waited to see if anyone would step into the open space, but no one did. To make sure, she remained several minutes longer before ascending the incline onto the ridge.

A decade earlier, she and Lester had named this path Cumbersome Trail, for the circuitous way it meandered south along the valley's rim—above the homes, fields, and farms. There was a transcendent view up here. In the far distance, she saw small bursts of lightning, as though towns on the other side of the Earth's curvature were practicing for Independence Day. In the near distance, beneath her, three large farmsteads splayed across the valley floor, with eighty and even one-hundred-acre fields. The heavily wooded, hilly Driftless Area didn't usually allow for such expansive cropland, which was why farming with 600HP tractors and combines with twelve-row corn heads never caught on. Most of the fields were too small for the big equipment to even turn around. By most Illinois, Iowa, and Nebraska standards, the farms beneath her weren't really farms at all; they were agri-hobbies, historic reenactment projects, or, in the case of Amish-owned operations, grounds for daily ascetic exercise. But to Driftless farmers themselves, and many of the people around them—like Ivan Bookchester and, when alive, Lester Mortal—the undulating, rocky area provided welcome refuge from a wider, more mechanized culture they very much wished to avoid, and they felt about the eroded hillsides, small towns, isolated homesteads, curving roads, and mixed hardwood and evergreen the same way dickcissels and bobolinks felt about prairie land.

As the moon rose higher in the sky, Hanh walked along an extended stand of conifer trees on a cushion of needles. The sensation resembled stepping on pine-scented blankets. Above, the canopy seemed like a sheltering roof, and a purpose began to form in the back of her mind.

Hanh saw a cluster of lights beneath her and recognized the unincorporated village of Words, spilled out along a creek—a haphazard collection of about sixty houses and somewhat larger number of garages and sheds. She followed a cow trail down the incline until reaching the road and walked along it in among the homes.

Unlike the restless people she'd seen earlier, the inhabitants of Words— though awake—remained indoors. This was probably because of living in town, she thought. Here, going outside was a public act, and before going out, you had to think about how you looked.

After a short time, the Words Repair Shop came up on her left, currently run by Ivan's father, Blake; he had taken it over after August's father, Jacob, retired. Years ago, Hanh had been inside it many times and still regarded the old cement block building fondly.

Inside nearby houses, faces looked at her through windows with partially drawn shades.

A dog resembling a beagle ran out from underneath a porch and followed her. A short time later, she arrived at the Words Friends of Jesus Church. The dog returned home. Distant thunder provided an aural background. Several houses away, someone started a motor, then turned it off.

The windows in the church were dark, the adjacent parking lot empty. She looked up at the front of the building. August's mother had preached here, and in earlier years Hanh had attended potlucks, participated in youth activities, and sat beside August while his mother talked about impending church-related events and preached about the importance of humility, hope, faith, and kindness.

Hanh tried the front door, and it opened. Apparently, the board of trustees had decided in favor of access over indemnified risk.

Inside, the high, open room seemed extraordinarily quiet, waiting and dark, as though sentient creatures had recently gone into hiding. The light seeping through the two banks of windows did not reach beyond the narrow side aisles, and she could barely make out the columns of pews with a carpeted center lane running between them.

She went ahead, stepping carefully. The old wooden flooring beneath the carpeting sagged and groaned.

Up front, to either side of the lectern, rested an upright piano and an electric organ. Hanh sat on the bench before the organ and stared at the flat rows of plastic keys. During her childhood, Lester had insisted that she take keyboard lessons, and a number of private teachers schooled her in finger placement, chording, musical notation, rhythm, and the dynamics of pitch. Eventually, though, her lack of enthusiasm wore down her instructors; Lester finally stopped insisting and sold the keyboard.

Right now, however, an interest in music had captured her, and she'd been thinking about it for the last hour. The grief she experienced over Lester's death seemed too large to contain and she wanted to free herself from it, to release it, move her obliterating sadness outside and into the world—express it. Perhaps then the feeling could be dealt with. Perhaps hearing it would offer remedy.

No one else needed to be included, and Hanh had no intention of sharing her sorrow; in fact, the idea of involving someone else was repellent to her. That's why she chose the organ. The sound of the piano was too hard to control, at least for her—too sharp and brisk—and her feet did not reach the damping pedals.

Organs were different. You could play them at whatever volume you wished, and besides, the feelings she hoped to express seemed better suited to the thick tones of an organ.

One of Hanh's music teachers had talked at length about the importance of affective tonal quality—the resonant personality of a particular group of notes due to their harmonic relationships. Each of the seven musical keys, she said, had a unique character, and composers took advantage of these qualities when writing music. C major possessed an open, cheerful, childlike tonality that songwriters often used for light and merry compositions. The key of D major was better suited to heartier sentiments, victory marching, belligerence, and, in general, redder emotionality. Those seeking more global ranges of expression—capturing the lows and highs within the same family of notes—often found a home in F major.

The minor keys conveyed darker and more brooding subjects, and the tensions held within them were tinged with sadness and longing. C minor, for instance, shared with C major the openness and naivete reminiscent of childhood, but also evoked some of the more uncomfortable associations like lovesickness, disappointment, and fears of inadequacy.

The chord Hanh searched for was D sharp minor, reserved for the most profound sorrow and utmost distress. As her former music teacher had once remarked, "If spirits of the dead could make a sound, they'd cry out in D sharp minor."

Maddening grief, it seemed, had been built right into the world of sound.

She cautiously located the keys (D#, E#, F#, G#, A#, B, C#), placed her fingers above them, and lightly touched their cool, flat surfaces. Her hands remained posed, and then she carefully pressed down, feeling the resistance of the keys pushing back, but no sound came out.

She searched along the organ front, found the ignition switch, and rocked it forward. A hollow, popping sound followed, and several insect eyes burned red and green on the front panel. Further research revealed a volume adjustment slider, and she moved it down to the far left. Then she carefully repositioned her fingers above the keys, closed her eyes and gently applied pressure.

Again . . . more silence.

Beneath the glowing red eye, she discovered a Standby button, and depressed it until it snapped into position. The red eye turned green, and a low hum filled the building.

She checked the slider, repositioned her fingers and carefully pressed down, exploding the darkness with earsplitting sound in D sharp minor.

Apparently, she'd turned the volume control all the way up.

Hanh snapped off the ignition switch and hurried through the building.

Before opening the front door, she inhaled a cubic yard of anxiety, listened to the last dying of the sound—the decrescendo—and went out.

Every functioning yard light in Words, it seemed, had been turned on, and the town's occupants, who had earlier been inside their houses, had come out. Most of them quietly stood just beyond their front doors, their hands at their sides or shoved into pockets. All faced Hanh as she looked back at them from in front of the church.

A figure came toward her from the road.

"What are you doing here, Ivan?"

"I don't know. Coming over just seemed like a good idea," he shrugged, and she knew he had followed her from Lester's house. His footsteps on the road. She'd thought she might have been mistaken. But she hadn't.

"I don't like anyone stalking me."

"There's such a thing as being too much alone. Where do you want to go now?"

"Back home."

"Do you mind if I come?"

"Why are all these people outside?"

"The organ woke them up. They were already awake because of the odd weather, but the sound of the organ gave them permission to feel strange about it, and they came outdoors."

"Why are they staring at me?"

"They think you might have made the sound."

"I didn't mean to. The volume went the wrong way. No one else was supposed to hear."

"It's all right. They wanted an excuse to be outdoors."

"Why did they turn their yard lights on?"

"It was the kind of sound you'd want lights on for if you heard it again."

"I never felt accepted around here. Everywhere I go seems like trespassing. I wasn't ready for the old man to die and I don't think I'll ever get over it. It feels like my spirit is looking for him, looking for the new place he's found for us to live—a place that feels like home to both of us."

Some of the yard lights were turned off, and five or six people went back inside their homes. Others talked to their neighbors. Three men and a woman sat at a picnic table and dealt out playing cards, and a number of children lit sparklers and ran around shrieking.

"Can I make a confession?" asked Ivan.

"I already know you followed me here from Lester's house."

"Yes, that too, and I miss Lester very much, but there's a part of me—whenever I think of him—that feels relief. He was—"

"I know. His body was giving out, and he was ready to go. I know all that, and there's a part of me that is glad I don't have to feel guilty anymore for not spending more time with him and not taking better care of him. But there's another part of me that feels like the rip in the world that began when he died will keep tearing."

Ivan took a deep breath of warm air. "Look," he said. "I need you to let me love you, because if you don't I can't go on living much longer. My dad has a loaner car somewhere. I know where the keys are and I can drive you home."

"Okay."

They walked the three blocks to the shop and Ivan found the keys to an old Focus. After checking to be sure the tires were inflated, they left.

Hanh opened the passenger window for fresh air. They drove over a hill, down into a valley, around a corner, and onto a gravel road. "I can feel you thinking about sex," she said. "Is that what you think will happen when we get back to my house?"

Ivan drove uphill and said, "I hope it isn't wrong to say this, but I wish someone could explain why sadness ends up wanting sex."

"It's not just you," said Hanh. "Brothels do more business in wartime. Losing people you love makes you want to make more. Or maybe it's just a good diversion. All I know is that when Americans and Vietnamese were killing each other like there was no tomorrow, it didn't prevent my grandmother and grandfather from making my father."

Ivan pulled into the muddy drive leading to Hanh's house.

"We should stop at Lester's. I think I left the front door open."

"I already closed it," said Ivan.

In front of Hanh's home, they stayed inside the Focus for several minutes.

"Does it ever bother you," began Hanh, "that when Lester was out here freezing to death that you and I were maybe, at the same time . . ."

"I've thought about that."

"Doesn't it somehow seem, well, bad?"

"Not really. During any hour of the day or night there're probably millions of people dying and millions of others doing what you and I were maybe doing when Lester died. Both things happen all the time. They're living's bookends."

THE SERVICE

THE OBITUARY FOR Lester Mortal had already been posted, and Winnie had received a number of calls asking when a service would be held. Soon, very soon, she told them.

Lester's house needed a lot of attention before anyone should be allowed inside.

Today, Jacob jump-started Lester's truck and hauled away three loads of refuse—old carpeting, bottles, plastic recyclables, discarded clothing, linoleum, leaves and dead branches—and this was just the beginning.

Then it rained again, and the mud-choked driveway became nearly impassable.

Winnie panicked, and while Jacob removed old magazines and books from the corners of Lester's house, Winnie drove over to the Gate to find August. On the way, she thought about how strange it seemed to be going to one of her gardening client's homes to talk with her son. She had not imagined that April and August would be attracted to each other—never really considered it—because April and August existed in separate worlds in her mind, yet here she was, driving toward the previously unimagined.

She waited momentarily for Gate security to receive authorization to let her in before she continued on to the house.

August opened the door after she knocked and they stood just inside the front door of April's house, out of the rain.

"Is it possible for you and Ivan to help?"

"Of course," August said. "I'll talk to Ivan, and Tom will help too. We'll come over as soon as the weather clears. You shouldn't have waited so long to ask."

"Ask what?" asked April, walking toward them.

August explained, "Hanh wants the memorial service held in Lester's house and Mom says there's a lot to do before that can happen."

"Is that true?" April asked, turning to Winnie.

"Yes," she confirmed, rainwater running out of her hair and down her face in wavy, transparent lines.

"In that little house?"

"It's what Hanh wants."

"And how many people does Hanh think will come?"

"That's not something she cares about."

"And you?"

"I'd like a good number to show up. People need an opportunity to show Hanh how much they—in the privacy of their own hearts—respected the man, even though their approval of him, and her, was mostly mute."

"Let me be clear on this, Winnie," said April. "You'd like to have many people come?"

"That would be good for everyone."

The velocity of the falling rain increased.

"I'll come with August, Tom, and Ivan," April told Winnie. "Now let me fetch a towel. I'll make tea while you dry off."

The following day, April drove over to Lester's house to help the others prepare it for the public. After working a very short while, she left.

Several hours later, a landscaping company arrived and spread sixty yards of fresh gravel along the driveway leading to Lester's house. Then levelers evened out the crushed rock and rollers packed it down.

In early afternoon, three trucks drove over the new gravel and workers erected an enormous tent—four times the size of Lester's house—and connected it to the front door with an open-sided awning. After filling the tent with chairs and tables, a second group of workers strung up lighting and sound equipment from the scaffolding poles. Porta-potties were placed outside.

The next day, an article appeared in the local shopper. It recounted Lester Mortal's death in last week's snowstorm, his military service, and a paragraph about the Vietnam War and the social forces it unleashed within the United States. It ended with brief mention of the ten a.m. memorial service on the following Saturday, and the brunch provided afterward by Gate Foods: three-cheese omelets with mushrooms, green peppers, and onions; buckwheat pancakes with whipped butter and maple syrup; biscuits with sausage gravy; orange, apple, and cranberry juices; and coffee. Everyone was welcome.

The unusually warm temperatures held for another couple days, and in response to such unseasonal weather, many trees began pushing out green buds along their naked limbs. Forecasters warned of an impending cold front from the west, but in the meantime, windows were thrown open to the fresh air, and dog-walkers, deliverymen, and everyone else walked around outdoors without coats, gloves, or hats.

By 9:30 a.m. Saturday, the cars parked along the newly graveled driveway extended for a hundred yards. Food service employees inside the tent were handing out meals as quickly as they could prepare them. Some of those consuming the food were dressed in traditionally somber clothes, others much more casually, and a few as though they'd spontaneously acted upon the idea to attend while cleaning out their garages. Lester Mortal's half dozen veteran friends huddled around the memory board, inspecting photographs and examining the memorabilia put together by Winnie and Hanh inside Lester's house. In the tent, there was standing room only.

Winnie was greatly comforted. The turnout revealed several reassuring things: people read local flyers; the Vietnam War still had some relevance to people reading local flyers; a free meal brought folks out of their homes like nothing else. She could feel the anxiety she'd lived with for the last week lifting, and she carried this blessed sense of relief as she walked toward the makeshift lectern at the front of the tent. At exactly 10:00 a.m. she snapped on the sound system, greeted everyone, prayed for grace, and talked for twenty minutes about Lester and how his life exemplified the universal virtues of courage, loyalty, and moral conviction.

More people seeking brunch continued to arrive and Winnie offered the microphone to anyone wishing to share thoughts about Lester. A few friends and neighbors came forward to recount anecdotes involving the deceased as the tent continued to fill with the aroma of steaming pancakes, frying sausage, and onions. After returning to the microphone, Winnie offered a closing prayer and asked that traveling mercies might be granted to those on their way home.

Thirty minutes later, the brunching crowd had thinned down to about eight people. All the old vets were gone and had either walked or been wheeled out of the tent and driven back to their homes by the hired transportation service; after they left, April told the Gate Foods employees they could stop serving in fifteen minutes.

Ivan set a glass of orange juice and a bowl of fruit in front of Hanh. He carried a plate of pancakes and sausage to his father and an omelet to his mother; they ate seated next to Jacob, who drank cranberry juice and sipped coffee. April's brother Tom sat beside August, eating biscuits and gravy. Ivan carried three cups of coffee over and sat next to them.

More people drifted out of the tent, and an afternoon serenity settled in.

Satisfied that a groundswell of vital human empathy had been publicly exchanged, and experiencing an overwhelming relief over bringing Lester's memorial service to a conclusion, Winnie tried to find a private moment with April to explain how thankful she was. Clearly, the event would never have happened at all without the resources that April had sponsored. And the tent, Winnie believed, was such an inspirational idea that it must somehow have been motivated, at least in part, by a divine knitting of events; she wondered if April would perhaps agree and felt almost certain that she would. On top of that, for April to hire a catering service and provide a free brunch . . . well, no rational person anywhere on earth could reflect on those two brilliant insights without seeing the hand of the Divine Weaver at work. And for someone familiar with Christian traditions and references, a community of people harmoniously eating together most certainly evoked visions of Jesus and the loaves and fishes.

But the harder Winnie tried to isolate April and present these thoughts to her, the more other circumstances demanded April's attention. The chief of the catering crew complained that the heat controls on the grill were no longer working correctly; parts of the grill were hotter than others, and there was some likelihood that the entire unit had been damaged by the substandard wiring inside the tent. And then April's phone rang, and a truck driver said she would be an hour late in picking up the chairs, but to not begin breaking down the tent before she got there.

And at this point Chopra Scarborough walked inside the tent with two large men in dark suits—one on either side of her. August rose out of his chair and moved forward, and the rest of the tent's occupants turned to look at her.

Chopie absorbed their attention like a plant processing sunlight. She strode in her tall, leather boots with imperial confidence, as though knowing that everyone admired the way she walked, and would, if they could be seen, also admire her feet.

The two middle-aged men beside her surveyed the room like they were looking for people who owed them rent.

"Hello, Chopra," said August.

"I see you're still around, Mr. Late Summer," observed Chopie, her voice suggesting she had just made a very amusing joke. "I frankly didn't think you'd last this long." She stopped walking and opened the front of her faun-colored leather jacket as though granting a dying man's request to display her new green-and-amber outfit. "We thought we'd take advantage of the warm weather and pop on over. My friends Lewis and Gordon are fond of pancakes."

"You're in luck," said August. "The grill is still open, and along with the excellent buckwheat cakes, I'd recommend the Peruvian coffee."

Chopie's hands made a nearly imperceptible gesture that resembled a butterfly batting its wings and the two men moved away from her, toward the food.

Tom stood beside August and studied her like an expensive piece of stolen art. He asked, "How about you, Ms. Chopie? Can I get you something?"

"No, no, dear boy, I'm here to talk to your sister, and speak of the devil, there she is."

August turned and watched April and his mother walking toward them along a narrow aisle between the chairs. April smiled.

"Chopie, you came."

"I hope this isn't inconvenient," said Chopie. "I called yesterday."

"Yes, I got your message."

"I brought a bereavement card," she announced, and pulled a thick, sealed white envelope from inside her jacket. "And I sent a donation to Veterans for Peace, like the obituary suggested." She handed it to August's mother.

"Thank you," said Winnie. "I'll make sure the family gets this."

"Let's sit over here where we can talk," said April.

They all followed her to an empty table. After a minor clothing adjustment, Chopie settled into a chair.

"I don't know *him*," she said, nodding toward Ivan.

August said, "I should have introduced you. Chopie, this is—"

"Because I don't know him, I don't want him here."

Ivan raised his hands in a submitting gesture. "That's okay. I was actually hoping to join Lewis and Gordon with a stack of pancakes." And he walked away from the table.

"First, let me assure you," began April, "I'm not sleeping with your husband."

"Oh, don't worry," Chopie said dismissively. "I'm not here about *that*. Everything changed between Denny and me. He shaved his head, took a vow of poverty, and joined a monastery. He's gone."

"What?"

"I know, it's a lot to take in. He gave his businesses to me—all of them—signed them over just like that. Said he wanted to do something else with the rest of his life and joined a Buddhist monastery. I sent all his personal things to a charity. And those two fellows I brought with me, Lewis and Gordon, they were his driver and bodyguard. They'd both worked for him for fifteen years. Denny just said, 'You take them.' And when I said, 'What am I supposed to do with them?' he said, 'Do anything you want.' I couldn't just let them go. They wouldn't know what else to do."

"Where's the monastery?"

"An island off the Burmese coast."

"Dennis Scarborough is no longer dedicated to my destruction?" asked April.

"No, he gave up on that. And I'm sorry about the vandalism in your home. It wasn't really Denny's fault, or mine for that matter. Though in some way I suppose maybe it was, because I might have talked to this one person and maybe he thought about what I said in the wrong way and somehow got the idea that I didn't like you and wished for something unfortunate to happen to you, and, well, three or four weeks later I guess he must have thought he could score some points with me by doing something and maybe Denny would then reward him with a job in Chicago working in the shipping department, and, well, it's fortunate that no one was really hurt. I'll pay for all damages and, like I said, I apologize for what happened. I'll send a contractor over on Monday and you can direct him however you choose. He'll replace everything on the first and second floor if it's your wish . . . rip out the walls down to the studs, anything you want. But that's not why I'm here."

"Dennis was a Buddhist?" questioned August.

"No, dear boy, he had no familiarity with Buddhism whatsoever before three weeks ago. He attended a party in Madison thrown by one of his business rivals—an even bigger braggart than Denny. At the party, Denny was introduced to five monks on a cultural exchange tour, and to impress the host he invited them to return with him to the Gate for a couple days."

"Were you at the party?" asked Tom.

"No, I try to avoid social events thrown by Denny's business rivals. They bring out the worst in him. I was asleep when they arrived. Denny told me to get up and attend to them, which of course I did. Though the monks were quite nice in a rather childish way, it wasn't easy talking to them. Their names were impossible to pronounce and they were not at all impressed with our home. I offered drinks, but they said alcohol was forbidden. The domestics set out trays of food and the monks politely nibbled on raw nuts and giggled among themselves. They didn't want to swim in our pool because the water smelled of chemicals. And they politely declined to watch anything in the theater room. Denny told me to play some music and dance for them, but this seemed to horrify them."

"You danced for them?" asked Tom.

"Well, yes. Then I showed them a few of the latest high-resolution simulation video games. I demonstrated how the controls worked and the proper way to engage the ejectors and blasters, but they simply weren't interested."

"What time was this?"

"Sometime around midnight. Denny was becoming more and more frustrated with them. Then, just before they went to their rooms, they told Denny about a monastery, which they referred to as a *kyaung*, on an island near Burma. I guess it made an impression because Denny looked it up and kept talking about it even after his guests went back to Madison. And then, later—in the middle of the night—he sat up in bed, announced he was leaving for a while, flew over to Burma, found the monastery, talked to the head monk, donated a bundle of money, and pledged to join. The next day, he came back here, told me he didn't want any hard feelings, called his lawyers, shredded our prenuptial agreement, set up a trust to avoid paying excessive taxes, turned everything over to me, looked one last time around the house, decided he never liked anything about it, and left."

"A Buddhist acolyte seems a little out of character for Dennis—at least from what I've been told about him," said August.

"Not really. It's Denny playing on a new game board. Someone challenged him. They explained the goal and rules and let him know they thought he wasn't up to it—that he couldn't possibly succeed. That's all it took."

"Most people don't think spiritual pursuits are competitive," Winnie said, "but I suppose it could seem that way to someone. John Milton framed the challenge over five hundred years ago in *Paradise Regained*, when his Christ scoffs at Satan's offer of wealth and power as worthless attainments compared to owning, and directing, one's own passions. And hundreds of years earlier than that, the thirteenth-century Sufi poet Rumi compared all sources of available joy to different wines. Everyone was a wine drinker, and the most blissful inebriation, for Rumi, came from spiritual fruits."

"Honestly, I didn't need to know any of that," Chopie said. "Good Lord, no wonder your son is useless. April, I don't understand why you'd keep people like these around. They're a hindrance to useful conversation."

April smiled. "Yes, but they grow on you."

"What a blow—for your husband to vanish like that," said Tom, his eyes exploring Chopie like an endangered pilot looking for a safe place to land. "You were really blindsided."

"No kidding. Thank God other people run his companies. But now they call me at all hours of the day and night, and I don't know a good jolly about what to say to them. Lawyers need signatures every time they turn around. The other day one was waiting for me to come out of the bathroom. He met me in the hall with an ink pen. I didn't even know he was in the house. There's a stable of racehorses somewhere in Kentucky, and a warehouse of slot machines in Korea that should have been sent to Hong Kong, and I know nothing about either situation; there's even a hockey team, and though other people oversee them, they call and ask questions. Everyone, of course, wants to talk to Denny, but there's no talking to Denny now. He has no phone. He has no computer. He doesn't even have body hair anymore—anywhere. And he doesn't talk . . . at all. He took a vow of silence and changed his name to Maha."

"So why did you want to talk to me?" asked April.

"I need your help," said Chopie. "I want you to set up an organization to prevent girls from being sold into prostitution by their families."

"Where?"

"In Thailand, to begin with—Bangkok."

"Isn't that where you're from, Chopie?" August asked.

"I first lived in Calcutta, and then Thailand. Denny was born in Thailand, though both his parents were American."

April said, "You want to create a nonprofit to work against human trafficking?"

"I hate the term human trafficking. It implies constant motion when, in fact, after the girls are delivered, they often spend the rest of their short lives within a single neighborhood, mostly inside one squalid building."

"I need to know exactly what you want from of me," persisted April.

"I want to prevent, or at least try to prevent, families from selling their daughters to people who have no business owning them. I want a team to work against that, starting in Thailand, and I want to begin as soon as possible. I know you mostly fundraise for already-existing organizations, but I also know you have experience in starting groups."

"Initial expenses will be high," cautioned April, "setup costs, licensing, registration fees, bonding, and depending on how you structure the organization—"

"I've been thinking about this most of my life and already have ideas about how it will work," said Chopie. "A lot will depend on the age of the girls we find, their skills, education, and general resourcefulness. Parents sell daughters out of desperation. They don't see other options. For some families, simply relocating them will help; others might need medical care or legal protection; as a last resort, we'll pay parents directly for the daughters they're intending to sell and then place the girls in foster homes, find them jobs. I understand how to identify vulnerable families, and I know people who can locate girls who have recently been sold. They know how to recognize them. And the girls themselves, once they're cut loose, fed, sobered up, and healthy, many will want to join us in freeing others. If we get them before the physical abuse, drugging, STDs, and malnutrition, they will still have functioning brains. Will you help? I'll pay whatever you ask."

"I'm not sure we'd work well together," said April.

"Why not?"

"Let's just say it's a feeling I have."

"Look, April, I absolutely never apologize, but I'm sorry about the vandalism. I am. I don't know exactly what happened between you and Denny, and I don't even want to know, but I need your help."

April took several measured breaths, and said, "The most—and only—involvement I'm willing to consider would be to help you incorporate and structure your project. After that, everything will be on you. I don't want any responsibility for staffing, consulting, or anything else."

"I already know most of the people I'd like to work with."

"Good, but I don't want any part in recruiting them. I'm already overcommitted to other projects."

"How long will it take to set up the organization?"

"Hard to say. Government wait times vary. Registration fees and licenses are often euphemisms for bribery . . . even in this country. We'll need legal help, and possibly a lot of it."

"I have lawyers. They call me all the time."

"We'll need attorneys of a certain kind—practicing in Thailand. And I need several days to consider this before I commit to anything."

"I'll wait."

Chopie looked around the tent and asked, "Who's the woman sitting by herself looking at the photograph album?"

"That's Lester's daughter, Hanh," said Winnie.

"Is she the one with gourmet honey, filberts, and ginseng?"

"Yes."

"Her face is scarred."

"A childhood injury."

"If we all had our scars out where they could be seen . . . oh, never mind. Please make sure she gets my card."

"Of course."

"In the trade, girls who cause trouble have their faces disfigured as examples to others. Do you think it would be all right to ask her if she has any basswood honey on hand? I recently ran out."

"That would be extremely inappropriate at this time," said Winnie.

"Well, yes, I knew that. Oh, it looks like Lew and Gordo are finished with their second round of pancakes, so it's time for us to leave."

"I'll get back to you and let you know my answer," said April.

"Call me at home. If both lines are busy, keep trying. If I don't hear from you soon, I'll send Gordo over to check."

"Ice hockey?" asked Tom, swiveling in his chair.

"Yes, one of the things Denny walked away from was a team in Michigan. I'd like to sell them as soon as possible, but don't yet know how to go about doing that."

"Which team?"

"The Sliders."

"Are you joking? You own the Michigan Sliders?"

"Yes, do you know them?"

"I've followed them since they reorganized and moved to Warren. They're a young team with speed and a lot of potential. If there's anything you'd like to know or—"

"I'd appreciate whatever help you can lend," said Chopie, standing up and adjusting her clothing. She closed her leather jacket with a gentle pat, like shutting the lid of a jewelry box. "Come over sometime."

"When?"

"Soon, but only after your sister agrees to help me."

"Nice to see you again," said August.

"The pleasure was mostly mine." She turned and walked out of the tent between her two large companions.

April, August, and Tom watched her leave.

"You seemed a little hesitant to help her," August remarked to April.

"I'm still angry about my house."

August's father joined them. Jacob announced that outside temperatures were expected to fall forty degrees before tomorrow morning.

Ivan came over and reported on his time eating pancakes with Lewis and Gordon. Both men, he said, talked freely about the challenges of their work. Being a professional driver and bodyguard, they said, involved a lot of dead time—looking alert while doing absolutely nothing. To be successful, you needed effective mental strategies for how to deal with prolonged inertia. Isometric exercise was one technique, and another was replaying—in as much detail as you could recall—security-related episodes from the past.

Winnie said all people—whatever they did for a living—could benefit from having mental strategies for dead time, and a vibrant prayer life had always served her well. Some of her most enlightened experiences, she said, had been precipitated by life-threatening boredom. Over the years she'd trained her thoughts to focus on methodical breathing at the first sign of mental impatience.

Jacob looked at his watch and said he should probably drain the water pipes in Lester's house before he left, because of the approaching cold front.

Ivan assured him that wasn't necessary because he intended to stay in Lester's house for a couple nights, and he'd make sure to drain the pipes when he left.

"Why do you want to stay there?" inquired Jacob.

"I'd like to watch a wood fire and take a couple days to just remember Lester. Since he died, the old man has grown larger in my mind, and I need to remember him down to normal size. I'd also like to toast some marshmallows and chocolate over graham crackers, but I can't remember what those are called."

"S'mores," said August, Winnie, Jacob, April, and Tom.

A crew of workers came into the tent, spoke briefly with April, and began folding up the tables and chairs and stacking them in the back of a panel truck. Several other workers took down the sound and lighting equipment.

Hanh closed the photograph album she had been looking at and carried it out of the tent and into Lester's house.

Ivan's father, Blake, talked to August's father about replacing the battery in Lester's truck, putting on a set of new tires, having the cab vacuumed out, the outside washed and waxed, and putting it up for sale. "Right now, it looks a lot worse than it is; there really aren't many miles on it."

"Hanh doesn't want to keep it?"

"She's the one who asked if we could sell it for her."

"Does it run?"

"It will."

"I'll tell Dart to give Winnie a ride home, and I'll meet you at the truck in fifteen minutes. We can drop it off at the shop."

"Okay. You know it doesn't seem right—Lester being gone."

"I know it. I know it."

April promised a bonus to Gate Foods employees if they could do a good job of cleaning up and be gone in the next hour.

Ivan asked his mother why his grandfather and grandmother had not come to the service.

"I don't know," said Dart. "When we talked to them, they said they thought they'd come."

"Neither of them answers the phone," said Ivan. "I'm going to drive over and check."

"I'm sure they're fine," said his mother. "Beulah's rheumatism probably flared up, and Nate doesn't like leaving her alone. But go on ahead and take Hanh with you. She needs some diversion. Nate made a custard pie yesterday that he's very proud of. He'll want to try it out on both of you."

Two hours later, and nearly everyone was gone. The sky began to darken. Temperatures fell fifteen degrees. A west wind blew two handouts from the memorial service across the empty front yard.

August watched the taillights of the last truck disappear down the driveway, taking the tent with it.

He picked up the handouts, opened one, and in the evanescent light glanced again at Lester's picture, read his abbreviated obituary and two Emily Dickinson poems. He slid the pamphlets into his pocket and walked into Lester's house.

At the kitchen table, April leafed through some receipts. August stood beside her and put his hand on her shoulder. She seemed tired and a little depressed.

"Is everyone gone?" she asked.

"Yes. Ivan and Hanh drove over to his grandparents' place. They'll probably be back in a couple hours, but everyone else is gone for good. Your brother took your car and said he'd be in La Crosse until sometime tomorrow or the next day. Everyone sang your praises for organizing it all. Mom was in tears over your generosity and kindness. She and Dad want us to come for supper this week."

Lester's house groaned.

August and April listened to the silence that followed.

"I suppose you want to talk about what happened between me and Dennis Scarborough," said April. Her voice seemed defeated.

"Not if you don't want to."

"I want to."

August sat across from her and laced his fingers on the tabletop. "You were apparently right about Dennis being responsible for the vandalism, indirectly at least."

"There was never any doubt about that."

"What do you make of him joining a monastery?"

"I wish him every success in whatever he wants to do other than come after me. Look, August, I probably should have told you about Dennis, but—"

"If you don't want to talk about it, that's fine. It's none of my business."

"I thought you wanted transparency between us."

"I do, but we have the rest of our lives to achieve it."

"Last summer, I was emotionally raw, inconsolable. I'd lost my first husband to suicide and my second to insects. A neighbor invited me to a barbeque party at her home—built to resemble an ocean liner—and against my better judgment, I went. As many as fifty Gaters showed up that night to eat barbequed chicken and ribs and drink from the marble bar running along the front of her deck."

"I assume Dennis was there," said August.

"Yes, but by the time he arrived the party was already fizzling out; the band was packing it in, and some people were taking leave of the host and looking for their jackets. I ordered a last drink when Dennis came on to me from behind, leaning over my shoulder, dripping bourbon down my neck, blowing in my hair, joking about the way I smelled and laughing at my attempts to get away. I'd never liked the man and having him assault me—in front of Chopie, no less—excited my anger beyond its normal limits."

"That's understandable," said August.

"No, it's not," said April. "There's nothing good or even excusable about what I did. I knew what would happen if he succeeded in getting what he wanted from me, and I knew what the fallout could be."

"You were vulnerable. He took advantage of that."

"August, I let it happen. After Chopie went home, I should have gone home. But I got another drink and waited. Within minutes he was all over me again. He yanked me across the deck, shoved me along a hallway and into an empty room at the back of the house, and minutes later the deed was done. A couple weeks went by. Then he showed up at my house, drunk and incoherent. My housekeeper answered the door; he forced his way inside, and chased me from room to room, swearing and eventually shooting."

"You're not to blame for any of that."

"I am, though."

"No one is criticizing you."

"I'm criticizing me. I let someone I despise have sex with me."

"What he did doesn't count as having sex, and it doesn't change the way I feel about you," said August.

"Then you really need to understand that behind the idea of me that you're in love with lives someone as spiteful and ugly as anyone else."

"Maybe, but standing inside her is someone who goes out of her way to help people like my mother without asking anything in return, and I'll never forget that."

"Can we go home now?" asked April, gathering all her papers into a single folder.

"Sure. I'll get the car."

GENE CIRCLING

ON THE DRIVE back to her house after the memorial service, April stared silently out of the passenger's window. The ambience inside the car did not invite conversation, and August could discover no topic likely to succeed at amiably engaging her. Consequently, he let his mind wander through the last several hours: his mother officiating at the memorial service; his father shunning crowded areas of the tent and trying to avoid notice; Ivan's parents looking much older than the last time he'd had seen them; pictures of Lester as a much younger man, some of them with August and Ivan—in boyhood—standing nearby; recognizing many people at the service but not remembering their names, and smiling self-consciously again and again.

At the house they were greeted by April's dog, wild with joy at their return. When August volunteered to take her for a walk, April handed him a jacket from the closet. August thanked her and she smiled in a tired way.

Hannah wanted to take the trail behind the house, and August followed her. They walked for some time while August thought about his parents, Lester Mortal, and the memorial service. Overhead, the sky darkened, and the air grew cooler. He was glad for the jacket. After about a quarter mile, he noticed an uncomfortable knot forming along the perimeter of his mind, and the more he ignored it, the tighter it became, choking off the oxygen to his other thoughts.

Something April had said just before coming back from Lester's house didn't make sense: "There's nothing good or even excusable about what I did. I knew what would happen if *he* succeeded in getting what he wanted from me, and I knew what the fallout could be." August had let it go at the time, because he didn't want to seem overly interested in a subject that he had already declared none of his business, but this now seemed like a mistake. He should have asked questions.

"We're going back," he told Hannah, and they returned along the same path.

He found April in the kitchen and she pressed a glass of bourbon into his hand. "Let's go into the basement," she said. They carried their drinks downstairs, sat on the bed near the glass wall, and watched fish in the faint, greenish light. Their quiet, languorous movements seemed hypnotic, and the remarkable stillness of the big house amplified the effect.

August had eaten little in the last twelve hours, and the alcohol began to loosen the bootlaces of his nervous system. The thriving community of microbes living on the surface of April's skin, and imparting the unique, musky fragrance of being near her, seemed uncommonly pleasurable. He wanted to sit closer to her, but did not, for fear of disrupting the congenial mood that had enveloped them.

He took another drink. An uptick in his heart rate, blood pressure, and respiration accompanied the way she arranged herself on their shared bed; her hip outlined by tan slacks; the rhythmic breathing of her chest; and the scanning motion of her irises as they followed the aquatic life beyond the glass. She sipped from her glass of bourbon and August heard the internal, swallowing sounds in her throat. Refrains from old songs floated nonsensically in and out of his attention, and then—without language or words of any kind—the imminent possibility of carnal joy arrived in his mind and began to bully aside all other considerations. He took another drink and realized that a biochemical line had been crossed somewhere inside him; if asked what he was thinking about, he could no longer honestly deny that he wanted every permissible pleasure that his and her corporeal forms could discover together, and as soon as possible. And as a way of arresting this urge, or at least not acting on it until he was confident of an acceptable approach, he thought about how the boundaries of mutually respectful relationships were established. Where did the many tumultuous feelings swirling around inside him—some urging him on and others holding him back—come from? Many, and perhaps most, of the rules for precopulatory behavior were no doubt made available through very long genetic inheritances, and these were interpreted through cultural traditions and experienced through hormonally induced fear of social shaming, reinforced by parental training in childhood, information gleaned from friends, depictions of human sexual conduct in movies, novels, media outlets and other cultural expressions. Pornography also provided an influence through a catalogue of goal-oriented scenes with little practical advice on how to legally arrive there. And, of course, personal experience also contributed toward imagining how future intimacies might proceed: August's experiences with people other than April, and April's experiences with people other than August, informed them—and were informing them right now—about what to do next with each other.

He loved her immensely.

April took another drink from her glass and turned toward him. "We need to talk," she said. "Come upstairs."

In the first-floor study, April sat behind the desk. She opened a drawer and handed several photographs across the desktop.

"I haven't tried to explain this to anyone before," she said. "It's hard to know how to begin but take a look at these and tell me what you see."

August stared into the photographs—pictures of April in different positions, attitudes and places, wearing a variety of outfits. "Your hair's a lot shorter, and it looks like you're using more makeup than usual," he remarked. "And the clothes you're wearing often seem dated. For instance, I remember those hats from decades ago. My mother had one. But you look good, as always, maybe a little heavier than you are now, but you look good. You're naturally photogenic, which doesn't surprise me, and I don't recognize where the pictures were taken. Am I missing something?"

"Those are pictures of my mother. Most of them were taken around thirty years ago in New Zealand."

"They look like period costumes."

"Here's a picture of her today."

She handed another photo across the desktop and August studied it. "You've held up well," he joked, though neither he nor April laughed. "Was this taken in your kitchen?"

"Yes, and here's a picture of both of us."

"When?"

"Several months ago. She stopped on her way to California. We're at the marina. Leaves were still on the trees."

"It's an unnerving resemblance," said August, "though it isn't rare for mothers and daughters—or for that matter fathers and sons and sometimes grandparents and grandchildren—to physically resemble each other."

"There's a little more going on here."

"Tell me."

"I will, but you must first promise to listen . . . listen carefully, without interrupting."

"Okay."

"One year ago, I hired a University of Wisconsin-Madison research team to discover why the two men I had had sexual intercourse with both lost their ability and desire to have sex again. After about—"

"Wait a minute. You mean to say—"

"August, I told you not to interrupt."

"Sorry, but that research must have been terribly expensive."

"It was, but I needed answers, and you promised to just listen."

"Okay."

"Early last May, the primary investigator, Dr. Phillip Johnson, explained to me what they found. My genetic configuration, he said, was identical to my mother's. My mother and I shared the exact same genome."

"You're a clone of your mother," said August. "That possibly means . . . I'm sorry. Go on."

"Somehow, my mother's body conceived me without my father contributing a single chromosome."

"But . . . sorry again."

"Look, August, please just listen."

August folded his arms.

"Thank you." April deliberately took several deep breaths and continued. "Dr. Johnson reported that when the hormonal levels of my second husband, Doug, were analyzed, they closely resembled levels found in a relatively small human subgroup who are attracted to neither male nor female targets—people sometimes referred to as asexual. For these folks, erotic desire and sexual affection simply don't figure into the way they relate to others; they want companionship and friends just like everyone else, but sexuality plays no role."

April paused and concentrated on her breathing again before continuing.

August turned away from her, as though hoping to digest the information he was taking in by diluting it with lake scenes from outside the window; his attention followed one of the lines of shimmering light across the rippled surface to its source at the top of a distant light pole in the marina.

"August, every man who has slept with me—after being satiated—lost his sexual drive."

He turned back to her, raised his right hand, as though calling time out, and quickly said, "That's natural. After reaching orgasm men usually don't want more sex, not right away. It's understandable. The male machinery has to be reset."

"But after finding release through me the drive doesn't return, ever. There's gratification, yes, but then, later, the craving doesn't return. That's what Dr. Johnson explained. The hormonal expressions responsible for a healthy sexual appetite simply don't regenerate. There's no impulse to do it again. And the research team was confident that the same thing had happened to my first husband, Bradley."

August looked outside again, where a small, single-engine outboard slowly moved across the lake, severing light lines by moving through them.

"I'm not sure I understand," he said.

"August, it's this cloned body of my mother's—me. Having sex with me brings about epigenetic changes in my partner. They called it gene circling."

"Fascinating," said August. "Your former husband—the second one—is studying a similar phenomenon in insects."

"That's my understanding as well."

"He called it parthenogenesis. Apparently, some uniquely adaptable insects reproduce asexually under stress. Bees are quite versatile in that regard. Female worker bees sometimes lay unfertilized eggs, which invariably hatch into drones—male bees without stingers. And of course, feminization is unavoidable in cloning because only the female gamete passes along both X and Y chromosomes. I'm sorry, please continue."

"The lab report from Dr. Johnson concluded that, after he slept with me, testosterone, serotonin, and dopamine levels in Doug did not return to the motivational levels needed for arousing thoughts and sexual behavior. Or as my first husband, Bradley, used to say, 'The idea-feelings just aren't there.'"

"Was he ill?"

"Not in the least. He was an athlete at the apex of his game."

"But his genital reflexes didn't function?"

"Not after that first time. And remember, August, we were young—Bradley and I—and our gender-specific identities were extremely important to us. For years, our endocrinal expressions had been inspiring most of our waking and dreaming thoughts. And when Brad no longer had any sex drive, he felt something was wrong. His sensibilities shifted, and he became overly aware of things taking place inside and around him, and this concerned him. All at once his world had shifted. 'I used to just be,' he lamented. 'It all used to just happen.' He'd simply gone after whatever he wanted, without questioning where the motivational stimulation for his actions were coming from."

"Self-reflection can sometimes be detrimental." August wished he had something better to say.

"He stopped getting along with his teammates. His interests dried up and he dismissed many of the diversions he'd earlier enjoyed—like movies—as simply opportunities to watch attractive people mate, or prepare to mate. Brad complained at great length that many cinematographic themes appealed to males by fantasizing about eliminating sexual rivals and appealed to women by overdramatizing the role of female sexual selection in evolutionary processes. Popular songs, he said, mimicked foreplay through melody, and most novels, he said, reinforced the happy illusion that we make conscious decisions independently from biological dictates. And in his opinion, many team sports, like football, were modeled after, and drew metaphorical strength from, a single sperm cell running a fallopian gauntlet, making it into the end zone, and scoring."

"There may be some truth in all those observations," said August.

"When Brad suddenly stopped having sexual urges, he thought he was a freak of nature. He failed two of his classes, his scholarship was seriously threatened, and he began arguing with his coaches. All the important areas of his life collapsed."

"I was told he took his own life."

"Who said that?"

"Your neighbors."

"I guess it shouldn't surprise me, but for some reason it does."

"Is it true?"

"It is. On top of everything else, Brad was risk-prone, with quick reflexes. It was part of what made him an outstanding running back. And when Brad's doctors gave him antidepressants, the drugs disinhibited the few mental guardrails he had to avoid impulsive behavior. His dark moods continued and after about a year he went into the garage, sat in a lawn chair, loaded a handgun, and shot himself."

"That's brutal."

"Tell me about it. I found him."

"I'm sorry."

"I was only nineteen and I had desperately wanted to succeed at being a good wife. You have no idea how much it had hurt to watch him fall apart. You can't know. You're not female and no one ever drummed into you how you must make everything right—to create and maintain a healthy, cheerful home. Any problems your man has are your responsibility."

"I'm not disputing this, but it seems a little dated."

"That's the way I was raised. Maybe my success-driven mother wanted to nurture more traditional attitudes in me to make up for her rejecting them herself—I don't know. I tried to support my husband as much as I could, but he resented every attempt I made, and he resented me. He hated for me to be away from home and found me annoying whenever I was there. After a while we avoided each other altogether because it was easier that way. I still curl up inside when I remember those times."

"It wasn't your fault."

"Not all of it, no. As far as I knew my husband had just lost interest in me without any help on my part. I now know that sleeping with me caused him to lose his sexual drive, but I didn't know it then."

"Do you still have that lab report, and could you show it to me sometime?"

April nodded.

"And did the same thing happen to your second husband?" asked August.

"Yes, only Doug experienced it in an entirely different way. His personality, and brain, were differently structured. He felt liberated."

"Liberated?"

"His life improved, he always said. He stopped having mood

swings. Regrets and insecurities no longer bothered him. Grudges he'd held against former competitors, relatives, and colleagues—he simply let go of them. He could admit things to himself and others that would have embarrassed him before. Performance pressures, making a name for himself, taking responsibility for the family business, winning the approval of his older brothers and sister—he no longer experienced them. And when these drives went away, new possibilities appeared. He explained, 'My sexual appetites were acting like life filters, not stimulators.'"

"Doug said that?"

"He also said he never really knew me until he stopped wanting to physically possess me. He used a well-worn analogy: 'If a hammer is your only tool, everything looks like a nail.' Without his preoccupation with seeking out more and better sex, other activities drew his notice. He found enjoyment in even the most common activities and his fascination with insects returned."

"He told me his curiosity with entomology reached back into childhood."

"Yes, before puberty handed him a big hammer and began pointing out the nails."

"He stopped desiring you?"

"Yes. He still loved me, but without the desire part. We grew even closer. We cared very much about each other, and still do."

"Why are you telling me this now?"

"When you and I were in the basement just a little while ago, you were working up to something."

"You wanted to dissuade me?"

"Yes. You need to fully grasp the issue here, and see this from my side. I'm just as interested in you as you are in me, but I won't let you, or rather I won't let us, do something we will both regret. We can continue with the sexual tension between us, of course, but we must never act on it. If we did, you would surely blame me later."

"I would never blame you."

"You can't know that."

August stood up and paced in front of the desk, staring at April.

"If you're trying to discourage my interest in you, it won't work.

I admit what you've just told me seems significant. The effect you apparently have on men fortunate enough to share intimacy with you presents a novel challenge, but I want to be a part of whatever and whoever you are, and I want everything that involves you to include me."

"You need to think through this very carefully, August."

"I've been thinking about this since I was first able to think. It might not bother me at all to lose my sexual urges. I think I'd be happy to be rid of them. Most of the time they bring me nothing but grief. Like all other addictions that require more and more fermented juice for less and less satiation, so is it with sex."

"August, the urge comes back so you can act on it over and over again, which most people experience as a benefit—a solace to accompany them throughout life. It evolved to be pleasurable, and usually is."

"Many things are pleasurable—some in a more beneficial and enlightening way—but we ignore most of them because we're tunneling through life looking for sex."

"But you may never again feel the way you're feeling right now. I mean, if we dash down the hall and jump into bed you may have to live without this blissful need for the rest of your life."

"Fine with me."

"What would be left of your feelings for me? How much of your confidence in us being right for each other comes from the same genetic machinery that convinces you of the desirability of all women?"

"But you're perfect for me. Like this conversation—I can't imagine talking to anyone else on this level, having the raw elements of our lives spread out before us. It's like not being alone. With you, there's no need to abandon my most fundamental longing to know myself from moment to moment, to live an examined, reflective life, to understand as well as to feel. With each other we are free to be who we really are."

"I know you think that, but how can you be sure your animal impulses haven't simply underwritten your appreciation for my less tangible human features, like education, deportment, and executive skills—through a kind of associative projection, the way our culture sexualizes wealth, status, automobiles, food, clothing, shoes, entertainment, and even exercise?"

"Afterward, I'll feel exactly the same about you. I'm sure of it. Nothing will change."

"You can't know that. Obviously, people react differently. What some tolerate, others can't. Dennis Scarborough first decided to try to kill me, and then later became a monk. I just don't want you blaming me."

"I take full responsibility for everything I do."

"That's very gallant, but it's almost always the woman who is held responsible."

"I wouldn't do that."

"Look, I only found out about this four months ago, and I don't know what else to say to you about it."

"Okay, you didn't know about gene circling, and this is the first time you've had the opportunity to forewarn someone. I get that. Until recently you were unaware of the genetic stamp you could leave on someone. I completely appreciate that you wanted to talk through this. But I'm telling you, April, I'm fine with going ahead. I'm more than fine. I want to have sex with you more than anything else in the world, and it's because I love you."

April stood up and they studied each other across the desktop.

August's phone hummed. He took it out of his pocket and held it to his ear. Ivan's voice greeted him from inside the thin metal housing: "Gus, can you meet me at the shop tomorrow afternoon?"

"Sure, what's up?"

"I promised to clean out Lester's truck before they start working on it—you know, make sure there aren't some personal things tucked away in the corners that Hanh might wish we'd saved. There won't be anyone else there because it's Sunday and I'd like to have some company while I go through it."

"I'll be over after lunch."

"Thanks. See you then."

August shoved his phone in his pocket and looked across the desk. April withdrew an unopened letter from the top drawer and handed it to him.

"This came for you," she said. "I need to get some sleep. It's been a long day and I've got a meeting early tomorrow morning in Madison. I'll be gone for most of the day. We can talk after I get back."

WE GREW UP TOGETHER

THE NEXT MORNING, after August had showered and dressed, he climbed the stairs. The main floor of the house greeted him with an empty stillness that spoke of April's earlier departure. To make sure, he checked the garage and saw that she had taken the green roadster.

In the kitchen, he ate a slice of buttered toast and drank several cups of coffee before reading the letter given to him the night before.

It was addressed to Mr. August Helm, c/o Ms. April Lux, Forest Gate, Wisconsin and appeared to be on University of Chicago stationary:

> *Dear August,*
>
> *We trust this letter finds you in good health. A promising start-up company in Atlanta, Georgia—Reion, LLC— is creating a library of quality recombinant antibodies showing high performance in targeting human transcription factors with multiple commercial applications. The project is headed by Dr. Cynthia Locus, known for her ribosomal sequencing work at Northwestern, and the search committee is currently looking for an experienced protein engineer. Dr. Peter Grafton submitted an enthusiastic recommendation of your work, and we encourage you to contact Research Recruitment Director Janet Branberry at the exchange provided below and inquire after the position.*
>
> *Wishing you all the very best,*
> *Lindiwe Sisulu.*

August read the letter several times before returning it to the envelope and inserting it into his shirt pocket.

When he arrived at the shop and went inside, Lester's pickup occupied the third bay, with both doors and the hood open.

"Gus, you made it," said Ivan, pulling a soda from the dispensing machine. "You want something to drink?"

"No thanks," replied August, closing the side door behind him. After inhaling, his head filled with memories inspired by the smell of oil and gasoline.

The shop had changed very little in the years since he'd last been inside, except for a new brand of digital diagnostic equipment parked at the end of the workbench. The tool cabinets, lifts, windows, cement walls, pressure tanks, lighting, and of course the smell were all the same as he remembered.

August and Ivan placed trash containers on either side of the pickup, put on rubber gloves, and began sifting through four inches of discarded items under the seat and covering the floor. Food wrappers were mixed in with receipt stubs, old gloves, grocery flyers, a pair of pliers, wasp spray, Medicare notifications, beer cans, fast-food coupons, half of a denim shirt, medication in unmarked bottles, expired credit cards, lyrics to the first two verses of "Amazing Grace" written on the back of an envelope, a deck of playing cards missing the four of clubs, the billfold Lester abandoned after Hanh gave him a new one on his birthday, containing old pictures—mostly of her—three dollars in cash, and car wash tokens from twenty years ago. There were also pieces of dried fruit, a flashlight corroded with battery lime, and a multipurpose utility knife rusted shut. And there was the occasional smell of the old man himself, a brief, unequivocal reminder of death's open door policy toward the living.

While they worked, the topic of sex and its clone-based repercussions with April gradually forced its way to the center of August's attention.

He wondered if it would be appropriate to talk to Ivan about the subject—discover his thoughts. Just as science benefited from rigorous peer review, another opinion might be helpful. And then he was reminded that scientists did not submit their theories until confident, or at least somewhat confident, they could withstand scrutiny. Also, the question of whether or not to have sex with April didn't seem particularly conducive to a free flow of enlightened opinion. Peer review in science worked because the topics under discussion were readily available for study, while the problem at hand seemed difficult to approach in an empirical manner.

The subject, August decided, was probably too complicated to talk about.

Then he did anyway.

"May I ask a theoretical question?" August inquired, tossing a handful of candy wrappers in the refuse bin.

"Sure," Ivan replied.

"Imagine two Bolivians—a man and a woman—discover that the more time they spend together the better they feel about each other. Before long, they begin to consider forming a more intimate and lasting relationship."

"Have they had sex yet?" asked Ivan, examining an old checkbook stained with something like tomato juice.

"They're considering it. The man is eager, but the woman worries the friendship they currently enjoy might suffer."

"Am I supposed to take sides?"

"Yes, but wait, there's more."

"Here's something." Ivan interrupted, holding up an old, spring-wound wristwatch with a brown leather band. "Remember this?" He twisted the stem several times and held it against his ear. "Still works," he said, and put it in his jacket pocket.

"Go on," said Ivan.

"Well, due to a quirk of nature the Bolivian woman's chromosomes are all female—every single one of them. Because of a cytokinesis irregularity, her genome contains nothing of her father. She's a clone of her mother and this has unusual consequences for her lovers. When she has intercourse with someone the satisfaction is so complete that—afterward—the male ceases having sexual desires. His batteries never recharge. The hormonal inducements that inspire men to feel like men are no longer expressed by his endocrine system."

"Wait a minute, Gus."

"Should I go over it again?"

"Let me put it in my own words. The woman you're describing has a double set of her mother's chromosomes—an extra portion of female. She's not only like her mother, but even more so. Her curves are no doubt are curvier, extremely big eyes, with soft skin, and her hair smells even more fragrant. And being more female, she's more appealing—at least to anyone with their orientation dials turned all the way north—yet her genetics also make her something like the castrating goddesses that sky-god worshippers used to be so frightened of. Am I understanding the situation correctly?"

"It's not exactly castration. Nothing is cut or removed. Intimate contact with her simply turns off sexual desire and leaves her lovers perpetually satiated."

"Then it's chemical castration."

"I suppose it could very, very, loosely be called that, very loosely."

The truck's rubber floor mat was now visible in places and August rolled the Shop-Vac over.

"How does this woman living in Bolivia know this will happen?" asked Ivan. "Maybe she overrates her own powers."

"It's happened before. In earlier years she slept with three guys—at different times, of course—and after experiencing supreme concupiscent joy, they didn't care anything for sex. They went on living in an extended postcoital state."

"And how did they feel about that?"

"One of them didn't like it; another felt released from a biological obsession that had been consuming most of his energy, and the third was somewhat undecided. So, knowing what you know about these Bolivians—the man and the woman who are in love—do you think they should have sex, or not?"

"Absolutely not."

"Why?"

"It's too dangerous. Losing his sex drive would cut the man off from nature's ultimate source of comfort and fun. Think about it: everything is connected to sex. There isn't a single thing that doesn't depend on it."

"Of course there is: mathematics, mountain climbing, and baseball immediately come to mind."

"Okay, maybe I exaggerated a little, but the only reason those things exist is because they don't seriously interfere with people having sex. If they did, mathematics, mountain climbing, and baseball would probably be outlawed. We think about sex all the time. It keeps our minds busy and our bodies healthy. If those thoughts went away, what would possibly replace them?"

"Better thoughts?"

"What could be better? Our greatest experiences are orgasmic. Time stands still when we're having fun, and with sex—at least with good sex—time ceases. And even when we're unhappy, at least we can imagine sex. Don't you think we should sweep it out first? I mean, before we hoover it up?"

"I suppose. Looks like there's a couple quarters and a nickel over there. Still, I think you're wrong. Most sexual thoughts aren't good; they induce temporary states of emergency that aren't based on anything real, like pranksters setting off fire alarms. Anxieties, frustration, regret, desperation, hopelessness, fear, urgency, and empty longing characterize most sexual thoughts; they act on us like mental uranium. And besides, the question I'm asking is whether the Bolivian guy's love for this woman—who he presently adores—would change if his physical attraction to her suddenly changed. I personally don't think it would. I'm certain he'd continue to love her and maybe love her even more—more honestly—without all those hormone-fueled neurotransmitters firing across his synapses."

"Not that long ago you were telling me that love *was* neurotransmission."

"I don't believe that anymore, though it's probably true on some level, and I'm convinced that a state of indefinite satiation would work out well for the Bolivian guy. The pleasures available to him through sex would find expression in different ways. His life could be more fulfilling. His interest in the design of female posteriors and the imagined bliss of erogenous foreplay would fade away. There'd be more time for friendship, reflexive conversation, innovative social policies, the problem of inadequate urban housing, medical research, equitable resource distribution, community sustainability, reading, baseball, stargazing, and discovering how primal cosmic dust eventually gives rise to congeries of electrochemical reactions resulting in conscious sensibilities. There are so many mysteries waiting, so much to learn."

"Gus, this is dangerous," said Ivan, standing up on the other side of the truck. "You can't possibly know how losing your libido might turn out. It could seriously mess with your mind. Sexual instincts aren't just pinned to us like clothing accessories; they channel down so deep they're part of who we are and how we think. It's too risky. I'll sleep with April first."

"Ivan, I was talking about a hypothetical situation."

Somewhere in the distance, a truck geared down to climb a hill and the sound seemed like groaning.

"No, Gus, you're talking about April. For some reason you always forget we grew up together. You can't fool me. Whenever you try to picture yourself somewhere, I mean when you were a kid, Bolivia was always your choice. It probably came from that book we read about the bat caves of Bolivia. You're talking about April. I see that. There's something agreeably alarming about her, and she's a magnet for erotic thoughts. It's not exactly like she's from another species, but there's clearly something different about her. Most people can see it, I think. Lester did, and he told me so. And I do. She's intimidating. It doesn't surprise me to learn she's been assembled along different lines and that her naked assemblage might have unusual effects on anyone coming too close."

"Implacably irresistible is the phrase I came up with."

"Implacably?"

August plugged the shop vac in. "I thought you were against the idea."

"I was, at first, but the thought keeps improving. I hope I haven't offended you."

"You haven't, and the part of me that bristles at your suggestion . . . well, it shouldn't. See, that's what I'm trying to say. Once the basic urge for sex goes away, maybe jealousy, possessiveness, and greed will disappear as well. There are so many adverse entanglements dragged along behind sexual desire."

"Yes, but what if you also lose your appreciation for beauty, humor, honor, generosity, or friendship?"

"Those aren't grounded in sexuality."

"How do you know they aren't?"

CLIMAX

MOST FUNDRAISERS ATTENDING the Sunday meeting in the
Dane County convention center overlooking Lake Monona did not relish working on the weekend and hurried through the items on their
agenda. They agreed to postpone discussion of disaster relief for several
southeastern states until the following week, and referred the problems of rape, crime, and starvation along migration routes throughout
sub-Saharan Africa to the executive committee. Breakout groups on
resource sharing were limited to hour-long presentations and the time
scheduled for the catered lunch was cut in half.

By 2:30 p.m. April found herself back in her car and heading
home. The traffic was light—even for a Sunday—and after driving out
of the city she set the autopilot and felt herself relaxing. Gradually, her
thoughts began to slowly spiral around several cheerful themes.

At the meeting she'd talked to several people who seemed perfect
for designing a project aimed at ending female genital mutilation. The
project could begin by building a scaffold of support for all women in
a given community, not just the children. Encouraging a culture to
include more opportunities—even on a small scale—would expand
traditional envelopes. These new contacts she'd met in the breakout
group had the needed language skills, experience, and temperament
to meet women where they were and walk with them into a less restric-
tive way of living. A combination of education, economic independence,
and friendship would succeed, she was sure of it.

She wondered if August was back yet from helping Ivan clean
out Lester's truck. Would he have time to take Hannah for a walk?
She could call Skylar; it had been a while since their dogs had played
together. But it was Sunday and Skylar usually spent her weekends with
Janet . . . if Janet was home.

When April arrived, she asked a guard at the Gate entrance if
August had returned yet and learned she was only seconds behind him.
He'd just come through.

They met inside the house.

August had a sack of tacos he'd picked up for dinner. The tacos were still warm and they ate them at the kitchen table with mugs of hot tea.

April told him about meeting the people she hoped to work with in the future, and he asked about the project.

"It's too early to talk about yet," said April. "My ideas are just beginning to come together, and I don't want to hex them by explaining too much. It's just that I worried that the meeting would be a waste of time, but now I'm glad I attended."

August took the letter from the University of Chicago from his pocket.

"Is something wrong?" asked April, sitting across from him at the table. "You seem tetchy."

"This is from the undergraduate lab manager in the Chicago lab where I used to work." August tossed the letter across the table. "She says Dr. Grafton has recommended me to a start-up in Atlanta."

"Well, that's good, right?"

"I suppose, but how would she know to send it here—your address?"

April poured some more tea.

"Is it possible you talked to her, April?"

"Who?"

"The woman who sent the letter—did you talk to her?"

"Yes."

"How did you know where to contact her?"

"Public records. You told me about losing your job and, well, it didn't seem right. I called her and asked why the funding for your position had dried up. We didn't talk very long."

"You gave her this address?"

"She didn't know how else to reach you."

August tasted the tea again, and again decided it was too hot.

"You still seem upset," said April. "Did you not want me to call her?"

"I'm fine with that, and I'm impressed your call prompted Lindiwe to tell me about a position and Dr. Grafton to recommend me for it."

"Will you apply?"

"No, I won't. I'll find something closer, in Madison or Milwaukee. I have real friends here, and my parents, and you. If I must commute long distances, that's okay. This is the place for me."

"What do you mean?"

"I'm staying here. You found a position for me in a distant city to test how resolved I am to stay with you."

"August, I'm not going to sleep with you. I won't take the chance."

"And I've told you nothing will change—"

"I won't do it. I've twice committed to someone who started out wanting me, loving me, and ended up going away. I'm not doing that again."

"I would never want to live without you. I'll never leave you."

"August, this might sound a little dismissive, but I've heard that before."

"The South American research project—the one exploring *Wolbachia* in insects—you found it for Doug, didn't you?"

"He had a deep fascination for bugs, and he no longer wanted me. But he was too good a man to violate his commitment without cause."

"So you found him a way out, and he took it."

"August, I'm not going to sleep with you. I probably should not have given you any hope. Yesterday, the memorial service and people talking about Lester—especially your mother—hardened my resolve. A relationship with me runs contrary to normal living, and I have an enormous potential for disrupting anyone who gets near me."

"I don't think gene circling will ever take hold in me, and if it does, I won't care."

"It would change you. Count on it."

"Then I'll change in a way I've always wanted."

"You're not seeing this in a comprehensive way. When it changes you, it changes us, and I don't want that."

"I can't promise to no longer have sexual feelings for you, and if I did, I'd be lying. Priests and many others have been breaking that same promise for thousands and thousands of years. Isn't it better to just find out right now what will happen, tonight?"

"Then once again I'll have become deeply intimate with someone who ends up not wanting me. I won't do it."

"There must be precautions we can take--prophylactic films, barriers, masks, and creams."

"I'm not taking the chance."

"There must be some avoidance."

"It would be irresponsible of me. I understand my decision is probably unacceptable to you."

"And do you also understand that a single afternoon of eating tacos and drinking tea with you—talking from our hearts—is worth more to me than a lifetime of sexual pleasures with any number of other people?"

A beast of silence lumbered through the kitchen.

"So, where does that leave us?" asked April.

"Right here—sitting across from each other, enjoying every second of each other's company."

They fell silent again until their second mug of tea cooled down.

"Besides, touching eyelashes couldn't hurt," said August.

"What?"

"If our eyelashes touched, my masculinity probably wouldn't be damaged."

"I suppose not, but—"

"And ears. If our ears brushed against each other, I'd still be fine. And hair, I mean, I could touch your hair, and toes."

"What are you doing?"

"I'm asking about touching your toes. That couldn't hurt, could it?"

April smiled. "No, I don't suppose that would hurt."

August tore off a blank corner of the letter, turned it over and wrote something on the back.

"What are you doing?"

"Writing something down."

"What is it?"

"I'll show it to you later." He put the piece of paper in his pocket. "Now I'm thinking about your hands."

"What about them?"

"Touching them. You have great hands."

"Everybody does."

"And then there are your knees, and neck."

"Stop."

"I can't stop. There are too many places belonging to you that I hope to visit. I could vacation for years and never leave your left shoulder."

"What did you write down?"

"Do you really want to see it?"

"Yes, I do."

August took the piece of paper out of his pocket and handed it across the table.

"What is this?"

"It's a date."

"October 2073. What does it mean?"

"By then I'll have become familiar with nearly all of you. I'll know about the back of your knees and the way your face looks when you're sleeping. I'll know all your favorite foods, and all the adventures of your childhood. You'll have told me about your recurring dreams and how hot you like the water when you shower. I'll know your dress and shoe sizes, and the name of your first-grade teacher. We'll know almost everything about each other. Our lives will be maximized around each other, and at that time, in October 2073, we'll talk again about the benefits and risks of gene circling. Until then, I won't bring it up or do anything that will force you to think about it. I promise. I just want to be with you, April. Always."

"We'll be oldened then, August."

"Yes, and I'll have happily loved and wanted you every single day between then and now. You'll know it and I'll know it and we'll know it together."

"And what will happen then?"

"Anything and everything we want."

EPILOGUE

THE MANY YEARS that April and I have shared together have been filled with happiness. We are friends, advocates, and custodians of each other. The dialogue between us never ends, and in fact, has never even abated; the strength we draw from each other has been invaluable in helping us endure great social unrest and global change.

But before I describe these species-wide challenges, it may be beneficial to explain the phenomenon of gene circling more fully. The accepted nomenclature for the manner out of which April Lux was conceived on Christmas Eve in the Wellington Hotel in Wellington, New Zealand, where her parents had taken a holiday, is called sperm-dependent parthenogenesis, i.e., the successful development of an unfertilized ovum into an embryo, initiated by the presence—but not the direct participation—of a sperm cell. That night in the hotel, following intercourse, the mere proximity of April's father's sperm to her mother's egg triggered an asexual reproduction event ending in a gamete-zygote attaching to her mother's uterine wall. And though this may seem extremely odd, it is not at all unknown within nature at large. A few other vertebrates can reproduce in this way. Sharks and Komodo dragons have both been known to replicate through parthenogenesis, and within the insect and plant worlds parthenogenesis is widespread. There are over two thousand species that wholly or partly reproduce through parthenogenesis.

Cloning during parthenogenesis takes place solely within the mitosis process, followed by the nullification of the telophase and cytokinesis cycles of meiosis, wherein the successful division of the female gamete into two separate haploid nuclei normally takes place. With parthenogenesis, the separation never occurs, and a viable zygote is formed with only the mother's chromosomes.

Surprising to both April and I was that her situation was by no means unique; though no one knew at the time, there were other humans who had been conceived through sperm-dependent parthenogenesis. The reason for this was obvious: few individuals could afford the costs incurred by April to discover her chromosomal inheritance. Only about a half dozen other wealthy women—acting independently—had funded research into why their lovers were losing their amorous ambitions, and each assumed her circumstance was entirely unique. And for clearly understood reasons, they kept their studies private.

But all that changed several years after April and I were married, when a few research microbiologists ignored the nondisclosure agreements signed with their clients and—though they did not reveal their clients' identities—quietly shared their data with other scientists. When numbers correlated, excitement levels rose: something was happening within the general population. Soon afterward, salient portions of the studies were shared with journalists.

At the first glimmer of what the scientists were saying, news outlets went wild with stories of female clones with emasculating powers; speculations of every conceivable description clogged the internet. Programing directors placed purported experts before eager audiences, warning about the dangers of gene circling. Church leaders proclaimed the End of Days. Others blamed extraterrestrials.

Everyone wanted to know: Who were these clones? How many were there? Where did they live? How could you identify them? If someone looked like her mother, did that mean she *was one*? And if someone looked a *little* like her mother, did that mean she was part clone? Could you lose your libido simply by standing near a clone and making eye contact?

April's privacy was never compromised, thank goodness, but the names of two women who had commissioned similar studies (in Los Angeles and Paris) were discovered, and every scintilla of their personal lives was unearthed, exposed, transmitted around the planet, and endlessly discussed. The hounded women went into hiding, and their disappearance caused even more rumors and conjecture.

Congressional leaders convened hearings and intelligence agencies came under pressure to identify existing clones and propose policies for how to deal with them. State laws mandating genetic testing were passed. Lawsuits were filed against them, and the courts—at all levels—devolved into judicial frenzy. Many Orthodox Jews, Christians, and Muslims removed their male children from coed schools; families prevented sons from dating girls who resembled their mothers.

While the courts weighed the constitutionality of mandatory testing, the question of how gene circling caused male sexual dysfunction was being explored through government and privately funded studies. In the beginning, most researchers inclined toward the hypothesis that a retrovirus responsible for male hormonal inhibition was being transferred during sexual intercourse.

But this theory soon expired. The retrovirus itself—a brief sequence of RNA hidden beneath a thin protein sheath—could be found within everyone, even in the oldest known genetic samples. Hominids of both genders had carried it—in its dormant form—since the Neanderthals. What remained a mystery was the mechanism for mobilizing the retrovirus and prompting its RNA sequence to express reverse transcription enzymes, which could then be copied into the working DNA, where chromosomal editing took place.

The social crisis became even more acute when select members of the scientific community learned of two women who had conceived parthenogenically *without the presence of a sperm cell.* The first was nearly thirty years old, living in Somalia; the other was fifteen, in Maryland. Both had spontaneously cloned. No intercourse, or insemination of any kind had been involved. The reproductive cycle in these women had simply initiated itself. Virgins had become pregnant and, after nine months, gave birth.

This startling discovery spurred hundreds of billions of dollars in research grants to discover the possible environmental triggers for parthenogenesis. The idea that nature was wresting reproductive control away from mankind was not acceptable and a British service agent famously remarked, "The Yanks haven't employed as many scientists since the Manhattan Project." One hypothesis mostly rejected by researchers, yet popular within the public, explained the arrival of human parthenogenesis as a Gaia effect—the planet itself limiting human populations for the sake of all other living things.

Social anxiety around gene circling also led to the formation of citizen groups dedicated to the sanctity and protection of normal sexual reproduction. Though their language was apocalyptic, most of these reactionary organizations did not physically threaten women and girls conceived through parthenogenesis; they simply wanted their

disapproval of species reproductive changes to be noticed and the subject of human parthenogenesis to be banned from schoolbooks at all
levels of study.

One vigilante group, however, Mother's Little Assistants, threatened violence against clones and anyone supporting, or tolerating, them.
It was hard to know how much public support the secret society of
Assistants enjoyed because their meetings were restricted to members
only, and their membership lists remained under lock and key. MLA
attempted to identify as many clones as possible (government sources
estimated there were likely between 67,000 and 92,000 within the con-
tinental US) and publicly harass them. Some clones were assaulted and
beaten; one woman was burned, and several others hanged.

For years, even when faced with open violence, local authorities
often remained reluctant to vigorously enforce laws protecting clones as
long as their citizenship status was being challenged in courts. When
crimes were committed against them, police and government officials
responded by appointing study commissions and refusing to comment
because of ongoing investigations.

In response to this official apathy, informal organizations throughout the world quietly formed to provide assistance and relocate women
and girls targeted by MLA. These groups worked closely with each
other to decode communications sent between MLA members and,
over time, thousands of threatened clones were quietly moved to more
secure locations.

Then, almost as abruptly as it had begun, MLA disbanded; the viru-
lent hatred directed at clones quieted down, tapered off, and disappeared.

April and I were frankly a little surprised that the extreme social
reactions to parthenogenesis and gene circling did not last longer. But
after the demographic numbers were published, the public seemed to
take a deep breath and accept what had been generally known for years:
the only danger posed by clones came from losing sexual motivation
after sleeping with them, and no one was forced to sleep with them.
And as though to drive this nail home with an especially big hammer,
after the gene-circling phenomenon became public knowledge, clones
(and women suspected of being clones) were inundated with men (and
women) wanting to date them.

In 2037, there were 3,623,145 babies born in the US, and among them were an estimated 8,000 clones. In 2038, there were 3,256,498 newborns, and about 15,000 clones. In the following year, there were 2,995,269 newborns, and roughly 29,000 clones. In 2040, 55,000 clones numbered among 2,546,243 newborns, and of the cloned newborns were 3,214 whose mothers had been cloned before them. Parthenogenesis had gone multigenerational. The clones themselves had begun cloning.

The facts were inescapable: while the US population steadily declined overall, the number of cloned newborns were increasing at exponential rates.

Similar rates were observed worldwide. Even countries known for high fertility rates experienced population declines concurrent with burgeoning numbers of clones. And although there were some boys among cloned newborns, between 94 and 95 percent were infant girls.

After 2040, overall populations continued to decline—in some countries precipitously—and the number of clones continued to rise, though both rates eventually became less pronounced. As I write this in September 2073 there are approximately 700 million human clones living within a total human world population of 4.8 billion. Less than 40 percent are male.

These were the facts, and in acknowledgment of these living statistics, laws were passed, and the courts affirmed that clones were entitled to all constitutional rights granted to other citizens.

The low birthrates shifted national priorities. Expectations for continuous economic growth, rising consumption, and global housing shortages were replaced with hopes and prayers for sustainability and strategies for maintaining existing living standards.

The value of human life rose, leading to a virtual consensus that something needed to be done about shortened life expectancies for workers who were needed to continue in the labor force for as long as possible. Government and private foundations rallied around the elimination and management of heart disease, cancer, respiratory infections, diabetes, mental illness, and dementia. And in seeking to extend life and productivity, the need for diets with higher nutritional content, lower sodium, and fewer heavy metals became clear. Environmental standards rose and renewable energy sources outpaced those depending on already-stored hydrocarbons.

Along with a focus on lowering mortality rates, the importance of children—all children—became painfully evident. Investment in fertility clinics skyrocketed. Bidding wars erupted inside adoption agencies, and deference to infants and young children was reflected in law and endorsed throughout popular culture. Refusing to give up your bus seat to a pregnant woman became a felony in most countries, and, in some, an invitation for mob violence. Support networks for children broadened and the practice of godparenting extended to god-families and even god-neighborhoods. Government policies made clear that no child should be undernourished, uneducated, or vulnerable to preventable diseases. And when Hanh and Ivan had a baby girl named June, there were more people lining up to help take care of her than could fit inside Hanh's house at one time. April and I were among those clamoring for time with her.

Workers were needed in every industry. Training programs were instituted even within county jails. Reforms swept through the criminal justice system and prison populations dwindled. Crime rates fell.

A cure of sorts, or at least proven management plans, were found for most forms of Alzheimer's, and I even played a very small role in fabricating one of the many needed antibodies, along with several other scientists in my Madison lab. I'm proud of this accomplishment, and I'm equally proud of the success our hobby group has enjoyed in combatting white-nose syndrome in bats. Local bat populations have been slowly rebuilding, and the threat posed by the *Pseudogymnoascus* fungus is no longer quite as serious to those strange yet wonderful nocturnal creatures.

I'm even more proud of April. Her work on behalf of women and girls has been widely recognized, and the model she created for anticipating migration patterns due to climate change has been adopted by several government agencies. Today, one of her nonprofits is meeting in our home to prepare for the arrival of a small group of sub-Saharan refugees in Wisconsin. A dozen or more business leaders are petitioning for the immigrants to be placed within their respective districts.

I'll be meeting Ivan at Lester Mortal's old place, where we come together once a month to share a meal, drink coffee ground from skillet-roasted beans, and indulge our friendship. Ivan's daughter June is currently away at school in Chicago, and Hanh is delivering hazelnuts and honey to retailers in Madison. Ivan will fry up too much food, and I'll provide a banana cream pie made from one of my mother's recipes. I'll bring him up to date on what April and I have been up to. He'll talk about Hanh and June, and about how Lester's old place really brings back memories. And then we'll both go on about one thing or another, complain about getting old, and recall a time when we could swim like river otter and run like deer. The wood stove will have warmed up by then and I'll take another drink of hot coffee, settle back into my chair, and let Ivan's stories lull me into a state somewhere between imagining and remembering. It doesn't matter that I've heard all his stories many times and raised innumerable objections to most of them. It doesn't matter because we simply like to be together. Both of us remember a time when many people, perhaps most, eschewed deepening friendships out of fear of losing their personal, true identity; but for Ivan and I, we found ours in each other. April insists that most people maintain their internal equilibriums through replaying familiar thoughts and reviewing benign themes over and over. She's right, of course, but once a month I let Ivan conduct the reviewing for both of us.

Tonight, I'm hoping he'll want to talk about how people relate to each other and the world, and why those relationships began to shift. He has an explanation for this, and I'm looking forward to hearing it again because it touches upon a couple areas of adolescent and preadolescent mythologizing that I sometimes forget about when considering the fundamental agencies of change.

It's important to me to have some explanation—however speculative—for why I was there when the human story first began to take a different direction. No, it didn't have to be that way, and if circumstances had been only a little different, I would never have gone to Forest Gate. Frankly, I'd never heard of April Lux and would probably never have learned of her at all except for a haphazard collection of other events, which at the time seemed purely accidental.

Ivan says the new way of looking at the world—the one that sees all other living organisms as part of the same dreamworld that dreamed us and is still dreaming—first came walking into the Driftless area in the form of a solitary traveler, a man in his twenties that hitched a ride from an older man pulling a cattle trailer behind his pickup from a bumper hitch. The young guy had no relatives or friends here, but after he was let out of the pickup in the middle of the night, he could think of no reason to go anywhere else. So, he slept in a cemetery until morning and went looking for work. He stayed here, saved what little money he made, and a decade or two later bought a small farm and milked a dozen Jersey cows. His name was July Montgomery, and it wasn't so much what he did, or how he looked, or the friendship he shared with my dear dad, or how he lived and died that was important—it was how he thought. One way to explain it, according to Ivan, pictures July Montgomery sharing his mother's womb with a twin. For nine months they grew together, developed fingers and toes and ears and hearts and brains. Everything one of them heard, the other heard also. And everything one tasted, the other tasted. Everything one felt, the other felt. Though doctors often remind us that a fetus isn't capable of thinking, these twins shared whatever it is that comes before thought. Whatever one emerging mind was doing before it could think, the other emerging mind was doing it too.

For nine months July Montgomery was never alone, and in as much as he possessed even the most rudimentary aptitude for knowing anything at all, he knew this. Then, his always-there companion died during the birthing process, and suddenly, July was breathing air all by himself. And for the rest of his natural life, his first instinctual response to everyone and everything he initially met—in the opening nanosecond of cognition—was to greet that person, or that animal, or that fish, or that plant, or that bug, as the remedy to his isolation. And though it might not seem like a very profound influence over how others think and act, really, what might it feel like—for even a fleeting moment—to realize a stranger believes you and he could be whole together.

ACKNOWLEDGMENTS

Painting Beyond Walls took a long time to complete, and I frequently despaired over finishing it. The future setting seemed confining somehow, and I experienced difficulties in imagining scenes that hadn't yet taken place. In addition, the subject matter both compelled and intimidated me, and the narrative voice driving the story forward often seemed in open rebellion to whatever I wanted to say. Though some characters were cooperative and spoke before their lines were even written; others refused to talk. Working all day might yield three sentences . . . or two . . . or one . . . and the following day only a deletion.

But all the anguish encountered in the work was eventually silenced by the joyful deliverance of finishing, and I'm especially grateful to those who offered support, encouragement, and assistance to the enduring venture. Without them, the book certainly would never have happened.

My former agent Lois Wallace was still alive when I first began thinking of the storyline, and her enthusiasm gave me the needed courage to present an outline to my editor, Daniel Slager. Daniel's support, and his nearly infinite patience in waiting for the first draft to appear on his desk, were as welcome as his incomparable skill in helping to shape the narrative, resuscitate weak scenes, and craft a dimly understood dream into a book. I'd also like to thank Milkweed's managing editor, Broc Rossell. Robin Straus, my agent, has been very encouraging as well, and I appreciate her help.

A recurring theme in *Painting Beyond Walls* draws upon biological relationships on macro and micro levels and required a great deal more familiarity with cellular science than I had. Thankfully, Zachary Schaefer, a microbiologist working at that time in cancer research in Chicago, allowed me a glimpse into his world of mitochondrial energy conversion, protein expression, transmembrane signaling, and countless other wonders. His patient help was indispensable, as were the ongoing encouragements from his partner, Emily Rhodes. All the credit for the science in the book belongs to Zachary, and all the errors in writing about it belong to me.

I'd also like to acknowledge Dr. James C. Noland, a good friend since early childhood. He consistently encouraged me in writing the book and read many evolutions of the manuscript. His insights into the origins of romantic love and advice on composition and tone were invaluable. And he kindly allowed me to glean from our correspondence over the years some of his short, poetic phrases and insert them at the beginning epigraph.

Appreciation is due to Edward Schultz, who made many valuable suggestions early in the manuscript, and offered many helpful insights into further developing themes. Similar thanks go to Dr. Paul Schaefer, whose friendship and support have been invaluable.

I began writing this book before I was diagnosed with stage-four bladder cancer, and Dr. Yousef Zakharia, MD, Clinical Associate Professor at the Holden Cancer Center at the University of Iowa Hospital, kept me among the living. Though I was reluctant to participate in (or even learn about) another treatment regimen after chemotherapy and surgery had failed to retard my cancer's metastasizing, Dr. Zakharia succeeded in convincing me to enter a new immunotherapy clinical trial. He explained that the treatment had not yet found FDA approval, but reams of data had already been collected on the drug, showing promise in cases like mine; dosage levels had been established and adverse reactions could be monitored. My chances were most certainly better, he said, than entering the hospice program. With Dr. Zakharia's help and the undefeatable efforts of his skilled and compassionate staff—the nurses, physician's assistants, aides, technicians, schedulers, and others—my life was spared.

And finally, I thank my wife, Edna. Without her openness to the original idea for the book, insight into every conceptual phase, and suggestions for better word production, the project would have collapsed under its own weight. In addition, Edna advocated for me with doctors, managed every aspect of my daily care, and transported me to and from the hospital for treatments and countless other procedures (one year there were roughly two hundred visits). No words can possibly express the extent of her self-sacrificing efforts or the bottomless depth of my appreciation.

Anna Weggel

As a young man, **DAVID RHODES** worked in fields, hospitals, and factories across Iowa. After receiving an MFA from the University of Iowa Writers Workshop in 1971, he published three novels in rapid succession: *The Last Fair Deal Going Down* (Atlantic/Little, Brown, 1972), *The Easter House* (Harper & Row, 1974), and Rock Island Line (Harper & Row, 1975). In 1976, a motorcycle accident left him paraplegic. He continued writing, but did not publish again until 2008, with his celebrated novel, *Driftless*. Several years later, a sequel, *Jewelweed*, was published to wide acclaim. After another decade, he returns to American letters with *Painting Beyond Walls*, his first to be set in the future. David Rhodes lives with his wife, Edna, in Madison, Wisconsin.

milkweed
editions

Founded as a nonprofit organization in 1980, Milkweed
Editions is an independent publisher. Our mission is to identify,
nurture, and publish transformative literature, and to build an
engaged community around it.

Milkweed Editions is based in Bdé Óta Othúŋwe (Minneapolis)
within Mní Sota Makhóčhe, the traditional homeland of the Dakhóta
people. Residing here since time immemorial, Dakhóta people still
call Mní Sota Makhóčhe home, with four federally recognized
Dakhóta nations and many more Dakhóta people residing in what is
now the state of Minnesota. Due to continued legacies of colonization,
genocide, and forced removal, generations of Dakhóta people remain
disenfranchised from their traditional homeland. Presently, Mní
Sota Makhóčhe has become a refuge and home for many Indigenous
nations and peoples, including seven federally recognized Ojibwe
nations. We humbly encourage our readers to reflect upon the
historical legacies held in the lands they occupy.

milkweed.org

Milkweed Editions, an independent nonprofit publisher, gratefully acknowledges sustaining support from our Board of Directors; the Alan B. Slifka Foundation and its president, Riva Ariella Ritvo-Slifka; the Amazon Literary Partnership; the Ballard Spahr Foundation; *Copper Nickel*; the McKnight Foundation; the National Endowment for the Arts; the National Poetry Series; the Target Foundation; and other generous contributions from foundations, corporations, and individuals. Also, this activity is made possible by the voters of Minnesota through a Minnesota State Arts Board Operating Support grant, thanks to a legislative appropriation from the arts and cultural heritage fund. For a full listing of Milkweed Editions supporters, please visit milkweed.org.

Interior design by Tijqua Daiker and Mary Austin Speaker
Typeset in Adobe Caslon

Adobe Caslon Pro was created by Carol Twombly
for Adobe Systems in 1990. Her design was inspired by
the family of typefaces cut by the celebrated engraver
William Caslon I, whose family foundry served
England with clean, elegant type from the early
Enlightenment through the turn of the
twentieth century.